S0-AZF-933

Love and Death

IN BROOKLYN

Also by Glenville Lovell

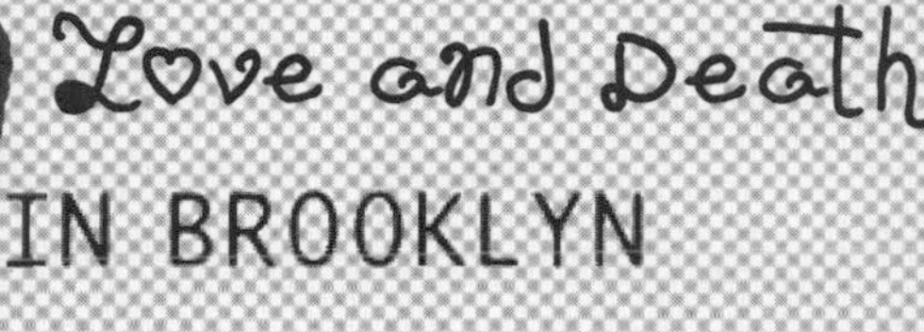

IN BROOKLYN

GLENVILLE Lovell

G. P. PUTNAM'S SONS
NEW YORK

This is a work of fiction. Names, characters, places, and incidents either are the product of the author's imagination or are used fictitiously, and any resemblance to actual persons, living or dead, businesses, companies, events, or locales is entirely coincidental.

G. P. Putnam's Sons
Publishers Since 1838
a member of
Penguin Group (USA) Inc.
375 Hudson Street
New York, NY 10014

Published simultaneously in Canada

Library of Congress Cataloging-in-Publication Data

Lovell, Glenville, date.
Love and death in Brooklyn / Glenville Lovell.
p. cm.
ISBN 0-399-15197-4
1. Private investigators—New York (State)—New York—Fiction. 2. Brooklyn (New York, N.Y.)—Fiction. 3. African American men—Fiction. I. Title.
PS3562.O8624L68 2004 2004044392
813'.54—dc22

Printed in the United States of America
1 3 5 7 9 10 8 6 4 2

This book is printed on acid-free paper. ♾

BOOK DESIGN BY MEIGHAN CAVANAUGH

Love and Death
IN BROOKLYN

ONE

That Sunday in church I cried thankful tears of happiness for the eight-year-old daughter I didn't know I had until nine months ago. But that Sunday in church I cried most of all for my friend Noah Plantier.

One week earlier eight of us had gathered at Bulawaya, a South African restaurant in Brooklyn, to celebrate Noah's sixtieth birthday. His wife, Donna, had brewed a cocktail of surprises for her husband of thirty-eight years, beginning with hiring a limo to take seven of us to the Brooklyn Center for the Performing Arts for a performance of the National Song and Dance Company of Mozambique, a company she and Noah had seen in its homeland while on their African junket ten years ago.

Stuffed into the limo along with Noah, his wife, and myself were four other friends, all members of Noah's Fellowship of Harlem Playwrights Workshop. At Noah's urging I'd joined the workshop a few months after resigning from the NYPD, full of resentment and anger. He thought it'd be a good place to channel my hostility.

I do not really expect to become a writer. In fact, despite Noah's encouragement and insistence that everybody had a story to tell, I'm confident that I'll probably never finish a play. But back then I had a lot of time on my hands and a wife urging me back to therapy to get a handle on my anger. I hate baring my soul to strangers and hated therapy the first time around. Never again. The workshop became my excuse to get her off my back. Good move, because I enjoyed the workshop enough to stick with it, even taking a few college courses with Noah, a theater professor at City College. I actually started a few plays. All about missing fathers. Surprise. And my wife hasn't bothered me about therapy lately, so something must be working.

The performance of the National Song and Dance Company of Mozambique was electrifying. I was incredibly moved by the dramatic *In Mozambique, the Sun Has Risen,* done with traditional dances, choral and instrumental music, accompanied by poetry and storytelling. I'd never seen anything like it before. It stoked my imagination as well as my spirit enough to have me humming some of the songs in the lobby at intermission, where I joked to Noah that perhaps it was time for me to make my pilgrimage to Africa.

After the show we loaded into the burgundy Mercedes limo and cruised up Flatbush Avenue, jabbering like teenagers at the top of our voices, cutting one another off in our eagerness to express our views about the show, making more noise than elephants in a stampede. We'd all been dazzled to the point where we would've followed the company to the next city just to see them perform again.

Donna had made reservations at the restaurant, located on the ground floor of a brownstone in Fort Greene. We were welcomed at the entrance by a tall man, handsomely dressed in traditional African clothing that shimmered under the pale light. Two large rectangular tables had already been set side by side for our party. The interior was warm and cozy and the mutedly lit white walls were exquisitely decorated with African art. Exotic-looking cooking pots and pans dangled haphazardly from the center of the ceiling, and a collection of colored glass jars and conch shells decked the various ledges. Juju music echoed from ceiling-hung speakers and before long we all were humming, smiling, and tapping our feet like schoolchildren. Spiced aromas swept through the room from the kitchen to our right, a hint of things to come.

Sweet music. Fine food. Great art. All present in this small establishment. Could there be three more fitting symbols of man's genius?

Still glowing from the high-voltage dance performance, our spirits surged to new highs when Donna unearthed a thirty-year-old bottle of Pouilly-Fuissé she'd been hiding in her bag. I joked to her that the bottle of wine must've cost as much as their new Harlem brownstone.

That's when Noah's son, Ronan, walked in. Noah's eyes ripened with surprise; you could've plucked them out of his head and he wouldn't have noticed them gone.

Something had happened to cause a rift between them; Noah would not discuss it with me, and for a long time, he and Ronan had not spoken to each other. Ronan was now something of a celebrity in the black community. A year ago he'd been elected to the city council and his first bill sponsored was one calling for reparations from the government for the atrocities of slavery. As expected this bill caused much furor in the media, and it did not go unnoticed in black America. Soon Ronan was all over the tube, on talk shows, on local news shows; he was quoted in newspapers, he was sought after to speak at local black churches. I knew Noah followed Ronan's achievements and nothing would've pleased him more than to be on speaking terms with his son again.

For a few moments he just stared at Ronan as if witnessing the second coming of Christ; then he looked at Donna, whose eyes were flushed with glee. She was clearly enjoying Noah's shock. Slowly Noah rose from his chair and walked over to his son, whose bony frame was sheathed in an expensive-looking brown wool suit.

There was a mysterious twinkle to Ronan's earthblack eyes that alerted you that he knew something the rest of the world didn't; that behind the mask of his gentle smile and his smooth brown face with its strong jaw, behind the flash of light escaping the gap in his front teeth and the slight rocking of his hips when he walked like the sway of a calypso song betraying his Caribbean roots (his mother was born in Guyana), that behind all that was a mind that had visited the ancients, dueled with monsters and seduced princesses, a mind that was as strong as the slaves who made it across the Middle Passage, a mind that understood how civilization jumped off the blackness of his skin.

And based on his credentials there would be no reason to doubt that. Having earned a master's degree from Harvard by age twenty-two, he went on to graduate with an M.B.A. in finance and marketing from Princeton, later making a fortune on Wall Street before jumping to politics.

After exchanging hugs, father and son moved to the bar where they conversed for some time, heads bowed together like monks in prayer. We couldn't hear what they were saying to each other but in a short while there were enough smiles and laughter and hugs exchanged between them to cure all the hatred and misunderstanding in the Middle East. Finally, they joined the table, sitting next to each other at Donna's right.

If you ever go to Bulawaya I would recommend the blackened salmon flavored with onions, tomatoes, and fresh greens. Along with that we also ordered curried shrimp, couscous, barbecued chicken, plantains, and brown rice, which came on large silver platters.

As we ate Ronan explained how he defeated Baron Spencer for the seat in the 41st District. Running on a platform that he promised would make black neighborhoods strong again, Ronan used his experience in market research to target communities which had historically produced poor turnout in elections and spent money and time conducting town meetings using PowerPoint slides to illustrate how he would turn their neighborhoods around. Their increased turnout proved decisive in helping him unseat the one-term Democrat.

Throughout the meal Noah beamed as if he'd been handed the winning ticket in the lottery. His fleshy round eyes flushed with pride and he kept running his hands over his son's head as if Ronan was ten years old and about to go into his first basketball game at the local Y.

Having pulled off the impossible by getting Ronan to attend his father's birthday dinner party, Donna sat back with a broad smile watching things unfold, her peanut-brown face plump with satisfaction. I'd known Donna for almost as long as I knew Noah. I knew her when her hair was tar black; it was now threaded with an abundance of silver strands, which she vowed never to conceal. I knew her when she was model-thin; she now had more meat on her bones than a buffalo. But she was no less beautiful and her smile was still bright enough to warm a dozen winter days.

I leaned over to Donna. "I've never seen Noah so pleased."

"Not in the last ten years," she replied.

"What did you say to get Ronan to come?"

"That's between Ronan and me."

"Mother's secret, huh?" I said.

She laughed and swept her right hand to partially cover mine. "I've spent twenty years running my own business. I didn't have time to doubt myself. If I did I would still be a nurse's aide. They're both stubborn men. Heck, Ronan is Noah, twenty-five years younger. I knew what I had to do to get them together and I did it."

We had finished our meal and the waiter had begun to clear away the dirty utensils from our table. Noah looked over to me and winked. He was eager to see the dessert menu. You see, Noah had a sweet tooth.

Pop! Pop! Pop-pop-pop!

I knew the sound of gunfire like I knew my face. Without looking around to see who was shooting or where the hell it was coming from, I dove for the floor dragging Donna with me. She tumbled on top of me, her black eyes spiked with fear, opened as wide as a subway tunnel. The room had erupted in shrieks and shrill voices, the ricochet of plates breaking and the frightening sound of scampering feet.

I flipped over onto my stomach, one hand clamped firmly on Donna's head to keep it down, my eyes raking the room for the shooter. A figure in a long black coat was fleeing through the door. Everyone else was on the floor. I assessed the room quickly. Broken plates, cutlery, broken glass, and twisted bodies were everywhere. Tables had been overturned as if flung about in a storm.

Everyone from our table was pasted stomach down on the floor or cowering cocoonlike behind chairs or tables.

Except Ronan. He was still sitting in his chair, his legs just a few feet from my face. Yellow flecks of couscous had spilled on the shiny surface of his pants. There were specks of brown sauce on his tan shoes. I grabbed his trousers and yanked. He did not move. I yanked again, as hard as I could. Then I felt something dripping down on my fingers. I looked at them. It was blood and bits of brain. First I froze; then I jumped to my knees. Blood oozed from the back of Ronan's head where a large-caliber bullet had exited, leaving a hole you could put a fist through.

TWO

Between Noah and myself, we had over twenty years of law enforcement experience, most of it spent patrolling New York's tough streets, and yet at this most crucial time that training had not been enough to protect our loved ones. Neither of us had sensed the danger. Neither of us saw the shooter.

At the sound of the first shot we both dove for cover and by the time we'd retrieved our experience and training from under the table the stealthy shooter had dissolved into New York's abyss, leaving behind a young man with one eye and part of his brain scrambled on the restaurant wall.

It all happened so fast. Not one person in the restaurant or anyone on the street got a good look at the shooter. Some swore he was over six feet. Others claimed he wasn't very tall, but slender. Some were certain he wore a red hooded sweatshirt. Others saw a black mask. The only thing anybody could agree on was that none of them got a glimpse of his face.

Donna had fainted and was being attended by EMS, who wanted to take her to the hospital. Torn between going to the hospital with his wife and keeping vigil over his dead son's body until the coroner arrived, Noah stood staring at me, his shirt embroidered with Ronan's blood, his face sagged, eyes vague as fog, his mouth opening and closing like a thirsty fish beached on the sand.

"You gotta go with Donna," I whispered. "I'll stay here."

He nodded silently, fingering his thinning gray hair, but did not move. I pushed him into the ambulance, which drove off with a wail of sirens and whirring lights.

I returned to the restaurant where detectives were still questioning witnesses—those who weren't too scared to speak or hadn't skipped away into the darkness the first chance they got. In this neighborhood gang-related killings were common, and to some of the witnesses who knew the terrain, this killing would fit that profile.

The police had arrived quickly; the restaurant sat on the doorstep of the 88th. The lead investigator, Detective Riley, was a moose of a man, standing about six-four with a square head and nose and forehead scaled so sharp you could downhill slalom off his face. He questioned me in a carefully measured voice, as if he was reading from a teleprompter, recording everything on a miniature electronic recorder.

When he was finished he put the device in the pocket of his brown wool coat and ran his fingers through his white-streaked hair. "We're gonna find the fucker who did this."

Then he gave me his card.

Accepting the card, I looked at him, but couldn't think of anything to say.

I LIFTED the black cloth covering Ronan's body. Blood and mucus had congealed in the eye socket, which had been blown out by the slug; the other eye was frozen open.

The thing that got to you about a dead person were the eyes. You can't begin to understand death until you gaze on the empty eyes of death. That look was something that permeated your soul. You can never forget it.

This was not the first time I'd looked at a dead body. Each time I witnessed a death I'd felt dirtied by the experience, especially if I was the one who'd done the killing. But even in the aftermath of a killing when my sleep rumbled with bad dreams, I knew that the sedative of time would one day restore my good humor. This one would be different. As I stared at Ronan's body quietly growing rigid under the pink light reflecting off the near wall, which made garish purple shadows on his cold face, I felt as if someone had pinned me to a tree by the roots of my hair. I would not quickly or easily recover from this experience. And I knew the healing would only begin when I found Ronan's killer.

THREE HOURS LATER, after the meat wagon rolled off with Ronan's body, I called Brooklyn Hospital and was told that Noah and Donna had left there an hour earlier. No one was answering the phone at their home and I left a message for him to call me. I thought of driving over there but I didn't have my car. I asked for and got a ride home with a cop from the 88th.

It was a short ride to my house on Maple Street and the only conversation that passed between us was the kind of small talk that fell between cracks of your consciousness as you waited for the world to get up to speed with your corrosive pain.

I kept thinking of Donna. Never would I forget the look of shock and horror on her face when she got to her knees on the floor and saw blood gushing from the back of her son's head. She let out one long sustained scream that cut through me like broken glass. Then her voice died completely as she clutched at Ronan's body repeatedly, as if her fingers had lost their sensitivity or as if she was touching fire. Then his body fell out of the chair into her arms.

It had taken Noah and me fifteen minutes to pry Ronan's head from her fingers.

Standing in the street opposite my house I watched the detective's Impala drive off. My body was sore, as if someone had slit my veins and let all of my body fluids drain away. Even the ripple and pulse of the New York night could not reenergize me. Cars filled with shadows buzzed past. But everything seemed to have shrunk away. I stepped out of the street and walked as if blindfolded to my door.

A YEAR AGO I settled a civil-rights violations suit with the NYPD for $2.5 million. Some of that money was used to buy this house on Maple Street from a disgraced congresswoman. That settlement also allowed me to invest in Voodoo, a nightclub in downtown Brooklyn featuring reggae and soca acts from the Caribbean, with an English-born radio personality who also dabbled in concert promotion. My other business, a music store on Nostrand Avenue, which I owned with a former calypsonian from Trinidad, was still holding its own, though it was growing increasingly difficult to compete with pirates who were not afraid to set up their street bazaars on the sidewalk outside the store to hawk their stolen CDs and DVDs.

The love of my life was not expected back before next week. I had asked River Paris, the woman who managed Voodoo, to stay with my eight-year-old daughter, Chesney, while I was out.

I'd met River six months earlier at my club on Lawrence Street. She was lusty-looking and full at the hip with a sharp tongue. Just the kind of person my partner and I were looking for. She'd come to us to drop off a demo tape, hoping to book a dancehall artist she was managing into the club. In a black silk mock-turtleneck shirt and with her python-thick thighs threatening to bust out of their black leather cages, she looked like she'd just stepped out of an *Essence* fashion show. My partner in the club, Negus Andrews, was smitten right away. I was prepared to be more cautious. The three of us spent the night together at the club drinking and swapping childhood stories.

She'd recently arrived in New York from Miami, where she'd managed a club not unlike ours. We couldn't believe our luck. Later as we stood outside her car parked on Jay Street, we offered her the job. She accepted on the spot.

River was sitting in my living room watching a movie with the lights dimmed when I walked in. It was minutes past two in the morning. I had called her from the restaurant to let her know I would be home later than planned, but I did not tell her why.

She got up from the sofa and came toward me. "Jesus, you look like you just saw your best friend gassed."

I screwed up my face and said nothing. She didn't know how close she had come to the truth. She held a glass in her hand and offered it to me. "Scotch."

I took the glass and drained it.

"Damn!" She leaned forward searching my face in the soft light, a stony smile of concern fixed on her face.

"Get me the bottle," I mumbled.

She turned away, taking the glass with her. I stood for a moment lost in my own house, remembering the first time I'd entered this house a year ago to speak to the congresswoman about her daughter, who'd been killed in my apartment. It was a beautiful house and I fell in love with it then. When it went on the market a few months later I jumped on it.

River returned with the bottle of Black Label and two glasses. I snatched the bottle from her hand and sank the spout into my mouth. She leaned against the balustrade watching me intently as I gulped half the Scotch in the bottle.

"Can I have some now?" she said gently. Like a thirsty woman scouring the desert for water, her eyes swept across my face searching for an explanation to my odd behavior.

"Sorry." I wiped the spout and handed her the bottle.

"What happened?" She put one glass on the end table, then poured two fingers into her glass and passed the bottle back to me.

Shock had finally conquered my mind and I stared at her silently. My brain felt like it was exploding in my head; my body so stiff I thought it was encased in brass. I heard her question, but my brain was having a hard time comprehending simple words. Everything in this room, including her, was part of a cyclorama of colorless images.

The cushion of experience I often used to suppress my inner feelings had been stripped away. I was on the cusp of tears.

She held my gaze in her spotless brown eyes and after a moment she said, "Chesney wanted to stay up for you."

"I'm glad she didn't."

"You don't want to talk about it, huh?"

I shook my head.

There was a long pause, like a wasted promise. "Well, I'm leaving." She hesitated. "Unless you want me to stay."

I shook my head again.

She turned and picked up her bag from over the arm of the sofa and then sauntered to the closet to get her coat. I watched as she covered herself in black leather. She turned to face me, her dark face tight.

"Thanks for staying with Chez."

She meandered to the door and stopped. "Let me stay with you. We don't have to talk if you don't want to. I've never seen you look like this."

"I need to sleep."

She unlocked the door and went upright into the night.

UPSTAIRS, I walked down the hall and into my daughter's bedroom. She was curled up under the Mickey Mouse comforter, her favorite toy—a fluffy white teddy bear—nestled against her face. As I kissed her softly on the cheek Donna's pain-scalded face flashed before me. My stomach knotted instantly. For a long time I stood looking at my daughter, observing the tiny twitching of her body as it danced in sleep. Then, not knowing why, I curled up on top of the comforter next to her.

CHESNEY'S ARRIVAL in my life was, to put it mildly, a shock. I'd met her mother, Juliet, nine years ago while vacationing in Barbados.

My love affair with the island of Barbados began long before that visit, even before my first visit at the age of ten with my father. My paternal grandmother was born there and after living in Panama for a number of years she moved to New York in 1922. My early years growing up in Brooklyn revolved around the elaborate family dinners she created in her Crown Heights home on Sundays where I was introduced to calypso music, curried chicken, sorrel, conkies, spicy baked pork, and a variety of crimpy old men and women who instilled in me a love for stories with their incredulous tales of myth and magic, all told with a casualness that only certified my awe.

After I got out of the Marines I went down to Barbados to decompress and to relax before deciding on my next move. I loved walking along its tiny roads at daybreak as the sun burned off the night's dew. My days were spent splashing about in the mystical blue sea or eyeing clusters of silver fish swim in unison like children holding hands. At night I drank beer, ate grilled fish, and watched the locals interact with each other with leisure and comfort, as if they were all from one family. Sometimes as I lay in bed listening to the sea pound its chest against rocks under my window, I'd remember the stories of heroic fishermen told to me when I was young by my grandmother and her cohorts.

Now I visit the island every chance I get. Recently my father relocated there to escape ghosts from his past. Since then he has unearthed legions of relatives, which has made visiting the island even more delightful.

On one of my visits I stayed at a hotel on the South Coast where I took a few scuba diving lessons. The instructor was a striking woman with a compact athletic body and a laugh that bubbled and crested like lava flowing from a mountain. Juliet Rouse was her name. We began an affair after my third lesson, capped off by an underwater lovemaking session in scuba gear the night before I left.

I promised to call as soon as I got back to New York. I don't remember why, but I never did call or write to Juliet. In fact, there was no contact between us after that affair. The next time I visited Barbados was on my honeymoon. I had no idea that Juliet had had my daughter until nine months ago when I got a call from Chesney's uncle, Gregory.

Juliet had gotten into an accident while on a shopping trip to Venezuela. The car she was traveling in flipped a number of times on a highway and Juliet was killed. Though Juliet had never contacted me, she'd put my name on Chesney's birth certificate—apparently you can do that in Barbados without the father's permission. Finding me was easy, Gregory said. My phone number was served up by the Internet white pages. I agreed to meet him at a restaurant in the city.

Of course I asked why Juliet had not gotten in touch with me. Gregory, stiff-faced, with a snobbish turn of his upper lip, laughed and said, "You obviously didn't know my sister." Juliet, he said, took her idea of independence to the brink of obsession. That, along with a ripe vindictive streak, not only propelled his sister to success in business, it also allowed her to get satisfaction by keeping Chesney's birth a secret from me as punishment for not calling her when I returned to New York.

Still skeptical, I asked him if he had a picture.

"I can do better than that," he replied. "Chesney is here in New York."

Anais had been away doing a play in Houston and was due back in New York the next night before heading out to Los Angeles to test for a John Singleton movie. That night I picked up the phone to call her and changed my mind about three times before deciding to wait until she came home.

Anais's flight parked at the gate shortly after midnight. The reasons why I fell in love and married Anais are many, but when I saw her walking toward me in the damp arrivals hall I was never happier to see her and proud that she had chosen me to be her husband. She was simply a remarkably beautiful woman. Always rain clear, her black eyes never lost that elusive hint of a smile, and her long strides, loaded with confidence and sensuality, made me think of a loafing show horse. Even before we embraced Anais's uncanny ability to sense disorder in my mind had sniffed out that something was amiss.

"What's the matter?" she said, after kissing me.

I picked up her bags. "Let's get to the car. It's a long walk to the lot."

She gripped my elbow. "There's something bothering you. Let's have it."

"We'll talk about it when we get home."

It was summer in New York. The air was thick and the night bled the odor of smoke as we left La Guardia. The sky off to our right was carroty-streaked, and black smoke spiraled above the low buildings. The old Volvo whined like a starving puppy when I tried to coax more speed out of it on the Brooklyn Queens Expressway.

"Why didn't you drive my car?" Anais said.

For her birthday I'd bought Anais a brand-new BMW X5, but I'd owned the Volvo for eight years. It was still the best car I ever drove, the soft leather and incredible sound system of her SUV notwithstanding.

I flicked the wipers on as raindrops splattered on the windshield like chunks of overripe grapes.

Anais unbuckled her seat belt and turned to face me. "What's bothering you? I can't wait until we get home."

"Get your seat belt back on," I said, without taking my eyes off the road.

"Talk to me, Blades."

"Just put your seat belt back on, okay? Jesus! Why do you always have to be so damn dramatic about everything?"

"Because you're always so damn mysterious about everything."

"I think I might have a daughter," I blurted.

"What?"

"She's coming to the house tomorrow."

"Hold up. Back up a minute. Did I hear you say you think you might have a daughter?"

"Yes."

"How do you *think* you might have a daughter? Isn't that something you either have or you don't have?"

"Her name's Chesney. She's eight years old. And it's possible she could be my daughter. I had a relationship with her mother in Barbados. Before you and I met."

For a second I took my eyes off the road to look at Anais, who just stared at me, her mouth quivering, and I knew she was trying to keep her temper under control. I knew it was a battle she would lose, which was why I had wanted to wait until we got home before I hammered her with this news.

Moments later I felt her purse slam against my head, the sudden blow causing me to swerve dangerously close to the median. Anais screamed for me to stop the car, but I kept driving. She struck me again and grabbed the steering wheel. The car swerved into the next lane. I slammed on the brakes and the car screeched to a stop on the shoulder.

"I can't believe you didn't know about this," Anais screamed.

"I swear."

"She's not coming to my house."

"Excuse me. Our house."

"No goddamn way, Blades."

"She could be my daughter."

"Oh, and you can't wait to see her."

"Is that what you think?"

"It's in your voice, Blades. You want her to be your daughter. And here I was thinking all this time that you didn't want children."

I looked away, my eyes trailing the low ghostlike buildings of Queens.

"We could've had our own child by now, Blades."

"Come on, Anais. You don't have time for children. You're always away. You're always busy. You made it clear. Acting was more important to you."

She threw her purse at the windshield and fell back against the seat with a whalelike bark, and I thought she would start crying but after that she was quiet.

We fought all the way home. She threatened to leave me but I was determined to see Chesney no matter what. Finally, Anais agreed to end our feud if I agreed to have a blood test done as soon as possible. To me, it was a small price to pay for peace.

CHESNEY CAME into my life on an unseasonably cool July day, the temperature never rising above sixty-five degrees. Arriving with her uncle early in the morning as the sun climbed high in a washed-out blue sky, she wore jeans and a thin black vinyl jacket, her thick black hair caught under a red baseball cap. The corner of her mouth was smudged from the chocolate muffin she was eating.

I took one look at her and knew a paternity test was unnecessary. From her dark placid eyes, to the layered lips and the high slope of her cheekbones, there was no doubt that Chesney was my child.

Two weeks later, after I'd convinced Anais that it was the best thing for my daughter, I contacted my lawyer to begin paperwork for citizenship, and Chesney moved in with us after her uncle returned to Barbados.

THREE

The morning after Noah's son was murdered I looked out my window and the sky was soaked indigo. At some point the previous night I must've left Chesney's room and come into my own; I didn't remember it happening. Beads of moisture collected on my face and chest as the sun steamed past the blinds. Were we in for another seventy-degree winter day?

It was only March, but Spring had been playing cat and mouse with Winter all season. Whether it was due to global warming, as some environmentalists and scientists claimed, or a sign that the end of humanity was near, as some religious people had declared, there was no doubt that the seasons were all fucked up. Most of February and March the temperature had been about fifteen degrees above average. Was it spring? Was it winter? Whatever the season, nothing much changed in Brooklyn.

By the time I brushed my teeth, threw on a pair of jeans and a thin blue cotton sweater before looking in on Chesney, it was after eight. She was not in her room, which surprised me. Chez was on vacation from school. The girl never came out of her room before midday on non-schooldays after watching her favorite cartoons on her in-room television, and then only came downstairs when she became hungry.

I went back to my bedroom and called Noah's house. Nobody answered. The phone rang and rang as though they'd turned off the machine. I tried his cell phone. No answer there either.

I found Chesney in the kitchen sitting at the island eating Eggo waffles and drinking chocolate milk.

"Morning, Daddy," she chirped.

"Morning, baby." I kissed her cheek softly. "You're up early."

"Of course. Don't you remember?"

"Remember what, sweetie?"

"You're taking me to Grandma's this morning."

"Oh, my goodness. I forgot about that."

I half-filled the water tank and put some Blue Mountain beans in the burr grinder of the Capresso coffeemaker Anais had bought a few months ago and pressed the brew button. This thing was so high-tech everything was supposed to happen at the push of a button. But the damn thing had so many buttons I still got confused with which button to push.

Chesney giggled behind me. "You can't forget. You promised. Grandma said she bought me a present from Paris."

"I'm sorry, Chez. Something happened last night. It just took my mind away from everything else."

"You still gonna take me, ent you?"

"Of course. In fact, I have a better idea. How would you like to stay over?"

"For how long?"

"I'll pick you up tomorrow night."

"What's the matter, Daddy? Why you look so sad?"

"Nothing's the matter. It's just that I . . ."

Chesney had stopped eating.

I sat down next to her on the stool. "A friend of mine was killed last night," I said, putting my arms around her.

"How did he die?"

"Someone shot him. I haven't been able to stop thinking about it."

"When people die you think about them all the time." She leaned her head into my chest. "I think about my mommy all the time."

"I know you do, honey."

Sunlight stormed through the round-arched windows Anais had wanted to replace with bay windows, but the architect told us we couldn't alter the outer design without written approval from the Midwood Landmark Preservation Committee. Such approval, the architect informed us, would be difficult to secure since all of the houses in this community were designated landmark treasures. Anais wasn't pleased but there was nothing we could do.

"When is Auntie Anais coming home?" Chesney said.

"In a few days."

"Sometimes I think she don't like to talk to me."

"Doesn't," I corrected.

"See, you agree with me."

"No, I was correcting you. It's *doesn't,* not *don't.* And I think perhaps it might be time for you to stop calling her Auntie."

"What should I call her?"

"Mommy. She's your mommy now."

"But she ain't my mommy."

I didn't want to argue. "Okay, we'll talk about this some other time."

"Are you going to send me back to Barbados if I don't call her Mommy?"

"No, dear. I'm not going to send you anywhere."

"Promise?"

"I promise. She loves you too, you know."

"Did you love my mommy?"

"Your mother was very special."

"She was in love with you."

"Did she tell you that?"

"She had pictures of you and her. She showed them to me. She said you were handsome." She giggled and milk trickled down her chin.

Chesney lifted the blue ceramic bowl to her lips, draining the milk from the bowl before dancing over to the sink. The bowl with its white painted giraffes rattled around in the sink after she dropped it, and she turned to me with an apologetic smile on her face because she knew I frowned on her throwing things into the sink. I didn't have the heart or the strength to reprimand her today.

She ran past me and out the kitchen. I stood smelling the soft air and listening to the coffee gurgling behind me. I imagined myself standing at the base of a volcano listening to the roar of molten lava come driving down a mountain. And then the bubbling red lava became blood exploding from a busted vein. I got up and shut the coffeemaker down.

MY MOTHER was standing on the front porch of her townhouse in Bloomfield, New Jersey, when I swerved around the park twenty yards away. I slowed down as two chipmunks in the middle of the road rose up on their hind legs as if to protest my disturbing their habitat. When the Volvo got a few feet away, they separated to opposite sides, wiggling their tails.

Wearing an oversized New Jersey Devils jacket over black jeans, her silver-blond hair bound into a ponytail, my mother began walking to the car even before I parked behind hers in the driveway. She stood waiting for me to kill the engine, the smile on her face as bright as a New York night.

"Hello, Carmen," she said, after I'd rolled down my window.

Other than my father and my sister, Melanie, my mother was the only person who still called me Carmen, the name she gave me at birth. I changed my name from Carmen Blades to Blades Overstreet before I went into the Marines. Can you imagine a young black kid from Brooklyn going into the Marines with a name like Carmen Blades?

I couldn't either.

I opened my door and felt a smile creep across my face like a lazy larva. My face has always been tea leaves to my soul in my mother's eyes and she must've read *pain* the minute she saw my smile shrivel up because hers evaporated just as quickly and the expression on her face became solemn.

"What's the matter, Carmen?"

I stepped out of the car. "Who said anything's the matter?"

Chesney had unbuckled her seat belt and now was skidding across the driver's seat to get out of the car. My mother bent to catch her as she tumbled outside. "What's my sweet granddaughter been up to?" she said.

Chesney threw arms around my mother's neck. "Where's my present?"

My mother beamed, lifting Chez into the air.

"You better be careful. She's a little big for that," I said.

"Well, I was deprived when she was a baby so I'll take my chances."

After a few moments of straining to keep Chesney aloft my mother settled her on the ground and with a groan and a grin, hobbled over to me, holding Chesney by the hand. "You want breakfast?"

"I gotta get back to New York. Is Jason asleep?"

"He's not here."

"Where is he?"

"Virginia."

I folded my hands into my pockets. The last thing I needed now was a Jason crisis.

"Don't worry," my mother said. "He's gone to see his father who's working on a project for the Navy."

"I'll be back to pick her up tomorrow," I said.

"You still didn't tell me what's on your mind."

"I don't want to get into it right now, Mom."

"His friend died," Chesney chirped.

My mother looked at me with a reproachful curl of her lip, but her eyes were sympathetic, reminding me of when I was seventeen and I lied to her about what my girlfriend and I did after our prom. That time, after she found out we had stayed in a hotel room in Manhattan, she lectured me for hours about what makes a man a man.

She walked over and hugged me, riffling her fingers through my hair. I closed my eyes and inhaled the fresh-snow smell of her hair. At six-one, I towered above her. When I opened my eyes I was looking down at her scalp. Her hair was beginning to thin out at the top and I could see the white roots.

My mother released me and stepped back, her eyes searching my face in an attempt to mine my tendency to break down under her scrutiny.

To avoid her inquiring eyes I bent down and drew Chez to me, kissing her on the cheek. "You behave now, okay?"

"Don't forget to come back for me," Chesney giggled.

"Would I do that?"

"What time will you pick me up?"

I thought for a minute. "How's five o'clock?"

"Don't be late."

I turned to my mother. "See what I have to put up with."

"Wait until she reaches thirteen," my mother said.

"I love you, Daddy," Chesney said.

"I love you too, baby."

My mother was still watching me intently. "You sure you don't want to talk, Carmen?"

Behind her the massive skeletons of hibernating oaks stood aloof, and silent. I shook my head. My mother believed in talking things out. Her approach was that of a Renaissance woman, a mixture of New Age yoga, hugs, and chanting. Right now the oaks were silent. When the season was right they'd flush away sleep and come alive with leaves and blossoms. I was like an oak tree. And it was the season to spring to life. I couldn't waste time talking when it was time for action.

SIPPING COFFEE in a doughnut shop in lower Manhattan half an hour later, I freed my cell phone from my belt clip to call Milo, my

Trini partner in the music store. Almost midday. Milo took his sweet time answering the phone.

"Good morning. Caribbean Music City."

"Hey Milo, are you jerking off over there?"

"Blades! So nice of you to remember that we have a business together. Where the hell you is, man? I just called your house. You need to come to the store right away."

"Can't, Milo. Something came up."

"What you mean you can't? You don't understand. Some crazy dancehall singer came in here this morning. Said he heard we been selling bootleg CDs of his music. Said he was coming back with a gun and I better give him all the copies we made and the money we took in off his CDs."

"Sounds like a shakedown. There's a Baretta in the office. Next time he comes around ask him why isn't he hassling the pirates on the sidewalk and then shoot the fucker."

"Very nice, Blades. If you want to take the business for yourself you can buy me out, you know. You don't have to set me up to go to jail."

"Sorry, Milo. I guess I'm in a bad mood."

"Blades, man, you gotta come here."

"I'll see if I can swing around later."

I hung up, finished my coffee, and left the diner.

SHORTLY AFTER ONE I parked outside Noah's brownstone on a Harlem hill, a few blocks from City College. Noah and his wife had only moved in a few months ago, having endured two years of construction screwups before the house was finally renovated to suit their expectations.

The result was well worth the wait and wrangling. But Noah, being the hard-ass tyrant to commitment, refused to pay the contractors because they had signed a contract obligating them to finish the work in one year. The matter was now in litigation.

Back in the '20s the house had been owned by an African-American writer who gained fame during the Harlem Renaissance. One of the reasons Noah bought the place. He got wind that a white couple was about to purchase it from the elderly Jamaican couple pining for their tropical paradise. Noah went to them and urged them to consider the cultural damage selling the house to whites would visit on Harlem. Noah wasn't always known for his subtlety.

Must've all sounded like mumbo jumbo to the poor Jamaican couple. They laughed in Noah's face and showed no signs of changing their minds until Noah outbid the white couple by $20,000.

The ornate wooden wall trims and moldings had been stripped and redone; a rickety balustrade had been carefully reconstructed. Looked brand-new now. Shiny hardwood floors had been installed and by the time Noah moved his awesome collection of African art into the house it had taken on that crisp, haunted look of a museum.

I trudged up the steps, knocked on the steel door, which had been camouflaged to look like oak, and waited. From down the hill came the sound of animated Harlem commerce on 145th Street, a street flavored with restaurants, clothing stores, real estate offices, and sidewalk vendors who couldn't find space further downtown, as well as small theater companies struggling to bring humor and creativity to the folks uptown at affordable prices. The Diaspora Now Gallery on the corner of Convent and 145th sold art created by black artists from around the world.

After a few minutes the door opened. Noah stood there dressed in black slacks and a mauve blue sweater; his face was puffed up as if it'd been injected with silicone, his eyes red and blank as the sky before dawn.

We looked at each other without speaking. He twisted his body foolishly, a man in a trance. I stepped into the foyer and for some reason immediately felt as if I was in a church. I looked up at the ceiling expecting to see stained windows. But all I saw were the high white ceilings of Noah's brownstone.

Noah closed the door and stood leaning against the wall, his hands hanging limp, his body slack and self-contained.

"How's Donna?"

He lifted his eyes off the floor. "Alive. Though barely."

"She's asleep?"

"Drugged would be more accurate."

"I'm sorry, Noah, but I was worried. I tried calling."

"You want a drink?"

"No. Some coffee."

"Too early for coffee. All I got right now is Scotch."

I watched his face to see if he would chuckle or laugh. He was serious.

"Okay, I'll have a Scotch."

I followed him into the ballroom-sized living room, a room so spacious Noah once joked that he didn't have to rent a theater to do his plays because he could stage them in his living room. Wide bay windows overlooked the street. Drawn thick purple curtains held bright day at bay.

Noah had gotten a head start with the alcohol. He picked up a half-filled glass of whisky off the table, sipped, stared at me a few moments, then walked to an antique table docked against the side wall to fetch a glass. He uncorked the whisky bottle and quarter-filled my glass. I took one short sip. The alcohol set my empty stomach aflame. I sat down. Too early to be doing this shit.

"I wish I could take drugs like Donna. I'd rather be sleeping," Noah said.

I nodded. *Blades, this would be a good time to comment that alcohol was a drug.*

"I'm not taking this well, am I?" Noah tried to smile.

"Does anybody?"

"I used to think I was tough, Blades."

"You're tough."

"Why Ronan?"

"Have you talked to the police since last night?"

"I haven't talked to a soul since last night. Not even Donna. I've got a thousand messages on my machine. I don't want to see anybody."

"Everybody needs comforting, Noah."

"I don't want anybody here until Donna is at least able to grieve without throwing up all over herself."

I took another sip. The room was getting warmer. Noah walked over to the window and pulled the blinds. Sunlight flooded the room. He gulped his whisky and poured another.

"How many of those things have you had today?" I said.

"None of your business."

"You want Donna to wake up and find you on the floor?"

"Who tells you Donna wants to wake up at all?"

"Is there something you're not telling me?"

He looked at me and his eyes popped open wide. "What?"

"What? That's what I'm asking you."

"How many people you killed, Blades?"

I didn't answer. I didn't want to lie to him.

"In the line of duty," Noah continued.

"I don't remember."

"I never killed anybody. I was shot at. Many times. Pulled my gun no more than ten times. Never killed anybody. It's not that I couldn't. It just never came to that. You understand."

"I understand. You've told me this already."

"I just want you to understand."

"I understand."

"Well, remember it. Remember I said it today, because it might be the last time I will get to say it and be telling the truth. I swear I'm gonna find the muthafucker who did this and give them a free ride to hell."

I didn't say anything. I wished I could say something smart, something rational, something different. Unfortunately I was thinking the same thing.

He turned to face me. "You know what he told me last night?"

"What?"

"We were at the bar. Well, you saw what happened. I was overwhelmed. It was such a shock seeing him there. He didn't hate me, he said. Never did. I always thought he hated me. Ever since he was a teenager he was fascinated with the Black Panthers. He read all the books: *Soul on Ice. Soledad Brother.* But he didn't know the truth. One summer he came back from college and I decided to school him. I told him what I knew about the Panthers. I told him about the good stuff they did and I told him about their fuckups too. I told him about the two Panthers who killed a friend of mine in an ambush. But he didn't believe me. He laughed at me. Told me I was a pig in those days and was out of touch with the revolution that was going on. I hit him. Shit, Blades, I smacked him so hard I broke his jaw. We never talked again. At least not a polite conversation. And then last night he said he'd forgiven me. He said he missed talking to me."

"Do you know of any threats against him?"

"He was my son, Blades. But I can't tell you a thing about his life. Ain't that a fucking shame? That's why I gotta find his killer."

"You're too damn old to be running around playing detective, big man."

I set my glass down on the table and got up. I left him sitting there with a dazed look on his face and went out the door.

FOUR

After I left Noah's house, I made a call to someone whose awareness of every ripple in the odious subterranean swamp life of New York City, especially Brooklyn, kept him one step ahead of the law and his competition; it also made him a valuable informant on the lifestyles of the criminally famous. Except for pickpockets and petty thugs, Toni Monday could connect the dots to almost any criminal activity of substance in Brooklyn. He wasn't home and I left my cell phone number.

Walking into my music store on Nostrand Avenue shortly after three that day, I was greeted by the bounce and rattle of kettle drums propelling the hypnotic beat of a popular Tuk song, background music to the activity in the store. Good to see so many customers buying rather than loitering. Over the years we've seen our share of loiterers, mostly men hanging out, listening to music and nothing more.

When I joined the NYPD in 1988 my partner, Leroy James, was a caretaker at the academy. Out of our love for calypso music—I grew up listening to it in my grandmother's house—we developed a business idea. Five years later we opened Caribbean Music City selling tapes,

CDs, and records, losing so much money the first year we almost closed. Later our product line expanded to include videotapes, DVDs, and cell phones. Today we made a meager profit, allowing us to hire two part-time assistants who rotated days and weekends.

After observing a few transactions for CDs and DVDs I walked into the office to find Leroy—who I affectionately call Milo—sifting through bills, a pile of catalogs on the desk. Because of the club, I was spending less time at the music store, but Milo was real cool about it, never hassling me.

He looked up when I came in. "You late, man."

"Late for what?"

"I called the cops. When that guy showed up again they arrested him."

"See, I knew you could handle it."

"Looks like I handling everything around here now, right?"

"And doing a right good job."

"That's not how it was supposed to be."

"What's bothering you, man?"

"Nothing."

"Okay then, I'm gone."

"Where you going?"

"I got some business to take care of."

"Nothing to do with this business, I bet."

"Personal."

"We don't get to hang out, man. Shit. I used to see you at the store every day. Now if I see you twice a week I'm lucky."

"Have you read the newspaper today?"

"Not yet. Why?"

"Remember my friend Noah?"

"Yeah, the professor?"

"Somebody killed his son last night. Shot him in the head. I was there."

Milo was silent, just looking at me. "That's fucked up."

"Listen, I got things to do. We'll talk later."

"Yeah. Be cool."

DINNER THAT EVENING was nothing special; just some lentil soup and falafel I'd picked up on my way home from a Middle Eastern restaurant. River Paris showed up on my doorstep as I was finishing. There was a seductive glow to her smile as I stared at her standing under the outdoor light affixed above the door.

She was dressed in her trademark leather; rich cream pants and short black jacket, her smoldering purple lips threatening to ignite the rest of her. She waved a bottle under my nose.

"What're you doing here?"

"Blades, I'm hurt," she cooed. "I have a very expensive bottle of wine here. And no, it didn't come from your collection at the club. Do you wanna have a drink with me?"

She eased past me into the house. I closed the door, following her into the living room. She set her bag down on the sofa and unbuttoned her jacket.

I said, "This is not a good time, River."

She smiled. "Don't look so scared, Blades. I'm here as a friend. That's all."

"I'm sorry, but I can't drink right now. I've got some things to think about. Alcohol's only gonna mess me up. I need my mind to be clear."

"I saw the newspaper. Why didn't you tell me last night?"

"I didn't want to burden you."

"When is Anais coming back?"

"Next week, I think."

"You okay?"

"I'm fine. Thanks."

"If you wanna talk, I'm here. You know that I like you a lot . . ." She stopped and dropped her eyes to the floor. "Shit."

"What?"

"Nothing. I almost fucked it up."

"Fucked what up?"

"You know, when I met you I was glad that you were married. Now I'm not so sure." She laughed and picked up her bag. "What should I do with this bottle of wine?"

"Save it. I'm sure we'll get a chance to drink it sometime."

She tugged idly at her dreadlocks. "I suppose you're right." She came toward me and stopped a few inches away, looking deeply into my eyes. "How does Anais keep other women away from you?"

I laughed. "That's not her job."

She winked. "See you at the club."

I watched her walk out and followed her graceful stride down the driveway to her car.

WATER CONSERVATION had been the political theme song all winter in the city. At every press conference the new mayor urged New Yorkers to limit their water consumption. The reservoirs were so low a drought emergency had been called because the city's Department of Environmental Protection had calculated that it was impossible that the reservoirs could be at one hundred percent capacity by June 1.

From around ten o'clock that night it rained. Heavily. Water thudded through the streets and raced across my roof like wild horses. At any moment I expected my house to collapse around me. I faded in and out of sleep, never getting more than ten minutes of shut-eye at any one time.

By morning the streets were flooded; the mayor must've been happy. It was still raining when I left my house.

FIVE

Toni Monday was a six-foot, three-hundred-pound transvestite whose long blond hair (that was the color the last time I saw him) and charcoal skin made him more of spectacle than the clothes he wore, if such a thing was possible. Toni's mother died when he was ten, leaving him in the care of his tough-talking Trinidadian grandmother, who started a roti shop in her basement and in ten years had built up a restaurant business boasting three locations in Brooklyn.

Before he was thirteen Toni realized that not only was he attracted to boys, he was also convinced that he was meant to be a girl: a discovery he couldn't share with his ultra-religious grandmother. From then on Toni lived a double life. At the High School of Performing Arts he studied dance, though his grandmother thought he was being trained in music. He also got turned on to drugs. Addicted by eighteen, his weight ballooned and he gave up dance.

His grandmother died when he was twenty, leaving Toni a business worth nearly half a million dollars. It took him just over a year to run the restaurant into the ground because Toni was more interested in selling dime bags than rotis. By the time I'd collared him for drug possession the restaurant was bankrupt.

He became my snitch, helping me break up a drug ring run by the Bloods in the Washington Houses. In return I got him into rehab and stayed on him until he was cleaned up. Toni was now a hairdresser, with a unisex salon in Brooklyn and one in Manhattan catering to many Broadway stars.

Toni may've gotten off drugs but he didn't get out of the business. He became smarter, elusive, ruthless, trusting no one, but kept plenty of people on his payroll if only to get information before it became stale. The salons became fronts for his other activities.

I drove through Prospect Heights, reaching the corner of Underhill and St. Marks where I hoped to find Toni in his salon. The rain was only spotting now. The mayor and the DEP might be rejoicing, but not the drivers I passed. Many streets were submerged under eddies; in some places the water rode above the fenders. Cars stalled. Fortunately I was driving the SUV.

Toni was not in his salon. I was told he was eating lunch across the street at a small restaurant called The Nob. I spotted someone with red hair at the counter. As I crossed the street the person stood up, wiping his mouth with a yellow napkin. Toni.

He tried to smile when he saw me, but I could see he was having difficulty. His mouth was too full. He chewed rapidly, trying hard to swallow.

I hadn't seen him in about a year. His permed hair was now cut short and dovetail-shaped in the back. Heavy makeup had turned his face into a flawless satin mask and his drooping eyelids threatened to obscure the green lenses hiding the true color of his eyes.

He batted his long eyelashes and finally swallowed. "Blades, I could've choked when I saw you. You look so fucking good! Come here and give me a hug, baby."

"Hello Toni."

We pounded. Sweaty alcohol fumes evaporating from his pores threatened to intoxicate me. I stepped back to look at him again.

"What?" he said, and his throat trembled. "I know. I'm getting fat.

I can't help it. It's my fucking genes. You shoulda seen my grandmother. A bear. But I'm going to have my stomach stapled."

I sat on the stool beside him.

The cheerful smile painted on his face never dried. "You been working out, haven't you?"

"A little. My wife is into hard bodies."

"So am I, honey. You look awesome."

"What happened to your hair?"

He took a sip of his Snapple. "I got tired of all that mess all over my neck."

"I like the new look. But red?"

"My boyfriend doesn't like it, but he can go to hell. He's too controlling if you ask me. He doesn't want me to have the operation, you know."

"What operation?"

He put his hand to his mouth in drama-queen surprise. "I didn't tell you?"

"I haven't seen you in a year."

His eyes lit up, he started to laugh. "It's the most important thing to me, Blades. You know me. What's the most important thing to me?"

I paused. "Oh that. Are you serious?"

He cupped his breasts. "These aren't fake anymore. These are mine."

I stared at him with doubt in my eyes. He grabbed my hand and put it to his chest.

"Touch them," he said. "You don't believe me? I started taking hormones six months ago."

I withdrew my hand. "I believe you."

He laughed. "I told my boyfriend I needed to do this. He said he'll leave me. That if he wanted a woman he would've married one. But I'm doing it. Even if he leaves me. My dream is to live my life as a woman."

I couldn't think of a response to that, so I said, "What's that you're eating? I'm hungry."

"Pesto chicken sandwich. You want some? I went out all night last night. This is breakfast."

I waved to the guy behind the counter, a tall man with a light complexion. He left his conversation with a ruddy-faced white man at the other end of the counter and came over.

"Coffee. Black. No sugar," I said.

"Anything else?" the man said. His eyes were hard and unfocused, as if he wanted to chide me for drawing him away from his conversation.

"That's all for now."

He turned away with a muted grunt.

"So did you come looking for me or were you just driving by?" Toni said.

"You didn't return my call."

"You called me? When?"

"Yesterday. Left a message."

"I'm sorry. I haven't been home in a while. Let me give you my cell number." He opened his purse and took out a purple card and handed it to me.

"I want your opinion on something," I said.

"What? You planning to let me get my hands in those curls?"

I waited until the counter guy had settled the cup of coffee in front of me and had walked away.

"Who would want to kill an important politician?"

Toni stared at me, his eyelashes flickering. "How the hell would I know?"

I took a sip of coffee. It was too hot. "Who would know?"

"I don't hang around people like that anymore, Blades. I got a successful business."

"This is important, Toni. I really need your help."

"Christ! I thought you were my friend, Blades."

"I am your friend."

"So why you here trying to dust off my old fingerprints?"

"I'm just asking you what's on the street."

His shoulders hunched and his face clouded. "I used to sell drugs. I used to be an addict. You know all about that. That's in the past. I certainly don't know anything about a hit on a politician."

I ran my hand through my hair and smiled. "Toni, I'm here as a friend, not a cop."

Sweat began to deface his creamy mask. "You're beginning to piss me off, Blades."

"Look, Toni, I'm exhausted. I didn't sleep but a few winks last night. There's this thing on my mind. It's not doing anything for my disposition. Don't make me spoil your day. Don't make me come into your hive and drag you out."

"Ha! Ha! Very fucking funny," he mocked. "Where'd you hear that one? Letterman? You've already spoiled my day, Blades. I don't want to talk to you anymore."

He got up to leave.

I grasped him firmly by the wrist. "Sit down, Toni."

"You gonna arrest me?" His mouth twisted in aped shock. "Oops, I forgot. You can't do that anymore."

Then a black veil of anger descended on his face. He flicked my hand away and picked up his bag from the counter, staring at me all the way before walking out. I slapped two dollars on the counter and followed him into the street.

"I know your drug outfit is still in place, Toni."

"You better back off, Blades."

"I also know you iced Fat Joe."

"What was that?" He stopped in the middle of the street to let a car go by. For a second I thought he was going to continue across. But after the car passed he turned and trudged back to where I was standing on the sidewalk.

"Fat Joe controlled the action around the Marcy Houses. A year ago someone burned his bacon while he was getting a haircut. Ironic, huh? Two men walked into a barbershop on McDonald Street and shot him three times. Weeks later you're controlling all the action in the Marcy Houses. My guess is that's no coincidence."

"Your guess? Fuck you, Blades. We're not on *Hollywood Squares.* I don't care about your guesses."

"A politician was killed in a Fort Greene restaurant two nights ago. Have you heard anything?"

His face remained stiff, his mouth twisted as a corkscrew, but he said nothing.

"This is important to me, Toni."

"I told you, Blades. I don't know anything."

"Toni . . ."

"Just leave me alone, Blades."

I watched him cross the street and enter his salon. The rain had all but stopped. Only the slightest of drizzles now. But the sky was still engraved with dark clouds moving in circles like spinning black disks descending from some alien spaceship. A few feet away an emaciated black-and-white cat lapped from a pool of clear water. Deeply I breathed in spent carbon monoxide from cars idling in shoals of water, filling my lungs with millions of invisible toxins, which, if you believe the experts, would one day form an army and stamp out my life. But right now I wasn't interested in my life ticking away. I was thinking about doing bodily harm to Toni Monday. That sudden flash of irrational anger scared me. I was going down that lonely road again. A trail I hoped to avoid after I'd left the NYPD. A trail I last walked in Miami.

I WAS FIFTEEN when my father dropped out of sight. That was twenty-two years ago. When I caught up with him in Miami after years of searching he tried to explain to me why he'd run away. It was not a believable story.

He must've thought he'd found the perfect place to hide on Miami Beach. One of his artist friends owned a house that was hardly ever used. The house had been built in the 1940s and had been redesigned by a famous interior designer. From its grassy courtyard to its concrete fireplace and its gourmet kitchen with graphite black slate from Brazil, it was a house no one would've expected to find my father living in.

Just after sundown about a week later we were walking on the beach about half a mile away from the house. Quiet whimpering waves shadowed our trail. The beach was empty for most of our stroll until a man in a tracksuit wearing a wide Panama hat, a cigar fixed at the corner of his mouth, passed us, nodding as he went by. I had noticed him coming toward us in the distance, walking with his head down until the moment he reached us. That's when he lifted his head, made eye contact, and smiled. I turned my head to watch him go past, a habit acquired from working New York's streets late at night. The man had stopped and was unzipping his sweatshirt. I saw the gun flash in his hand. Instinct took over.

I pushed my father to the ground and dived to the sand, clearing my gun from my waist. The quick movement startled and flustered the man. He got off one shot at my father, which was off the mark. My shot severed an artery in his neck.

My father thought he recognized the face but it was a little too dark to be sure. We left the scene quickly, sure that no one would've been able to identify us, even if anybody had seen what had gone down.

The next day we read that the man was Carlos Peterson.

CHESNEY WASN'T happy that I arrived late. But I knew the box of chewy chocolate cookies hidden behind my back would be enough to mitigate my error. Soon she was hugging and kissing me the way grateful children do.

I chatted with my mother for a while, listening to the latest triumphs and conquests of my brilliant lawyer sister out in California. She had recently been made a partner at the firm she'd been with since graduating law school. My mother was proud, and though our relationship sucked, I was proud of my sister.

We left New Jersey just before nine and met little resistance as we clipped through the traffic back to New York. Chesney fell asleep as we approached the tunnel and didn't wake up until we'd reached home.

It was past ten when I parked the Volvo in the garage and entered the house through the side door from the attached garage with Chesney in my arms.

She woke up long enough to get herself ready for bed, kissing my cheek before sliding under the covers. I crawled back downstairs where I flicked on the television to watch the news, which was half over. I watched three badly written horror tales passing for news stories about murder and rape, including a surveillance tape of a man who kidnapped a Columbia University student, raped her, and then forced her to withdraw money from an ATM before killing her. I turned the television off in disgust as the phone rang.

"Hi, baby." Anais's cozy voice settled into the empty space in my brain reserved for her pitch, immediately soothing me.

"How's it going, superstar?" I joked.

"Let's see if my scene makes the final cut before you go nominating me for any awards," she said. "I miss you."

"I miss you too. When're you coming home?"

"Tomorrow."

"Really. I thought you had another week."

"They're wrapping early. How's Chez?"

"She asked about you yesterday."

"Really? That's nice. How're you? You don't sound like yourself."

"Missing you, that's all."

"Save some of that loose saliva for when I get home, bad boy. Something's wrong. Let's have it."

"Everything is fine. Do you want me to pick you up at the airport?"

"Blades, the last time I went away I came back to an eight-year-old stepdaughter. I'm almost afraid to think of what you might be hiding this time. Out with it."

I attempted a disarming laugh, but my voice failed me.

"I'm not joking," Anais said. "Tell me what's going on, Blades."

I paused, struggling to find words to tell her what was on my mind.

"Blades? You still there?"

I sighed loudly. "Noah's son is dead."

Anais gasped, then I heard her breathe out loudly. "Jesus! What happened?"

"Shot in the head. I was there. I saw it happen."

"Was it an accident?"

"Murder. It was a hit. The shooter got away."

There was a long pause before Anais spoke again. "I know exactly what's going on in your head, Blades. And I want to tell you right now to forget it."

"I'm sorry, Anais. I can't."

"No, Blades. I'm not going to stand for it."

"Noah is my friend. He's like a father to me."

"Let the police take care of this shit, Blades. You're a father yourself. Remember?"

"Yes, I know that."

"Well."

"What time should I pick you up?"

"I'm not done, Blades. I want you to promise me . . ."

"Not this one, Anais."

"Don't bother picking me up. I'll take a cab. Good-bye."

Anais had hung up the phone.

SIX

A white limousine had picked her up from the Bronx at nine to take her to the airport. Though it was cold outside she rode the heated leather seats in the back of the limo with the windows down. Soggy wind splashed through the window, flailing her loosened locks and tickling her nose cavity, making her smile because it reminded her of sea-spray at the beach. Snow was in the forecast and she hoped it would wait until she and her lover were securely ensconced in his Queens home, where they could watch the snow fall after what she hoped would be a night of intense lovemaking. She'd been horny all week.

Judging from his accent she suspected the driver, a tall thin man, was of European origin. With a leaden tongue he asked if she wanted the window closed, repeating it a number of times before she understood what he was saying.

No, she said, and leaned her head out the window as the car pounded across the Triboro Bridge, heavy and solid as an armored truck.

They reached the American Airlines terminal at JFK airport around nine-forty. A black Lexus cruised slowly by. Its driver eased his window halfway down and smiled. She saw his eyes and immediately felt a chill course through her.

As she exited the limo the Lexus drove off.

The cramped arrivals hall was bright, but damp and dusty. JFK airport had been under major renovation for years and dust was everywhere, making her cough several times. Just as she decided it might be better to wait outside, even in the cold, the man she was expecting appeared.

He was about fifty, handsome in a colonial way with a clipped mustache and well-dressed in a black buttoned-down wool suit. The product of a British high school and university, he walked stiffly, without that air of casual rhythm that might've identified him as being from the Caribbean. But she liked this about him. It was his camouflage. He wasn't stiff at all; far from it. But in keeping with his professional stature as deputy ambassador, his public demeanor was always businesslike.

Excited, she waved her hand in the air to get his attention. She did not see the man who blindsided her, knocking her to the ground in his haste. But he was nice enough to help her up and then he looked so intently into her eyes she thought he would kiss her. Then he was gone, rushing outside. Her eyes followed him for a brief second, then returned to the tall man coming to greet her.

Maxwell, grinning like a teenager, swallowed her up in his long arms. She twined hers around his neck, kissing him unrestrainedly. Over a week since she last saw him.

"Not here, honey." He uncurled her arms from around his neck.

Trying to check her passion was like attempting to stem a tornado with a flag.

She reattached herself to him. "I missed you so much."

"I missed you too, darling, but we're in public."

"I don't care."

A laugh came from his chest, deep and resonant as a dog's growl. Flattered that his absence for a week could have this effect on her, he returned her kiss, experiencing a familiar surge of energy in his crotch.

"Let's get to the car," he said, sucking on her earlobe.

Linked arm in arm, together they walked toward the exit. To anyone watching they were an elegant couple. He walked upright, his head tilted gently as if listening to a special rhythm; the same rhythm she created with her high prancelike steps.

"How was the flight?" she asked.

"Horrible."

"Really? What happened?"

"I was sitting next to this clumsy idiot, that guy who ran you over just now. He spilled coffee all over my suit."

She stopped and turned to face him, examining the front of his suit. She saw the stain on his pants leg, a patch the shape and size of a mango just above his knee.

"I went to the bathroom to try and get it out but couldn't," he said.

"It's not that bad," she said.

Outside, puffy flakes settled on their heads. The limo pulled up next to them.

"Come on," she said. "This is it."

As they got inside she saw the black Lexus roll up and stop behind them. Maxwell immediately closed the glass partition separating them from the driver. She thrilled to his hasty, though expected attack. His lips smacked against hers; she opened her mouth for his tongue, which butterflied around hers with fluttering strokes. His wide mouth clamped hers open, his tongue scraping the back of her throat. The limo swerved onto the highway. Max parted her legs, his fingers beginning their seductive dance on her inner thighs seeking the warm thicket of her crotch.

Spreading herself out on the leather so he could remove her panties, she tried not to think of the black Lexus or the possibility that someone might be following them. She lifted her left leg and leaned on her side to give her lover access to her pussy, which had been wet ever since she got into the limo. He leveraged himself against the front seat and entered her forcefully. After a few thrusts she told him she wanted to sit on him.

He did not argue and leaned back in the seat. Facing the rear window, she eased herself onto him. But it was not the position, she soon discovered. It was her mind. She was distracted and no matter how vigorously she bounced up and down on his dick, or rocked back and forth, she could not find a rhythm or become fully engaged in his sexual zeal. Getting her freak on had never been a problem. Especially not with Max. His voice alone could get her juices flowing. And fucking in the limo was one of those perks she looked forward to when he came to New York. But try as she might, she could not shake the sense of foreboding that had dropped like a wrecking ball on her head ever since she saw the eyes of the driver of the black Lexus.

While she absorbed his climax—she figured she could get her groove on later—she peered out the back window to see if the black car was following them. In the frosty darkness she saw knuckles of snow dissolving into the cavernous night but little else. She rode him as well as she could; he came quietly, effusively, leaving a trail of thick cream on her leg and skirt.

Ten minutes later the limo slid to a stop in the wet snow; they had arrived at their destination. She peered outside. Forest Hills Estate was one of the better neighborhoods in Queens, its redbrick houses and immense thick-hedged gardens reminding her of England.

She watched tiny cotton balls float to the ground. The once naked boughs of thick elms had sprouted white blossoms, swaying and bending in the wet breeze. The sidewalk was a white carpet. Throughout the neighborhood houses were dark and quiet.

The driver got out to open Maxwell's door. She scouted the floor for her panties. Still on hands and knees she heard a vehicle approaching. How did she know something was wrong at that instant? Instinct. What wasn't right?

Lights! The approaching vehicle had no headlights.

She bolted upright as the first shots rang out. Kicking open the door closest to the sidewalk she dove outside head first. Several more shots exploded in the night. A jolt of fear zipped through her stomach as breaking glass crackled and metal chinked under the impact of bullets.

She vomited.

Hunched near the rear wheel of the limo she peered under the car. Maxwell and the driver were sprawled on the ground. Neither moving. A car had stopped several yards behind the limo. She saw the grill. It was a Lexus.

Someone got out and began walking slowly toward the limo. In the frightening quiet gunshots echoed in her brain. But the shooting had stopped moments ago.

Her feet were wet and cold. She'd left her shoes in the limo. The thought of dying here in the snow without her shoes gave her an instant headache. She heard herself breathing and her chest tightened as the heavy sound of boots crunching snow got closer. Mouth open, she snatched air to calm herself. Snow-thickened air burned her lungs.

The sharp sound of boots biting through snow came closer, obliterating the echoing fear. She ripped her purse open trying to block out the sound of death approaching. She threw the bag into the car after yanking the snub-nosed .38 automatic from inside. Bracing herself on her knees, she held her breath.

How close was he?

A whiff of his cologne.

Close enough.

Like a black cobra she sprang up firing, the .38 jerking, spitting deadly venom.

The man fell to a knee, rolled over a few times, and rose up firing. She ducked down until he stopped to reload. Up she sprang again, firing angrily. He tried to run, stumbled a few more steps, then slumped to his knees.

The Lexus sped away. Left hand to right wrist, the gun held stiffly in firing position in her right hand, River kept her eyes glued to the fallen shooter, advancing slowly toward him. Her heart bounced against her chest like a rubber ball.

She stood over him. At the flicker of an eyebrow she would blast him again. He wasn't moving.

Retrieving his silver-handled .45 from the ground, she ran back to the two men sprawled in crimson snow behind the limo. Both dead. The limo's trunk was open, Max's luggage still inside.

She slammed the trunk closed. Lights were popping on in the surrounding houses like bulbs on a Christmas tree. In this neighborhood it would not be long before cops arrived.

The keys were in the ignition. She fired the engine, flicked on the wipers, and floored the gas. The white car plowed through the snow like a Hummer.

Taming her ragged breathing was more difficult. Her whole body trembled as if she was in a vibrating chair. She fought the urge to glance behind for one last look at her lover.

She abandoned the limo at the first subway station she came to after retrieving her belongings. All except her panties, that is, still couldn't find them. She threw the gun into the sewer and went to catch the train.

SEVEN

"Why did you come to me?"

I needed to hear this story like I needed to get an audit from the IRS. It seemed too incredible to believe. But my skeptical mind couldn't deny her presence in my house, bleeding; her face scorched with what looked like the evidence of her experience. Her hair was wet, her sweater ripped in the front; her black knee-length leather skirt covered in mud. Secluded under long curled lashes, her dark eyes were fixed remotely on my face.

Unable to stand her cold stare, I got up and went to pull the thick yellow damask curtains. The ground outside was marbled with wet snow. Bright light reflecting off the snow filled the room with an intense orange glow.

She had told her story in a gentle and strangely calm voice. That in itself was unsettling. How could she be so calm after killing a man?

I began to think back, searching for clues I might've missed, something to leaven the shock that I'd hired a killer to manage my club. I hated feeling like a jerk. But that's exactly how I felt.

She'd done such an excellent job running the joint I now had plenty of time to scout new acts for the nightclub with Negus. It never would've dawned on me that she was capable of firing a gun, far less shooting and killing a man. I didn't even know she carried a gun. I carried one, and had a permit to do so, though the last mayor had tried to have it revoked after I sued the city.

River sat with her back upright in the chair. She was looking in my direction, but her eyes were blank as if she were looking through me. I was having a hard time digesting what she'd told me. She'd been working for me for six months and I thought I knew her pretty damn well, but clearly not. She'd never mentioned a lover of any kind. And we'd gotten drunk together on more than one occasion.

She stood up and walked toward me. "I'm having another drink. You okay?"

I looked up. "Am I okay? About what?"

She turned. "Your drink?"

I nodded. She stumbled when she leaned over to pick the bottle off the table and clutched at my arm to steady herself. I held her by the shoulder and she straightened up, her eyes locking onto mine with a fire that appeared to have no end. There was a savageness, too, about her face, about her eyes, something I'd never noticed before, that compelled me to stare at her. She was a tall woman, almost six feet, with immense hands. Skin the color of nutmeg. For the first time I noticed blood on her elbow and forearm where the material of her sweater had been ripped away, hanging like flesh from a wound. Her perfume was sweet with a snatch of wild flowers.

"Thank you," she said, blinking repeatedly, as if her eyes were blurred. She poured her drink and went back to her seat.

"You didn't answer my question," I said.

"What question?"

I sipped my drink trying to bridle the self-righteousness that was beginning to soar though me like an overflowing river. What was I supposed to do now?

Her muffled voice, muted as if coming from inside a paper bag, stopped the train of my thoughts. "I can't go to the police."

Usually, it does not take long for me to adjust to shifts in personality, but with River I wasn't sure if I was walking on the bank or slipping into a riptide. The savagery of her face had disappeared, replaced by a look of egg-white innocence, a look even the Marquis de Sade would've pitied. I didn't know what to say.

"And I can't go to my house. I'm sure they'll be looking for me there," she said.

"Who're they?"

"The people who assassinated Maxwell."

"And who're these people?"

"I don't know exactly."

"They know you, know where you live, but you don't know them, is that what you're telling me?"

She coughed hard; her body shook. Hunched over her knees, her body looked like a ball of solid iron.

"Are you okay?" I said.

Still coughing she rose, unfurling herself like a bad memory, and walked to the window. I turned my head to follow her path and saw that she limped slightly, but not from injury. The heel of one of her shoes had come off. She turned in a circle like a tired animal after a bruising fight and looked at me. Behind her I could see the brilliant snow dripping like hot wax from the trees.

"They must've followed me to the airport."

"I'm still trying to get past who're *they.*"

She licked her lips slowly, ignoring my tone of annoyance, speaking as if I was no longer part of the conversation. "Which means they know where I live."

I sniggered. "Is this the part where you tell me you're leaving town?"

She smirked. "Why're you being such a dick?"

"I am being a dick?"

"Yes, you are."

"You come into my home, tell me you shot a man to death, and expect me to act like we share some kind of bond?"

Her voice snapped like a firecracker. "You've never killed anyone?"

"This is not about me. Don't act like we went through boot camp together. I don't recognize you. You're not the woman I hired."

"Yes, I am. You just didn't know everything about me."

"I've heard enough, thank you."

"Sometimes I moonlight as a diplomat's bodyguard. What's wrong with that?"

"A diplomat with enemies. That doesn't explain why you didn't wait for the police."

"I couldn't."

"I've got that down. I'm still trying to swallow the rest. The *why* part. Why would anybody kill a diplomat from the Bahamas? Does anybody in this country even know where the Bahamas is?"

She leaned forward, shook her long locks, and let out a sigh. "Look, Blades, these people know where I live. There're not above assassinating a diplomat on the streets of New York, what the fuck you think they'd do to me if they find me? Once I go to the police I'm a sitting duck."

"You may not have heard of it, but there's such a thing as police protection, you know."

She rolled her eyes. "Trust me, Blades, I know as much about the police as you do. They can't even protect themselves against the common cold. All I need is a place to lay low for a while. You're the only friend I've got in this town."

"Would you like to hide under my bed?"

She cocked her eyes and smiled mockingly. "That'd be fine with me, but I don't think Anais would want me to listen to you two make love."

"Why didn't you tell us about this gig when we hired you?"

"It was a part-time thing. Only when he was in New York. And he wasn't here that often. He was stationed in D.C. I didn't see the need."

"You didn't see the need?"

She glared at me as she walked back to the couch, her eyes like hot branding irons. "No. I didn't see the need."

Somewhere outside a dog began to bark. I reframed the images I'd stored of her scrambling about in the snow, shooting her way out of trouble. And the calmness of her eyes as she related the story came back to me. Perhaps I didn't want to admit that I admired her courage and coolness.

I didn't want to care what happened to her. And I suppose I had good reason to feel that way. At the very least she misled me, and may've lied too. Shit like that pissed me off. Not only was it disrespectful, it was a sign that she thought I may've been a chump. And I never thought of myself as a chump.

Besides, whatever she'd gotten herself involved in, she'd done knowingly. Why the hell should I care what happened to her. But I did. Maybe I was a chump after all.

I looked out the window. The redbrick church across the street stood out against the white-blossomed trees, its spire rising like Excalibur in the lake. The dog continued to bark and I felt a nausea stirring in my chest, the kind of treacherous feeling I used to get when I prepared to go out onto the streets to set up a buy and bust. Behind me I heard a droning sound. I turned around. River was sitting on the couch curled up like a hermit crab. She was crying and clawing at her face like a wild animal.

EIGHT

There are parts of Brooklyn that look like wasteland. Especially on a rain-clouded day. Even though you know that before you stands a structure designed to hold inhabitants: a store, a restaurant, an apartment complex; there is something about the scarred face of these buildings, the dingy dust-colored bricks, the cracked, oil-caked sidewalks that shriek of neglect. Many of these areas are in East Flatbush and East New York, home to many immigrants who become victims of crime.

A sixteen-year-old girl on her way from school in East Flatbush was snatched off the street and raped several times before being thrown down a flight of stairs. With information gathered at the scene and the girl's account and description of her assailant, the police quickly nabbed the suspect. This young girl was one of many such victims who found their way to Susan Zenaro, director of the Crime Victims Counseling Center at Long Island College Hospital, but she was not the person I drove up to CVCC's offices to see.

Susan once worked for the Crime Victims Unit of the NYPD and we've been friends since then. She knew as much about me as any woman outside of my mother and wife. During that bleak period of my life after Anais left me to live on the West Coast I spent quite a few boozed-up nights in Susan's company, but throughout our relationship remained platonic. She was hard on men, but tougher on booze, with a capacity to drink copious amounts of alcohol without getting drunk.

A year ago I helped her secure temporary rental space in Carroll Gardens on the second floor of the building owned by a friend of mine, while a permanent home for the Crime Victims Counseling Center was being constructed on the campus of the Long Island College Hospital.

The woman Susan had called me about that Thursday morning had bitten off her boyfriend's penis after he tried to force her to perform oral sex. I wonder if he'd considered the tradeoff beforehand.

The trend of warm winter days had not been broken, and today the temperature hovered near fifty degrees. I was dressed in black jeans, a thin black leather jacket, and a blue Dallas Cowboys cap.

I found Susan behind her desk eating tabouli salad when I walked into her office shortly after three o'clock. Black wire-rimmed glasses perched on her nose tip, she got up to greet me, trying to smile through a mouth full of food.

"Sorry," she mumbled, putting her hand to her mouth. "You told me you'd be here about three-thirty."

"I got through at the bank earlier than expected."

"It's just that she isn't here yet," Susan replied.

She covered the plastic bowl and pushed it behind a gold paperweight against a pile of papers at the back of her desk, then came over and shook my hand.

"You want me to come back?"

"You kidding? I get to see so little of you. Do you want some salad?"

"No, I ate lunch late. Still full."

Susan stood a head below me and looked up at me through grainy-blue eyes. Her silver crew cut smelled like shampoo and her perky smile exposed a gap between her front teeth. Even though her job brought her in contact with people who'd endured unspeakable horrors at the hands of criminals, I've never seen Susan without her perky smile. Today was no exception.

"How's Noah doing?" she asked.

"Barely holding on. Tell me more about this girl."

"Don't stare when you see her."

"Why, is she deformed?"

"It's temporary, thank goodness. Her boyfriend beat her up pretty bad."

"You said something about her reaction when she heard about Ronan's killing?"

Susan focused her eyes on my face. "It's a hunch. But you used to say a hunch is a cop's best friend."

"That's right."

"She was being interviewed by a detective from the Seventy-second."

"Anybody I know?"

"A woman."

I chuckled. "You implying I don't know any women detectives?"

Susan wagged her finger at me. "They weren't many in narco."

"Narco is tough on women."

"Chauvinist."

"So what happened?"

"The news was on. And they were showing footage from the scene of Ronan's murder. You should see the way her eyes and face changed. Stricken like she was having some kind of attack. She started shaking and stopped answering questions and ran into the bathroom and refused to come out."

"Maybe it reminded her of something else."

"Maybe. I had a hunch and called you. She was very disturbed by those pictures. I can't describe the way her face changed. Maybe she knew Ronan personally. Maybe she was there and saw something. I acted on a hunch."

"Okay, I'll play. What's her name?"

"J'Noel Bitelow."

"Are you kidding me?"

Susan laughed. "You can say she was born for this role."

"Is her boyfriend in jail?"

"The police can't find him."

"What about the hospitals?"

"Personally, I hope they find him dead. He's better off as fish bait. Jail's too good for people like him. Something weird is happening in this city. We've been seeing a lot of violent domestic rapes lately. Don't know what it is. Some of them are very sadistic."

"When'd this happen? J'Noel's attack?"

"The night before Ronan got shot. She spent the night in the hospital and checked herself out the next morning. She didn't even call the police. The attending physician, she called me and I took the police around to see J'Noel."

The phone on Susan's desk rang. She picked it up and glanced in my direction and nodded just after she identified herself to the caller. The conversation was brief. After she settled the phone into its cradle she picked up a pen and scribbled on a notepad.

"That was her," Susan said. "She can't make it. Said she doesn't have anyone to look after her baby. I think she's lying. I don't think she planned to come. Here's her address, and telephone number."

I took the paper she handed me and scanned the information.

Susan reached for her salad. "It's a long shot, but you never know."

BY THE TIME I reached the address Susan had scribbled for me, the blade of the afternoon sun had slashed Brooklyn in half. A salty wind disturbed plastic shreds on the dust-filled streets outside the three-story apartment building on Lincoln Place in Crown Heights where J'Noel Bitelow lived. I buzzed apartment 3A and waited on the slab of broken concrete outside the black metal door.

A chorus line of women carrying Bibles and *Watchtower* magazines shuffled shoulder to shoulder down the wide sidewalk, pausing to offer me something inspirational to read. I declined with a polite smile and they continued down the street, their eyes weary but resolute, for Brooklyn was overtaxed with sinners waiting to be saved.

A woman came to answer the door, a pudgy sour-faced toddler at her hip.

"J'Noel?" I questioned, after she had swung the heavy door back.

"Who're you?"

"Blades Overstreet. A friend of Susan Zenaro at CVCC."

"You a cop?"

"No."

"What you want with me?"

"Can I come inside?"

"Why?"

"Please, I don't want to talk out here. Susan's very concerned about you."

She never blinked as she stared at me long and hard, then she broke off her gaze and stepped back as the toddler began to cry. I passed through and she released the door. It clanked solidly behind me. Her head skillfully wrapped in cloth that matched her red glossy lipstick, J'Noel jingled like an African percussion band whenever she moved her right hand, which was encased up to the elbow in gold bangles. She might've been a pretty girl before her boyfriend got the inspiration that he was Mike Tyson. She had an apple stuffed in her jaw on the right side and a grape-sized chunk of flesh was missing from her left ear. Her left eye was so black it looked like she had a patch over it.

She walked unbalanced, as if the lump on the right side of her face was too heavy to bear. I followed her one flight up a narrow, dark stairwell, cluttered with crushed empties and butts. She picked up Spiderman from the ground in front of her apartment and gave it to the youngster, who quickly stopped bawling, then pushed the door open. I followed her into a sparsely furnished room that was a spectacle of breezy living: shoes, toys, clothes, and children's books scattered about like pieces of a puzzle.

"If you here to get me to go to that victim's place, you're wasting your time. I ain't no victim." Her voice was whiny, not much thicker than her kid's.

"Can I sit down?"

She pulled back a Bugs Bunny comforter to reveal a plush brown recliner, which had obviously found better usage storing toys.

I shifted Spawn, the Hulk, and Wolverine out of the way and sat at the edge unbuttoning my leather jacket for comfort. She snuggled into a loveseat with the giggling little boy climbing up her back.

"What's the big guy's name?" I said.

She stared at me, her eyes blank and lost.

"Your son," I added.

"Oh . . . Malcolm Junior. His father named him after himself. I wanted to name him Stephon after the basketball player. Stephon Marbury. You know him?"

"Not personally. Good player, though."

"He's from around my way in Coney Island. I should've named him Stephon. Now I have to call him by that muthafuckin' name: Malcolm. I hate that sonofabitch."

"A lot of great people are named Malcolm."

"The only great thing about his father is when he ain't around. Then I have a great time."

I chuckled. You gotta love a girl who still has a sense of humor with her face looking as if the kicker from the Dallas Cowboys had tried to put it through the uprights from fifty yards. She looked to be about twenty-five, but with her face so distorted it was a wild guess.

"Did Malcolm do this to you?"

She winced trying to smile. "You should see him."

"Yeah, can't look like much of a man without his johnson."

"His what?" She laughed. "Oh . . . you can say his dick. It's all right. I ain't shy. He didn't have much use for it anyway. Not even Viagra could get that shit hard. Come here all the time talking about suck it 'til it lift. I'd be dragging on that shit like a dope fiend on a crack pipe and still the shit be soft as ice cream."

"How long you known him . . . Malcolm?"

"About seven years. He used to hang out around my school. He always had money to throw around. I didn't get along with my mother and he was cute so I started going to his house after school. Then I found out I was pregnant. I had an abortion, but he was good about it. Said he would marry me and shit. I moved in with him after I graduated."

"Where'd he get so much money? Was he dealing?"

She eyed me suspiciously. "You think every black man with cheese be dealing?"

"No," I said.

"He ran with a crew out of the projects in Coney Island. That's where I used to live with my dad. I moved in here by myself a year ago. Couldn't take his friends. Bunch of muthafuckin' know-nothing idiots. He's been coming around trying to get me to move back to Coney Island. He's good to Malcolm Jr., though. That night he came up here I wasn't in the mood. He got mad. He'd been drinking or something. We started to fight. He bit my ear. Pulled out a pistol. Said he would kill Malcolm Jr. if I didn't give him some. I couldn't believe he said that. About his own son. Even if he was joking. Shit! How you gonna say shit like that about you own son? I told him if he left Malcolm alone I'd give him a blowjob. I bit off his dick and left him here screaming and took Malcolm and ran."

"Did you know Ronan Peltier?"

Her eyes blew open wide. "Who?"

"The politician who was shot in Fort Greene the other day."

"What's that got to do with me?"

"I want to find his killer."

Her face slouched; her good eye dimmed. Sunlight faded through the unwashed window. The red lipstick was beginning to smear and she looked as if she'd been drinking blood. "Who the fuck are you? I don't know what Susan say to make you come over here but I don't know nothing 'bout that shit. You must be crazy."

"Were you in that area that night?"

"I wasn't anywhere near there."

"Susan said you got very upset when you saw the news about Ronan."

"She don't know what upset me. I wasn't even looking at that shit."

"If you know something about Ronan's death, please help me."

She scratched her neck with blunt fingernails. "You a cop, ain't you? I bet you a cop."

"I'm not. But I used to be. If you know something but you're afraid to speak because of a threat, the police can offer you protection," I stressed.

"Yeah, like they protected my brother."

"Your brother?"

"A few years ago my brother witnessed a drive-by in the Pink Houses. The police said if he testified they'd protect him. He testified at the grand jury but never made it to the trial. Got parked having waffles at IHOP one morning."

"That politician was a friend of mine."

"So? Why should I give a shit about you or your friends? I don't know you. Get the fuck out my house." She stared at me, her red lips trembling.

I was too stunned by the suddenness and hostility of her expression and the broken cadence of her angry fluttering eyes to get up immediately. When I recovered I got up and opened my wallet, taking out one of my cards, which had both the numbers to the club and my cell phone. I handed it to her. "If you feel like talking I'd appreciate it if you got in touch with me."

She took the card and ripped it into two pieces, dropping them to the floor next to her. "You can let yourself out."

I CRAWLED DOWN the dark stairwell feeling as is someone had just beaten me about the heel with a crowbar. I'm sure J'Noel would protest my feelings of pity, but what did the future have in store for a woman like her? She might get some measure of satisfaction withholding information from me, but would she survive her next brush with an abusive boyfriend? Would she be able to break out of that violent cycle? I hated to think of what I would do to the man who tried to abuse my daughter that way.

NINE

On my way home I picked up Chesney from the Brooklyn Children's Museum, where she'd spent the afternoon with her friend from next door. When we got home Anais was already there, having made good on her threat to take a cab instead of letting me pick her up. Chez was very happy to see her; even happier with the bag of goodies Anais presented her after they'd hugged. Then she bounded up the stairs to unload the tropical fish Anais had bought for the tank she kept in her room.

With Chez upstairs I took the opportunity to fill Anais in on what had transpired between River and me. Already fuming over my plan to hunt Ronan's killer, she was even angrier about my decision to stash River in my old co-op in Carroll Gardens.

I'd bought that apartment when Anais moved out west. We lived in it together for a short while after she returned, but it'd been empty since we bought this house on Maple. I had not yet made a decision about whether to sell or lease it. Since it was just there gathering dust at the moment I saw no harm in letting River stay until she figured out what the hell she was going to do. Of course, I could've done it without telling Anais, but by telling her I hoped to remove any appearance of impropriety. Anais had a tendency to think that every beautiful woman who smiled at me was itching to get inside my pants. I didn't want to aggravate her already jealous nature.

THAT NIGHT we ate dinner at a Malaysian restaurant in the Park Slope neighborhood where I grew up. Memories of my childhood came flooding back as we walked along President Street past four-wheel-drives parked on both sides of the busy streets—the vehicle of choice in this mixed middle-class neighborhood, home to many college professors and artists—past potted plants jammed in ground-floor windows of restored brownstones, past couples strolling with their children. I remembered racing my brother, Jason, along this same street on our way to Prospect Park. Often, without our parents' permission, we would head in the opposite direction: to the park on Fourth Avenue. Once we crossed Fifth the neighborhood changed abruptly. Stately brownstones gave way to brightly painted row houses; the pavements, no longer well maintained, were full of cracks; there was laughter and cursing on the streets; women and men kept the stoops warm, drinking from long bottles of beer; the passionate voices singing love songs on the radio were in Spanish. We preferred this part of the neighborhood. It was more alive, more mysterious.

Anais loved to dine out. And food had always been my secret weapon whenever I need to break down her resistance. Plying her with exotic food and wine had always worked to get me out of messy situations. I'd even called ahead to make sure my order of flowers had arrived and were placed at our table. Nothing was working tonight. She brushed aside my questions about her trip with indolent stares and monosyllabic grunts.

Unable to engage her in any meaningful conversation, I finished my chili shrimp in coconut sauce and sipped my Chardonnay. She toyed with her pan-seared sea scallops in silence. I tried to make eye contact but she ignored my searching gaze. Once in a while I would catch a spark in her brown eyes behind the look of torment plastered on her face. In her current mood the possibility was faint, but the thought of making love to her later was never more tantalizing.

WHEN WE reached home Chesney was already asleep. The sitter, Jovan, a sixteen-year-old Brooklyn Tech student from next door, was watching TV and yacking on her cell phone in the living room. I paid her and she left.

"Would you like a drink?" I said to Anais.

She was halfway up the stairs when she stopped and turned her head just enough for me to catch a glimpse of her drained face. "No, I'm going to bed."

I began to unbutton my shirt at the foot of the stairs. "Look, Anais."

Maintaining her distracted expression she turned completely around and sat down on the stairs leaning her head on the rail. "What?"

Edging up to where she was sitting I stood over her, reaching down to finger her blue silk scarf. She folded her lips into a tight ball and looked up at me. Her eyes were tired, but the gloss of her dark skin was still new, like the shine of a freshly minted coin.

I reached down and traced her mouth with my index finger. Her body stiffened, but she did not move. Had to circle the warm flesh of her mouth several times before she relaxed, releasing her lips from their self-imposed prison. Slowly she stood erect, licking my finger. Leaning my body into hers now, in the most affectionate manner I knew. We stayed this way for a long time. Then her arms curved around my back and she rested her head on my shoulders.

"I know this is a lot to have to deal with your first night back."

"I only have one question. Are you fucking her?"

"I love you too much," I said.

"A yes or no is what I'm looking for."

"No."

She smiled weakly. "I missed you."

. . .

OUR BEDROOM looked out onto a patio and below that a garden surrounded by a high evergreen hedge. In our king-sized bed we took turns undressing each other. When my turn came I could not help but feel lucky. Her body was as firm as when I met her ten years ago and if anything she was even more beautiful today. Over the years the confidence she had developed as a woman and her awareness of her own beauty had become a part of her physicality, producing a sensuality cauldroned in playfulness and candor. As I peeled off her black silk shirt I admired her flat hard stomach. While she wasn't a gym rat, Anais took care of her body with a daily regimen of exercise and dance classes.

When she kissed me I could feel the release of tension built up in the weeks we'd been apart as the dust of our misunderstanding floated away. She brimmed with peppery sensuality. One whiff of her sexual scent and I was frantic with anticipation. I hosed her taut body with my tongue, languishing for a long time on her fat nipples as she teased my manhood with her strong hands and talked to me, her voice mischievous with laughter. We spent a long time caressing each other, something she'd taught me to do, playfully prolonging the explosion we knew was coming.

She got on top of me, her eyes never leaving mine. It was a snug fit and with a hard sigh she settled onto my chest, her face flushed with urgent passion. Undulating her hips with a rhythm so deceptively gentle that it looked as though she was barely moving, she lay on my chest flicking her tongue over my nipples. That drove me crazy. My hands roamed her hard buttocks, urging her on, but she kept her rhythm smooth and contained, concentrating on teasing me into losing control. Her easy rhythm picked up pace and she began to buck, grinding her pelvis into me with sustained power. She sat upright, her palms braced against my shoulders, and began to rise up and down, steadily bouncing on my manhood. Her mouth fell open and guttural sounds she made spurred my passion even more. I incited her in a language beyond reason or respect. This pushed her into overdrive. She screamed and the fire flowed from her sex up through my stomach, into my brain and back to her. Ignited, we exploded together.

EVER SINCE I left the NYPD in a cloud of anger and frustration I've kept a low profile at police social events. The albatross of anger I had carried around over my shooting almost proved too heavy for my marriage, and it cost me a number of good friends in the department, but I still had a few left.

The next day, Friday, I called Terry Doyle at the 112th in Queens shortly after 10:00 A.M. Promoted recently to captain, Terry came from an Irish-American police family. Father was a cop. His uncle too, until he was caught shaking down drug dealers, and Terry's son was about to graduate from the Academy.

On one of the few occasions when I gathered with other cops since leaving the department, I celebrated Terry's promotion with him and some of his buddies at a pub on Steinway Boulevard. Only a handful of the cops present knew anything about the shooting that led to my resignation, and I liked it that way. I was able to relax and have a good time.

A few minutes passed before I heard Terry's chirpy hello.

"Terry, Blades here. How's it going, pardner?"

"Blades, you son of a gun! I better check my lotto tickets. Whenever I hear from you I win something. The last time you called me on the job I got promoted the next day, remember?"

I chuckled. "That's why they call me Santa Claus."

"Who calls you that, your wife?"

"Never mind."

"So what's shaking, dude?"

"A couple of squirrels got squashed in Forest Hills night before last in a drive-by. What your boys got on it?"

"Forest Hills. Can you freaking believe that? What's your angle, big man?"

"Straight up. A friend of mine was caught in the crossfire."

"With her panties down?"

"Come again?"

"Somebody did. All over the seat of the limo. Was she the one playing horsy?"

"I never said it was a woman."

"We found the limo with semen stains all over the seat. Found a pair of panties too. That would suggest a woman was present. Your friend got a name?"

"This person wants to remain *this person* for now."

"Achew!"

"Bless you."

"Excuse me," Terry sniffled. "Caught a cold from my niece."

"Robbie's daughter?"

"Yeah. She's been spending a lot of time over at the house lately."

Terry's twin brother, Robbie, a firefighter, died in the World Trade Center terrorist attack.

"How's the family doing?" I said.

"Robbie's wife still can't sleep in her own bed. She's basically moved into my house. Practically housebound. Gave up her job. Just sits around watching soap operas."

"How's your mom?"

"She wants to move to Dublin. Too many bad memories here, she said. First Joe, and then Robbie."

"Is she from there? I mean, was she born there?"

"No. Her father was, though. She was born here, but her mind is locked in mourning."

"Your father, he's retired, right?"

"Yeah."

"Is he moving too?"

"I don't know. It's one big drama right now, you know. She says she's moving with or without him. She's got a sister there and lots of relatives. My father says he ain't running away from America. Look, Blades, would love to stay and chat, but I've got a precinct to run."

"Gimme some love, Terry. What you got on the people who got chopped?"

"Three down. All males. Two Caucasians. One black. Excuse me, African-American."

"He wasn't American, anyway."

"How'd you know that?"

"Come on, Terry. Don't make me beg."

"The investigation is ongoing. That's the official word."

"Fuck the official word."

"A bone for a bone, Blades. Who is she?"

"This person is just an innocent bystander."

"Then bring this person in to talk to us."

"There's gotta be something you can share with me, Terry."

"One of the body bags was a low-level diplo from the Bahamas. He calls the limo company from the airport in Arizona to pick up someone at a Bronx address. The house, we discovered, is rented to RL Investments. A full year paid for. RL Investments happens to be a shell company owned by our dead diplo. The other two bags were the limo driver and a clipper from out of town. Russian. We believe he was part of the hit squad and got chopped down himself. We have no theory yet on how that happened. There may've been bodyguards in the limo. We got several species of slugs at the scene."

"What do Russian mobsters want with a third-rate diplomat? Was he dirty?"

He hesitated. In the short break I heard his heavy breathing. He coughed.

"What, Terry?"

"You want any more information talk to the Feds."

"FBI?"

"FBI. State Department. It's their show. The FBI might've been watching this diplomat for a while."

"A sting?"

"I don't know what was going down."

"Thanks, Terry. Say hi to the wife."

"You bet."

AROUND ONE O'CLOCK that afternoon I got my hair cut at Shirley's Salon on Rutland Road, where I listened to Shirley and his crew discuss cricket and Caribbean politics. I heard all about the debate in Barbados over one Lord Horatio Nelson, a British naval hero, and whether or not the Barbados government should remove his statue from its place in the center of the capital, Bridgetown, because it was a symbol of imperialism and colonialism. Most of the regular patrons, older men in their fifties and sixties waiting for their weekly trim, argued that the statue should stay since it had become a popular tourist attraction, but one fire-tongued youth with cornrows said he would volunteer to go down and blow up the statue himself since the man it memorialized hated black people and had been a slave trader.

ANAIS SHOVED her head into the family room where I was listening to Mingus. It was just after four. She asked if I wanted to walk with her and Chez to get roti on Flatbush Avenue. Ordinarily, when I was troubled, Mingus's music had a way of speaking to me, leveling out the rough edges of my emotions. For some reason I wasn't feeling him today. Perhaps I was just too tired. I agreed to go with them.

Looking west I saw a sky stippled purple and orange as the sun played hide and seek with tall buildings. The air was smoky gray from a fire somewhere in the neighborhood, and as we walked past the large apartment building at the corner of Flatbush and Maple the smell of pot wafted through an open ground-floor window. From overstuffed garbage bins along Flatbush refuse had overflowed onto the oil-speckled sidewalk serving up fetid fumes of decayed fruit and meat.

The condition of the sidewalk so disgusted me, I wanted to turn around and go home, but Chez had her mind set on roti, and new to this role of father, I relented.

Straining to pull a shopping cart behind her, an old woman in a multistained red coat with a white dirt-caked wool cap pulled over her face, slipped past mumbling to herself. I turned to see her rifling the garbage bin, retrieving the lofty prize of a half-eaten McDonald's burger.

The roti place was crowded. As we waited on line for Chez's beef roti my cell phone rang.

Noah grunted at me in a deep voice from the other end. "I just called your house. Where're you?"

"I didn't know I was under house arrest."

"Not in the mood for your smart-ass talk, Blades," he barked. "Meet me in Manhattan in an hour."

"What's shaking, Noah?"

At the mention of Noah's name Anais's eyes turned on me, her face rapidly tightening with displeasure.

"If I wanted to discuss it over the phone, I wouldn't ask you to meet me, now would I?"

"Where you want me to meet you, old man?"

"Joe Lilly's. I'll be at the bar. And I warned you already about that old man crap."

I rang off and clipped the phone back onto my belt. Anais's eyes were demanding an account of the conversation.

"Noah wants to see me. I gotta go to Manhattan."

I didn't wait for any further questions to filter through her insistent eyes. I bent down and kissed Chesney. "I gotta go to see a friend, Chez. I'll see you later."

"Why can't we come?" Chesney asked innocently.

"Next time, baby."

She giggled. "You always say that."

"Your father says a lot of things he don't mean," Anais chimed.

I crossed my eyes at her. "Don't say things like that to her."

Anais folded her hands over her chest. "When're you coming back?"

"I don't know."

"Should I wait up?"

"You bet."

I tried to kiss Anais on the lips; she turned her face and my lips fell on her moist cheek. Chesney giggled at our childishness.

TEN

The thought of driving crossed my mind but only for a second. Prospect Park station on the B line was a block away and I felt adventurous, a prerequisite for descending into the New York subway. Like many of the B-line stations in Brooklyn, Prospect Park was under renovation. Here, the tracks, while below street level, were open to the elements. The token booth was not underground as it was in many of the other stations, but housed in a dilapidated building above ground.

The ground beneath me shook as a Manhattan-bound train rumbled into the station. I swiped my Metrocard through the computerized turnstile and slid through, racing down the steel stairs as the train screeched to a stop.

I found a seat in the last car and immediately wished I'd brought a book. New York subway rides were never boring; there was always someone begging for money or food, or a struggling singer armed with a guitar eager to share his talent, or some loud fool who sought his fifteen minutes of fame on the train. I would prefer not to be an eavesdropper on other people's conversations, or be a witness to the many subterranean dramas, familial and otherwise, but the alternative was taking on the congestion above ground. No picnic that.

Seated next to me was a woman eating fervently from a large bag of Wise potato chips. Opposite her, a man reading the *Times*, his round pink face like an inflated balloon. Intermittently he glanced at her suspiciously, until he could no longer stand the noise of her chomping jaws and got up. The only other seat in the car was between two black men. He looked over in their direction, then walked to the far end to stand against the door.

I got off the train at West 4th Street and walked briskly down the underground tunnel, past rows of movie posters defaced by scribblings of pubescent youngsters in all likelihood bragging to themselves and anyone else bored enough to try to decipher their hieroglyphics about girls they probably never saw naked. The walls of the New York subway system were tainted with many such testosterone-inspired fantasies.

Joe Lilly's on Carmine was one of Noah's favorite joints. The margaritas were dirt cheap and got me adequately inebriated, but I didn't like the food, which could only be described as maudlin Southern, everything fried and smothered.

I found Noah at one end of the long mahogany bar, his back to the door. Alongside him was a woman whose blond hair flopped at the nape of her neck like crushed silk. She was applying rouge to her cheeks with the visual aid of a compact, a glass of white wine set on the bar in front of her.

Noah dragging carelessly on a bottle of dark beer.

The woman leaning toward him to say something.

It was clear he'd been drinking for a while. He tilted away with the stiffness of an over-the-hill boxer as if he didn't want to hear what she had to say.

I came up on his right shoulder and tapped him. He must've sensed my presence before I touched him because he didn't turn around right away. Instead, he lifted the Samuel Adams bottle to his mouth and drained it, throwing his head back with uncompromising abandon, the act of a man bordering on drunkenness or done to establish some external term of reference for someone's benefit.

The seat next to him was empty so I sat down. Noah turned in my direction, his eyes dull as a piece of gray cardboard.

"What you drinking, Blades?" he said.

"The usual."

He laughed, then hollered to the bartender. "One margarita over here, Pedro. Easy on the salt. This man is very health conscious. And bring me another beer. Make sure it's cold. The last one was too warm. Warm dark beer tastes like shit." He launched into a raucous laugh. Other people sitting at tables around the restaurant turned to look in our direction.

"Are you okay, Noah?"

"Am I okay? You tell me, Blades. You've known me a long time. Am I okay?"

Noah wasn't drunk but he wasn't himself, which was understandable. My friend was still fighting the chokehold of shock and it was almost as painful to watch his inner struggle as it was to remember the tragedy that dispatched his mind into this state of confusion.

"Blades." Noah's face was suddenly serious. "I want you to meet someone."

He stood up and took a few steps back from the bar so that the woman sitting next to him could see me clearly. As our eyes met for the first time I was impressed with the steadiness of her gaze. Her hazel eyes never wavered from my face and there was a purposefulness to her demeanor that suggested someone who was not easily distracted, someone who knew when and how to take charge of a situation.

"Billie Heat. This is Blades Overstreet," Noah said.

I got up and stepped close enough to shake her hand. Her handshake was all business: firm, brief. Throughout she kept eye contact with me, smiling at the last moment when I mouthed that it was nice to meet her, but she said nothing.

"Miss Heat is a therapist," Noah continued. "Why don't we exchange seats, Miss Heat? That way you can talk to both of us."

"Actually, it's Dr. Heat, and I'm a psychologist. But call me Billie, please." She stood up for the first time to take over the seat previously occupied by Noah. She was tall and straight as an exclamation mark, her skin bright as a hologram.

The bouncy olive-skinned bartender brought my margarita. I used to think he was the owner but Noah had told me that he was a cousin of the owner's wife, whose name was not Joe Lilly; to tell the truth I can't remember the owner's name, but he was an ex-cop, someone who worked with Noah back in the day.

I rubbed the lip of the glass to distribute the salt evenly, allowing myself a moment of indulgence as my fingers lingered to absorb the sensuality of salt grains on a frosty glass. The salt burned my lip on the first sip. But I expected that. My lips chapped in cold weather and I often forgot to apply balm to keep them moist. I licked my lips, dissolving the remaining salt, and took another sip of my drink. Then I put the glass on the bar-top and turned to look at Dr. Heat, whose snooty demeanor was beginning to crackle my blood.

Noah began to speak. "Dr. Heat . . . Billie called me yesterday after she read about Ronan. I want you to hear what she told me."

Dr. Heat turned to face me. She spoke in a clear authoritative voice. "Ronan was a patient of mine. As recently as two weeks ago he talked about fearing for his life. He intimated that somebody might've been stalking him."

My eyes were fastened on the tall woman's eyes as she spoke, an old habit left over from my days in the NYPD. Drug addicts were notorious liars and since I used many of them as informants I had to be sure they weren't feeding me chicken shit. By carefully analyzing their eye movements I discovered that I could quite accurately determine when they were lying. Ever since Ronan's assassination I'd gone into investigative mode, where I approached everyone and everything related to Ronan with skepticism.

"Did he say who might've been stalking him?" I said.

"No," replied Dr. Heat.

"Do you know if he went to the police?" I asked.

"I don't know."

"Did you suggest it?"

"I should've, I suppose."

"How long have you been treating Ronan?"

"About six months."

"Did you take his concerns seriously?"

She paused and lifted her glass to her mouth, sipped, then put the glass back down and sighed. That gentle sigh, the pause to catch a breath, made her seem human, finally. "I couldn't tell. At times he appeared paranoid."

"What are the signs of paranoia?" I asked.

Her eyes flickered violently and then she smiled. With bony fingers she combed her treacle-thick blond hair, then flicked her head, flashing her shiny mane through the air. She looked at me and her eyes were sharp enough to do bodily harm. "I can tell you don't like psychologists," she said.

"How's that?" I said acidly.

"Your tone. It's very aggressive. Combative."

"I'm sure you didn't come here to analyze me."

"It's not an analysis, Mr. Overstreet. Just an assessment."

"Meaning what? A judgment without cause?"

"No need to get defensive."

"Are you telling us that Ronan was suffering from paranoia?"

"I didn't say that."

"Then what are you saying?"

"Ronan had a lot of issues."

"Don't we all?"

Her eyes grew eager. "Don't you feel a need to talk sometimes? Ronan did."

"What are some of the things Ronan talked to you about?"

"I can't go into details. I'm sure you can appreciate that. But I can tell you this. He had a deep distrust of some of the people around him. He often said he was surrounded by spies. He fired his personal assistant because he thought she might be a spy. He believed someone would try to assassinate him because of his views, the way they did Malcolm X."

"Is that what he said?"

"Yes."

"Did he say who this personal assistant was spying for?"

"No. But he did say he had to call the police to get her off the premises. She became belligerent and abusive."

"Did she threaten him?"

"Yes. But I'm sure he didn't take her seriously." Her eyes wavered. "Ronan came to me because he needed help with personal problems. In hindsight I realize the threat he felt must've been real. At the time it didn't seem that way. I'm sorry about what happened to him."

"Is that why you're here? You feel bad?"

Instead of answering she picked up her wine glass. I picked up my margarita, which looked even more appealing after staring into Dr. Heat's cold eyes. I licked the lip of the glass once then drew a mouthful of the tangy liquid. I could feel the slender woman's eyes on me.

Noah got up. "It was good of you to call me, Dr. Heat. Thanks for coming."

She stood up. "No trouble. I'm very sorry for your loss. Ronan was an extraordinary man. I just wish . . ." Her voice trailed off.

They shook hands behind me.

"Thank you," Noah said, and walked over to the rack to get her coat.

"I wish we could've met under more pleasant circumstances," she said. She turned to face me and was smiling. "Likewise for you, Mr. Overstreet."

She extended her hand and I took it. It was small in mine, and her skin had a cracked luminosity under the yellow light.

"Same here," I said nonchalantly.

She looked at me and her mouth moved as if to say something; nothing came out. Stiffly, she turned to Noah, who was holding her black wool coat in his hands. For a moment it looked as if she wanted to take the coat from him. She placed her pocketbook on the chair and allowed herself to be fitted.

She walked crisply out, her flowing black coat almost touching the ground.

Noah ordered another beer and scooted over into the seat next to me. "Why the hell didn't you rip out her throat while you were at it?"

I turned to face him. "What do you mean?"

"What do I mean? Jesus, could you've been more contemptuous? If I didn't know better I would say it was something personal. What's wrong with you?"

"I don't like her."

"That's no reason to try and stuff your dick down her throat."

"Do you believe Ronan was crazy?"

"Look, Blades, you need to be more open-minded sometimes, you know."

"Open-minded about what?"

"Therapy does help some people."

"Did it help Ronan?"

"How the fuck should I know? The boy didn't talk to me for years."

"I'd like to talk to this personal assistant he fired. Can you find out who she is and how I can get in touch with her?"

"I'm sure his office would have that information."

"How's Donna holding up?"

"Her sister just came up from Detroit. And her brother is flying in from California. There are times when having a big family helps."

"Have you decided on a date for the funeral?"

He shook his head slowly. "You hungry?"

"Not hungry enough to eat here."

He laughed. "Man, you need to come down off that gourmet high horse. Your mom's from New Orleans, isn't she?"

"She was born there, yes."

"She grew up there, too. And your grandmother was West Indian, so I know fried food can't be foreign to you. What the hell do you have against food that comes with a little grease?"

"Lots of grease and no taste, that's a bad combination."

"Nothing tastes better than grease. Ask the folks who eat at McDonald's."

"I'm not eating here, Noah. There's Tutta Pasta down the street. And there's Jyoti's Indian Palace on Seventh Avenue South."

He crinkled his eyes. "I'm not hungry anyway. Haven't had an appetite since this shit happened."

"Did it surprise you that he was seeing a psychologist?"

Noah tied his brow into a dark knot. "I don't know. It's the thing to do now, I guess. You can't function in this country now without a therapist or pills, it seems. I mean, that's the way white people been doing it for years. Black people who couldn't afford a therapist have been reaching for the bottle and the occasional crack pipe. Either way, everybody in this country is on something. Something to get them high. Something to get them around the monsters of life."

"Have you ever been in therapy?"

"Naw, I'm old school. I'd rather drink."

"Why're we so unhappy, Noah?"

"That's what capitalism does to people, man."

"Capitalism makes people paranoid?"

"You can never be happy if your moral base is tied to the production of capital and convincing other people that they can't be satisfied with what they have. That they must always have more. That it's their right to have more than the next guy. That in order for the system to survive they need to buy more. Even if they don't really need it. It's the American way, but it's fucked up and wasteful."

"Look at the alternative."

"What?"

"Look at what happened in Russia."

"Who says that's the alternative?"

"Then what's the alternative?"

"I don't know. Maybe there's no alternative. I know this. We gotta rediscover the meaning of the word contentment or this planet is doomed. Contentment is a word whose true meaning runs counter to the rampant acquisition of capital. 'Cause if that's your purpose in life how can you be happy? You can get rich, but that don't mean you'll be happy."

"It don't mean you'll be unhappy either, professor."

"Yeah? Professor this." He grabbed his crotch.

We both laughed.

Noah continued, "Suppose after all the buying and accumulation of capital and stuff, you're still not happy. What then? You start looking around for answers, asking questions. Then somebody calling herself a therapist tells you it's because of your parents. And since you can't do anything about your parents, since you can't go out and punish them for fucking up your life, for turning you into a consumer, there's only one thing left to do. Sedate yourself. That's why the rich and poor alike make drug dealers rich. Some legal. Some illegal."

I always got a kick out of Noah's riffs on American society. I didn't always understand or agree with him but the thing about Noah I loved was that he never held back. His tongue was always loaded and he sprayed everyone.

"You think Ronan was blaming you?" I said.

He looked at me then his eyes wandered off. "I just read a book called the *Founding Brothers.* You should read it."

"What's it about?"

"The Founding Fathers. Get it? Washington. Jefferson. John Adams. Alexander Hamilton. That crew. The people who put slavery and liberty in bed together and begat America. Land of Freedom and Racism. You don't think those contradictions are enough to send us all to the funny farm? It might all make some sense if a president had the balls to stand up and offer a real apology to black people for the holocaust of slavery."

"I thought Clinton did that."

"Then I musta missed it." Noah was now pretty drunk.

"So we're not eating, right?" I said.

He laughed. "We're drinking."

"Not anymore."

"You've only had one drink."

"I'm done. So are you. In fact I think we should leave."

"If you wanna leave. Leave."

"I said we. Did you drive?"

"We? I ain't married to you."

"I'm taking you home, Noah. Where's your car?"

"You ain't taking me nowhere."

"I'm not letting you drive that truck in your condition."

"What's wrong with you, boy? You lost your mind? You don't know nothing about my condition."

"Do you want me to call Donna?"

He turned away from me and got up off the seat. I watched him sift through the pockets of his lined jacket, coming up with a bunch of keys, which he threw at me.

"If you ever threaten to call my wife on me again I'm a kick your ass."

ELEVEN

Saturday. I took Anais to Danielle B. on 57th Street in Manhattan, where I bought a diamond ring for her birthday, which had fallen on one of the days she had been away. Afterward we lunched at Fireman's, a hotbed for tourists, a place I would not ordinarily be caught dead in at lunchtime, but Anais's cousin was the director of sales and, well, the lunch was free.

Anais leaned over to kiss me soon after the waiter had delivered our appetizers and left. The dark pupils of her eyes sparkled as bright as the diamond on her finger and I got an irresistible urge to ride my fingers along the ridge of her clavicle. The thought induced me to smile.

"What're you smiling at?" She reached across the red tablecloth and clasped my hands, linking her fingers through mine.

"I love you," I said.

"In that case, you wouldn't mind telling me what Noah wanted last night?"

"He just wanted to talk."

"Any genius could've figured that out," she responded with a wry grin.

I picked at my salad. "He's my friend, Anais. What do you want?"

"I want you to look at me."

I turned to face her. A splinter of sunlight bounced off the wall, splattering haphazardly on her neck, highlighting the smooth swell of her jawline. She chewed patiently, as if waiting for me to say something.

"I've got to help him," I said.

"Help him do what?"

"Get through this. He's hurting right now."

"And you didn't discuss investigating Ronan's murder?"

"Back off, Anais."

"Blades, you've got your own family. You've just become a father yourself. You hardly know your daughter. You expect me to be a mother to this girl that I don't even know. I'm not complaining about that. But don't you think you should let the police find Ronan's killer and concentrate on keeping this family happy?"

"Noah is like family."

She released my hand. "There's no reasoning with you, is there?"

"Just give me some time, Anais."

"You're like a damn pit bull, Blades. When you clench your jaws around something you'd rather die than let it go."

"I cannot desert him now, Anais. I just cannot."

"What about me? You'd rather desert me?"

"Let's just drop this before . . ."

"No, damn you! I don't want to drop it."

I jumped up. "Fine, then I'll drop it!"

Heads snapped in our direction at the raising of my voice. I picked up my hat. Anais looked at me stunned, but her eyes never left my face. I felt as if I was on stage and didn't know my lines. Fumbling for words that wouldn't come, I flopped the black Kangol backwards on my head and went to get my coat.

IT WAS stupid of me to storm out of the restaurant leaving Anais behind. I knew it the moment I stepped out onto the sun-washed pavement, into the thicket of New York tourist traffic. I turned around to go back to apologize but before I could move I saw her coming out. Expecting her to approach me, I stopped. But she passed without a glance in my direction, in fact, as if we were strangers, bustling down 57th in the direction of Broadway. Too surprised to do anything I stood bewildered for what may've been no more than a few seconds, but what seemed like minutes, before I set off after her.

I caught up with her at Broadway and 57th, as she was about to enter the drugstore on that corner. Clutching her arm, I tried to arrest her flight, but she slithered out of my grasp and went inside.

I remained outside. The carvings on the new hi-rise art-deco apartment building across the street spat sunlight into my face, though not enough to burn away the humiliation I was feeling. Roadwork in progress a few blocks south on Broadway created a traffic jam, piling cabs on top of limousines, and buses on top of delivery trucks. Impatient drivers honked their horns, competing with the jabbering jackhammers for decibel supremacy.

Anais did not stay long in the drugstore. She came out with a small gray shopping bag in her hand, the color matching the scowl on her face. She stood on the steps looking down on me; the whites of her eyes clear as fresh snow.

"I'm sorry," I mumbled.

"What did you say?"

"I said I'm sorry."

"What do you think would happen if you went skydiving without a parachute?"

I stared mystified. "What's that supposed to mean?"

"You figure it out."

She walked past me and stood at the curb and stuck her hand out to hail a cab.

"Where're you going?" I said, my voice still apologetic.

"Home."

"Why're you taking a cab? The car is parked two blocks away."

"Because if I got into a car with you right now we might end up in the East River. I'm not going to listen to you try to convince me that what you're doing is honorable. I don't want to hear it, Blades. You still think you're a cop. Be a cop, then. But don't expect me to load your gun."

A dirty-looking yellow cab pulled up close to the curb. I strained to find a suitable response to delay her flight, but Anais wasn't about to wait for bricks to fall from my clogged brain. Before I could reply she jumped into the cab, which drove away with a spurt of blue smoke.

IN MANY parts of the country the onset of darkness prompted citizens to rush indoors. Not my city. The absence of daylight in New York City was celebrated by the unleashing of a mad rush of creativity; thousands of volts of electricity pouring into golden filaments hanging all over the city powering zillions of electrons, driving the wheels of commerce. Dazzling floodlights on Broadway shows. Dizzying strobe lights in discos. Office lights on Wall Street. Blue lights in jazz clubs. Dim romantic lights in restaurants. The glow of crack pipes heating up.

As the sun was disappearing I went running in Prospect Park. The park's lilac lights spread through the empty arms of giant oaks and sleeping elms, stripped of their foliage since November. The evening was raw and cloudy, the wind whipping around me with the fervor of a spurned lover, quaking leafless branches, stirring up dirt and dust along the path. It wasn't good running weather, but I needed to shake off my anxiety. I hadn't seen Anais since our fight this afternoon. She hadn't come home and hadn't answered any of my calls to her cell.

I ran about five miles, almost twice around the park. Despite the weather, there were enough runners and cyclists to keep me company. Running hard, I pounded my anger into the asphalt with such passion that my knees hurt, but I continued running until my chest ached, my heart throbbing violently against my rib cage. Gloveless, my fingers burned as if on fire and the wind scraped my face like the knife of an angry mugger.

I finished my run and tottered in a stupor down Lincoln Street.

Opposite the Prospect Park subway station I stopped, hunched over, my chest heaving, trying to stave off the prickling urge to puke as I scarfed frigid air into my lungs.

Underneath my black tracksuit the fitted biker shorts and sweatshirt were soaked through. My wool cap was damp; my wet face was chilling quickly. Babbling riders spilled from the subway station. I stood upright, having scuffed the urge to gag, and zigzagged through the crowd on the sidewalk, crossing Flatbush.

About ten yards away from my house I sensed someone coming up on my left shoulder. I turned abruptly.

"Blades Overstreet?"

Her voice was rich and deep, which seemed about what a voice coming out of such a large body should sound like.

I stopped walking. "Do I know you?"

She brushed aside my gruffness. "Did you enjoy your run?"

"I'm sorry, but my mother told me not to talk to strangers."

She spooned yogurt from a plastic cup. "Sallie Kraw. FBI."

"You're alone? I thought you feds traveled in herds."

She smiled, licked her lips. "Budget cutbacks. But as you can see, I'm a big girl. I can take care of myself."

She opened the way for a million other intriguing questions. Like, how did a big girl like her get mixed up in that racket. But I was out of deep questions. And I was tired as hell. I just wanted to get into my damn house, take off my wet clothes and have a shower before supper, and with any luck my wife might actually be inside waiting for me.

I rubbed sweat from my neck. "Are you lost or something?"

"I was waiting for you. The young lady in your house said you'd gone running. I'd say she's too old to be your daughter."

"Babysitter."

She licked the white plastic spoon. "Yes. So, how was your run?"

"Lonely."

"You know, there's nothing that appeals to my instincts more than a man with sweat running down his face. Reminds me of my father.

He had a farm in Michigan. Every morning he would come into the house after working for more than two hours in his fields with sweat streaming down his face. It was beautiful."

"That's very nice. But I'm already married."

"But does your wife like to see you sweat?"

I chuckled. "I didn't realize sweating was a spectator sport."

"This is America. We're all a bunch of bored nuts. Everything is sport. Everything is entertainment."

"So you're here to see me sweat. Is that all?"

A lefty. The yogurt cup she was holding was lost in the palm of her right hand.

"I bet I know what you're thinking. You're thinking I have very large hands," she said.

Volcano bubbling in my stomach again. "I was thinking I'd love to stay and watch you eat but . . ."

Stirring the spoon into the bottom of the cup, she said, "Tell me about Maxwell Burns."

"Who?"

"The Bahamian deputy ambassador to the United States. We found him last night shot to death in Queens."

"Did someone tell you I knew him?"

"We found your card in a limousine he left the airport in. Perhaps he visited your club sometime."

"It's possible."

"But you don't remember?"

"Can't say I do."

"Would you walk with me to my car?"

I stared at her, uninspired. "It's a pretty safe neighborhood, Agent."

She crumpled the yogurt cup in her hand. "I was thinking if you saw a picture of Mr. Burns it might jog your memory. I have one in my car. It's right over there. Only take a moment."

She turned and walked briskly to a car parked about ten feet down the block. For a big woman she was as nimble as a show horse, walking on her toes, it seemed. I followed reluctantly. She opened the passenger door and scooted across the seat to the driver's side. Leaning on the open door I peered into the black Impala.

"Get in," she said, her voice weighted with confidence.

I hesitated, not particularly taken with her bossy attitude. She opened a manila envelope and took out a large photograph. She looked up and saw that I hadn't moved.

"Please, get in," she said.

I slumped into the seat and she dropped the picture in my lap. The car's roof light illuminated the photo, which I examined with little interest. As River had said he had a handsome face, though not as handsome as I'd expected. His eyes looked tired and scornful, his ears far too big for his small face. Then again, it might not have been a good picture.

"Does that face do anything for you?"

I shook my head.

"You've never met him or had any dealing with him whatsoever?"

"None." I couldn't hold back the sneeze. "Achew!"

"Bless you! How do you think he got your business card?"

"When you find out thank whoever it was that's drumming up business for me."

She took the picture from my hands and started the car. "Thank you."

"I'm free to go now?" I said.

Her teeth were bright when she smiled. "They told me to watch out for you."

"Who told you that?"

"My momma always told me not to kiss and tell."

"Someone should've told you this town's full of liars."

"Good night, Mr. Overstreet."

The car drove away and I stood watching, no longer feeling fatigued. The crisp air that I inhaled seemed to be sharpening my senses. I locked my fingers together under my chin and that's when my stomach erupted.

. . .

THAT EVENING I cooked dinner for Chesney and myself. She ate hardly anything. She pleaded for a beef roti, but I was too tired to walk to the roti shop on Flatbush and they didn't deliver. I ordered her to eat what was on her plate. That's what my grandmother would've done.

I had wanted to cook fish but one of the things we were discovering about our new neighborhood was that fresh fish was a scarce commodity. The two fish stores we found reeked of stale fish as soon as you stepped through the door. We just couldn't give them business under those conditions.

Chesney picked reticently at her chicken, her mouth high on a mountain. I got tired of her antics and excused her from the table. Not hungry myself, I stopped eating soon after she disppeared upstairs.

I cracked open a bottle of Banks beer—which to my delight I had found available in this neighborhood—and went into the living room, where I sat staring at a painting I'd bought in Barbados from one of my father's friends, a young painter named Neville Crawford. Detailing two young boys wrestling on a beach, their scrawny backs reflecting the sun's rays while a group of older boys looked on, this oil on canvas was one of my favorite paintings. As I drank the Barbadian lager, the tropical flavor of the painting set my mind flowing across the Atlantic sea and for a moment I felt the sun's rays bearing down on my bare back.

The phone rang, shocking me back to the cold. It rang twice before Chesney picked up and called down from the top of the stairs.

"Daddy, it's Auntie Anais," she said.

I walked into the family room behind the stairwell and picked up the cordless lying on the sofa.

"I've got it," I hollered to Chesney, and waited for the click of her phone settling into its cradle. "Where're you?" I said to Anais.

"On my way home."

I waited a second for her to elaborate as she breathed unevenly into the phone. But she said nothing more.

"I was worried about you," I said.

"Sorry. Should've called earlier."

"Where'd you go?"

"The movies."

"Long movie."

"No need to get sarky."

"Sarcasm or tears? Which do you prefer?"

She gave a little laugh. "Tears from you? Now that would turn me on."

I clucked my tongue twice mockingly. "Now who's being sarky?"

"I'm sorry about this afternoon, Blades. Why don't you open a bottle of wine and light some candles in the bedroom. I'm feeling quite penitent tonight. It's a night when you could probably do anything you want to me."

"Anything?"

"Anything your little heart desires."

I laughed out loud. "You sound like you're drunk already."

"See, there. You can take absolute advantage of me."

"I didn't know they served alcohol at the movies."

"I ran into some old friends after the movie."

"Anybody I know?"

"I don't think so. People from the theater."

"I know people in the theater."

"The only person you know in theater is Noah Peltier. And he's not really in theater. He's a professor. More interested in theory than practice."

"I think Noah would dispute that."

"If he didn't he wouldn't be Noah. But nobody can dispute this, Blades, my love. I'm horny as hell. I'm drunk. And I'm ovulating. You know how I get when I'm ovulating."

I didn't say anything.

Her voice echoed wetly in my ear. "Did you hear what I said? I'm ovulating."

"I heard you."

"I'll be home soon. You still gonna be mad at me?"

"We'll see."

"No, Blades. Let's finish it now. You can start something else when I get home. Something that'll give us both some pleasure."

"See you when you get here."

Her voice turned silky. "I love you, sweetie."

Like a centipede those words wormed into my ear, sucking the fight out of me. "I love you too, baby."

I waited for the thud of dead air before sliding the phone away from me onto the sofa. I don't know if it was anger or confusion, but there was something clawing deep in my chest and I was afraid to release it. Has Anais been mysterious about where she'd been or was I being paranoid?

The pale light from the street shone through the window. I got up to draw the blinds and happened to glance across the street. There was a man standing in my garden who had absolutely no business being there.

TWELVE

I kept an empty nine-millimeter Glock locked in a desk in my bedroom. I grabbed my keys from the rack in the kitchen and hurried upstairs. Unlocking the drawer, I pulled out the nine, fitted a clip into the grip, uncatched the safety, and yanked the slide back to send a pepper into the chamber. I took one more peek out the window to see if the man was still there. He was staring up at me and I thought I saw him smile.

As I made my way to the stairs with the gun in my waist I stopped to make sure Chesney was in her room. Her television was on and she was lying across the bed already in pj's. I continued down the stairs and opened the front door.

The man had disappeared. I ran into the street, looked left and right, but the street was empty as far as my eyes could see. I walked south one block. A group of young men approached on foot, laughing and jabbering excitedly about sports, their arms flapping wildly. They breezed past me without a glance in my direction. My eyes followed them until they turned down the next block. Then the street was quiet and empty. I turned to walk back.

A yellow cab, one of those new Honda SUVs, with a neon ad for an upcoming movie starring Denzel strapped to its roof rack, pulled up in front of the house the same time I got there. I stood in full bore of its headlights as the passenger got out. Anais.

She dropped the shopping bags and stood looking at me as the cab spun its wheels and zoomed down the block. I could not make out the expression on her face, but as I walked toward her I realized she was smiling, the soft curled-lip smile she unleashes when she gets high.

When I got within distance she reached for my hand. "What're you doing out here?"

"Waiting for you," I lied.

Her smile broadened, showing rows of even teeth. "Really? That's so sweet."

"It's my job to be sweet to you."

"Does that mean the candles are aflame?"

I drew her into my arms. "What do you think?"

"I think we should go upstairs and get wicked."

I picked up her bags from the sidewalk. "You went shopping?"

The soft curled-lip smile again. She was drunk all right. "Didn't you say we were out of *Maxim?*"

She walked ahead of me. I watched the sensual swing of her high-stepping jig. She turned and crooked her finger, beckoning me inside.

STARVED, AND still tingling from the long night of lovemaking with Anais, I wolfed down a tower of blueberry pancakes the size of hubcaps at breakfast. I caught Chesney staring at me as I gobbled my food. Embarrassed by the probing eyes of my daughter, I slowed down, sipping hazelnut-flavored coffee.

She has my eyes, Chesney does. Every day I see it more and more. The adjustment to New York, to a new school, and to a man she'd only known roughly nine months—a man she now had to call Dad—had been difficult for her. In the first few months there were times when I wondered if it'd not been selfish of me to bring her to New York knowing that not only would she have to adjust to a new city, making new friends, but also a stepmother who had no children of her own. Though Anais sometimes spoke in wistful buzzwords about not having a child—*I've still got time; I'm too busy right now*—the issue, I suspected, would one day hit critical mass as she raced toward the big four-O. Did she need to be confronted with my daughter, a reminder that her clock was ticking?

Anais and Chesney took off for the Prospect Park skating rink after breakfast. Half an hour later I left the house.

FLATBUSH AVENUE was as lively as any marketplace—double-parked cars and streaking dollar-vans honking their musical horns, women pushing strollers crossing the street against traffic. I drove along tapping my foot to bebop on WFUB, the lone jazz station remaining in the New York area.

I reached Downtown Brooklyn, parked in the lot on Livingston Street, and walked back one block on Smith to the Brooklyn Tabernacle. I had not seen the inside of a church since I got married. Grandma Blades would've been horrified at how I turned out. Until her death when I was ten, she made sure I went to church and Sunday School every week.

The Brooklyn Tabernacle was located a few blocks from Voodoo. I passed it every time I went to the club, and it was the first church that came to mind this morning when I woke up and felt a need to give thanks for the daughter I didn't know I had nine months ago. I'm sure Anais would've gladly gone to church with me that morning, but it was something I felt I needed to do alone.

It was after twelve when I left the church. I was scheduled to meet Negus at the club around two. Enough time to pay River a visit.

The sky was a graveyard of gray clouds, as if everyone who'd ever had a broken dream had climbed up and hung their busted heart on a cloud. I reached my old neighborhood and parked a block away from the apartment and walked along President, a walk still very familiar to me, whistling "Papa Was a Rolling Stone."

I'd given River my keys so I buzzed and waited. Before River could let me in, a man appeared in the lobby and came outside singing "Papa Was a Rolling Stone."

We looked at each other and began laughing, realizing that it was one of those inexplicable coincidences. I slipped inside, singing now instead of whistling, and climbed the two flights to the apartment. I knocked three times on the door.

Low voices in the apartment.

Muffled giggles.

A man's voice.

River was not alone.

"Who is it?" Her malt-thick voice trickled through the heavy door.

"Blades."

Feet shuffling quickly inside, furniture shifting, feet scampering across the floor, then River's voice at the door, high pitched trying to sound calm, the voice of a woman trying to stifle sexual energy.

"Blades? What you doing here?"

"Need to talk to you."

"I just got up."

"You alone?"

"Gimme a minute, Blades."

"If you're not alone I can come back."

Hands fumbling with the lock. The door opened and she stood before me wrapped in a black and gold African-style robe, her eyes jumpy and bright. She twitched uncomfortably and wiggled her eyes around, which made her look as though she was having some kind of spasm.

"Are you okay?" I said.

She was striking in that flowing gown, her impressive height more commanding somehow, her skin the color of strong black tea, and her broad face more expressive than I'd ever seen it. "I'm fine. Look, you wanna come back later?"

I stared at her without speaking, the undeveloped gentleman in me telling me to turn around and walk away. But the devil was coaxing me to find out who was inside my apartment with River.

"You aren't alone, are you?"

"If you must know . . ."

A voice boomed from deep inside the apartment, "I'm here, man."

It was my partner Negus. River pushed the door open; the effort caused her gown to open slightly. She was naked underneath and though I wanted to turn my head away, I stared as if seeing an accident occurring before my eyes.

"Come in," she said, drawing her gown around her.

I stepped into the apartment, into the sweaty scent of coitus interruptus, into a cloud of memories. I'd bought this apartment on impulse after I sold the house in Queens. I'd wanted to move closer to Manhattan and while I couldn't afford Brooklyn Heights, this neighborhood offered the same delights without the rent surcharge—restaurants, bars, bookstores, and one of the best fish stores in Brooklyn—with its own charm, its own unruly, uninhibited nightlife on Smith Street, and dark claustrophobic side streets where shady figures cohabitated under the wings of the 76th Precinct.

"Listen, River, perhaps you're right. I should come back."

She turned to me and laughed, the high-pitched song of a kettle boiling. "You look like you've seen a ghost. Come on in. I'll make some coffee."

Negus appeared from the bedroom in black slacks and body-tight cream sweater, his size filling up the space in the tight corridor, his linebacker shoulders hunched, his eyes inspecting the floor as if he were a guilty schoolboy.

River had already turned and gone into the kitchen. Negus and I looked at each other, the awkwardness of the moment as titillating as a punch in the gut. I had no idea she and Negus were fucking each other, not that I cared, but I wished I didn't have to find out this way. Actually, this was good news for me. I could use this to convince my wife that River was just an employee in trouble who I was trying to help, nothing more.

"I guess we can have our meeting here," I joked to Negus.

"Look, Blades, I . . . Ah . . ."

"Hey, you don't need to explain anything."

River chirped in from the kitchen. "I think what he's trying to tell you, Blades, is that there's really nothing going on between us. It was just a fuck, that's all. I came out of the movies last night and felt like talking to somebody. I called him and he came by. We had some wine and things just got freaky."

"Look, I really think I should go," I said.

River came to stand in the kitchen door. "You came to see me, what did you want?"

"It can wait."

She stared straight at Negus. "If anybody is leaving, it's Negus."

Negus demurred. "Yeah, I should go. We still meeting at the club?"

"Yeah," I said. "We gotta talk about the show this weekend."

"I spoke to Papa Smooth last night. He's very excited," River said.

Negus spun and went into the bedroom. He returned with a black leather jacket slung over his shoulder like a limp piece of cloth and walked past me. He stopped at the door.

"I'll see you at the club then," he said to me.

River said, "Negus, thanks for last night. It was fun. Oh, and this morning, too."

Negus smiled awkwardly. "I'll call you later." He opened the door and went out, leaving it ajar.

I walked over and closed the door.

"You should get dressed," I said.

She looked at me for a second, her expression turning stony, as if she thought I was admonishing her. "I'll be back," she whispered, with an exaggerated twist of her mouth. As nonverbal a "fuck you" as I've ever seen.

Before I'd moved out I'd sold most of the furniture; the only pieces remaining in the living room were a bruised coffee table with burns from joints left unattended and an old recliner. I plopped myself into the recliner, staring out the tall windows at the drifting clouds. I looked around the room. It looked larger now with all the furniture gone.

River returned shortly, dressed in velvet slacks and a purple sweater. The pants fitted snug against her hips, and the power hidden in her legs was quite evident. She carried two white mugs of coffee in her hand. One of them she handed to me. I caught a whiff of dried sex-sweat on her body. She moved to lean against the wall by the window overlooking the street. Resting her cup on the window ledge she began to twist her dreadlocks into two braids.

I slurped coffee inhaling steam and spicy chestnut. "The FBI came asking about your boyfriend last night."

The information seemed to roll off her back like oil off marble. She turned to me, still twisting her hair, her eyes lazy and fretful. "A diplomat murdered in the city . . . that can't be good publicity for the city. For the country."

"Let's just cut the bullshit, okay!"

"Are you shouting at me?"

"What's going on with you and Negus?"

"I told you. He came by last night. We got into a little something."

"He's my partner . . ."

She smiled, her eyes cagey. "Fucking your partner is illegal now?"

"I'm just trying to protect my business."

"What? Fucking Negus is gonna hurt your business? We're not talking Fortune Five Hundred here, Blades. This kind of thing happens all the time in clubs. I didn't know you were such an uptight dude. Back off. Stop acting like you're my man."

"I hired you to manage our club, only to find out you're also a hired gun. That's enough to make anyone uptight."

Her almond-shaped eyes widened. "Why're you letting me stay here?"

I sipped coffee and said nothing.

Her eyes raked my face for an answer. "I don't need you to feel sorry for me," she said.

"Oh, really? When did you have this epiphany? After you got the keys to my apartment, I suspect."

"That is so classless."

"You're an enigma. I don't like enigmas."

She grunted. "We're even there. You're a pretty much an enigma yourself. And an angry one at that."

"What do I have to be angry about? I'm happily married. I've got a beautiful daughter."

"What about your father? Aren't you still angry about him for leaving you when you were a boy?"

"My father and I . . ." I hesitated. "Who told you about that? Negus?"

"Your father and you, what? Have made up? Some people don't get a second chance."

I got up from the chair. She moved toward me. We stood a few feet from each other and for a second I felt a strange adversarial tension between us, as if we'd been in some kind of struggle before today. Long before today. Something left over from a previous battle.

She reached out and took the mug from my hand. "Listen, Blades, I know I come off a little stubborn sometimes."

"Evasive is more what I'm thinking."

"If you knew me you'd understand why."

"School me."

"Not now."

"In the meantime what do I do with you? You've put us in a bind at the club. The police are looking for you. The FBI is asking about your boyfriend and you refuse to tell me what's really going on. I feel like I've got somebody else's shit all over my shoes and I don't like the smell."

Her tone turned angry, defiant. "Do you want me to leave?"

"I wish you would."

"I'll be out of here by this evening."

I didn't wait for her to change her mind. I turned away and without looking back, walked to the door, opened it, and went out.

THIRTEEN

My meeting with Negus did not take long. We discussed security for the upcoming show with Papa Smooth, a dancehall artist, and Toxic, the soca band from Antigua. Toxic was wildly popular with teenagers and we anticipated a large number trying to sneak into the club. And since our manager was now in hiding, I would have to handle the day-to-day operations of the club for the time being.

Negus's other gigs as a radio DJ on a Caribbean radio station and fledgling promoter brought him in contact with many top reggae, hip-hop, R&B, and soca artists. This was the main reason I wanted him as partner. While I loved music, and while many of the soca and reggae artists came to my music store, I knew very little about the business of booking artists, contracts, dealing with managers and that sort of thing.

I met Negus when he came to the music store asking to use my store as a community ticket outlet for a reggae show he was promoting on Randall's Island. He seemed to be a confident fellow, not pushy, but sure of himself with a big booming laugh. Perhaps his self-confidence came from being a radio personality. My guess was that it grew out of his size. He was a big man, bigger than me, going about six-three, fit-looking with a clean-shaven head and dull, pokerfaced eyes.

He'd been born in England to a Bajan father and Jamaican mother who were both med students at the time. They returned to the Caribbean when Negus was five, moving around doing research in various islands, first Barbados, then Jamaica, then Trinidad, ferrying Negus from island to island, from school to school, preparing him for his radio moniker: Negus "Caribbean Man" Andrews.

The office was upstairs where the restaurant I had planned as an extension of the downstairs club was under construction. Negus was jittery throughout our meeting, but I didn't give a fuck. As banal as it may sound, business was business. Getting involved with River was a bad idea. I didn't tell him this, but I'm sure he got the message from my cool manner throughout the meeting.

We'd finished our business and I got ready to leave. He leaned against the desk sipping a beer that he'd had throughout the half-hour meeting. I could feel his eyes on me as I packed away the tape recorder into a desk drawer. We recorded our meeting on tape so there'd be no confusion in the future over who said what. You get the idea. I don't like bullshit, especially when it came to business.

"It's no big deal, you know," he said.

I closed the drawer and locked it. "What're you talking about?"

"River and me."

"Then why you bringing it up?"

"Because you're sore for some reason. I don't know why."

"If you don't know why, then drop it."

"I ain't married. Neither is she. What's the big deal?"

"Look, Negus, it's none of my business."

"Then why're you sore?"

"Business is business, Negus."

"Business is business? I know business is business. What else could it be? She called me up, Blades. What was I supposed to say, 'Sorry, business is business'? You can't tell me you don't think she's fine. You can't tell me that if you weren't married you wouldn't want to tap that ass. It's no big deal, man."

"Were you thinking that when we hired her?"

"I'm a man, Blades. I think about pussy a lot."

"Lots of women come through this club, Negus. And I have to admit most of them come because of you. They hear you on the radio and they want to meet you. Fresh eager pussy every weekend. Why you wanna mess with somebody who works for us? Who's managing our club?"

"If I didn't know better I'd say you're jealous."

"Do what you want, cuz."

I tucked my bag under my arm, grabbed my coat and hat off the rack, and left. Outside the sky had turned over and its bright bluish side was now showing, wafer-thin clouds sailing along quietly.

AFTER DINNER Chesney went next door to play with her friend Mila, with whom she attended school in Boerum Hill. Mila's sister Jovan was the student I employed to baby-sit Chesney on occasion. The girls' father was an ophthalmologist from Guyana who'd escaped an attempted kidnapping in his country five years ago. He had vowed never to go back there.

I called Noah but got his machine and decided not to leave a message. It was around seven o'clock. Sitting on the sofa in the living room with my legs stretched on puffed pillows, I booted the television with the remote and started flipping through channels. It was cool in the room.

Anais came downstairs wearing wine-colored sweatpants and a white turtleneck cotton sweater. She sat next to me and picked up a magazine from a pile on the floor. She flipped pages, then threw the magazine back onto the pile and sighed hard, which made me turn to face her.

"I'm sorry," she said.

"What's bothering you?"

"Nothing. I'm just . . . When is Ronan's funeral?"

"I just called Noah but he's not home or not picking up. There's a pastor in Brooklyn he's talking to about the service."

I looked at my wife and thought how beautiful her pupils were, so dark they were almost transparent. The first time I met her I thought she was the most beautiful woman I'd ever seen. It was a rainy summer day in Central Park. I'd just crossed the finish line at the Citibank AIDS 5K and was hunched over trying to catch my breath when I sensed someone standing over me. I looked up and there she was, handing me a bottle of Gatorade. She was a volunteer with the race sponsors. I took the yellow bottle from her hand and looked into her eyes and smiled. She asked me how I felt; I said fine. She could've turned away, on to the next spent participant near her, but she smiled back at me, water dripping from her black Citibank parka, her dark pupils shiny as a cat's, and waited until she saw that my quickened gasps for air had subsided.

Before the day was over we'd exchanged phone numbers, and I wasted no time calling her the next day. She accepted an invitation to the movies and later took me to a billiards room in the Village where we played until the sun came up.

She got up from the sofa and walked halfway across the room before stopping; she turned, lips pursed. "There's something I have to tell you about last night, Blades."

I adjusted my position on the sofa so I could look at her directly. "What is it?"

She returned to sit beside me on the sofa. "Do you remember Pryce Merkins?"

"Not really. Who is he?"

"A businessman. He also produces plays. He's put some money in a few Broadway shows. I'd gone out with him a couple of times before I met you. I told you how he got me my first agent."

"I don't remember."

"Well, I had dinner with him last night."

"Really."

"I should've told you last night but I wasn't sure if you'd be jealous."

"Should I be?"

"No. It's just that he offered me a part in a play he's producing."

"That's nice."

She bit into her lower lip, holding the flesh between her teeth for a second as she stared out the empty window. "He also asked me to go to bed with him."

"A lot of men want to go to bed with you."

"Should I accept his offer?"

"To go to bed?"

"No, I mean the play."

"Do you like the script?"

"Yes, it's a revival. Good solid characters. Starts off-Broadway, but could go further."

"You've never asked me to make career choices for you before. Why now?"

"Pryce Merkins is a very persistent man."

"You want me to have a word with him?"

"No, that wouldn't be necessary."

"Then what do you want me to do?"

"Nothing. Forget it." She stood up.

"Negus is sleeping with River Paris."

"Why doesn't that shock me? There's something about that woman. I knew she was after one of you. I thought it was you. Perhaps she decided to settle on Negus because she couldn't have you."

"I hope he hasn't bitten off more than he could chew."

"Negus is a big boy."

"She's a tough customer."

"More rough than tough, I'd say. Bordering on uncouth."

"What has she ever done to you?"

"I just don't like the way she looks at you. I'm going upstairs to read."

The phone rang once and Anais picked up the cordless from the side table next to her and greeted whoever it was in her warmest voice.

"It's for you," she said, and handed me the phone.

"Hello."

Toni shouted at me from the other end, "Blades, I got some information for you."

"Why're you shouting?"

"I'm in a bar. Meet me at Longfellow's in half an hour."

"Why can't you tell me over the phone?"

"What the hell's wrong with you, Blades? You know I don't talk business over the phone."

"What's Longfellow's and where is it?"

"A bar."

"What kind of bar?"

"A gay bar on Seventh Avenue."

"I'm not meeting you in a gay bar."

He giggled. "Sorry. Forgot you're not out yet."

"What?"

"Just kidding. Hold on to your jock. There's a bar for weirdoes like you on Twenty-sixth and Park. It's called Crow Bar. Half hour."

"Don't keep me waiting."

I walked up to Anais standing at the foot of the stairs. "Honey, I gotta go out. Chesney should be home by eight. If she isn't call over there."

"Where're you going?"

"To meet Toni Monday."

"Does it have anything to do with Ronan?"

"Not now, babe."

I kissed her on the lips and went upstairs to dress.

CROW BAR was a funky joint. Tight spaces filled with lithe bodies, all young, all good-looking, all yuppies. But the music. Pow! Retro as a '60s Caddy. When I walked in Marvin Gaye's "What's Going On" was funking up the joint. Who said yuppies didn't have taste.

Sipping his drink slowly, Toni Monday sat at the farthest end of the bar, in a deep alcove all by himself. He was not dressed as flamboyantly as I've known him to dress; still, a 300-pound man in pink pants and skintight blue sequined shirt was as inconspicuous as a giraffe on Park Avenue. I wondered if that was why no one sat next to him.

I braved the predictable stares and slid onto the stool next to him. He turned to look at me and smiled knowingly, but it wasn't his usual flirtatious smile. There was a cool edge to his eyes, which were perfectly made up for any photographer who might've happened by to catch him in costume.

"Martini?" I asked, knowing that to be Toni's favorite drink.

He nodded, then turned his head around to follow the trajectory of a young man heading out the door. "How're you, Blades?" he said after the man had exited.

"I'm fine. You?"

"Lousy. My boyfriend is driving me crazy."

"I didn't leave my hottie wife to come listen to you complain about your boyfriend, Toni."

"Can I get a little sympathy from you, Blades? Why you gotta be so tough all the time?"

"Truth is, Toni, I'm not nearly as tough as you."

He laughed. "Anybody hearing you would think I'm Gotti or something."

"You said you had some information for me."

The bartender sauntered over and stood staring at me. His face was spread flat as a waffle and sour white like curdled milk; his thin lips curled insolently up at the edges. But it was his eyes. The stare he gave me. As if he thought it beneath him to have to ask me what I wanted to drink.

"You drinking, pal, or you here to soak up the sunshine?" he said with a smirk.

I didn't like the tone right off the mark and I continued to ignore him. I knew if I opened my mouth I would say something nasty.

"I'll have another martini," Toni said. "What you drinking, Blades?"

"Bourbon with ice."

"Who do you think you are?" the bartender scoffed.

I gathered he was talking to me, but I refused to give him the satisfaction of a conversation.

"Go do your job, G-man," Toni said.

The bartender waited another second, I suspected to see if I would speak to him, before turning away and back to the rows of bottles on the shelf.

"What's it about you, Blades?" Toni said.

"Come again."

"What's it about you that gets people so riled up?"

"Must be the company I keep."

"Are you referring to me?"

"I'm not here to look cute, Toni. Nor to get eyefucked by some jerk in an Islanders jersey."

Toni finished off the martini he was nursing and pushed the glass to one side. He massaged his right ear, lingering on the gold hoop hanging from the lobe. "Talk is that your politician friend had bad karma. Your boy pissed a lot of people off, starting with that former Black Panther he defeated in the election. He called the man a jailbird. And a woman-beater. In public. But that was only the start of his shit. Word is he had a spy in the man's camp. Because of her your boy got the state attorney's office to investigate the ex-Panther's finances. Claimed he was taking kickbacks from contractors bidding on city contracts. Nothing came of it, but the bad press fucked up his campaign. To top it off she was fucking the ex-Panther and your boy at the same time. You got all that?"

"Lemme see if I follow you. Ronan had a woman spying on Baron Spencer?"

"That's right."

"And this woman was fucking both Ronan and Spencer?"

"You got it."

"Who's the woman?"

"I didn't get a name. Spencer threatened to dump your boy in a dumpster if he ever caught him alone. You know how those ex-Panthers are. Underneath their new millennium suits they're still sixties thugs."

The bartender returned and plopped the drinks down before us with such carelessness that Toni's martini splashed out onto the bar.

Toni jumped up. "Hey! What's up with that? If you don't wanna serve us, just say so. We can spend our money somewhere else. Otherwise you treat us like we're your lovers."

"Yeah? Or what?"

"I'll be so far down your craw your stomach will think I'm dinner."

"You and what other Halloween leftovers?"

With an agility that belied his bulk, Toni vaulted the bar, slamming his body into the bartender, sending the fella parachuting into the rack of bottles before he knew what hit him. Toni grabbed his head and cracked it into the wooden bar-top. I saw the man's eye whirl around like a loosened Slinky, then close. Toni released him and he drooped to the floor.

Before anyone else could react Toni leapt back over the bar, grabbed his coat from the back of the bar stool, and with a flick of his wrist knocked the martini across the bar. He started for the door.

I was right behind.

At the door a short rotund man stepped in front of Toni as if he were a power forward taking a charge. Toni didn't wait for the man to say anything. A chrome-plated automatic pistol appeared in Toni's hand with the precision of a David Copperfield trick.

"I don't think you want to fuck with me, Shorty," Toni said.

The man hesitated, then quickly stepped aside. Toni pushed the door and cool air slammed into us as we tumbled onto the sidewalk. We walked about a block down Park Avenue at a brisk pace before I grabbed his lapel.

"Why the hell did you do that?" I demanded.

"I hate when people spill my drink," he said coolly. "That was the second time he did it too."

"My car's on the next block. I'm going home."

"I told you we should've met in the gay bar."

"You know that guy had a point. You are dressed like it's Halloween."

"This is the way I dress. So fuck off. You want me to dress like the pope."

"That's no better than this," I said. "That's a Halloween costume too."

Toni laughed and lifted a pack of cigarettes from his coat pocket.

"You have a permit for that thing?" I said.

"I'm a businessman, Blades. I need to be able to protect myself."

The street was alive, people going by in clumps, some in animated conversation, others bunched in silence cowering against the cold. We reached my car parked opposite a closed pizza parlor. A couple of kids leaned against the corrugated gate smoking a joint.

I stopped next to the car. "Did Spencer order the hit on Ronan?"

"I don't know."

I got into my car, started it, and leaned out the window. "You better keep that gun in your pants, Toni."

Toni lit a cigarette. "That's the same advice my boyfriend gives me every morning I leave the house. I didn't know you felt that way about me, Blades."

I drove off laughing. In the rearview mirror I saw Toni fixing his shirt.

FOURTEEN

I dreamed I was a child folded into a box like a dress. And blood was oozing from my eyes and my ears. It wasn't the first time I'd had that dream. When I went to visit my father in Miami several years ago that dream had plagued my nights there, occurring as frequently as a morning erection. It had troubled me no end back then because one time I woke up from the dream and found myself bleeding from a cut on my face. What terrified me was that I didn't know how it got there. My fingernails weren't long and it was unlikely that I had cut myself in my sleep. It was difficult to get back to sleep after that, and for the duration of my time in Miami I had trouble sleeping.

I left the house before Anais and Chesney woke to go to the gym in Flatbush. It had just opened when I got there at six. After changing into black cotton shorts and tee I did the circuit before spending another half hour with free weights, working on chest and arms. Then I went upstairs and ran five miles on the treadmill. I ran hard, away from the dream. Sweat streamed off me and when I was done I felt used up, but my mind was relaxed.

I left the gym shortly after eight, rewarding myself with spinach and codfish patties for breakfast from Allan's Bakery on Nostrand.

Leaving the bakery I decided to profile Baron Spencer's office on Empire Boulevard across from the Roller Rink. I didn't expect him to be there, but since I was in the neighborhood, what the heck.

Cruising along the weather-warped asphalt of Empire Boulevard I passed the yellow flat building housing Baron Spencer's community outreach office with its mural of Malcolm X on the front wall. I made a U-turn, pulling in behind a black Explorer with tinted windows. I got out, chewing on a codfish patty, and walked toward the truck, an icy wind licking my face.

I leaned forward to peer inside the truck. The windows of the Explorer were so dark I could only see my reflection.

Two men standing outside on the sidewalk.

One leaning against the front of the Explorer sipping from a white Styrofoam cup looked to be in his forties. Wide as the truck, with a face that looked like it'd been pile driven into the ground by Hulk Hogan, he eyed me with casual disinterest through dark square glasses. Taller and somewhat older, perhaps fifty, but nothing much to look at himself, with a nose that was too flat, a mouth too wide, and eyes too small, the other man stood leaning on the Explorer's front door stuffing his face with a glazed donut, a Styrofoam cup in his other hand. His ears moved up and down like a dog on alert; I didn't know humans could do that and I chuckled out loud. Hearing my chuckle he turned and stared at me.

"What you laughing at, homo?" the tall man grunted.

"Homo? What is that? A variation of *Homes*? Is that the way brothers are greeting each other nowadays?" I teased.

They reached over the hood and pounded.

"A homo is a faggot," the broad one said. "What kind of brother you are if you don't know that? Brother from another planet."

I chuckled as I chewed carelessly. "I'm just fucking with you idiots."

The tall one spat out his donut and took a fighting stance. "You better be bringing some funk with that kinda talk."

I decided not to answer. Stuffing the last piece of my patty into my mouth I wheeled toward the ground floor entrance of the office. The linebacker moved quickly to cut me off.

"Where you think you're going?" he said, backpedaling.

I stared into the dark glasses covering his eyes. "That office right behind you."

I heard Styrofoam hitting concrete with a half-filled thud behind me.

"What's your business there?" the tall man said.

"My business is my business. Why you so goddamn nosy? Is your name Oprah?" I said.

"Mr. Spencer doesn't see anyone without an appointment," the broad one in front of me said.

I took a step back and to the side, squaring up so that I had both of them in my sight. I was still in the crossfire of their spittle but at least now I could see it coming.

"He'll see me."

"You don't look like the president of the United States. Even then you'd still need an appointment," the broad one said.

"Then give him a message for me. I heard he had a beef with Ronan Peltier. I'm sure you ho's know who that is. The man who took away his seat. If I find out he tried to blow up that beef by taking Ronan out, tell him I'll do my very best to make sure he spends the rest of his life playing hide-the-soap with other convicts."

The broad man's eyes locked on to mine with a nuclear stare, his mouth twisting into a frightening snarl. I took a step forward so he could see my eyes, see that I was not about to be intimidated by his ugly grille.

The right passenger door of the truck opened and a slim man stepped out wearing wire-rimmed glasses and a long black coat. His shoulders were hunched slightly, as if he was bearing up some incredible weight. He looked to be in his fifties, but he could've been older. Head cleanly shaved, as was his face, his dark skin was without blemish, and looked soft, like the skin of someone who had regular facials and visited spas for relaxation.

"Do I know you?" he said, addressing me.

"Do you wanna know me?"

"What's with the tough guy act? You a cop?" His voice plopped like heavy stones hitting the bottom of a well.

"Did you have Ronan Peltier killed?"

His laugh was measured, controlled, as if it was some luxury imported from Iraq. "You a comedian, I see. Since you're providing the morning's entertainment, the least you could do is tell me your name."

"Blades Overstreet. Ronan Peltier was a friend of mine."

"Sorry to hear that."

"I bet you're not sorry he's dead."

Baron Spencer began to limp away toward the entrance of his office; it was the only part of his deportment that showed signs of weakness. "I let the dead speak about the dead, my friend."

I said, "Did you have him killed because he took your seat or because he was boning your girlfriend?"

The broad man took two steps toward me. Spencer barked at him and he stopped like a trained puppy.

Spencer smiled, but his face was tight. "See you around, joker."

The taller of the two clowns unlocked the door to the building and the three of them disappeared inside.

I SPENT the next few hours at the club making phone calls. First order of business was catching up on my other commercial venture, the music store. Milo wanted to fire the cashier because he thought she was stealing. I told him to do what he had to do. Then I told him to hire his mother, at least we knew we could trust her. Milo wasn't amused at all by this since his mother lived in Trinidad and had no intention of leaving.

I had a beer while going over the publicity package Negus had assembled on Papa Smooth. Already Negus's connections have been paying dividends. A blurb had appeared in the *Daily News* just yesterday and *Carib News* had a full article planned for the weekend.

I'd seen Papa Smooth once at a show Negus promoted in Prospect Park. I wasn't all that impressed with his act, but the women seemed to love his curious blend of dancehall lyrics and stone-love crooning. It was his popularity with the ladies I was hoping to capitalize on.

Negus had more ambitious plans for Smooth. Looking to start his own record producing company, Negus hoped to sign Papa Smooth to a contract.

My mother called to tell me that my brother Jason was on his way to New York to see me, but she wouldn't explain why. I hated when my mother got mysterious about Jason. It usually meant that something was up. And right now the last thing I needed was a Jason emergency.

Jason was older than me by three years. My eldest sibling, Melanie, was a lawyer in California. Melanie and Jason were children from Mom's first marriage to a white man. My father, a black man, married my white mother in the sixties, the decade of radicalism and experimentation in America. And I suspect that at the time they both thought they were being hip when they decided to get hitched. Perhaps they were. Perhaps in time unions such as theirs might be judged as catalysts for real racial harmony in America. But theirs proved a bad marriage for everybody; none more so than Melanie, who blamed everything that's ever happened to her and Jason, from her first zit to not having a date for the prom to Jason's depression and drug abuse, on my parents' marriage. Or more correctly, on my father.

I used to idolize my brother. But after he was expelled from UNC, where he played one year on a baseball scholarship, he came back to New York and almost died from a heroin overdose. One day I caught him scoring coke off a dealer on Fourth Avenue; I decided there and then I wouldn't rest until I'd gotten rid of every drug dealer in the world. I was fifteen. And like most teenagers, idiotically idealistic. Years later I would join the NYPD, becoming an undercover narco.

When I resigned from the Department after five years of buy and busts I had made not even the slightest dent on the drug problem in New York.

Never quite able to hold a steady job, Jason has spent the better part of his life in and out of drug rehab. Were it not for his family—my mother, sister, and me—he would be homeless, though for the past six months he'd been sticking to his meds and keeping appointments with his therapist.

I left the office an hour later and made it home before Jason arrived. Anais and Chesney had not yet returned from their excursion to the Botanical Gardens.

I fixed myself a cheese and turkey sandwich and flicked on the television in the family room downstairs. On the walls were photos of Chesney falling on the ice in Prospect Park the first day she put skates on and pictures of Anais taken when she was still a dancer performing with a company in Germany.

I'd just plunked myself down in front of the television when the bell rang. I walked to the front door chewing my food. Normally I'd get the party outside to identify themselves before opening the door, but thinking it was Jason I twisted the brass knob and swung the heavy oak door open.

The thickset man standing before me had the kind of eyes that could curdle a thought as if it were sour milk. They opened no wider than slots in a coin machine, as if he'd mastered a way to prevent people from identifying the color. His hair was silvery blond with a too earnest sheen, the gloss of hairspray. The jutted clay-colored forehead looked like it'd been abandoned by the rest of his body and he had dark pig-snout lips. I'd bet my house he'd never get a call to model for Calvin Klein.

"Can I help you?" I muttered.

"Blades Overstreet?"

"And you are?"

"You don't need to know who I am."

"Then get the fuck off my property."

"I want the girl. Her boyfriend was in possession of some property that was ours when he was killed. She's got it. We want it back."

"Get the hell off my property, you ugly fuck!"

"Even the ugly have a place in this world, Mr. Overstreet."

"Not here you don't."

His face expanded into a half smile, his eyes squeezed even tighter. "Consider your family, Mr. Overstreet."

I threw the sandwich in his face and slammed the door. I ran upstairs to get my gun. I figured he'd be gone by the time I returned, but the fucker had more balls than an elephant. He was still standing there, his expression as calm as if he'd come begging sugar, his face frozen in that half-dead smile.

I pointed the Glock at his face. "I'll give you five seconds to get off my property."

He wheeled and like a rhino with hemorrhoids, walked not too jauntily into the street. A black SUV drove up and stopped. A door opened and Lizard-Face got in. I watched it drive off and then I realized I was trembling.

FIFTEEN

I could taste anger in my mouth. Bitter. Acrid. The taste of fear. My tongue was a piece of wet leather. Something about the iciness of that man's voice and the ease with which he walked right up to my house and threatened me and my family with the reptilian look of death in his eyes had scared me to my core.

I did not have long to dwell on my anger. Before I could close the door Jason's blue Honda Civic swung into the driveway. There was a woman in the car with him. He drove up to the very edge of the garage and stopped.

A balmy wind had sprung up, jangling the needles of the pine tree in the otherwise empty garden. Jason stepped out first in baggy blue jeans and puffy blue and white Giants jacket, a black L.A. Dodgers baseball cap on his head. He leaned against the car waiting for the woman to get out, smiling in a wayward, off-kilter fashion, his lips not really parted but stretched across his teeth as if he was trying to veil a flaw in his dental work, which was not the case, because unlike Melanie and myself, Jason had perfect teeth. Never had a cavity in his life.

Delicately, the woman got out the car, first one foot as if to make sure the ground under her would not give, then the other, the way a diva would step out of a limousine in a movie. When I saw the rest of her I realized the gingerly manner in which she got out was not a fashion induced by delusions of grandeur, it was necessitated by her size.

She wore the long yam-colored sheepskin coat with aplomb, the color melding with the soft honey dye of her processed hair, which fell to the nape of her neck. After a few seconds looking around, as if surveying new property, with a lacquered smile on the globe of her face, she leaned over and gave my brother a bold open-mouth kiss. He giggled like a schoolboy.

They walked toward me holding hands. Jason was a big man, but she made him look positively Lilliputian. Her gait was unsteady, as if she was dizzy or suffered from vertigo, legs spread apart, a gladiator walking from the arena after a fierce battle.

Their nonchalant funeral pace ratcheted up my impatience. That visit from Lizard-Face had let loose worms of dread waggling in my head. I didn't know who the hell he was, but he knew me, knew where I lived, and had threatened my family. Had I still been a cop I might not have thought twice about shooting him. A man like that would've been packing weight. It would've been easy to set up as a clean shoot.

Jason and his woman friend finally made it up to the front door. The gleam in his eyes dazzled so much I wanted to run into the house for my dark glasses. The woman was smiling, a smug skein of satisfaction like the flameout at the end of a Macy's fireworks display. Her eyes were glazed and watery and I knew right away she was an addict.

Damn it! What was Jason up to now?

Across the street a shaggy dog leisurely combed the sidewalk as its owner strolled amiably along, a dark leash hanging from her fingers. A police cruiser slowed down as it got to the woman, the driver said something, the woman laughed, and the cruiser picked up speed and disappeared. Blue-tinged twilight reached its talons across the front of the house, scraping the red wall to reveal blue undertone. Wind whistled like a crooning love-struck bird.

I hugged Jason and we held each other for what seemed like a long time. Anyone who knew our family would tell you that the river of our history has never been sprinkled with sacred water. But what family's history was? Even when you try to lock skeletons away in closets, somehow light seeps through awakening those freckled bones and the avalanche of misery taints the river even more. My family was as fucked up as families got. The struggle to get Jason off drugs and leading a productive life had been going on for all of my adult life. All of his, come to think of it. We'd shipped him off to as many rehab centers as there were stars in a New York sky. Getting him to stay with his therapy, or keeping track of whether he took his medication, has been a full-time job for Mom. Though he was older I often found myself thinking of him as my little brother.

As strong as my bond with Jason was, my relationship with my sister, Melanie, was the opposite. Don't get me wrong, I love my sister. But we were both too strong-willed to accept the other's narrative of our family's history. Mine being that she disliked my father because he was black and transferred that hatred onto me, his son. Hers being that my father broke up her happy family, sending Jason spiraling into mental disorder.

"How're you, Jason?"

He giggled schoolboyishly. "It's all good, nigga."

"Jason, what'd I tell you about calling me that?"

"But it's cool, man. We brothers, ain't we?"

"Yes, we are. And if you want to stay my brother you'd better lay off the ghetto act."

He began to laugh and I knew he was on something. His eyes weren't as glassy as the woman's but his laugh was as cracked as a crocodile's skin.

"I want you to meet my woman, Marsha."

I stuck out my hand. "How you doing, Marsha?"

Her eyes shifted slowly to mine. "I'm awright." She looked me over carefully, as if contemplating whether to offer me the extent of her wisdom. "So you're Blades. Damn. You a good-looking muthafucker." She exploded in laughter, a hoarse, deep-throated baying. I waited until she was finished.

"Come on in," I said.

I closed the door behind them. Marsha stood in the atrium looking around, again with that smile of satisfaction on her face. It made her seem almost ghoulish. She took off her coat and handed it to me. Jason took his off but kept it in his hand. I led them into the family room behind the stairwell.

"Do you want me to hang your jacket, Jase?"

"No, it's okay. You know who signed this jacket, man?"

I pretended not to know. "Who?"

"Guess."

I'd given him the jacket so I knew who'd signed it. "Phil Simms?"

"Eeengh!"

"Michael Strahan?"

"Wrong again. Man, who's the greatest Giant ever?"

"Lawrence Taylor."

"Right oh!"

I left to put Marsha's coat in the closet. When I returned they were sitting together on the sofa kissing as if locked in some passionate yearning left over from a Jackie Collins miniseries.

"Can I get you guys something to drink?"

"I'll have a beer," Marsha said, unlocking her lips from Jason's.

Jason leaned back and leered as if he'd been caught loitering. "Me too."

"You're not supposed to drink, Jason. Remember?"

"Oh yeah." He looked at Marsha and they both giggled.

"I have V8 Splash. You like that," I said.

"Yeah, gimme some Splash."

I left them and went to the kitchen. Today I had no patience with

Jason's silliness. How many times can you lead a horse to water and stand there waiting for him to drink, only to have him puff and grimace and turn to stone? I heard the wind clucking away outside, bullying the eaves into an uncivilized whimper.

Toting two tall bottles of Coors and a glass of tropical V8 Splash on a tray, I returned to the den. I almost felt like clearing my throat to alert them to my coming. To my surprise Marsha still had her clothes on as this time they were merely holding hands.

Marsha took one Coors and Jason the V8. I watched Marsha cram the beer bottle in her mouth, which seemed to lodge in the dimples of her jaw. Her body quaked as she gurgled the beer without a ripple of her throat. I sat across from them and sipped my beer slowly, looking at Jason. He was watching her with puppy eyes.

"Mom called to tell me you were coming to see me," I said.

He pulled his eyes away from Marsha's suctioning mouth. "Yeah. I wanted to ask you something."

"Shoot."

"What do you think of Marsha?"

I waited for a second before speaking. "What's there to think?"

"You like her?"

"She seems like a nice person."

"Why you two talking about me like I ain't here?" Marsha burped.

Jason leaned over to kiss her. She giggled, combing her fingers through his blond hair.

Impatience was getting the best of me. "What's going on, Jason?"

"I wanted Marsha to move in with me."

"Move in with you where?"

"Jersey. Mom said no."

"And you want me to talk to her?"

"No. I was thinking. This house is pretty big. You got lots of room. It's only you three living here. You could let Marsha and me stay here for a while. I've got a job. I want to save some money and get my own place."

"When did you get a job?"

"Today. I interviewed last week. They called me today to tell me I got the job."

"Where?"

"The mailroom of a law firm in Manhattan. I'm gonna go back to law school."

"That's a lot of work, Jase."

"I'm feeling it, man. I know I can do it. I feel good. My head feels clear. This new medication I'm taking, it's working great. I feel on top of the world. And Marsha here, she's the best, dude."

"Where do you live, Marsha?"

Marsha showed me a lazy eye. "I just lost my apartment."

"So where're you staying?"

"In a shelter."

"You doing drugs, Marsha?"

Anger quickly melted the glassiness of her eyes. "Who you think you are, muthafucker?"

I replied calmly, "Just trying to protect my brother."

She jumped up. "Later for you, nigga!"

"I'd prefer if you don't call me that."

"What? You think you too good?"

"Get her out of here, Jason."

"Blades, come on . . ."

"Fuck you, nigga," Marsha shrieked. "Come on, Jason. We don't need him."

Jason hesitated, looking foolishly at me then Marsha.

Marsha slapped his face. "You gonna stay here with this stuck-up nigga?"

"But where're we gonna go?" Jason protested lamely.

"I got friends," she snorted.

"Blades, please, man. She gets a little emotional sometimes."

Marsha pushed Jason roughly. "I told you not to talk like I ain't here."

I could feel my anger growing but I sat where I was. Jason was a big boy. He should be able to take care of himself with Queen Kong.

"Jason, I don't have a problem with you staying. But she can't stay in my house. Not if she's doing drugs."

"She'll be good. I promise."

"I don't wanna stay here anyway," Marsha said. "So I don't know what the fuck you two puppies barking about. Get me my muthafuckin' coat."

Before I moved I glanced at Jason to see what he would do. He sat silent as stone. I left the room to get Marsha's coat. When I returned they were in each other's arms, Marsha's pulpy body mashed down on top of Jason stretched out on the couch. With some difficulty Marsha lifted up off Jason when she realized I was back in the room.

Jason grinned sheepishly. "Marsha changed her mind. She doesn't want to leave right now."

"What does that mean?" I said.

"She wants to stay here with me."

"I told you, Jason."

"I don't do drugs, okay," Marsha piped. "You think every black woman living in a shelter be doing drugs? Man, you as racist as them crackers out there. Hell, anybody would think you the white one and he the black one." She started to laugh, the rasping cackle of someone who didn't give a damn what you thought about her.

I set the coat down on the arm of the couch. "You working, Marsha?"

"They got me doing workfare. In the fall they had me doing stupid shit like clearing leaves from the parks. Nothing but slave work. Now the leaves are gone they ain't got shit for me to do. I gotta find me a real job. Maybe I can work at your club."

I said nothing; just stared at her in amazement.

There was a self-contained unit in the basement with two bedrooms. I might've been able to convince Anais to let Jason stay, but no way in hell would she agree to having his screeching paramour along, not even for entertainment.

Before they left I told Jason I'd give the matter some thought. At the very least I could let them stay in the apartment in Carroll Gardens once I made sure the current transient had moved out.

SIXTEEN

When someone threatens your family your first thought is to neutralize that threat as fast as possible. It was with that determination that I stormed my apartment on President Street to confront River. I rang the bell several times and when I got no response Negus's house was the first place that came to mind.

Ever since I left the NYPD, I've been searching for a new way to live. What I've discovered is that there are no easy ways of seeing the world, and no matter how clever you are, no new ways to tell a story that didn't have an end. But there are new ways of dreaming. And since I had the bounty of dreams, a beautiful wife and daughter, I was determined to find a new way to live, away from the ugliness and the brutality that ruled my life as a cop. Seeing drug addicts die in their own pee. Seeing innocent children pimped by their relatives for a fix. Seeing mothers wail for young men and women who died trying to live the only life they dared dream: the life of a gangster, the life of a victim.

An earlier search for a new way to live had led me to seek out my father who had disappeared when I was fifteen. What I found was another story. New dreams and old deaths. Here I was faced with another ugly story. Another threat to finding the peace of mind I sought.

It took me ten minutes to get to Negus's on the other side of Flatbush in Fort Greene. His crib on South Oxford, recessed from the street on a rise and surrounded by trees and a high iron fence, was practically invisible from the street. I parked the Volvo on the inclined street, got out, and opened the gate leading to the steps. At the top of the first set of steps Negus's yellow house came into view. His silver BMW and black Bronco were parked in the driveway.

I reached the house and hopped into the verandah, which circled halfway around the two-story house. Negus lived upstairs. I rang his bell.

He came barefoot to the door dressed in a black jogging suit, his expression betraying no surprise at seeing me. He unlocked the door and stood like a sentry, his body stiff, his feet planted hip wide.

"Is River here?" I said.

"What makes you think she'd be here?"

"Don't play yourself, man."

He swiveled his head, shifting his gaze to the top of the stairs. "Come in."

I stepped through the door and waited for him to close it behind me. Then I followed him up the stairs, the old staircase creaking under our collective weight. At the top of the stairs he turned right and walked along a thin corridor between walls covered with posters of popular reggae and soca artists, most of whom Negus had worked with at some time or another.

The living room looked out onto the front lawn. It was a busy room with lots of chairs and cushions and pictures and speakers. The furniture was very modern, shiny and new. Negus lived alone and I think he decorated this place with the help of a *Modern Living* magazine. There was a mishmash of colors: reds and grays, mostly. A large-screen television in a corner and a print of Bob Marley holding a guitar as if it were a gun on the wall above.

River was curled up on a stone-colored sofa watching television in a sea-blue dress of wrinkled cotton, her locks collected in a bun and twisted at the top of her head. It was odd to see her dressed so femininely. No leather jeans. No boots. No sweaters. She kept her gaze focused on the television when I entered the room, as if she'd been expecting me.

"Can you leave us alone for a moment?" I said to Negus.

He stared hard at me then to River as if seeking her approval. She did not acknowledge his yearning in time to save him retreating in embarrassment back along the corridor we had come.

After he left I walked over and switched off the television. River kept staring at the blank screen for a moment and then rose up and smoothed her dress, which had bunched around her buttocks.

"So you're living here now?" I said.

"You wanted me to leave. I left."

"Have you explained to Negus why you can't go home?"

She sat down and drew her legs under her carefully. "What do you want?"

"Do you know what you're doing?"

"Look, I'm sorry I got you involved."

"You're sorry. Is that what you're gonna tell Negus when Lizard-Face shows up with piss in his eyes?"

She tilted her head to one side and there was loneliness in her eyes. "What're you talking about?"

"This guy shows up at my house this evening. He walks as if he's got a catheter stuck up his ass and is as endearing as a maggot. He says you've got his property. And either I give you up or my family pays the piper."

Her eyes receded and she gulped hard. "Did you tell him where I was?"

"What is he looking for?"

"I don't know."

"He seemed pretty sure you have it."

"Fuck him. I don't. He's looking for me because he thinks I might be able to identify him as Maxwell's killer."

"He said your boyfriend stole his property."

"I wouldn't know anything about that."

"You think I'm here to fluff you? This sonofabitch threatened my family. I will protect my family, you hear me? From any danger. If you know anything about this shit, then you better clean it up."

She glared at me, her eyes wide and dewy. "I'm sorry I got you into this, alright? But don't you be talking to me like I'm your maid. If you're concerned about your family why don't you take them on a vacation? Just leave me the fuck alone."

I wanted to smack her in the mouth. "I don't believe you're telling me the truth."

"I didn't know you were my priest."

"What about Negus? Do you care what happens to him at all?"

"Nothing's gonna happen to Negus."

"Oh, you can guarantee that, huh? Well, if you can guarantee his safety, what about my family's? Can you guarantee theirs too?"

"Just leave it alone, Blades. I'll take care of my own problems."

Negus came into the room looking lost, a bag of Tostitos chips in his hand. "What's up, Blades? Why you shouting, yo?"

"Why the hell you think I'm shouting, Negus?"

"Relax, man," he squawked.

I turned to speak to River. "I'm not going to let anything happen to my family, you understand? Unless you lay the shit out so I can understand, I'm gonna tell them exactly where you are if they come back."

Negus looked at me, bewilderment scrawled over his brow. "What is your problem, man?"

"You should be careful what you let crawl into your bed, Negus."

River jumped up and marched from the room. I watched her go, my anger gaining momentum. I took a step to follow her.

Negus stepped into my path breathing heavily through his flared nostrils as if he wanted to blow me down. "Why'd you have to say that, man?"

"I could've said worse."

"I think you should leave my house, cuz, before I have to put you out."

"C'mon, Negus, the pussy can't be that good. Don't be an ass over this bitch."

"Where you get off being so disrespectful?"

"Negus, this woman's trouble. You don't know her. You can't handle her shit."

"You're jealous, aren't you?"

I could've stood there and argued with him, but the cold hard look in his eyes told me there was no point. I don't know if it was love or lust, but River had his balls in her mouth. There was no one more irrational than a man who was balls deep in a woman.

NEXT DAY Anais had a breakfast meeting with prospective investors in the play she was thinking of doing. After running a number of errands I met her for lunch at the Kitchen, a seafood place in Boerum Hill. When we lived in Carroll Gardens we often ate dinner in their garden in summer. It was too cold for the garden today, but the interior was cozy, even at lunchtime, with its crisp white walls and red linen.

Anais had pulled her hair back into a ponytail, exposing the dramatic curves of her angular face. She wore a tawny brown pants suit that hugged her body pleasingly in just the right places, the pearl necklace and matching earrings giving decisive accent to the outfit. No way to miss it. She was stunning. And when she walked in I forgot my troubles for a moment and wished I could've made love to her right there.

I got up to pull her chair out. She kissed me and we sat down. Our table was positioned in a corner near a window where we could look outside. The sky was filled with charred clouds, and the sound of construction going on a block away was intrusive enough for us to comment that we should've gone somewhere else.

We each ordered a glass of merlot, which came two minutes later.

"You look lovely."

She beamed. "Thank you."

"Frankly, I would rather be home eating you right now."

"You have such a dirty mind."

"I can't help that my first impulse is always to ravish you."

"You can help. You just don't want to."

"Well, why should I? You're my wife. And you taste first-rate."

"You're gonna make me self-conscious."

"I don't think that's possible."

She gurgled a laugh. "I don't like the sound of that."

I sipped my wine. "It's a compliment."

"One never knows with you." She opened the menu. "What kind of fish are you having today?" After she said it she looked at me and winked. "On second thought, don't answer that." Then she laughed out loud.

"So how'd your meeting go?"

"The people I met with today have so much money I wanted to hide in one of their pockets so I could pilfer some loose change. I was almost beside myself listening to them talk about takeovers and IPOs like they were discussing sex."

"Maybe to them it is. Are they gonna invest in the play?"

"I don't know. I got the sense that they're not as excited about the project as Pryce is. I think that's why he set up the meeting, so these people could meet me. I think he was hoping I could seduce them with my enthusiasm."

"I can't see how they could resist your charm."

"You're assuming that there were mostly men in the meeting."

I chuckled. "Not really. You could seduce a woman as easily as a man."

Anais muttered, "Can we talk about something else? Talking about seducing a woman doesn't whet my appetite."

"What's your gut say? Is the play gonna come off?"

"Pryce Merkins is wealthy enough in his own right to produce the play. I don't know if he wants to take the risk himself. He would if . . ."

"If what?"

"Nothing."

"Evasiveness is not the biggest club in your armory, my sweet."

She sipped from her wine. "He wanted me to have dinner with him tonight. It's the way he keeps bringing up our past relationship. It's creepy."

"Has he tried to touch you?"

"No. Nothing like that."

"You telling me the truth?"

"Blades, don't get that tone."

"What tone?"

"That tone. You know what I mean. That 'Do-I-have-to-go-fuck-this-guy-up?' tone."

"Well, do I?"

"Listen to yourself, Blades."

"I can't hear myself when I'm angry."

"I shouldn't have told you anything."

"Tell him if he ever touches you I'm a come break his fucking fingers."

"Blades, this guy owns a chain of pharmacies. He went to school with the mayor. He contributes to hundreds of charities in the city. He's on the board of three hospitals and several large corporations. He volunteers in the AIDS ward at St. Vincent's every Thursday night. He has campaigned with the governor. With that pedigree you don't want to breathe too hard on this guy, lest he accuses you of trying to give him a cold."

"No, I want to break his fucking fingers. He can get a cold in the hospital."

"You can't threaten people like him, Blades. He isn't some whacked out drug dealer you can intimidate. Jesus, sometimes I wonder who's crazier. You or your brother."

"Now why you wanna be saying shit like that?"

"I'm sorry. But you make me so angry sometimes. Remember when I came back from L.A.? Remember what you told me? You told me that the NYPD was out of your system. I'm beginning to wonder, Blades. Was it the system? Was it the NYPD or is it your nature?"

"What do you mean?"

"That violence may just be your nature. In your blood."

"You can't believe that."

"I don't know what to believe. You can't seem to be able to let go of that tough-talking crap. That kinda talk may scare rats but a man like Pryce Merkins would swat you like a fly."

"I think you should forget about this play."

"Why?"

"You just told me why."

"No, I didn't."

"This guy wants to fuck you."

"And I want to do this play."

"So what do we have here? Fuck and play?"

"Very funny. You know what, Blades? You're crazy."

"Don't tell me I'm crazy."

"Blades, I deal with idiots like Pryce Merkins all the time. Every day. Creeps like him are a dollar a dozen in this business. I think I've done pretty damn well without your intervention up to this point. What do you expect me to do? Wear a sign: Property of Blades Overstreet, Tough-Talking Ex-Cop."

"You're laughing at me."

"You should be too. You're acting like a jerk."

"If he touches you I'm still gonna break his freaking fingers."

"I'm not gonna talk about this anymore."

We dropped into a zone of silence until the waiter returned to take our order. Anais ordered scrod. I asked for grilled tuna. Rare. In my raw mood it would've been impossible to appreciate anything cooked.

SEVENTEEN

Pigeons lay dead on the tracks of the Q train. From the platform of the Cortelyou station you can see the soot-gray hi-rise apartment buildings above ground with antennas and satellite dishes jutting from all angles. I rose from the pared gut of New York and looked around. The corner of Cortelyou and Sixteenth.

Down the lethargic street I walked, a sense of anxiety deepening with every step. A man stood in the middle of the road pointing binoculars toward the scarred sky. Cars slowed down and incredulous drivers honked, but ignoring their irritation, the man kept his binoculars scoped heavenward.

I smiled at his recklessness, not really understanding why I found it amusing. Perhaps I'd already assumed that he was a madman, thus associating his actions with an inability to understand the consequences, which made them childlike and therefore humorous. I don't know. I was really more concerned with the state I would find Noah in when I reached the address he'd given me over the phone.

After lunch Anais went on home. I drove to a recording studio in Queens where a Barbadian soca artist named Archie Miller was laying down some tracks. I wanted to talk to him about appearing at the club. Noah left a message on my cell while I was inside the studio. I called the number he left. He was with Dr. Christine Palmer, Ronan's ex-wife.

After sitting in traffic on Flatbush for half an hour I heard on the radio about a demonstration along Church Avenue to protest the killing of a young man who was shot in his car, allegedly by undercover cops investigating a stolen car report. Any major disturbance along Church Avenue was bound to clog the rest of East Flatbush. I wasn't feeling patient. I took the Volvo home and parked it. The Q train would be quicker and painless.

I reached Argyle Road, a narrow street with huge oak trees on both sides, whose empty branches merged high above the street. As I approached the large Victorian house halfway down the block two men came out and got into a brown Impala. Something about them screamed *detectives.* They drove away from me, down the tranquil line of houses.

I walked up the fractured stone steps to the front porch. After ringing the bell, I turned around to survey the block. All the homes looked much the same. Two-story Victorian houses, some over a hundred years old, with lots of windows and gables and good-looking lawns. Used to be a neighborhood of mostly white middle-class professionals not so long ago. Many African-Americans owned homes here now as well as Caribbean immigrants and lately a growing Muslim presence from countries like Pakistan.

The door opened behind me and I turned around. Noah stood in jeans and black sweater, his large eyes bulging as if about to leap out of his head. He looked up and down the street then ushered me into the bright living room; light flowing generously through two windows in the front and two huge windows facing west. Dr. Palmer lay on a chaise lounge, her eyes closed. She wasn't sleeping. I could tell by the way she was breathing: quick and shallow. She wore a long black dress that covered her ankles.

"Do you want a drink?" Noah said to me.

"A glass of water."

Noah looked at me questioningly. "You sure?"

"Without ice."

"Chris?" Noah said to the woman.

Eyes opened in the plum-dark face. "No thank you."

Noah left and I sat down in an insanely comfortable wood-framed leather armchair near a window. The room was spacious, edited down to essentials. A large beige leather-edged carpet covered the floor. The sofa was cream and so were the drapes. The beigeness of the room had a calming effect on me. A low mahogany-colored table in the middle of the room was covered with miniature African artifacts, with an arrangement of small stones off to one side. There were two large mirrors mounted on walls. On a tall drum-shaped table sat two huge African ceremonial masks. A mouse-colored cat curled up on the sofa.

"This is a beautiful house," I said to Chris.

This time she did not answer. Like a bad dream on two legs, she rose ghostlike from the chaise lounge, the black dress billowing around her. Her apple-shaped face was drawn hard and her faded eyes were as washed out as the moon at dawn.

"Tell Noah I've gone upstairs." With that she swept down the dark passageway and disappeared.

Noah returned and handed me a glass of water. Instead of sitting he leaned against the far wall next to a glass cabinet containing photographs, trophies, and African trinkets on shelves. In his hand was a short glass, which I would have bet did not contain Sprite.

"Dr. Palmer went upstairs," I said.

"She looks terrible, doesn't she?"

"I didn't notice."

"You don't miss anything, Blades, so don't bullshit me."

"What're you doing here, anyway?"

"Chris and I went to look at caskets today."

"I thought they were divorced."

He nodded. "Just because they were divorced doesn't mean they stopped being friends. She wanted to pay for his funeral."

"That's very civil of her."

"He shouldn't have divorced her. I told him so. She's a very special woman."

"Why'd they get divorced?"

"I don't know. Whatever it was, it was bullshit. You don't divorce a woman who loves you as much as Chris loved him. I don't think she ever stopped loving him."

"Why'd you wanna see me?"

"You saw the two men who just left?"

I nodded and took a mouthful of water. "Detectives?"

"Yeah. Somebody tried to kill me today."

I leaned forward and put the glass on the end table to my right.

Noah paced, then sat down a few feet away. "This morning I met Chris at the funeral home to pick a casket. Donna had wanted to come but she couldn't even fasten her own bra without getting the shakes. I called her sister and had to wait for her to come over. And that made me late.

"It didn't take long to choose a casket. I'd already checked some magazines. Before we could settle on the price Chris broke down. I took her outside to get some fresh air.

"I lit a cigarette. After a few hits I tossed the shit. Tasted like dirt in my mouth. I was about to go back inside when I heard what sounded like a backfire. I spun around. I see this black car slowing down. I saw a silver flash and my instinct took over.

"I grabbed Chris and dragged her to the ground. *Pop-pop-pop-pop.* Like firecrackers, man. Muthafuckers didn't stop, though. Just kept driving. I pulled Chris up and we ran inside."

WE SAT FOR some time in silence after Noah had stopped talking. The house was silent. A silence louder than thunder. Not a fly buzzed. Not even the cat blinked. I looked at Noah. His eyes were wide and keen. I began having flashbacks of Ronan lying in a dark pool of blood. Hearing his mother's scream. To rid my mind of such lesions I looked outside through the high glass window. An intense struggle was going on between the wind and the raw limbs of slumbering oaks. I got up and walked to the window. The empty branches snapped like an animal trainer's whip. A man leaned against the lamppost taking a leak. Two Mormon youths, toting Bibles and backpacks, stopped to proselytize. The man menaced them with his dick flapping and they scrammed.

"I don't like getting shot at, Blades," Noah said behind me.

I didn't turn around. "You thinking what I'm thinking?"

"What if Ronan was an accident?"

"What if it was you they were after?" I returned to my seat. "You got enemies out there, Noah?"

"Who doesn't?"

"Not me."

His chuckle never left his throat. "As much heads you busted open."

"Did you get a good look at the shooter?"

"With what? The eyes in my ass? I was flat on the ground, kid."

"Okay, big man. No need to spit in my eyes."

"Sorry. I feel like I've been walking through a dark valley and someone above me keeps cracking my head with a hammer."

"It's that juice you're drinking."

"It's either this or sobbing like a woman."

"Try sobbing once in a while. It's easier on your liver."

"My father drank all his life and smoked two packs a day. Know how he died? Got hit by a bus. At seventy-five. He had a gourd for a liver."

"Bad genes skip a generation. Maybe good ones do too. Any brass collected at the scene?"

"Forties."

"Ronan was cut down with forty-fives."

"So? Professionals carry an assortment of cookies."

"But the good ones stick to a brand they like. Were there any witnesses to this drive-by?"

"Two old women were walking by when it happened."

"Did they see the shooter?"

"The cops couldn't get anything sensible outta them. Too damn scared to organize their brains. One of them had to be taken by ambulance to the hospital."

"So we got zippo?"

"Essentially."

"Who wants you dead, Noah?"

"My wife. But she's grieving so hard she can't even take a shit by herself. Can't be her."

"Somebody you sent away for a long time, perhaps. Might be now getting out of jail."

"How you expect me to remember shit like that?"

"Who knew you would be at that funeral home?"

"Nobody I don't trust."

"Could they've been after Chris?"

"Chris? Who'd want to kill her?"

"How did Ronan make his millions?"

"How do smart people make money, Blades?"

"Stealing. Were she and Ronan involved in any business dealings together?"

"I wouldn't know that."

"I'd like to speak her."

He took a slop of his drink and looked at me. "What if my boy took a bullet for me, Blades?" His voice cracked and broke like the cry of a wounded animal.

"Has Riley turned up anything new?"

"You kidding me? He and the rest of the boys in blue are too busy pissing on the new contract they were forced to sign by the mayor."

"You talked to him?"

"Last night. Wanted to know if Ronan ever mentioned being

threatened by Baron Spencer. He might get lucky and solve this case but I doubt it."

"I'm sure he's doing the best he can."

"Blades, this guy lives on Long Island. When he's sitting on the Expressway in traffic do you think he's thinking about finding my son's killer or how he is going to get back to his suburban home in one piece?"

"Sometimes I wonder how you got that Ph.D."

"By saying whatever the fuck I want." He put his glass on the table. "What kinda heat you packing, kid?"

I reached under my leather jacket and pulled out the Glock, ejecting the magazine and racking the slide to empty the chamber before handing it to Noah.

He took it from my fingers and hefted it. "I haven't carried a gun in twenty-five years, Blades. I don't even own one anymore. Kept my service weapon for all of two years. I'm thinking I should get some gear. What do you think?"

I paused, studying his eyes. "It might not be a bad idea."

He handed the gun back to me. "I'll go bring Chris down."

I loaded the Glock and checked to make sure the safety was on before stuffing it back inside my waist.

Noah came down the stairs a few minutes later with Chris in tow. I hated having to question her under the circumstances. The way she looked I wasn't sure how coherent she would be. She settled in the chaise lounge and leaned back, dabbing sweat from her brow with a napkin.

"Dr. Palmer, Noah told me what happened this afternoon outside the funeral home. How're you feeling?"

She kept dabbing her brow. "You can call me Chris."

"Do you feel like answering a few questions?" I said.

"I already told the police everything I know." Her voice was squeaky and lifeless, like the computerized voice on an answering machine.

"Bear with us," Noah said. "Blades is a friend. I trust him."

"You don't trust the police?"

"Not like I trust Blades," Noah said.

She sighed helplessly.

"Did you notice anyone following you when you left home?" I said.

She lifted her head to look at me. "No. Not that I was looking, really."

"Any threats made against you?"

"No."

"I know you and Ronan were divorced, but Noah said you two were still good friends."

"He was my best friend."

"How often did you talk with him?"

"Almost every day."

"Did he mention feeling that his life was in danger?"

"No."

"Did he mention anyone stalking him?"

"Not that I can remember."

"I think that's something you'd remember, don't you?"

She turned slowly and stared at me. "He never mentioned it to me."

"Were you and Ronan involved in any businesses together?"

"No. The only business I have is the clinic."

I looked at Noah.

"Chris runs a clinic in Coney Island," Noah said.

"How's business?" I said to Chris.

"Fine."

"No money issues? No debt?"

"I don't understand what these questions have to do with what happened this afternoon."

"I know you're upset, Chris. But I'm just trying to help."

She rose from her seat. "I'm tired. And I have a headache."

Dropping the napkin in the chair she disappeared down the dark corridor again.

NOAH OFFERED to drive me home, but I said no. As I was about to step through the door, he remembered that he had the number for

Ronan's ex–personal assistant. Her name was Marjorie Madden. I took the piece of paper with the number on it and left.

It was freezing outside but I felt like walking. Buttoning my jacket up to the neck I stepped out into the crackling cold. The sharp wind set my ears sparking. It was a classic winter evening, the wind blasting with the hint of snow. I traded hellos with an Asian youth with a long angelic face heading in the opposite direction. I wished I could photograph the evening. It was that beautiful.

EIGHTEEN

The wind howled like a woman in labor. I reached the corner where the two Mormons I'd witnessed earlier facing off with the man impersonating a dog at the lamppost were deep in a debate with a dreadlocked youth. The light was red, but traffic was sparse so I decided to jaywalk. Before I could move off a black SUV pulled up next to me. I glanced over and saw the window slowly moving downward and I immediately hunched down clutching at my Glock.

"Blades." A voice echoed from the SUV.

I stood up. The window was all the way down and I recognized the driver. Special Agent Sallie Kraw.

"Come here," she shouted.

I strolled over and leaned into the window.

"Get in," she ordered.

"Do you get a kick out of ordering people into cars?"

"Just folks with pleasing smiles. Get in. I want to talk to you."

I got into the car. The traffic light turned green and she drove off.

"Nice ride. Is this what the FBI is doing with my taxes? Hooking up agents with hot rides?"

"This doesn't belong to the Bureau."

"Yours?"

"A friend's."

"So you're not on official business?"

She glanced at me quickly, the brightness of her smile caroming off my face.

"Where're we going?" I said.

"For a drink."

"Did you think you might want to ask me first if I have the time?"

We stopped at a light and she turned to me, her smile still as radiant as sun-baked stone, but there was now a distinctly condescending clear gleam in her eyes. Her big boned body seemed unduly passive this time around. Perhaps it was her clothes, the gray heather shirt and brown pants. Could've been the way her thick ginger-colored hair settled about her soft pale face.

"Can I buy you a drink, Mr. Overstreet?"

I don't know why I didn't say no. I just didn't. "How did you know where I was?" I said.

"First, will you let me buy you a drink or not?"

"I suppose."

She hiccupped a laugh. "You're a strange man, Blades."

"That doesn't explain how you found me."

"Your wife."

"You spoke to my wife?"

"Yes. A very beautiful woman. You've got great taste."

"Yes, I like to think so."

She chuckled. "And little modesty."

"There's enough of that in the world."

"You can never be too polite or modest for me," she said.

"I'll remember that."

"Have you recovered from your amnesia yet?"

"Didn't know I had that affliction."

"River Paris. Your manager? Do you remember where she is?"

"Nothing to remember. I don't know where she is."

"Somebody is going to find her, Blades. It might not be us. And that could be very unfortunate for her."

"That's her problem. Not mine."

"Do you know what Saizen is?"

"Never heard of it."

"It's a human growth hormone."

"I'm pretty grown as you can see."

"It's been touted as a fountain of youth. Legally it's given to people over fifty to replace hormones. Illegally, it's used by athletes to boost performance. A week ago we foiled a plot by some Russian crime figures to steal a shipment of Saizen worth about a million dollars. We arrested about five men, one of whom did some whistling. He told us about a shipment stolen about two weeks before in Arizona worth about one-point-five mil on the black market. With the information he gave us we set up a sting to bag some other mobsters trying to sell off that shipment. First they wanted us to buy the entire shipment. We couldn't float that kinda cash. We settled on half the load for seven hundred and fifty thousand dollars. The sting went bad. The suspects got away with the money and the growth hormones. They also killed one of our agents.

"The next day the man who was cooperating with us was kidnapped and killed. Dropped from the roof of a building. Very messy. He was a young kid. Nineteen years old. His name was Serge Konstantin. Arrived one year ago from Russia."

"So you're sympathetic to young Russians. Is that the point to this story?"

"I'll get to that in a minute."

We'd reached Park Slope without my taking notice. I didn't like that I'd lost track of where I was. She parked the SUV behind a yellow Ryder truck and killed the engine.

We both got out. We were on Seventh Avenue amid a flurry of young couples heading to bars and restaurants. At nightfall there was a beauty to New York's bustle even in winter that was stunning.

Youths drunk on their own beauty, ticking with sexual power, nuzzling on the aphrodisiac of the city's reputation for self-indulgence. Sometimes I wish I was twenty again.

We waited for a car to pass, then skipped across the street in front of a bus. A minute later we entered Pinter's Pub at the corner of Ninth Street, not the kind of joint I'd expect a woman like Agent Kraw to go for a drink. But what do I know?

It was a dank musty place. Not too big. Just right for people who took their drinking to the limit. Black walls. Muted lighting and tables immersed in shadow. Circular bar with shiny aluminum top.

We headed for the back of the room away from the jukebox. I slung my jacket over the back of the chair and sat down. It was dark and I felt a trickle of guilt at being in such a dark place with a pretty woman whose name was not Anais.

A young woman dressed in black pants and white buttoned-down shirt took our order: bourbon for me; rye and tonic for the lady.

I felt a train rumble beneath us. We sat smiling at each other as if paralyzed by the gloominess of our surroundings. Perhaps she didn't realize that Pinter's was a place where people came to forget they were alive, to disappear into the placenta of nothingness.

She reached into her bag and pulled out an orange lollipop. At least I thought it was orange. I wasn't trusting my ability to identify colors in this place.

"Want one?"

"No thanks."

Our drinks came and I took a big gulp of mine. It clawed at my throat with a soothing fire. The agent sipped hers slowly. She put her glass on the table and leaned forward. Her face was clean, her simmering eyes limestone clear.

"The money left Arizona. And it's here in New York."

As if waiting for me to ask a question she sat up and slipped the lollipop into her mouth. I sat motionless, not really thinking about what she was saying. The alcohol was leading my mind in circles. I saw

Anais floating on a cloud. Seeing the disinterest in my eyes the agent started speaking again.

"Maxwell Burns was the transporter. We believe he had the money when he was killed. We suspect that after Serge Konstantin began to cooperate with us this gang began trying to cover their tracks. That's why Deputy Ambassador Burns was killed. And I don't think they're done. We want the people who killed our agent and we want our money."

"Don't look at me."

"We'd like to talk to your friend, River, about our money."

"She's no friend of mine. And I'd say seven hundred and fifty large would be a good reason to disappear."

"She's still in the city."

"How do you know that?"

"A professional calculation."

"You mean you're guessing." I finished my drink and stood up. "Thank you for the drink. But I gotta be getting home to my wife. The alcohol's got me feeling kinda horny."

"You're not too bashful, are you?"

"It's not a proposition, Miss Kraw."

"You think because I'm from the Midwest you can shock me? If you were propositioning me you'd be very disappointed, Blades."

"Well, I'm not."

"I see the fire in your wife, too, if you know what I mean."

I paused, trying to make my face as deadpan as possible. But inside I was feeling anything but calm. I took my coat from the back of the chair. "I'll take a cab."

"Blades, I'm sorry. I shouldn't have said that about your wife. Not very professional of me."

"You're not working."

"Still . . ."

"See you around, Sallie. You don't mind if I call you Sallie, do you? I mean we do have one thing in common."

I left her staring expressionless into space. Outside I breathed New York; its gnarled black energy; its snarling wind; its dry smell of boiled cabbage. I looked up at the lights above and saw sparks fizzling through the white waves of light. I buttoned my jacket and hailed a cab.

NINETEEN

About two-thirty the next afternoon Marjorie Madden finally returned the three messages I'd left on her machine. We arranged to meet upstairs at Cane, a pretentious after-work club in downtown Manhattan where players of all stripes and species convened to practice their charm and takedown techniques mingling with celebrities and wannabes in entertainment, a joint where jazz and comedy in the upstairs cafe lounge competed with booming hip-hop and reggae joints on the downstairs dance floor. I knew the place well. Great atmosphere for showing off new threads and snaring starry-eyed honeys, but I didn't like its admission practices and had promised myself not to party there. But Marjorie insisted on that spot, saying she was meeting a stand-up comedian friend who was performing that night.

Wanting to stake out an area quiet enough where we might be able to speak without swapping globs of saliva, I got there ahead of her and had no trouble getting past the hue police at the door since I had that certain look this club craved. You know the look I mean. The one often projected in rap music videos which begged the question of the asswipes who produced these celluloid gems: Aren't there any dark-skinned black people left in America?

Perhaps one day color in America will be as benign a subject as horseracing. But today, it is still as frightening as the firing of a loaded gun in a crowded subway car, the report as deafening to whites as it is to blacks. The one-drop-equals-black equation still simplifies things for whites. For us, the equation is an exponential one that keeps growing, becoming more baffling as we try to incorporate variations and gradations of hue taken on through interracial mixing. My feelings are that we should just stop searching for a homogenous way to define ourselves. Why is it easier for me to get into a club like Cane than a dark-skinned brother who is not a celebrity? For all our fancy handshakes and superfluous ways of greeting each other we're still mired in the color-coded muck created by whites. We may call each other brother and sister but our degree of intimacy and acceptance can change depending on the hue of our skin.

I found a quiet table and ordered bourbon to sip while I waited. I had gotten there at seven and had half an hour to kill. A group of men on the tiny stage were tuning up instruments but it was clear no performance would be taking place anytime soon.

Around seven-thirty Marjorie rolled into the club. I said rolled because her physical appearance was that of an inflated balloon, from her face to her ankles. She wore a long black dress and looked beautiful in it even in her advanced stage of pregnancy. It was hard to miss the sister standing at the top of the stairway looking around. I left my drink on the table I had corralled near a window and went over to introduce myself.

Her face flashed a passive smile as she took my hand. A faint trace of her flowery perfume slipped the short distance between us. Its hint of spice tickled my throat. Colorful streamers twirled above our heads as we walked back to my table and bodies weaved around us like choreographed criers in an Alvin Ailey ballet.

We settled into our seats; it took Marjorie awhile to get comfortable. Then she leaned over and touched my arm and smiled as if to reassure me she wasn't quite ready to drop, her full dark face radiant as a moon.

"Would you like some coffee? Tea?" I said, a little surprised by her friendliness.

"A cup of hot chocolate would be nice. And a big fat brownie." She giggled as if the thought of the brownie triggered some pleasurable memory.

I tried to get the attention of a waiter but the place was filling up fast and either they were short of staff or some of the waiters were hiding in the bathroom because there were only two people servicing the entire room.

"It's probably quicker if I go get it myself," I said.

"No, sit down. I'm sure somebody'll be over in a minute."

"It's no problem," I replied, and got up. I made my way over to the long shiny aluminum counter where I placed my order with one of the four people working there. I was back at my seat five minutes later with the brownie on a small plate and the hot chocolate in a thick white mug, which I set down in front of Marjorie.

She beamed. "Thank you." Delicately, as if she was folding back the edge of an origami design, she broke off a piece of the brownie and her tongue extended to receive it. "Mmmm! I've wanted this all day." She looked at me chewing slowly. "So tell me, Mr. Overstreet, what terrible stories have you heard about me?"

"I'm always the last to hear things. What terrible stories are out there?"

"I thought that's why you wanted to talk to me."

"I'm talking to all the people who were close to Ronan. You were close to him, weren't you?"

"Is that what you heard?" she said, her eyes becoming cagey.

"Is it true?"

She put her hand to her mouth and turned her head away as if she was about to sneeze. When she looked at me again her eyes were shiny with emotion. "I loved him."

"Did he love you back?"

"Did he?" She gave a whimsical girlish laugh. "I don't know if he loved me but he certainly took full advantage of my love."

"Meaning?"

"You're a man. What would you do if you were him?"

"But I'm not."

"You would've done the same thing, Mr. Overstreet. What man wouldn't?"

"You were having an affair?"

"Why am I here, Mr. Overstreet? So you can humiliate me, huh? I am carrying a child. And I can assure you his name wouldn't be Jesus."

"Are you saying you're carrying Ronan's baby?"

She rose from her seat too hurriedly, her bulk making it difficult. Her knee struck the table, which rocked tipping the cup. Chocolate flashed onto the table.

"Shit!"

"Please, sit down," I said.

"Why? So you can laugh at me some more? You don't think Ronan could love somebody like me, is that it?"

I quickly mopped up the spilled chocolate with paper napkins. "I'm not trying to offend you. And for the record, I don't see anything wrong with you. You're a beautiful woman."

She brushed something from her dress with the cotton napkin and sat down again. "We would've gotten married if he had lived."

"Did Ronan ask you to spy on Baron Spencer?"

"I wouldn't call it spying."

"What would you call it?"

She tilted her head contemptuously, as if annoyed by the question. "I met Spencer at NYU where he was delivering a speech on the role of the Panthers in the civil rights struggle. We went out for coffee and really hit it off. One thing led to another. It was nothing to me really. But it sorta never went away, you know. I don't know why. I wasn't in love with him. And it wasn't the sex. There wasn't much of that." She giggled, took a sip of her chocolate, and continued talking. "He just was simply a very interesting man. He loved to talk. And I loved to listen to him. He wanted to buy me things. Real expensive stuff. Stuff I didn't think he could afford. Diamonds. He even wanted to buy me a house. So I asked how he was gonna get this money. He'd laugh and say he could take me places. That he had the means. So I told Ronan and he spoke to some people he knew in the state attorney's office."

"When did Spencer find out about you and Ronan?"

"I don't know." She broke off another piece of her brownie.

"Have you talked to him since the election?"

"I called him to tell him I was sorry."

"What did he say?"

"I don't want to repeat what he said."

"Why did Ronan fire you?"

She chewed slowly. "Because that woman told him to."

"Which woman?"

"That doctor he was seeing."

"You mean Dr. Heat?"

"Dr. Liar would be a better name for that bitch. She was supposed to be helping him, but she had him all confused. Told him it would destroy his political career if people found out I was carrying his child. She offered me a hundred and fifty thousand dollars to leave New York. I refused. I loved him."

"Why would she offer you money to leave?

"Because she wanted him for herself."

"Are you saying she was having an affair with Ronan too?"

"That's exactly what I'm saying."

"You know that for sure?"

"He didn't have a dog, Mr. Overstreet. Many times he'd come to my house after seeing her and he'd have blond hair wrapped around his balls. It doesn't take a degree to figure that one out. And I've got a degree."

"Did you ever threaten him?"

"She's been spreading those lies to anyone who'd listen. The police came to my house. Asked me that same question."

"So, did you?"

"No, never. You see, Ronan fired me from his office, but he didn't fire me from his life."

"Meaning?"

"Meaning, he was all up in my shit the night before he was killed. He wanted this child. He told me he had stopped seeing Dr. Liar. That he was going to find another therapist."

"Did he ever tell you what made him decide to see a therapist?"

"Not really. But I think it had something to do with his father. There were things he couldn't talk about."

"Who else knows you're carrying Ronan's child?"

"Other than Dr. Liar? I don't know."

"What're you doing now? Work-wise?"

"Teaching."

"College?"

"High school."

"Does that pay well enough to take care of you and a baby?"

Her eyes hardened. "I'll be fine. I don't need any help if that's what you're getting at."

"I was just wondering what Ronan's father would say."

"I'd thank you not to say anything to him or anybody in Ronan's family."

"I'll try to keep your secret. Do you have a name picked out?"

"If it's a girl I'm going to name her Sylvana. If it's a boy, Sylvan. That was my grandfather's name."

"Nice name."

"You have any kids?"

"A girl. Name's Chesney."

"I want a girl." She paused and sipped hot chocolate. "I don't know why. Just do."

I rose from the table. "I'll be getting along. Thanks for meeting me."

She looked up at me. "If you say anything about the baby I'll just deny everything."

I went down the stairs and out through the door into the hazy cold. For a moment I stood there watching as young men and women who likely didn't make the passing grade for entry milled about, hands in coat pockets, their faces screwed up against the bitter wind as if wondering if they might've had better luck if they'd brought a gift. I wondered if it would snow. It seemed a perfect evening for snow.

TWENTY

Pryce Merkins owned a town house on Charles Street in the Village. I'd bet he owned several other homes in different parts of the country. Men like him always do. According to newspaper legend he was one of those shrewd self-made immigrant millionaires trotted out by conservatives to tout the pervasiveness of the Almighty American Dream. Arriving from Russia at the age of six with his mother, he grew up somewhere in Brooklyn spending summers and evenings working in his uncle's hardware store, while studying computer science at Brooklyn College. Opened his own electronics store on Pitkin Avenue in Brooklyn at twenty-two. Sold that store before moving to Manhattan to start a software company. Made a ton when that went public ten years later. Became a darling with the black-coutured downtown crowd when he financed a fringe musical based on *Alice in Wonderland* with Alice as an immigrant Russian girl in Brooklyn to rave reviews, moving it uptown to Broadway. Plenty of champagne-filled parties later the show had won a Tony and Pryce Merkins found himself munching beluga with puff-shouldered Hollywood moguls, sleeping with coked-out, burnt-out stars, and playing dream-maker to young waifs with gold statuettes dancing in their eyes.

He made the most of it. People like him always do. He understood that Broadway was New York. And New York was Broadway. He staged free concerts in city parks throughout the boroughs and cozied up to politicians, getting himself sweetheart real-estate deals for his other businesses for enticing movie production to New York. He sponsored a theater scholarship in his name at The New School, pouring money into plays and musicals looking for that next Broadway hit. At one point he was even mentioned as a possible running mate for the governor.

But people like Merkins don't run for political office when they can stuff a few stiff-shirts into their pockets. From time to time his business dealings came under scrutiny. Investigated twice by the SEC for insider trading but no charges were ever laid. He never left a warm enough trail. People like him never do. Between offshore accounts and shell companies guarded by a bullpen of aggressive lawyers and accountants, Merkins's financial lair was so complex that even Theseus with his ball of twine would've had difficulty navigating that labyrinth.

Charles Street was one of those Village blocks where nothing seemed to be going on until you took a stroll down its narrow confines. Then you'd see the cozy restaurants or colorfully decorated stores selling old greeting cards and posters tucked away in basements. Merkins's town house at the end of the quiet block of redbrick buildings had wide ground-floor windows outfitted with rich purple blinds. The recently repaired cement sidewalk had been roped off but someone had already initialized the artwork with a handprint in the wet cement.

Carefully I balanced my way across the bridge of raised planks above the moat of drying cement and took the red steps to the front door two at a time. I rang the buzzer twice, stepped back, and waited.

A glancing wind swept off the Hudson River, whistling noiselessly through the empty branches and above the low apartments, rotting to nothing as it smacked into the high-rises on the east side. I glanced self-consciously down at my shoes and began to ruffle specks of dirt from the cuffs of my black corduroy pants as the door clacked open.

The man at the door barely reached up to my chest. He was much too young to be Merkins, flamboyantly dressed in a purple sweater and shiny green satin pants. He had raccoon eyes, his skin much too pale to be healthy, almost bleached to the point where there was no tone whatsoever.

"Yes . . . Can I help you?"

"I'm looking for Pryce Merkins."

"So's everybody else in theater. What's so special about you?" His voice was as pale as his face, high-pitched like the aftershock of an electronic flute.

"Name's Blades."

"Blade. Hmm! You don't look like Wesley Snipes. And the vampires around here don't come out 'til Halloween. Come back then."

I wedged my foot at the base to stop him from closing the door. "Tell him it's Anais Machel's husband."

His amber eyes floated over my face. "You have to get your foot out of the door."

"Will you tell him I'm here?"

He flinched. "Yes."

I let him close the door. For a while I just stood there staring at the detailed carving of the doorpost, then I turned to the street, fishing through my pockets for gum. It was moments like these when I wished I hadn't stopped smoking.

A couple was arguing on the steps of the building across the way. The woman, looking all business in a stone trench coat flapping over a hazy blue pants suit, was screaming and waving a newspaper back and forth under the man's eyes as if trying to deafen and hypnotize him at the same time. She'd caught him with her cousin in their apartment.

Loser!

He stood quietly, letting her perform her wronged-woman ritual, a scene out of a bad Ntozake Shange play.

People passed and stared, and one kindly old woman inquired of the woman if she needed assistance. I couldn't hold back a chuckle.

The door opened behind me and I turned around. The Harlequin imposter stood there hand to hip, his lips tight and pursed.

"Come in," he said.

I entered and he closed the door with a shot of anger. I towered over him, yet he took the time to look me over before moving past me and up the stairs. I followed, up the serpentine stairs with wooden handrails and iron spindles.

At the top of the stairs he turned left, marched a few feet along a wide corridor armed on both sides with large black urns. He opened the double wings of a black wooden door onto a large room with a terrace, which was flooded with light from large sunlamps. For a moment I thought I'd stepped onto a movie set.

The grand expansive room itself had a swirling high ceiling, perhaps twenty-five feet or more, framed with thick red timber. The walls were angel white, graced with large modern paintings. A chocolate German pointer was curled up on a yellow lounge chair next to a lacquered grand piano with antique legs.

Pryce Merkins was an aggravatingly handsome man. The thought of him slobbering over my wife made my head spin. I don't know how long I stood staring at him as if I was lost. He stood swirling cognac in a glass. It was a cognac glass, so I assumed it contained cognac. People like him would only put cognac in a cognac glass. He was dressed like a man who held himself in very high esteem, perhaps higher than he should, higher than most people would, in fact. The collar of his pink shirt was finely pressed and he wore cuff links that glinted in the sharp light. His pants were black, linen, shiny, and expensive-looking. He wasn't as tall as me, but being slender and holding himself aloof like a dancer, he appeared taller. The skin of his face crusted like overdone quiche, showing the effects of too many hours of leisure, too many hours under an ultraviolet lamp.

He beckoned me to him with a pompous wave of his hand, exhibiting long delicate fingers. His lips were full and dark, his chin curved; his small pulverized eyes the only mistake in an otherwise perfect face.

"I've always wanted to meet Anais's husband," he said, extending his hand.

I took his hand. His grip was powerful, assured.

"I won't take more than a few minutes of your time," I said.

"I have no pressing appointments," he said jovially. "Would you like a drink? Some cognac?"

"No thanks."

"Sit down then. Come . . . How about something to eat? You like caviar?"

"No, this won't take very long."

"Mister . . ."

"Overstreet. But you can call me Blades."

"Blades, I get very offended when people refuse my hospitality."

"That's all right. I'm used to offending people."

He smiled. "Yeah, you used to be a cop, right?"

"Five years. Narco."

"I bet you offended a lot of people."

"Only punks and shitbags."

"How is Anais?"

"You just saw her this morning."

His eyes wavered but he recovered quickly and smiled. "Yes, I did. And she looked fine. As always."

"Well, you see, Mr. Merkins . . ."

"Please call me Pryce."

"Well, you see, that's what I'm here about."

"What?"

"My wife . . . She told me about your lunch the other day."

He walked away to sit in a beige leather recliner. "Yes, I have this great play that we think would be wonderful for her."

I walked over and stood behind him.

He swiveled around to face me. "I'd rather that you sit, Blades."

"I want you to stay away from Anais."

He stood up. "Did she send you here to tell me that?"

"She doesn't know I'm here."

"I suspected that. I'm not surprised she left you awhile back, Blades. You seem like a man with little self-control."

"I use it when I need it."

"Then I'll let Anais tell me if she wants to see me or not."

"You don't understand. I'll break your fucking legs if you don't stay away from my wife."

His throat tightened and his nostrils flared. "Be careful. You don't want to threaten me."

"Just stay away from her."

I headed for the door leaving him staring into space.

"Mr. Overstreet . . ."

I turned around.

"Did she tell you about the time we spent in Los Angeles when you two were separated? Is that why you're so upset?"

I wanted to go back and punch him in the face, but I kept it together and went out the door and down the stairs. If my calculation about Pryce Merkins was correct the chance would come again. Sooner than later. With men like him, it always does.

TWENTY-ONE

Anais had gone to bed early that night and didn't hear me come in. After showering, I snuggled up to her in our canopy bed, listening to her even breathing, hoping she would wake up, but not wanting to be so obvious about my intentions. She must've been exhausted because ordinarily my presence this close would've stirred her. This time it didn't and I was forced to resort to more aggressive tactics.

She was lying on her stomach. Under the down comforter her short chamois had ridden up past her hips exposing her smooth ass. Leaning on my elbow I surveyed the mountains and valleys of her body; the high rise of her butt leveling off in the plain of her muscled lower back. I slid my hand along the back of her leg, up along her thighs, coming to rest on the peak of her buttocks. Her legs were far enough apart for me to dip a finger between the gulf of her thighs. She was moist. I became enthused by this discovery. But my insistent finger did not have the effect I hoped. She neither stirred nor sighed in any somnambulist pleasure. I gave up trying to wake her and rolled over to dream.

. . .

BROOKLYN IS the home of the bargain shopper. Walk along Church or Nostrand Avenues and the number of stores advertising the lowest prices in New York would make your eyes sweat with fatigue. From shoddy 99-cent stores to real-estate offices advertising foreclosure specials.

Next morning Anais and I strolled along Church Avenue charmed to smiles by the passion of the brilliant accents around us. Sliver clouds drifted across the sky like wayward gulls. A dog slept at the foot of an Asian youth sipping from a Snapple bottle, wearing Number 23 as fluently as any black kid in Harlem. The sound of someone playing keyboards drifted across the street. Inside a car a woman sat peeling a yellow-skinned mango with a smile on her face so elegant it could only be explained by conjuring images of angels. Old women hunched over to keep warm at the bus stop. Young men with the fabulous elongated bodies of athletes or models sauntered enterprisingly down the sidewalk, appropriating all the space without regard for the elderly couple approaching. The beautiful people chased around Manhattan by paparazzi didn't have anything on these folks.

We bought some vegetables and fruit from a Korean grocery and took a chance buying fish from a market next door before walking back to the car parked on a quiet side street a few blocks away.

I opened the trunk to put our purchases inside. Leaving Anais to pack and close the trunk, I went to open the passenger door. Having spent so much time as an undercover cop, I'd developed a great set of instincts. With my keys in my hand poised to open the door, I got one of those sixth sense flashes: *Somebody's watching you*.

I spun around. Across the street, standing next to a black SUV, was Lizard-Face.

Before I could do anything he raised his right hand. A silver flash. I flew to Anais screaming, *"Get down!"* For a second she stared at me, her eyes frozen in shock. I dragged her to the ground, groping for my Glock.

But Lizard-Face did not open fire.

I knelt behind the still-open car trunk. Anais was somewhere under the back of the car. I could feel her legs against mine. I fought the dizzying rush of blood to my head. Steadying the gun by bracing my left hand under my right wrist, I aimed it across the street.

Lizard-Face had disappeared.

Frantic, I scoped left and right along the drab street. No Lizard-Face. I scanned the block again. Passersby who'd heard me scream and who may've stopped to see what was happening had scampered when they saw my gun. I stood up and crossed the street at a dead run to the SUV. Nobody inside.

We were on a block of quiet flat red-bricked semi-detached houses. A clean-looking block. Lizard-Face could've slipped in between the houses and through a backyard and gone without anybody really noticing. I rushed back to Anais, still lying under the car.

Kneeling down, I spoke to her softly, "Come out, babe. It's safe now."

She was sobbing. "What the fuck was that all about, Blades?"

"I'll explain on the way home."

"I'm not coming out from under this car until you tell me what the hell is going on."

"I don't want to stay around here, sweet-pea. It might not be safe."

She stopped crying and slowly inched from under the car. The front of her coat was lashed with dirt. Her moistened cheek was speckled with granules of red sand. There was a laceration in the palm of her right hand that seeped a tiny amount of blood. She looked at her hand, wiped it on her coat, and hugged me.

"Are you okay?" she said, swiping her coat arm across her cheek.

"I'm fine. Let's go."

Her eyes were as wide as lakes and I wanted to throw myself inside. Just lose myself in all of her. I suppose it's normal for a man to feel this way after he and his wife have just escaped death.

. . .

AS I DROVE, checking my mirror for a tail, I told Anais about Lizard-Face coming to our home. In a span of three minutes the man had boiled me into a paranoid lather.

"Why didn't you tell me about this before?" Anais cried.

"I didn't want to worry you."

"I warned you about that woman, Blades. Didn't I warn you about her?"

"Don't blame this on her, Anais."

"Don't blame this on her! What's wrong with you? This asshole threatens your family because of some situation he got with this bitch and you telling me not to blame her?"

"I'll take care of it."

"Let the police handle it, Blades. What am I going to do if the next time that nut job sees you he just shoots you dead? What then?"

I glanced over at Anais. She will be forever beautiful in my eyes. But right at that moment as the crusader, the passionate champion for my safety, she was never more stunning with the handsome sweep to her forehead, insolent lips, and big wide-set eyes.

"Nothing's gonna happen to me, Anais."

"I don't want to hear that, Blades."

"I promise."

"That neither."

"Then what do you want?"

"You know what I want. I want you to go to the police. Tell them everything you know. And then we're gonna book a vacation."

"You can't be serious."

"Indeed, I am. Very."

"Anais, someone took a shot at Noah yesterday. His son's been murdered. I can't skip on this, Anais. Please understand."

"Blades, I put up with this when you were a cop because I didn't have any choice. But don't think it was easy. Don't think that every freaking night you left to go out there with your big gun and big ego that I didn't wonder, Was there somebody out there with a bigger gun? A bigger ego. Some shitface who could only get his dick hard by eating yours. Some nights I cried when you left. You could've been anything, Blades, but you chose to hunt criminals. Your mother is a college professor, for chrissakes. You had access to college. Your sister is a lawyer. But you wanted to go chase after lowlifes. I tried to understand because I thought I knew why. But you've left the NYPD and I wonder if this isn't worse. What drives you, Blades?"

I absorbed her raving because I knew it was cathartic for her. Every now and then we all need to take a laxative. Cleansing was good for the body and the soul. Not to mention the mind. Anais had been traumatized by the last fifteen minutes. Venting I could take. Oftentimes it was the unspoken words, fermenting like bad wine in the brain, which could be vinegar to a relationship.

We had recently wriggled out of a bad stage in our marriage. A stage where I indulged in some behavior I've been ashamed to own up to. The fights would bring on silences that would last for weeks. And in those silences I would imagine the worst. That Anais was having an affair. Or that she was planning to divorce me secretly. Or that she would disappear one night while I was sleeping and I would never see her again. So that when she left me and went to live in Los Angeles I nearly lost my mind. I drank every day. Too much of it. There was nothing cathartic about that. And the first night she lay in my arms after her return I was a vine climbing toward the sun.

Her stony words washed over me like a tide. I didn't say anything else until we reached home.

WE WERE not in the house five minutes before the phone rang. Anais picked up and said hello in a passive voice. Then she handed off the phone to me, her eyes moist and tentative, her faced masked in a strange gloominess. I was standing right next to her.

"Hello?"

"Today could've been your wife's last on this earth."

It took me a moment to realize where I'd heard the voice. "Listen to me, asshole! If I see you anywhere near my house or my family I will kill you."

He laughed and his voice sounded as if it was coming from hell. Then I heard the click of emptiness as he hung up.

I didn't want to look at Anais, but I knew she was staring at me.

"That him?"

I nodded.

"What are you going to do?" Her voice quivered.

"I don't know."

"I'm scared, Blades."

I turned and gathered her in my arms. Her face released the mask of fear and she leveled her eyes upward, floating them over my face, searching for reassurance. I had none to give.

I ran my fingers through her damp hair. "I think you should carry a weapon."

She pulled away from me. "What're you talking about, Blades?" Her voice rose and then crumbled as the weight of my suggestion settled on her.

I saw the resin of doubt cloud her eyes.

"You mean a gun?" she said, shaking her head. "No, Blades. I don't wanna carry a gun. I haven't fired a gun since you taught me how to shoot."

"For your protection. It'll make me feel better when you're out without me."

"Why don't we just go away until this guy is caught by the police?"

"What about your play?"

"They can find somebody else."

"We can't just run, Anais."

"You mean *you* refuse to run."

"Okay, I can't run. I don't know how to do that."

After a pause, Anais walked away to sit on the bottom of the stairs, her head tilted, leaning on the rail.

"Will you do it for me? I have a twenty-five caliber in the basement. It's small. Will fit easily in your handbag."

"Whatever you say, Blades."

TWENTY-TWO

New York is a city of insomniacs. But if it is a city that never sleeps, it is also a city that doesn't allow you to sleep, an overstimulated city where rapid-fire newscasts compete with ads, the Internet, restaurants, clubs, cafes, all-night parties, all-night delis, all-night noise. Garish commercial endorsements pock every inch of the city. Our brains are on information overload.

But it was none of these things which kept me from falling asleep. Before coming to bed I'd spent the better part of the evening drinking with Milo, who, despite the drinking and hard living he'd done in his youth, still looked much younger than his sixty-two years. At my urging he'd stopped dyeing the gray out of his hair. Now, bespectacled with close-cropped wavy gray hair, he looked as distinguished as a politician but was decidedly more honorable and honest.

More for laughter than anything else we recycled our lives over a liter of Old Oak rum. We ran the gamut from our glories to our trials and tribulations, disagreeing on each other's major failings, but agreeing that the reasons why we never seemed to find happiness despite all our efforts were not in ourselves but in the stars.

Milo downed glasses of Old Oak like he was swallowing aspirin. And I tried to match him knowing I would fail. Anais passed by, noticed what we were doing, and went up to bed with a smug look of disdain on her face. Yeah, I knew what she was thinking: *Blades was getting out of control again.* Common sense told me I should've stopped drinking when she shoved her head into the den to say goodnight. But I wasn't particularly impressed with what common sense had to say at that point. I wanted to hide in the cloak of drunkenness for one night.

Milo's brilliant drunken idea was that I should go searching for Lizard-Face. Why wait for him to come to me? To keep fucking with my family? Somewhere in the underbelly of New York he must've left a trail of slime. If he came from out of town, then he would need help from other reptiles on two legs wandering around this fine city. More trails of shit and slime to follow. Scum like Lizard-Face left distinct smells. And I had the nose for scum.

By the time I got to bed I was drunk enough to be rolled down a hill in a barrel. Anais had already conked out. She snores a little when she sleeps on her back. I listened to her soft snoring. I tried to go to sleep but Milo's words kept jerking at the tiny portion of my brain still functioning. And when I thought I was deep in the pit of sleep I was merely locked in an alcohol-generated hallucination.

I heard myself screaming for Anais to get down. Rapidly behind that came Ronan's blank eyes screaming death. And then the soul-rattling howl of his mother. That was enough. I jumped up shaking, my mouth parched, ears ringing as if I'd been sitting under the speakers at a Stones concert. I got up, got dressed in black, accessorizing with my black Glock in a shoulder holster under my jacket. Then I called Toni Monday. Anais hadn't stirred.

AS I WAITED at the Rogers Avenue lights after midnight, the March wind swept around me in swirls of paper. I could taste the bitterness of my drunkenness; my tongue a thimble of fire in my mouth.

In the hi-rise to my right, light beamed from windows like flares in a hurricane.

Life hung on such a thin string, what is money or beauty or glory by comparison? Six years ago I was a highly decorated undercover narco who almost died when a member of my own squad shot me by accident. Nine months ago I became a father for the first time, though I'd been a father for eight years and didn't know it. Now that's something to ponder, isn't it? Especially on a night like tonight when I wasn't sure if I was gonna kill or be killed. Again common sense tried to speak to me. *Hey, you're lucky to be alive. You've got a beautiful wife and a lovely daughter. Go home and get some sleep.*

But I wasn't smart enough to listen and I wasn't sleepy anymore.

Awhile back I'd promised my brother I was done with killing. But here I was, once again, feeling the tyrannical surge of power I used to feel when I strapped on my Glock and stepped out into the lights of New York City like Anthony Quinn in *Zorba the Greek* on Broadway.

The more I thought about my life, the years I spent as a cop, the more I hated the person it'd made me. And I honestly thought I could change. I wanted to change. Who was I? Was it inevitable that I would always be running from the past? Like an alcoholic who always returned to the bottle, would I always resort to violence whenever I felt threatened?

TONI MONDAY was waiting for me outside Junior's restaurant. He'd agreed to meet me here after I threatened to put his business on the police wire.

He leaned against a lamppost sucking on a cigarette. I was happy he'd left his flamboyant wardrobe at home. There was only so much of that I could take. And tonight it would've been tough. Not that he was dressed shabbily. The beige full-length sheepskin coat would've lightened most people's pocket. But Toni could afford it. He noticed me stumbling up to him and mouthed something in the wind. I was too far away to hear but I imagined he was cursing me. He took one last drag of his cigarette and flicked the butt away, pulled at the lapels of his coat and came erect.

"Man, I'm beginning to get real fucking tired of your act, Blades."

"Sorry, Toni. I had to do this."

"Do you know who you pulled me away from?"

"I don't even want to know."

"You're a whack job, Blades. You're the fucking devil. You know what you need, kid? You need a transfusion. You got devil blood in you."

"You wanna go inside out of the cold or you just like to see your breath flying in the wind?"

"What's wrong with you, Blades?"

"I'm cold."

I walked away, pausing at the entrance to Junior's. When I glanced back Toni was hurrying through the whistling wind behind me.

There were only a few patrons inside, mostly youngsters gouging on the desserts for which Junior's was famous. It was a large place, made up of cozy red booths. I sat at a booth near the window and Toni slide into the vinyl seat across from me. I took off my jacket and watched Toni peel off his expensive coat and drape it over the back of the seat, revealing a brown turtleneck sweater.

He stared at me as if trying to excavate an idea from the cave of my mind, his eyes shiny as polished brass. He'd dyed his hair again. This time it was the color of a golden sunset.

We both ordered coffee; Toni also ordered cheesecake.

"I need something sweet so don't say a goddamn word, Blades."

"I'm dumb."

"After what you pulled me away from, I need to indulge, baby."

"Indulge all you want. While you're in there see if you can come up with a name for me."

"A name?"

"Any mechanics from outta town looking for a woman who works for me?"

"Why're you always coming to me with your problems?"

"I'm not in the mood for your whining."

"I might've heard something."

"What did you hear?"

"Something about stolen cheese."

"Whose loot?"

"They aren't from outta town, I can tell you that."

"Who're they?"

"I don't know."

"How do you know they're not from outta town?"

"Don't ask me how I know shit. That's not your problem. They're not from outta town. They're from right here."

"Brooklyn?"

"Russians. You didn't hear shit from me, understand? I ain't got no beef with them."

"Where would I find these pinheads?"

He jerked up with a laugh. "You can't be serious."

"Serious or not. Where?"

"You ain't gonna go looking for these guys, are you?"

"Nobody threatens my family."

"Wake the fuck up, Blades. You ain't got that stupid piece of brass to protect you no more. A new set of rules are in effect, kid. Your family is fair game like anybody else."

"You oughta know better, Toni."

"Don't fuck around with these bozos, Blades."

"What would you do if somebody came to your house and threatened your family?"

"If I did have a family anybody crazy enough to do that wouldn't care about dying."

"You'd get rid of them before they harmed your family, right?"

"Let's get something straight, Blades. I don't get rid of anybody. I'm a businessman. But I'm all for good business practices. And that means taking care of problems before they escalate."

"Then that's what I'm doing. Taking care of a problem before it escalates. Where can I find these people?"

"I have to do business with these guys from time to time, Blades. I can't give you names."

"Come on, Toni. This is my family."

"Talk to Polly."

"Who's Polly?"

"He runs a bar on Coney Island Avenue. Near Kings Highway. The Humbert."

"What's he look like?"

"Big guy with a beat-up face. Used to be a boxer in the Russian army. Long scar like a river under his left eye. Whatever you do, don't mention my name."

The waiter returned with our order. Toni munched on his cheesecake. I drank my coffee in silence contemplating how I was going to walk into a bar called the Humbert on Coney Island Avenue and ask for a guy named Polly.

"WHO WANTS to know?"

"Tell him I got a message for a friend of his."

The bartender looked at me with feral eyes, his face a mask of shadowy wrinkles. There was a welt the size of a golf ball above his right eye, as if he'd walked into an iron pillar, or someone had struck him with a baseball bat.

He leaned across the bar, putting his face dangerously close to me. "I think you should take your nigger ass outta here." His breath reeked of decayed meat.

The Humbert was a lively little place. It wasn't really a bar, but a restaurant which had a tiny bar off to one side near the entrance. Everything in it looked fake. The black tubular chairs with plastic seats, the shiny drapes which gave it a funeral parlor ambiance, the piped-in ukulele music, the plastic tablecloths; the stringy blond hair, pinched mouth, and tartar-sauce-colored eyes of the bartender who thought my inquiry into the whereabouts of Polly funny enough to insult me.

I felt myself twitching as anger percolated through me, mixing with alcohol to make me feel like swooning. He didn't know how close he was to having his head split open. I twitched; I wormed about; I wiggled my eyes, everything to control my anger. He stared at me, his eyes narrowing. He must've been wondering if I was about to have a stroke.

"So he isn't here?" I said, getting my anger under control.

"What did I just say?"

"You don't want to be saying things like that to me, babe."

"Who the hell you calling babe?"

I reached out and tapped his face. "It's nothing. Just an expression we niggers use among each other."

His jaws caved in slightly and his eyes turned coppery. I knew what he was about to do.

With dodgy speed, I slipped my Glock from inside my shoulder strap. "Don't even think about it."

His mouth opened wide and he stood rigid.

I kept my eyes on him until I made it to the door.

CONEY ISLAND AVENUE stretched from Prospect Park to the Belt. It was a busy thoroughfare, a conduit to the highway which fed into Long Island, making it a favorite route of truckers. At night, however, traffic was usually light. Such was the case tonight.

I stood outside the Humbert trying to remember where I'd parked my car. Not such a smart thing to do considering what had just transpired inside. But I was being reckless. And for no good reason other than I was too drunk to think straight.

I paid little attention to the black Mercedes sedan that pulled up in front of me. The door of the Humbert opened and I turned around to see who was coming out. Two men, both tall and linebacker broad, exited wearing black full-length leather coats and nasty scowls on their faces.

One without a hat and stiff blond hair who seemed to have trouble breathing, whipped out a large shiny pistol from his coat. "Get in the car!"

I considered trying to reach my gun but thought better of it when he pointed the large bore at my head. Another man got out of the Mercedes and came up behind me. I didn't know which way to turn. A thick arm circumferenced my throat, snapping my head back. Someone kicked me in my groin. Unbelievable pain snaked down my legs and upward through my stomach, mushrooming through my chest and arms. My body went limp as a withered leaf.

Together they stuffed me into the backseat of the car, which sped south on Coney Island Avenue. It took a few blocks before my body began to recycle the blood that had shot from my lower body like scared rats from a cat. My balls still felt like they were resting on a hot grill, but at least I could feel my legs again. I could again feel the rhythm of my breathing. *Jesus! I'd rather die than feel that kind of pain again.*

Two men in the backseat with me. Two in the front. The four of them were jabbering in a foreign language.

The man in the front passenger seat turned around. He had a flattened face except for a sharp hawk nose. His eyes swam in a reservoir of pink humorless void. His nose trickled a thick colorless liquid and a hearing device curled behind his fleshy ears. A long thin gash snaked under his right eye.

"Who sent you?" His voice croaked like arthritic bones.

"Who sent me?" I couldn't hear my own voice.

"Do I hear an echo?"

The four of them laughed. I struggled to find a steady rhythm to breathe on.

"Why you looking for Polly?" the snotty-nosed man said.

"I was told he could help me find a man."

"What man?"

"Are you Polly?"

The slime draining from his nose was beginning to bother me. I wanted to tell him to clean his fucking nose. I had no idea where we were; I had a faint sense that I might've lost consciousness but I wasn't sure. I felt like my head was in a vise and someone was trying to twist my body into a corkscrew.

"Who sent you?" Nasal-Drip said. When he breathed he made a shallow nasal whistle on the intake.

"Nobody sent me."

"And Nobody's your name, right?"

"My name's Blades." Ah, the rhythm was coming. I could hear my breath.

His face twitched into a lopsided smile; if you could call the shape his liver-thick lips had assumed a smile.

"You came to see Polly all by yourself?"

I nodded. It hurt even to move my head up and down.

"You a cop?"

I thought for a second whether saying I was a cop would save me further punishment or even death. I decided it wouldn't matter. "No," I whispered hoarsely.

"Who's this man you're looking for?"

"Broad. Tiny fish eyes. Silver hair. Bullet forehead."

"What do you want with him?"

"He threatened my family. Frightened my wife."

The four of them broke into laughter. I didn't know what was funny about what I'd said.

The man on my right put a gun to my head and said, "We should kill him."

The car came to a stop on a quiet street. I tried to peer outside. An elevated train rumbled on old tracks not far off. Somewhere else close by the surf was up, a hollowed out sound as pure as a thought.

The back doors opened and the two men who'd boxed me in slithered out.

"Get out!" the man with the scar ordered.

I tried to move but the lower part of my body was paralyzed.

"Get out!" he squawked again.

The men outside the car grabbed my legs and dragged me outside.

My head struck the metal edge of the door. My body landed with a thud on the hard cold asphalt and the left side of my head was flushed with warmth. I didn't touch it but I knew it was blood.

Bright lights approaching fast. A vehicle stopped with a screech of tires. Voices. Orders. Somebody landed a kick to my ribs. I heard my breath zip out of me with the force of an exploding cannon. Before the blackness swept over me I smelled rubber burning on the asphalt. I heard more voices. Somewhere the sea was calling my name and I wanted to get there as fast as I could.

TWENTY-THREE

I woke thinking I was in the arms of my wife. That was before I felt the pain. And then I wasn't even sure where that was coming from. My head? My arm? My back? A golden light dazzled my eyes, making it impossible for me to see. I tried to call Anais's name but my tongue was wrapped around a stake. Then I heard a voice and the golden light melted away leaving silver tails in my vision.

"Blades?"

First I saw the smile, the long sharklike teeth, the pink lips stretched thin then slowly closing in an *o* around concern. It wasn't Anais. It was Special Agent Sallie Kraw.

"Where am I?" I struggled to get up.

"Don't move. Relax."

I looked around me, becoming aware of the shiny interior with small shelves and rows of blue and yellow packages. There were lights flashing somewhere. Was it outside, or inside my head?

"You're in an ambulance," Kraw said.

Ambulance. I let the word tumble around in my brain. *What the fuck am I doing in an ambulance?* Then I remembered the fall from grace and the blow to my head on the way down. I managed a smile. "You've been following me?"

"Somebody's gotta look out for you."

"Couldn't you've looked out a little sooner? Like before I became a football?" I realized I was lying on a stretcher. I tried to sit up again but could only get my head off the pillow.

"Don't try to move. You're hurt."

I closed my eyes and felt my mind reach out for darkness again. Then came a man's voice pitching through the blackness.

"Mr. Overstreet, how're you feeling?"

I opened my eyes. He was leaning toward me smiling that painted smile he was trained to give nervous patients. But his eyes were a million miles away.

"I'm fine."

"That's good," he said. "But we'd like to take you in to have you checked out. Can you tell me what happened?"

"I don't need to be checked out."

He'd already punctured a vein in my arm and attached a drip. I reached up and ripped it out. A small amount of blood seeped from the tiny perforation in my arm.

I grabbed Agent Kraw by the wrist. "Get me outta here."

"You were unconscious, Blades. You might have a concussion," she said.

"Just another name for a bad headache. That's what Excedrin was made for."

"I can't let you go until I'm sure you're okay, sir," the young attendant said, his voice firm and official.

I pulled myself to a seated position with Agent Kraw's help. "Are you gonna take me to my car or am I going to have to walk?"

She turned to the attendant in his wrinkled blue uniform. "He's not gonna go."

The attendant shrugged and peeled off his gloves. He leaned forward and said something to the driver in the cab of the ambulance. The engine surged to life.

With Agent Kraw's help I staggered outside and stood up in the street, my knees feeling like loose springs. She held me steady as the ambulance drove off, its lights whorling but without the wail of the siren.

"You want to go somewhere to clean yourself up before I take you home?"

"No thanks."

"What's your wife going to say if she sees you like this?"

"She's used to seeing me like this."

The agent looked at me with a bewildered grin.

"It's just a joke," I said. "Where's your car?"

"Across the street. You sure you're okay?"

I smiled weakly but with confidence. "Once I see my wife I'll be a thousand percent better."

TEN MINUTES LATER we were whooshing past darkened service stations and closed up restaurants along Coney Island Avenue. My head was beginning to lose its clogged up feeling, but the dull headache had grown in intensity. I was bleeding from a cut on my elbow and I knew I had a welt on my forehead. But I was alive.

"Why did you go into that restaurant?" Agent Kraw said, taking her eyes off the road for a second to glance at me.

"I love Russian food."

"Looked like you bit off more than you can chew."

I was slightly amused but did not show it. "Is that the best you could do?"

"You're playing with quicksand, you know."

"I only play with my wife."

"Tough guys don't last, you know. They die horrible deaths. Because there's always somebody more desperate. You're not dealing with streetcorner addicts here, Blades."

"Someone threatened my family. I'd sell my blood before I let anyone hurt them."

"Who threatened your family?"

"Someone who looks like he's been using his face to hammer out dents in a car."

"Oh that's real helpful."

"He's just ugly. Silver hair. Husky."

"Sounds like Parkoff. We think he's the one who threw Konstantin out of the hotel window."

We reached my car curbed at a bus stop on Kings Highway. Agent Kraw parked behind the Volvo and looked at me. "You smell like you showered in a still. You gonna be okay?"

I got out and spoke to her through the open door. "I'll never get drunk again. And you should stop following me around. I really don't know where she is."

She handed me a card. "Call me if you need anything, Blades. You're a liar but I don't want to see you dead."

I took the card and closed the door.

I felt like I'd been run over by a bus. My groin hurt and my legs were limp noodles. I managed to drag myself into my car with some effort, where I sat letting the pain stirred up by my effort dissolve. Agent Kraw was still parked behind me. I fumbled through my jacket pockets for my keys. It took me a few seconds but I finally got them out and poked the Volvo's ignition. The quiet purring of the old car's engine was a comforting sound. I tooted my horn and drove off.

TWENTY-FOUR

I slept like a man in a coma, opening my eyes around 10:00 A.M. the next day to a pain in my knee so severe I almost cried out. My mind still pitched in fog, I looked around for Anais before realizing I was not in our bedroom. I'd slept in the guest room.

It was Friday. The drapes had been pulled—Anais must've come in while I was asleep—still the room was gloomy dark. Outside a dense rain whipped ropes of water with stunning rapidity at the window pane, slapping hard and flat with a heavy thump, as if a giant hand was trying to break though the glass. Sitting in bed I watched the smooth sheets of water spill off the window like a waterfall as the rest of my body weighed in with its assortment of pains.

My mind was slowly emerging from last night's fog and I didn't like what was before me. I reached up and caressed the bulge on my forehead, which only registered a dull ache. There was also a pain in my elbow. That too was manageable. It was the sting of my ego that disturbed me more than anything. I was caught flat-footed last night because of arrogance and carelessness. How could this have happened to me?

I rolled over and looked at my knee. It was swollen to the size of a baseball. Fully awake now, and shamed by the memory of my folly, I tried a dismount from the bed that would've made an arthritic old woman laugh. Rolling to the edge of the bed I planted the good leg on the floor, standing up by grasping the headboard so I could lift the wounded knee off the bed.

I limped to my bedroom. Anais was long out of bed. In the bathroom I took a one-legged leak. I braved the mirror offering myself a smile of condolence. The golf ball on my forehead was now the color of raw beef. After brushing my teeth and gargling with mint Listerine I found Icy-Hot and a bandage in the medicine cabinet. I massaged the spongy gel into my knee. No afterburn.

Deciding to save the bandage for later I limped downstairs taking the allotted fifteen minutes for such a maneuver on one leg. My knee had warmed up some and was more flexible by the time I reached the living room.

Anais's truck was not in the garage. I hobbled to the study and tossed myself onto the couch. I was breathing heavily and I could sense myself becoming irritable. I was annoyed that Anais was not around. Irrationality was a sign of tension.

I picked up the phone and dialed my father's number in Barbados, a call I'd been contemplating for some time. He sounded as if he'd just woken up himself.

"What's up, Pops?"

"Blades! You're going to live long, son. I was just telling my friend here that the last time I heard from you I could still bend over and touch my toes."

I tried to sound amused. "What friend is that?"

"Lady friend."

"Listen, Pops, I've got some bad news."

He sighed softly. "Should I sit down?"

"It's Noah. His son was murdered."

His voice rushed out hoarse and quiet. "Ronan's dead?"

"And somebody took a shot at Noah three days ago."

"Is Noah okay?"

"Yeah, he's fine. Ain't easy to kill that old lion."

After a long pause, he said, "I can't imagine what state Donna must be in. When did this happen?"

I waited a second. "Monday before last."

"Fuck! And you're just now calling me?"

"Actually, I wasn't sure if I was going to tell you."

"When's the funeral?"

"In four days."

"I'm coming up."

"Did I hear you say you're coming up?"

"I'm coming."

"You're coming back for Ronan's funeral but you couldn't come back for me twenty years ago?"

"You're a grown man, Blades. To hell with it."

"I suppose I am," I said quietly.

After I hung up I sat thinking, wishing I could've been excited about seeing my father in New York. Seeing him in Barbados was one thing. New York presented a genre of problems far beyond anything I wanted to contemplate right now. The safety of my family was a bigger concern. The eagerness of his decision to return made me wonder if the idea hadn't been already in his mind. It sure sounded to me as if he'd been looking for any opportunity, any excuse. But why now?

AFTER BANDAGING MY KNEE I got dressed and left the house. Though I was hungry I didn't eat. Irrationality was getting the better of me again. A dark anger percolated through me like alcohol through a drunk. I was sitting on the kind of frustration I used to ride when a particularly nasty drug dealer I'd busted walked away scot-free because the D.A. screwed up, or as happened in several cases, the defendant somehow managed to imbue some lonely female juror with a sense of pity, thereby securing an acquittal. In the past whenever I felt like this I would take my rage out on some dim-witted drug suspect, beating the poor fellow until he was too afraid to do anything but shit himself.

I corked my anger long enough to call Anais's cell phone. I wanted to know where she was. She was at a meeting in Manhattan with Pryce Merkins. That bit of information didn't make me sparkle in the least, but I knew my wife was no pushover when it came to business or anything else, so I arranged to have dinner with her later and hung up.

My next call, to Negus's house, came up empty. I tried his cell. Nothing. I drove along Atlantic Avenue past stores selling antiques, past Middle Eastern stores growing in popularity for their spices and scented coffee, stopping outside Chesney's school on Court Street just for my peace of mind. Then I threaded the dense traffic to the club, where I planned to do some work.

I found Negus in the office chatting on the phone, his large feet, encased in brown Adidas sports shoes, tilted onto the desk. Didn't sound like business. His yellow linen shirt had a satin sheen. I'd seen him in that shirt before and liked it then. Today I wasn't liking anything about Negus.

I limped back outside for a cup of coffee, hoping to calm my ragged nerves.

NEGUS WAS still on the phone when I returned. I circled him like a hungry tiger and he looked up, his eyes leathery brown.

"You talking to River?" I said.

He whispered quick good-byes and hung up. "Couldn't you've waited until I was finished? Godammit!"

"She's in big trouble, Negus. Did she tell you that?"

He took his feet off the desk and stood up. "It ain't nothing we can't handle."

"We? Are you Batman and Robin now? You're in over your head, Negus."

"Get over yourself, Blades. You think you're the only one who knows how to handle shit?"

"You ain't even funny, Negus."

"Fuck you, Blades. We don't need you."

"Is she still in your apartment?"

"Don't worry you little head of curls, baby."

"I'm trying to help you, Negus. I'm trying to stop you from having your dick served to you on a spit."

"Man, what's your problem? Don't you already have a wife?"

I stepped back to look at his bone-bright face. "It's your dead, cuz."

THAT NIGHT Anais came to bed in a purple teddy smelling like a flower. Her locks were loose about her face, hanging black beads from a bearded fig tree. I was lying on my back naked from the waist up, my eyes open but my mind not in the room. She laid herself out on top of me, kissing first my cheeks then munching my lips. Securing a dark nipple in her mouth she sucked with fervor.

On any other night I would've risen with speed, ready to slay the dragon of my wife's passion. Not tonight. My mind was lost in a dank everglade of doubt and fear. I could not get Negus and River out of my mind enough to enjoy the sensations Anais's mouth was delivering to my body. Hell, I couldn't even feel them. I knew they were there because Anais was a great lover. She knew just how to kiss me and where in order to heat my blood. My blood was too toxic to flow tonight.

It didn't take her long to realize her machinations were useless. She leaned close to my ears. "What's the matter, honey?"

"I don't know."

She licked my ear. "Relax, baby."

"I'm trying."

Anais rolled off me; her left leg draped lazily across my groin. I breathed deeply, trying to bring my attention back to my wife. *Christ! I must be crazy thinking about Negus and River at a time like this.*

"Blades, you're thinking about that crazy guy from yesterday, aren't you?"

"I'm just tired, I guess."

She massaged the hair on my chest lightly. "You wouldn't be trying to hustle me now, would you my darling?"

"I can't imagine how I'd get away with that."

She pinched me. "You're right. What happened to you last night is nothing compared to what I'm gonna do to your ass if you don't have a good reason for turning me down."

"I'm sorry, honey. We've got a big show at the club tomorrow night."

"I don't want to hear about the club. I want to hear what's really on your mind."

"I think Negus is in trouble."

"Negus loves trouble."

"Big trouble. He's hooked up with River. He's got her stashed somewhere."

Anais sat up, got down off the bed, and walked to the love seat in the far corner. I twisted my head to follow her. She sat with her legs drawn up, her head bowed, touching her knees. A wedge of light cut through the parted blinds illuminating the outline of her muscular thighs. I could see the dark juncture of her pubic hair at the end of those thighs. For a moment I felt a surge of excitement. I loved when I caught her sitting like this.

"Blades, if Negus can handle the pussy let him handle the other shit this bitch is floating in."

"Her name is River."

"I do not care if her name is Ocean."

"Is it wrong to wanna help my friends?"

"Why don't you change your name to St. Bernard?" She got up and picked up her robe from the foot of the bed. Caped in the long black gown she strode stiffly out of the room.

TWENTY-FIVE

The two bodies were found the same day at almost the same time in different parts of Brooklyn. Marjorie Madden's pregnant body was discovered by police after a neighbor complained of a dog barking nonstop through the night. She'd been strangled and had been dead for six hours. The police were still gathering evidence and interviewing possible witnesses but it appeared to be a push-in robbery; the place had been ransacked. When I read the news story I thought of telling Noah about the child Marjorie had been carrying, but what would that accomplish now?

A SANITATION WORKER, walking his dog on a deserted stretch of the Coney Island boardwalk early in the morning before he set off for work, saw something in the sand that aroused his suspicion. It could've been a piece of wood. But driftwood that size was not common on that beach. He whistled for his dog and together they walked down the steps onto the sand. As he suspected, it wasn't driftwood. The naked frozen body lay face up and the sanitation worker wondered aloud to the police that only a crazy person would kill somebody and then cut off his dick. Cause of death had not been determined by press time.

I CALLED a trusted friend to do some digging for me. Semin Gupta, a respected Pulitzer Prize–winning reporter with the *New York Times,* and I went back a ways. She'd come from India on an H-1 visa contracted to work for a software company and after six months she'd had enough. She got married, and having always fancied herself a writer, she wrote a number of freelance articles on technology for webzines before enrolling in the journalism program at Columbia.

After graduation her technology background landed her a job at the *Times.* Soon her reporting skills were being noticed and she got to do feature stories, one of which, a series on brutality in the NYPD, brought her to interview me. We've stayed in touch ever since.

I asked Semin to find out what she could about Dr. Billie Heat. Did she have a track record of getting involved with patients? A push-in robbery seemed too convenient an explanation for Marjorie Madden's murder. I had nothing to go on other than Marjorie Madden's word that Dr. Heat saw her as a rival for Ronan's affection. Now Marjorie Madden was dead. And I wanted to be sure Dr. Heat didn't have a reason to kill her.

I WAS waiting for Baron Spencer when he arrived at his office that morning. A light snow flurry had begun, but if the forecast was correct it would only last a short while leaving barely a deposit of the white stuff. Spencer's two bodyguards stiffened like lead soldiers when they saw me standing outside the door, and from the change in their expressions I suspected they were beginning to harbor ugly thoughts about my demise.

The three walked toward me, Spencer behind, shielded by his two robots. They stopped no more than a foot away, their eyes hollowed out with repressed rage at my insolence.

"What're you doing here?" the broad-chested bodyguard said.

"Have you ever watched the snow fall through the air?" I said. "The tiny flakes look like a swarm of flies."

"Fuck you," the man said. "Get out of our way."

"Mr. Spencer, I'd like to speak to you for a couple of minutes," I said.

The cool air was like silk across my face, as the wisps of bright snow fell freely around us. A thin bluish line of smoke coming from a building about a block away trailed across the sky. I watched it thinking it was such a blemish to a beautiful morning, almost as much a blot as the faces of the two ugly bodyguards.

"What did we tell you last time you were here?" the older bodyguard said. He wore a thick down coat, keeping his hands in his pockets the whole time.

Spencer sliced through the two guards like a weary halfback, crouched and circumspect. "Are you a student of history, Mr. Overstreet?"

"You can call me Blades."

"What do you think America would be like today if the Black Panthers had succeeded in its mission to liberate black people in this country?"

"If they hadn't self-destructed, you mean?"

He took off his glasses and rubbed his eyes. "You're right, we self-destructed. We had a lot of help but we fucked it up."

"The history books are closed. You can't go back and change it now."

"But that's where you're wrong. We can't go back but history isn't done with the Panthers. Because the spirit of the Panthers isn't dead. Do you know what effect your father's betrayal had on our New York chapter?"

"I'm not here to talk about that."

"Do you know of the many programs we had thriving in this city? The free clinic. The breakfast program. The literacy program. Do you know what happened to those programs after our chapter was decimated by the fallout when our brothers were convicted?"

"You can't blame my father for that."

"We were afraid to trust anybody. Even our wives."

"Did you know Marjorie Madden was found murdered last night?"

"I knew your father. Fancied himself a ladies' man, you know. Dick Harder, we used to call him. He must've fucked half the women who worked with us in the breakfast program. I would never have suspected he'd flip like that."

"Did you think Marjorie Madden would flip on you? Sell you out to Ronan?"

He puckered his mouth like a blowfish and then spoke through a vexed smile. "Do you want to know what I did last night? I watched a program on TV called *Where Are They Now?*"

The wind changed direction and the fine snow drifted across my face, blushing against my cheek like feathers.

Spencer came closer to me, standing now just a foot away, his face tilted upward, his silent eyes radiant as a cat's. "I know you'd like to take me down. But you can't. Ronan tried. And failed."

"This isn't personal, Mr. Spencer."

"Then why're you harassing me?"

"You have a motive for killing both Ronan and Marjorie."

"Listen to me, Mr. Overstreet. My life's work, my mission until I draw my last breath, is to continue what the Panthers started. We had high expectations and fell short. But as long as I'm alive I will work to empower black people. Today I'm prepared to work within the system. Or make the system work for me. People like Ronan who only care about enriching themselves can never stop me."

Cars whisked by in heated surges of noise. Flickering swirls of snow blew past me as the diminutive Spencer followed his bodyguards into his office.

IT WAS LATE in the afternoon when I showed up at J'Noel's apartment unannounced. I had called several times but no one answered the phone. The sun had just tucked itself away in the folds of dark clouds and as I rang J'Noel's bell I was thinking to myself that I wished the show wasn't tonight because it meant I had to be out late and right now I was feeling like shit. My body was getting too old to recover from a beating without the benefit of three nights of solid sleep.

But J'Noel didn't answer her bell. I took out my cell to ring Susan Zenaro at the Crime Victims Counseling Center. Susan, sounding stressed and agitated as usual, informed me that she'd been trying without any luck to reach J'Noel for the last two days and suspected that she might've moved.

I walked back to my car parked one block away. My call to Toni Monday caught him coming out of the shower.

"Blades, I'm happy you called. There's an art show and party tonight at Leon Dupri's loft in Williamsburg. You wanna come?"

"Who's Leon Dupri?"

"I thought you were into Caribbean art, Blades."

"I've never heard of this person."

"He's a young Haitian artist. Very arresting stuff. Lots of bold voodoo imagery."

"I'm busy tonight. But it'd be great if you can help me find a girl, Toni."

"What kind of girl you looking for?"

"Young. Battered. With a little boy about two years old."

"Jesus! Blades, with your looks you can do better than that."

"You might've known her boyfriend. Malcolm Nails-Diggs. He was found dead on a Coney Island beach."

"What's this chick's name?"

"J'Noel Bitelow."

"What makes you think I knew this Malcolm Nails whatever?"

"He was dealing out of the Coney Island projects."

Toni cursed. "You seem to think I know every lowlife in Brooklyn."

"And some in Queens."

"I'm off to sample the creative talent of this city. Later for you, dawg."

. . .

RIVER HAD A certain look in her eyes that made you take notice of her even if you didn't want to. As if she'd already gobbled up half the night and planned to gobble up the rest when it suited her fancy. She watched me in sullen silence. I watched her in amazement. Her black eyes were restless as if under assault from the wind. There was something violent and stunning about the way she was dressed. All leather. Black. Stilettos. She looked like a large animal, a swift leopard resting before a journey across the plains.

I did not expect to see her here. She sat alone at my table in a dark bay near the stage. A little after eleven. Show was an hour away. The large crowd we'd anticipated had begun to arrive. People fluttered about the large space like butterflies among branches.

She twitched when our eyes met. The solemn mask that locked her face made her look gaunt.

I walked over and sat at the table. For a moment language abandoned me as we stared at each other. I felt as if the air had turned to ice. A memory weaved itself into my consciousness. Playing hide-and-seek with my father when I was a little boy. Why that memory I couldn't say. But like a fire it jarred my voice back from its cage.

"You're stupid to come here," I said.

"You look handsome, Blades." Her smile seemed to multiply in my brain and then it dispersed like rain.

"Cut the crap! What're you doing here?"

"Negus invited me."

"I don't want any trouble in my club."

Her body was tensed, her eyes intent. "Relax, I wasn't followed."

"You're trouble, River."

"Coming from you, I take that as a compliment."

"Take it how you like, but I want your ass outta here."

She blinked, her eyes becoming diaphanous spaces. "Are you ordering me to leave, Blades?"

"You bet your ass. You're a menace to my business."

"Did you consult your partner?"

"I don't have to consult anybody. Negus is a silent partner. On these matters he remains that. Silent. You haven't been straight with either of us, River. I've tried to be your friend but you have no respect for friendship. And I hope I'm wrong, but if you're not careful you're gonna get Negus killed."

"This thing will blow over soon, Blades. Trust me."

"Oh really?"

"Yes."

"Then I suppose the bear who just walked up to the bar is just here to bury his food for the winter."

She did not turn around, which told me something else about River. She'd spent some time on the street or had surveillance training. Most people would've fallen prey to their curiosity and turned around the minute I mentioned a mark. Only someone trained in surveillance techiniques or someone accustomed to being watched would've had the discipline to sit tight.

I said, "Does he know what you look like?"

"We've met."

"Get up and don't turn around. Walk past me toward the dressing room. If he turns this way I'll cut him off."

The DJ started to play Gabby's "Dr. Cassandra" as River got up and quietly eased past me. It amazed me how cool she looked. Inside my brain silent black explosions were taking place. A hollow fire had started in the pit of my stomach. A bad thing. There was no way to control the rage once I overheated. I was pretty close to blastoff. More than anything I wanted to throw that lizard-face fuck out on his head myself.

I was pretty certain he couldn't have made it past my security with a gun. Throwing him out might stifle the bile churning in my gut, but the commotion could also prejudice arriving patrons from entering, and hasten a stampede from the club. The best thing would be to get River off the premises quietly.

I turned to follow River, who'd drifted away to the back of the club toward the bathrooms and dressing rooms. Two exits back there led into the alley on Hoyt Street.

The tall woman's stilettos morsed a hauntingly defiant code on the hard oak floor. As I made my way along the narrow passageway near the main dressing rooms I kept hoping a vapor of clarity would make its way to my clogged brain to help me figure out why I kept pulling this woman out of shit. By the time I caught up with her my brain was still as soggy as a squeegee's sponge.

I turned to see if we'd been followed. No one behind us. River had stopped ahead. In the pale light the black walls on either side of us seemed to be moving, creeping closer, cutting off the air. I breathed deeply in and exhaled, as if to defy the shadows threatening to render me breathless. River's dark eyes lit up the passageway, and their defiant fire was reassuring.

She reached out and touched my arm. "I know the way out. You can go back."

"You got wheels?"

"Negus's Bronco."

"Where's it parked?"

"Don't worry about me, Blades. I'll be okay. Tell Negus I had to leave. I'll call him to hook up later. And thanks. Good looking out, babe."

She hugged me and her wispy perfume danced across my palate. I watched her dark silhouette disappear down the stairs leading to the exit before turning to make my way back to the dance area. I was halfway down the passageway when black-suited Lizard-Face appeared, blocking my path.

He halted when he saw me and in his eyes I saw the struggle to decide whether to stay and wage war or turn tail. His body stiffened. A decision to fight, I presumed. I was confident he was unarmed but I was taking no chances. Reaching back I slipped the Glock from my waist holster, holding it down at my side parallel to my leg.

I stopped two feet away.

He saw the gun and folded his arms across his chest in mock self-embrace, flashing large tobacco-stained teeth. "You know I'm unarmed."

I tucked the gun back into its sheath. A smile grew on his face, obliterating his tiny eyes. I feigned a left and when he stepped in to parry I smashed a right elbow into his beefy neck. His knees buckled. From a crouch he lofted a straight right at my face. I weaved left, crunching a right hook into his Adam's apple, a blow that would've knocked out most men. He sat on his ass coughing involuntarily. With a snort he swept his right leg out catching me above the ankle of my bad leg. Needles of pain shot through my knee and up my leg. I fell on top of him, my good knee burrowing into his chest. Air and spittle spurted from his mouth like the breath of a dying whale. Keeping him immobile with my knee in his chest I reached for my gun. He gasped for air, his slanted eyes vacant as a desert. I ground the nozzle into his forehead.

"All I want is the girl." He sputtered blood. "The longer you hide her the worse it's going to be for everybody." Grinding his face into a ball of anger, he spat more blood and grinned. Behind the red smile I could almost hear the murmuring of his rage at being humiliated. I eased off him as it was becoming too difficult to balance myself on my weakened knee. The pain there had almost numbed my leg. I steadied myself, keeping the gun aimed at his bullet head. He sat up, smoothing his hair. I reached for my cell phone, taking my eyes off him a second to dial 411.

The electronic voice asked: *What listing, please?*

I said, "Eighty-fourth Precinct."

Lizard-Face was now on his feet.

Hold for the listing, please.

"I think it's unfair that I know your name and you don't know mine," Lizard-Face said.

I grimaced in pain. "I don't wanna know your name."

He grinned and bit his lip, backing away. "It's Parkoff. We're becoming so intimate you can call me Andre."

I limped toward him. "Don't move."

He rippled a laugh. "You ever shot anyone in the back?"

He turned and started running along the tight corridor, his hips dipping and swaying disjointedly. I closed the phone and limped after him but couldn't keep up. By the time I reached the dance area he had filtered through the crowd. I saw him going out through the entrance.

Soca music had stirred up the crowd. The dance floor was jammed up with vibrating bodies, women gyrating ferociously as if their hips were pneumatically connected to the rest of their limbs. This tangle of flesh hummed together as if searching for some communal secret, a spirit that the ancestors had emptied or flung into the air which could only be retrieved when all of them came together like a flame.

I ordered security to call the police. Then I hobbled back to the bar. After swallowing a shot of Jack Daniel's I stood there, my mind suspended. I was a swimmer in rough seas unable to get a fix on the horizon. I had made little headway in finding Ronan's killer. Was he killed by a jealous lover or was his death the result of a political vendetta?

In the meantime I was sinking fast into the dark puss of some deadly mind game between River and Lizard-Face whose trail I did not have time to follow. Except that the black clot of this dangerous game seemed ready to close around me.

TWENTY-SIX

Papa Smooth's hourlong show was a charismatic mix of romantic lover's rock reggae and rueful self-effacing dancehall lyrics. He pranced and jumped and ran around the stage like a man in a voodoo trance delivering his iron lyrics with airtight precision. His style was that of an old storyteller, quick to compliment the women near the stage, but watchful that he wasn't dissing any of the brothers whose girlfriends might be the ones undulating to his hypnotic voice and over-the-top flattery. Then there was the cold hostility in his voice when he sang about growing up without a father in Jamaica, or the personal sorrow of having to watch his best friend die of a drug overdose.

The show left many people smiling and nodding their heads. They may've witnessed the first blush of a new reggae star.

I watched the performance alone from my table. Intermittently, I got up to scout the room to make sure Lizard-Face had not sneaked back in. Negus was nowhere in sight. I presumed he watched the show from the sound booth. After the show I went backstage to congratulate Smooth, and Negus if I saw him.

Negus was already in the dressing room along with several young girls in stretch-to-fit pants that couldn't possibly stretch another inch without bursting a seam. Some of them wore weaves of colors to match the rainbow. Negus was dressed as only he could, his freshly shaved dome shimmering in the harsh dressing room light.

Papa Smooth sat in a chair as if poised on a throne, his awkward skeleton of a body still dripping sweat. Negus had told me he ate only vegan. He looked like he could use a little meat. In front of him was a glass filled with a green pulpy-looking liquid, perhaps some kind of fruit mixture or vitamin drink.

"Commanding show, Papa," I said.

He looked at me with a smile, his eyes wide and tired-looking. Then he stood up. I shook his hand and he smiled again. His face was too broad and too long for his extremely slender body and his teeth were craggy. He had narrow dreamy eyes, the eyes of a child, quiet, as if they were still tangled in the bliss of sleep. The matching gold satin shirt and pants almost made him look like a circus performer. But his smile had the infectiousness of sunlight, with his upper lip curling back like a lily unfolding.

He was exhausted, seemingly too tired to speak. He sat down again and the sight he presented was amazing. For as tired as he appeared to be, he still sat as rigid and upright as a monument. Must be that West Indian upbringing, I thought to myself.

"The crowd loved you," I said.

He offered another tired smile. "Yeah, man." His Jamaican accent rippled like a warm wind.

"We should all have a drink together to celebrate," Negus said, his eyes planted on my face.

One of our waitresses sashayed by and I tapped her shoulder, stopping her. "Bring me a bottle of Courvoisier, Adriana, and some glasses."

"Sure thing," she said, and sailed off with a sassy swirl of her hip.

I chuckled. These Caribbean women always throwing their hips around like old news.

"My . . . River told me that a friend of yours was killed the other night." Smooth sipped from his glass, gulping to swallow chunks of pineapple.

"He could've been a great one," I said.

"Yeah, I know that story."

He sipped from his concoction and looked into my eyes. I saw a pain there that startled me. I averted my gaze.

"Were you two close?" Smooth said.

I turned to face him. "Not really. I'm closer to his father."

"Oh, yeah, the newspaper say his father used to be a cop."

"Yeah."

"Like you, right?"

"Yeah."

"You ever killed anyone?"

I don't normally find that question unsettling, but at that moment it was. I decided to ignore it. I turned to Negus leaning against a pillar in the middle of the room with a satisfied smirk on his face. "Did River call you?" I said to him.

He nodded.

Someone touched my shoulder. I looked around.

"Your brandy, big boss," Adriana said, letting her insouciant smile uncurl like an earthworm.

I took the tray; Adriana sashayed away. Setting the tray down on a table in the corner of the room I poured brandy into three of the glasses. Negus accepted the glass I offered with a smile and nod.

Smooth shook his head at the drink I held out to him. "Me don't drink strong, cuz."

I looked at Negus, who shrugged as if to say: *You shoulda known that.*

"Well, a toast to you, Smooth," I said. "You lived up to your name. You're as smooth as lightning."

Our glasses clinked together.

I CHECKED the street carefully to make sure Lizard-Face wasn't laying in wait when I left the club shortly after four. The street was quiet. The train of noise, which distinguished this city even in its deadest hour of the day from any other, came rumbling through the sky: a wailing police siren; the hoarse underground cough of subway cars; the screech of wheels scorching the track. A block away, garbage men ganged up on refuse cans to stuff them into the back of trucks. This was my city.

Vibrant.

Ugly.

Musical.

As I grasped the Volvo's steering wheel I wondered if I might get away with waking Anais.

EARLY NEXT AFTERNOON Anais, Chesney, and I walked along the lake in Prospect Park. We'd taken Chez to the rink, where she skated for over two hours. It was impossible to get her away, and we only accomplished this by promising to take her for cou-cou and flying fish at Culpepper's. Understandably Chesney was still attached to Bajan cuisine.

The rain had fallen earlier and misty air came sweet in its trail. A muffled echo rose up from the trees behind us followed by loud snorts. Mounted horses slowly emerged from the mist, one skittish roan jerking at his bridle, but the young rider kept her composure and soon calmed the lively horse down. As the group passed us Chesney grew excited, tugging at my arm.

"Can I learn to ride, Daddy?"

I looked down at her bundled together like a Christmas present in red corduroy coat and green pants, her hands as small as a doll's, her eyes as bright as a comet, and felt my heart jerk against my rib cage. Emotions still new to me currented through my body. But I have to admit that as strange as these emotions felt, there was something inspiring about witnessing the expression of innocent exuberance, not just in any child's eyes, but in the face of my own child, a face that spoke to me in an emotional language more poetic than any I've ever heard.

I laughed. "First we master the ice then we'll try a horse."

"But I'm a good skater," she protested.

"Let's ask Auntie Anais what she thinks of your skating."

"Oh, you're not going to trap me," Anais said.

"Don't you think I'm a good skater, Mom?"

Anais, who'd been walking ahead of us, stopped and turned. In the amber afterglow of the setting sun her face flushed with primal emotion. It was shock and bewilderment competing with the desire not to make a big deal out of one little word, which at this time had driving implications to us all.

"I think you're a great skater, honey," Anais said.

"See, I told you," Chesney exclaimed, wrapping her arms around Anais's leg.

And then I understood what a real Hallmark moment was. It was when two females ganged up on you.

"Okay," I said. "You can learn to ride."

Past Anais down the path she skipped. I caught up to Anais and we hugged, smiling into each other's eyes. On the lake gray swans searching for food raked the water with their sword beaks. A quick wind got under the treacherous ripples producing a current that corrupted the calm of the dark silvery surface. The swans took flight, lifting toward the sun, then plunging back to the lake with an air-rattling explosion.

After our late lunch at Culpepper's I tried to take a nap. I was close to drifting off to sleep when I got a call that would take me back to Prospect Park.

TWENTY-SEVEN

After leaving the club I met a girlfriend at Wharf Rat on Pier 23 where Negus met me around three. We left there two hours later. Negus had rented a room for me at a hotel in Paramus.

"We made love that morning. I was really hungry afterward so I ordered room service. Five minutes later there was a knock at the door and Negus went to answer it.

"I was thinking room service was kinda quick when I heard *phatt*, then a cry. I knew it was a silencer. I didn't wait. I jumped from the bed straight through the window. I don't know how I did it. Fear, I guess. I landed in a garden and started running to the Bronco.

"We'd come up with an escape plan for something like this. We had a tire stashed under the truck and a spare ignition key under the mat on the driver's side. I broke the glass and jumped in. Started up that shit and was banging. When I hit the highway I checked to see if he was following me. There was nobody behind me. I got to the first rest stop and called the police and told them to get an ambulance to the hotel."

It was late evening. We were sitting on a bench in Prospect Park near Grand Army Plaza. There was little foot traffic in the park as the sun had already hung its head in the forest of sleeping oaks for the night. The golden lights of the park lamps left shimmering halos above the stripped tree limbs. I didn't even want to look at her. The muscles in my jaw tightened. I tried rubbing them vigorously, but that only served to make my shoulders tense. I was a horse tethered too tightly and strained for release. But I couldn't lose it now. She had an agenda and I was curious to know what it was.

"So you don't know if Negus is dead?" I said stonily.

She squeezed her forehead as if trying to scare away a headache. "He's alive. I called Paramus police when I got across the bridge. They wouldn't tell me how bad his condition was but they said he's alive."

"What were you wearing when you got away?"

"A sweatshirt."

"That's all?"

"I'd just put on one of Negus's sweatshirts before the shit happened."

"Where'd you get those clothes?"

She was now wearing a leather bomber and thick corduroy pants.

"A friend."

"What friend?"

"What difference does it make?"

I leaned forward to peer deep into her eyes, hoping to catch a glimpse of what was really going on in her thoughts. It was like trying to see the bottom of the sea. "Just tell me one thing?"

"What?"

"Who the hell are you, really?"

"What do you mean?"

I leaned back, anger beginning to overwhelm me. "You're a killer, a liar, and maybe a thief. What I don't understand is why you chose to lay your skunk on me?"

She laughed and I heard a dark hysteria behind it. On the other side of her voice was the absence of feeling, of emotion.

"You're the only person I know smart enough to keep me in one piece until this thing blows off. If I knew this city I wouldn't need your help."

"Why should I help you?"

She squared her eyes, staring directly at me. "Because you don't abandon your friends."

"Who was your boyfriend working for?"

"I don't know."

I stood straight up and started to walk away.

She broke after me. "I'm telling you the truth."

I turned around. "I'm so over your freaking games."

"Listen, I didn't get into his business. I didn't need to have that information. I knew he was a transporter. That's all I know. And I didn't even need to know that."

I grabbed her jacket. "I don't believe you."

"Then fuck you! What the hell do you want me to do? Genuflect to your royal badass before you take pity on me? Well, I'm not going to do that for you or anybody. You either want to help me or you don't."

I released her. "I suggest you talk to the FBI."

"Forget them. All I need is a place to stay. Preferably outside the city."

"Your Russian suitor is known for some grisly stuff. He threw a man out of a building in Arizona to shut him up. Left a stain on the sidewalk they're still trying to wash out."

"I'm not running because I'm afraid of him."

"Is there anything you're afraid of?"

"We all got our weak spots."

"This life of secrets. Doesn't it get boring sometimes?"

She scratched at her face. "No more boring than yours."

"It's funny, I thought we hit it off so well when we met. Hiring you was easy. Gettting rid of you is like trying to get rid of the devil."

"A man like you, the devil is in good company."

"Why don't you go back to Miami? Don't you have family down there?"

"What if I told you no?"

"You've got to have family somewhere."

Her eyes met mine and there was no give. "What if I said no to that too?"

"I'd say that's impossible."

"Why? The slaves who were brought over here from Africa had to start a life without families."

"We're not talking about slaves. We're talking about you."

She took a step back and hung her head. When she looked at me again there was pain in her eyes. "We're talking about separation. Life is a series of separations. My mother is dead. My father is dead. I'm separated from everyone else. I'm alone and that's the way I like it."

I stared at her for a second not knowing what to say. To say that she was a very complicated woman would've been an understatement, but she was also as compelling a personality as anyone I'd ever met. Behind her a woman in a gray leather coat meandered into view, shaking her head as if she was talking to herself. Then she disappeared.

"I might know somebody with a place," I said.

"Thank you."

I unclipped my phone to call Toni Monday.

SEMIN GUPTA called me later that night as I was checking my e-mail.

"Did I catch you at a bad time?" Her voice was playful as always.

"No, Semin. Just cleaning out junk e-mail."

"This shouldn't take long. Your good doctor comes from a very stoosh New England family. Went to Harvard. Practiced in Boston before relocating here. About five years ago, two years before she moved to New York, she was investigated by the police for stalking one of her patients. Apparently they'd been having an affair and the man tried to break it off. Her family managed to get it hushed up but she had to leave Massachusetts."

"Don't you get your license shredded for stuff like that?"

"Not if your family's got money and connections."

"You just get run out of town to start somewhere else."

"Dr. Heat isn't a total deadbeat, though. She's done a lot of community work since moving to New York. She volunteers once a week at Rikers where she counsels violent inmates. And before that she worked once a week for the Children's Family Health Center. Gratis. Perhaps this man she stalked in Massachusetts deserved it."

I laughed. "Don't we all, Semin?"

"Some more than others," Semin said. "Is there a story here for me, Blades? Does this have anything to do with Ronan Peltier?"

"Why do you ask?"

"Politicians can't keep secrets. He was nailing her, wasn't he?"

"This is New York. Somebody's always whipping it out in the dark."

"I'm hearing some rumblings that his death might've been a hit by the Russian mob."

"Really? Where'd you hear that?"

"The police say they've bagged the killer. As in body bag. Some dude whose girlfriend seemed to prefer blood sausage to franks. His body was found on a Coney Island beach. According to police they found the gun that killed Ronan Peltier in this guy's apartment. They're saying this guy was used by the Russians to take care of any trouble they had in black neighborhoods."

"They're certain of this?"

"Hey, you used to work for the NYPD, do they make mistakes? You don't know anything about this, do you?"

"Thanks for the info, Semin."

"Anytime, babe."

I hung up from Semin and dialed Noah's number.

He answered the phone after the second ring, his large voice moldy with sleep, his growl a true minimalist delight. "Huh."

"You sleeping already, big man?" I said.

"What you want, Blades?"

"You didn't tell me the police solved Ronan's murder."

"Huh?"

"I just spoke to a reporter. She said the police think a gangbanger they found sleeping with the crabs on a Coney Island beach killed Ronan."

"Oh that. It's crap."

"*Oh that*. Is that your response?"

"Look, Blades, Detective Riley called me and told me they found the gun that killed Ronan. And the shooter was dead."

"Why didn't you tell me?"

"'Cause I want you to keep digging. Riley gets a tip from somebody who says the gun used to kill Ronan is at this apartment. They don't have a motive. Nothing."

"That doesn't explain why you didn't tell me."

"I forgot. I got a lotta shit on my mind, Blades."

"What if it's true?"

"What?"

"That this guy did body work in black neighborhoods for the Russians."

"Why would the Russians want to kill Ronan?"

"I don't know."

"Then find out."

After I hung up I sat staring at the computer screen for a long time deep in thought. Was there a connection between Ronan and the Russians? And who killed Marjorie, and why? Was I wrong in thinking their deaths were related?

I fished through my wallet for Detective Riley's card. It was after eleven in the evening. I didn't think I'd find him at the precinct but I called anyway. He wasn't there.

I called Noah back. "Do you have the detective's home number?"

Noah groaned. "Hold on."

I powered off my Mac as I waited. Noah returned shortly with the number.

"Thanks," I said, and hung up.

I dialed the detective's home. A woman answered the phone with a plush intelligent-sounding voice. In the background I could hear the scattershot drone of rain falling.

"May I speak to Detective Riley?" I said.

"May I ask who's calling?"

"Blades Overstreet."

"Hold a minute, please."

Riley came to the phone with a bounce in his voice, sounding the way I think I'd sound after a good bout of sex with Anais.

"Detective Riley, this is Blades Overstreet."

"Yeah, Blades. What's up?"

"Noah Peltier told me you got the fucker who did his son."

"Yeah, should wrap this baby soon."

"Do you have a motive?"

"We're working on that."

"What have you got?"

"Listen, Blades, I shouldn't be telling you this. We're looking at a Russian connection. Only the Russians would have the cojones to put a hit on a councilman."

"Who tipped you to the gun?"

"Some chick."

"A woman?"

"Isn't that what I just said?"

"Did you speak to her yourself?"

"Yeah, I did."

"Did she leave a name?"

"No name."

"What did she sound like?"

"I don't know. Young. Black."

"She sounded black, you say?"

"Sure."

The pause brought a heavy sigh from the other end. "What? I know what a black chick sounds like, so fuck you."

I replied calmly. "Didn't you wonder how she knew about the gun?"

"Look, Blades, are you married? My wife is here wearing the sexiest piece of lingerie you've ever seen. Do you know what that does to a man?"

"Enjoy yourself," I said, and hung up.

TWENTY-EIGHT

To some people on the other side of the East River, Brooklyn must look like shit when they gaze from their lofty towers across the tiny stretch of water. No Empire State Building. No Chrysler Building. No shiny glass skyscrapers. Just a tangle of low nondescript buildings.

But to Brooklynites brownstones are almost as familiar as the Empire State Building is to residents of Manhattan. In a city full of monstrous glass buildings, brownstones have a grounding influence and add an aura of community. Harlem is famous for its brownstones, but some of the most charming ones can be found in Brooklyn Heights, owned by many world-famous musicians and literary types.

Dr. Heat's practice in the Heights, as Brooklyn Heights is often referred to, was on the top floor of a beautifully restored brownstone on Clark Street. The bronze brick gleamed in the bowing sun and the intricate design of the heavy cornice flashed brilliant black.

Upstairs, the receptionist, a perky clear-eyed young woman in a warm yellow dress, showed me into a waiting room with stacks of magazines on a table. On the walls were prints or drawings made up of undefined squiggly lines, endless loops, and ropes flung every which way, the kinds of drawings four-year-olds do in art class. Closer examination showed them to be Pollock prints. Therapists have a fondness for Pollock, it seemed. The one I'd seen a couple of times way back when also sported Pollock's prints in her office.

The room was furnished more for high living than receiving patients, the red-stained floor set off the creaminess of the walls; the windows hidden by thick red drapes. I skimmed through the magazine stack finding nothing to my taste. I leaned back in the comfortable green-cushioned antique-looking chair to wait for Dr. Heat.

Twenty minutes later I was still waiting. To offset boredom I picked up *Psychology Today* and leafed through it not expecting any of the headlines to bestir my high intellectual curiosity. I began to read an article on the use of anticonvulsant drugs to control bipolar disorder when a smiling Dr. Heat popped through a door to my left in a rust brown pants suit with a cream silk scarf swaddling her throat.

"Good evening, Mr. Overstreet."

I put the magazine back on top the stack and stood up. She skated forward as if walking on oil and shook my hand. Hers was warm and comforting, a handshake well practiced to put people at ease, I'd say.

"Let's go into my office." She smiled and her cheeks expanded like rising dough.

I followed her inside the large office whose windows looked out across the East River onto lower Manhattan. This room, like the one I'd just left, boasted very high ceilings, a shiny parquet floor, and cream-colored walls with wonderfully detailed wood paneling. The dark leather furnishing and worn dark rug contrasted with the muted color of the wall, which held several black and white photographs of what looked like old European cities, giving the room natural warmth.

"Great view," I commented.

"Yes, but it can be distracting sometimes."

"How so?"

"Sit, please," she said, pointing to a gray leather sofa facing the window. She sat opposite me in a brown leather chair and crossed her legs. "Sometimes patients look out the window and all they want to do is daydream. Which I will allow in some situations."

"I don't blame them," I said, and sat down.

"But you're not here to daydream, are you, Mr. Overstreet?"

"Blades, please. Was Ronan a daydreamer?"

She blinked her eyes and smiled. "Now what do you think? You knew him."

"Actually, not that well. You now, you knew him quite intimately, didn't you?"

"It's my job to get to know my patients intimately."

"And just how intimately did you get to know Ronan?"

"As his therapist I got to know him quite well, if that's what you're asking."

"Weren't you also his lover?"

My bluntness smacked her hard in the face and she shifted her glasses farther up on her nose, squinting as if something was in her eyes. "You don't waste much time drop-kicking people you don't like, do you?"

I shifted in my seat. "Is that what you think? That I dislike you?"

"People relay more information in their intonation than you'd think, Mr. Overstreet."

She wasn't telling me anything I didn't know. Years of questioning lying, drug-addled scum taught me to listen closely to the way people said what they said. In this instance I noted the emphasis on the way she said *Mr. Overstreet,* as if she thought it might annoy me that she was refusing my offer to be familiar. "Why would I dislike you?"

She smiled again, this time it seemed forced. "I have no more patients for the day. Can I offer you a drink? Some sherry, perhaps?"

"No thanks. When did it start?"

She stood up, her body rigid. "Do you understand what you're asking me?"

"I think so."

"Your attitude is rather crude, but your crudeness aside, you're asking if I was violating one of the most sacred tenets of my profession."

"You're assuming I believe there's anything sacred about your profession."

"I'm disappointed in you, Mr. Overstreet."

"Did you have him killed because he ended the affair?"

"Why do you dislike me so much? You don't know me so it can't be personal. Did you have a bad experience with a therapist or something?"

"This is not about me."

"I think it is. Why're you so hostile? Aren't you comfortable in that mixed skin? I'm sure it must be a burden sometimes."

I could feel my skin crawling. "You take yourself way too seriously."

"I volunteered information that I thought would help you catch Ronan's killer. If I knew you were such a bastard I wouldn't have bothered."

"You pointed a finger at another woman who's now dead. What you left out was that Ronan had dumped you as his lover and his therapist. And that you had been investigated once for stalking a former patient."

Her eyebrows arched in surprise. "I don't appreciate you digging into my past."

"Did you offer Marjorie Madden money to leave New York?"

She smirked. "I bet she also told you that Ronan was the father of her child."

I sensed that she had more to say and waited.

"Ronan never had sexual relations with that woman. Can't you see? It's a classic case of transference. Ronan mentored her. Took her under his wing and dragged her out of the projects where she was destined to become nothing more than another welfare case. He got her into NYU. And then he gave her a job."

I had a strange desire to laugh but breathed deeply. "Were you in love with him?"

"I have nothing more to say to you." She marched to the door, her high heels clicking out hostility on the hard surface. She swung the door open with a vigorous tug. "Good day, Mr. Overstreet."

I got up and spoke to her across the breadth of the room. "You did some community work counseling inmates at Rikers, didn't you?" I didn't wait for her answer. "Was Malcolm Nails-Diggs one of your patients at Rikers?"

"Get out."

I walked to the door. When I got there I reached out and held the frame near the top. "You didn't seem surprised when I told you Marjorie Madden was dead."

"I read the newspaper, Mr. Overstreet."

"The police think she was the victim of a push-in robbery. I think you had her killed. I also think you hired Malcolm Nails-Diggs to kill Ronan. And when I get the proof I'll be back."

She stared into my eyes without answering. I went out past the receptionist's station and heard the door close behind me. The woman in the yellow dress was gone. It was after six o'clock and she might've gone home for the day. The hallway was hot with the artificial fragrance of pine.

I got on the empty elevator trying to shrug off the elephant's foot that seemed to be trying to plant itself in my chest. I needed a drink. There's nothing more depressing than finding out that someone you idolized was all too human. How was I going to explain the soap opera of Ronan's life to Noah?

I don't know that I believed the psychologist killed Ronan or Marjorie. It was possible but I had no proof. Malcolm Nails-Diggs did body work for the Russians, but that didn't mean he didn't contract himself for local fare. Worms like him ate whatever shit they found. The police had a murder weapon and a dead trigger man. Who the hell was Malcolm Nails-Diggs?

TWENTY-NINE

That evening the phone rang as Anais was putting the finishing touches on a dish she claimed was part Caribbean, part Cajun. Before my wife left Atlanta to study dance in New York she was quite proud of the fact that she'd lived her life without having to learn the nuances of food preparation other than *Pass the salt, please,* or *Can we have some more butter, please?* Over the years she'd come to accept that acquiring culinary skills did not make one a social misfit. In fact, from time to time, she would go on a creative cooking spurt, buying books and trying recipes with as many exotic-sounding names as could be found in the New York telephone book. For this meal she'd seasoned black bass with Caribbean jerk sauce bought from one of the Korean greengrocers on Church and had blackened it on the indoor grill. I could tell she was quite pleased with the outcome.

I picked up the phone in the bedroom.

"That girl's got an angel on her shoulder, Blades."

"Excuse me?" I said into the phone to Agent Kraw.

"The people around her don't seem to be so lucky however. Who's going to be next?"

"I'm about to have dinner with my family."

"You and I need to talk."

"I'm sure it can wait."

"It's about Ronan Peltier."

Pause.

Kraw twanged in her flat Midwestern voice. "Remember that stolen shipment of Saizen?"

"What about it?"

"Was heisted from a pharmacy co-owned by Ronan Peltier."

I waited to see where she was going with this thread. But she was stringing me along.

"Meet me on the Promenade in half an hour," she said. I could hear the edge trickle off her voice. Now it was cool, playful.

I hung up.

Anais was adding a layer of style to the dinner table with Indian-designed place mats when I came downstairs dressed in black corduroys, leather jacket, and boots. We met at the foot of the stairs.

"You can't be serious," she said icily.

"I'll be back as soon as I can."

"Where're you going?" Anais asked.

"It's business."

"Something to do with the club?"

"You can say that."

"I want *you* to say, Blades." Her voice was clipped and full of rancor.

"I have to meet someone. I'd rather not go into details right now. I'll explain later. But it's important."

"What are we supposed to do now? Wait until you return?"

"Go ahead without me."

"Aren't you picking up your father later?"

"Midnight."

I TRIED NOT to let my mind meander as I weaved through the streets of Brooklyn. But how do you parse information that might implicate someone you hoped was clean through a cynical mind without leaning close to the edge of doubt. Could Ronan have been involved in this Saizen scam?

If he was killed because of it, then Dr. Heat was innocent. The unpleasant realization came that I wanted her to be the killer simply because of her profession.

Ten minutes later I parked on Pineapple Street and walked along the narrow quiet block to the Promenade. Spotted Agent Kraw in a yellow windbreaker and black baseball cap, her back leaned against the waist-high iron rail. As I got close she trawled around in her jacket pocket and came out with a large box of M&M's. She peeled the plastic wrapper away and tilted the box to her mouth leaning her head back. Without a word said she offered me the box. I accepted and dropped two red pills in the palm of my hand, knocking them together like dice.

She smiled half-heartedly. "How's the family?"

"My wife's a little upset with me."

"I can't imagine anybody staying upset with you for too long."

I tossed the M&M's into my mouth. "Why is that?"

"You got that charm, Blades."

"Charm? Your antennae must be clogged."

"No. I'm pretty good at this."

"Pardon my saying this, but I didn't get the impression you knew a whole lot about men."

She snatched the M&M's box back. "Charmers come in all races, sizes, and sexes. It's not a male thing. But even if it was a male thing, I grew up among men. Charismatic men. My mom died when I was young. My father raised me. And he had lots of brothers. My grandfather came from Russia and lived on the Lower East Side. He moved west when my father was fifteen. My father got married when he was twenty-two. Divorced at twenty-three. Married again at twenty-four. To his first wife's sister. You need a lot of balls and charisma to pull that off."

"You speak Russian?"

She tossed M&M's into her mouth. "A few curse words."

"What's the skinny on Ronan's pharmacy?"

"A week before the shipment was stolen he and his partner took out additional insurance to the tune of three point five mil," she said. "We believe the robbery was timed to follow the insurance upgrade."

"An inside job?"

"His partner was Rupert Chernin."

I extended my hand for more M&M's. "Where do I know that name from?"

She dropped a few of the colored capsules into my palm. "Perhaps you cruise the obituaries."

I gave her a hard look and swallowed what I was thinking. "Dead?"

"Executed in his hotel room in Miami two days ago."

"Wasn't he implicated in the big junk bond scandal several years ago?"

"Never charged with anything. Seven years ago when pharmaceuticals were hot Ronan bought into a small chain of drugstores owned by Chernin. A chance came to cash out a few years later when a larger chain wanted to buy them out. But Chernin got greedy. Stocks were still climbing. He bought a few more independent stores intending to take the small chain public himself later. But before he could light his fuse the bottom fell out of the business. They started scrambling for additional investors. Nobody bit. Business kept dying. I think someone approached them with the Saizen offer and they couldn't refuse it."

"Somebody being the Russians?"

"We can't prove this yet. But after our agent was killed the gang might've seen Ronan and Chernin as weak links and decided to shut them down."

"Why didn't you tell me this before?"

"I don't have to tell you anything, Blades. You should be happy that I even bother to talk to you."

"It's not going to help you get into my wife's pants, you know."

She grimaced. "Is it your objective to be so crude that everyone you meet will hate you?"

"I don't care who hates me."

"Everybody wants to be loved. Even you."

I looked at her with curiosity, then I turned to walk away. Kraw grabbed my arm.

"Where's the girl? You're right. I'm not giving you this information because I think you're cute. It's called I scratch your back, you scratch mine."

"I'm not into that kinky stuff."

"You can go to hell, Blades."

Agent Kraw drew her face in under her baseball cap and walked away. I watched her descend the stairs leading to the street, then I turned around and cast my gaze on the East River. Its flat face, varnished by the brilliant lights of lower Manhattan, seemed to be beckoning me. I was in no mood for water sports.

I HOLLERED at Noah as I crossed Atlantic Avenue. The sky's dark ceiling opened up and rain dripped out. I flicked on my wipers and waited for Noah to pick up. Voice groggy, as if gurgling salt water in his mouth. I felt a heavy agony as I relayed the information from Special Agent Kraw. He listened until I'd finished, not interrupting once. When I stopped he sighed as if in pain, and spoke in a knotted voice.

"This don't mean shit to me, Blades. Do you believe this Nails-Diggs killed my son for the Russians?"

"I don't know."

"Then call me when you do. Just tell me who killed my son so I can rip the muthafucker's brain out and feed it back to him through a straw."

"I appreciate your honesty, big man."

"Anytime."

I heard the phone slam and cursed myself for calling him. Through the vacuum of his bluster I could hear the fragility in his voice, I could hear him preparing himself for tomorrow. Each time I spoke with him I wished I knew what to say to make the path he was walking easier, but each time my failure to construct any meaningful or profound sentiments made me realize that the English language was not gifted with words to explain nature gone out of balance. This was why music was created.

For some time I'd been planning to install a CD player in the Volvo. Still hadn't found time to do it, or have it done. The great thing about driving Anais's SUV was being able to play CDs. In the Volvo I had to settle for cassettes. I stuffed Bob Marley's *Catch Afire* into the deck and turned up the volume. As the music swelled I started to bob my head to the thumping bass. The Volvo slid silently through the dark streets of Brooklyn.

THIRTY

My father's flight arrived late. The one-hour delay gave me time to catch up on phone calls. I thanked Toni Monday for letting River use his safe house, one of three I knew about. I'm sure he had several more. This one I knew he would never use again. He informed me that he was leaving his boyfriend but had nothing on J'Noel Bitelow's whereabouts and he assured me that the Russians hadn't hired Malcolm Nails-Diggs to whack Ronan. My brother had called earlier in the day and I returned his call. He wanted to borrow money. Throughout our conversation I heard lots of giggles and laughter in the background, no doubt his exuberant girlfriend. I was almost reluctant to admit that she seemed to make him happy. But I still planned to keep a close eye on her.

Ten after one my father came strolling through the sliding doors of the American Airlines arrivals hall at JFK. He hadn't even bothered to dress for the weather, wearing only a short-sleeve tropical print shirt and sand-colored slacks with sneakers, looking like a tourist returning home who wanted to make sure everyone knew that he'd just left the tropics. The flesh on his sun-scrubbed face had lost its taut healthy look; the skin sagged and his eyes were sunken. He'd lost some weight; his hair was now scalp-shaven. He carried a small camera bag over his shoulder, and dragged a twenty-inch suitcase on wheels behind him like a beleaguered puppy.

When he saw me he flicked his eyes up and they were sad. He walked slowly toward me as if he was walking on sore ankles, with the slouch of a man carrying a camel's hump.

The reality of seeing him in New York jolted me. We hugged for a long time. I was thoroughly unprepared for this emotional kick to my system and my throat welled up. It was as if I was seeing him for the first time in twenty years. There was no explanation for my being so overwhelmed. I banked the rush of tears and emotion in the back of my throat as we measured each other for a time, like two prizefighters before the bell. He smiled, showing for the first time that familiar glint in his eyes, opening a crevice of memories in my brain.

"How're you, Dad?"

"Not as good as you, I'm sure. You look like you've been hitting the gym hard."

"Mostly running."

"My ass! You in the gym, boy. Your body as hard as a brick."

I laughed.

He dragged deep on New York's lung-clogging air. "This shit still smells the same."

I picked up his bag. "Welcome home."

WE PASSED OVER the Queens border into Brooklyn absorbing the spectacle of New York at night. Any New Yorker would tell you that when the lights went up on New York City it whirled and danced with the energy of a Broadway show. My father hadn't seen this in a while but it couldn't have been any less impressive. Thousands of lights sprinkled about the tall project apartments as backdrop to the myriad of crazy transactions taking place in dark alleys, on train platforms, in fast-moving cars, on buses slogging through downtown streets: the coke dealer negotiating a better price for smack; the prostitute holding to her asking price; the baby's father in the project negotiating to get pussy in exchange for the child support that was already six months in arrears; over dinner and a hundred-dollar bottle of wine, the banker sealing a deal uptown with the gift of a vacation in the Azores.

My father knew this New York.

What he didn't know was the brown-facing of the outer boroughs. The transformation of Brooklyn, Queens, and the Bronx (Staten Island was still ostensibly white) into Third-World America with immigrants who spoke in tongues that most Americans didn't know existed. What he didn't know were the tensions rising from the fear this created: the mosques burned, the abuse of undocumented Mexican immigrants (men beaten on Long Island or women forced to perform sex acts to keep their subsistence jobs), the Korean immigrant robbed in his greengrocery and told to go back where he came from, the Pakistani immigrants swept from their homes in Midwood in pre-dawn raids by the FBI and deported without due process. But then again, my father might call me ignorant. He might mention COINTELPRO. He might say those things were happening before he left, before I was born, but they were happening to black people. The more things change the more they remain the same. He might say again: *This shit still smells the same.*

The broad stretch of Atlantic Avenue lay before us. Overhead, the rumble of a train on an elevated track. My father rolled down his window and stuck his head outside.

"Damn! I forgot how noisy this city was," he exclaimed. But it was clear he wasn't complaining.

"I love the sound of New York," I said.

"I missed New York." He was silent for a while then he said, "How's your mother?"

"She's fine."

Silence wedged between us again, this time with a pocket full of change for the meter. I felt his eyes on me as I weaved through Flatbush. Then, just like that, an anger grew inside me that almost choked me. I did not know where it came from. My father must've seen my face mold to the new emotion.

"What's wrong?" he said.

I didn't answer. What could I say? Was I angry at him? If so, why? I had no explanation for the feeling that had just ambushed me. I breathed deeply trying to let the emotion dissolve. Slowly it left me. In its place came a memory of something my sister, Melanie, had said during one of our many fights.

MELANIE HATED my father. She made that clear to me on more occasions than I care to remember. Heavily influenced by her own father's views, Melanie couldn't forgive Mom for marrying a black man who just happened to be my father. The more I grew into my father's image, the more she directed her fury at me. I'd never said it to her, but I'd often wondered if she hated him because he was black. Melanie, equipped with a 175 IQ, didn't have to be led to that conclusion, however.

We were having one of our weekly verbal dart-throwing bouts about a year after Mom had gone back to the university to get her master's. My dad had been gone about two years. Melanie had come into the house from a ballet class. I was looking through a box of my father's things, looking at photographs and some sketches he'd done. Melanie made a comment that Mom should throw all my father's things out of the house.

"They're my things now," I shot back.

"Your things?" she taunted. "I bet you turn out just like him."

"What's that suppose to mean?"

"That you'll be a bum."

"Better a bum than crazy."

"Better crazy than missing. I know where my father is. Where's yours?"

"Leave me alone, Melanie."

"Face it, he's a bum. He abandoned you like a sick dog."

"Leave me alone or else . . ."

"Or else what? You'd hit me? Go ahead. It's what your father would do."

"My father never hit you."

"My dad would've killed him if he did. But don't pretend you never seen him do it to Mom."

"You're lying."

"You saw him."

"You're such a liar."

"Pretend all you want, Carmen. You know you saw it too."

I GLANCED at my father; he was deep in thought. Despite Melanie's claim I never recalled an incident where I saw him hit my mom. I remembered the arguments. I remembered the tears. And I remembered the night he left. It was in September, not long after Labor Day. My parents had had one of their arguments. I remembered that there was mention of another woman, one of Mom's friends, and then Dad left. I thought nothing of his leaving at the time. It'd happened many times before, the fights, the screaming, the doors slamming. I was sure I would wake up the next day and he would be there having his plate of eggs and bacon and sausage, talking to Jason about baseball scores.

But he wasn't at the breakfast table the next morning or the one after that. I didn't see him again until fifteen years later.

Why did the memory of that conversation with Melanie surface now? There was never any doubt in my mind that the physical violence Melanie accused my father of never took place, that she had made it up to get me angry. And I'd never wavered from that belief.

I'd kept the secret of my dad's whereabouts from my mother for the past seven years. When I told her that he was returning to New York for Ronan's funeral she showed no emotion. Then she confessed that she'd known where he was for some time. The secret came out in my body language, she said. She knew after I came back from Miami that I'd made contact. And I realized then that my loyalties had been woefully misplaced. There was no reason for me to have been that loyal to my father, the incident in Miami not withstanding. When I considered the agony my mother had suffered over the years raising three dysfunctional children, I wondered if she would've made the same decision to marry my father if she had to do it over.

"Are you going to see her?"

"If she wants to see me." His voice drooped with doubt.

"She wants to," I said coolly.

"What does she expect, though? She knew I wasn't coming back."

"Then why didn't she file for divorce?"

"Heavens knows, son. I sure as hell don't. Look, Carmen, the truth is, the marriage was over whether I left New York or not."

"Can I ask you a question?"

"Shoot."

"Did you ever hit her?"

"What?" He was silent for a while. "Did she tell you that?"

"No. She didn't tell me that."

"So why're you asking?"

"I'm just asking."

"You're just asking?"

"Yeah, I'm just asking."

"For no reason you're just asking?"

"Okay, Pop. Forget it. Forget I asked."

"Is that the way you greet me on my return to New York? You ask me if I ever hit your mother? That's just great."

"Don't let's fool ourselves, Pop, okay."

"What do you mean by that?"

"You know what I mean. I was the one who came looking for you, don't forget that."

"How can I forget that?"

"Okay. That's the way it is."

"There's no point in staying mad at me."

"I'm not mad at you. I just want you to be clear about our relationship."

"I love you. You're my son. That's our relationship. I can't change the past. Neither can you."

I didn't know what to say to my father so I stayed silent. I didn't want him to think that I was unhappy to see him. Far from it. I wanted him to be here. From the time he'd intimated that he was coming I'd looked forward to his presence, for despite our reconciliation after the long lapse I've still never felt whole with him, the chasm his leaving left has never been bridged. Even when I saw him in Barbados last year he was still my estranged father to me. I felt myself wanting more, wanting him to say something to dull the pain of all those years, at the same time I chided myself for being such a sissy. I'd gone through the Marines, was shot at and almost killed in the NYPD, what did it matter that my father didn't feel the need to comfort me for those years we missed together. After all, I was a man, thirty-seven years old, with a wife and an eight-year-old daughter. Why would I still need validation from a man who disappeared from my life without even saying good-bye? At the same time why couldn't I forget about it and just move on?

"I never hit your mother," he said.

"Forget I asked, okay?" I said.

"Well, you did, and you got my answer."

THIRTY-ONE

The memorial service for Ronan took place at the historic Emmanuel Baptist Church in Brooklyn, ironically just a few blocks from where he was gunned down. I was hoping to get there early with my father, who wanted to see Noah before things got started. We got held up in traffic; by the time we arrived the parking lot was full and throngs edged the sidewalk and the stairs leading to the church. A large portion of the block had been cordoned off, reserved by police for vehicles bringing the mayor and his entourage, and we had to park several blocks away.

Emmanuel Baptist, an intimidating structure outlaid in ornate Romanesque style with a soaring tower, was listed in the Register of Historic Places of New York, and I gathered that many tourists came to Brooklyn to see it. As I entered the spacious courtyard I saw why. It was a soaring monument to creativity and workmanship with rusticated stonework and heavy cornices that I read somewhere had been imported from Italy. I saw a number of familiar public faces among the large crowd milling about. Ronan had been a popular figure in the small but growing world of black entrepreneurs and liberal intellectuals, and even among black conservatives, though his reputation might've taken a hit with this group because of his demand for slave reparations.

On the outskirts of the wave entering the church I felt a light hand on my shoulder and turned around. It was Milo. Now in his sixties, Milo typified that West Indian philosophy that clothes and manners made the man. Today, attired in a crisp black suit with matching black shirt and tie, Milo was indeed the black knight.

"Hey Johnny," I greeted him sportingly.

"Johnny?"

"Johnny Cash. All you need is a guitar and a cigar."

"If we weren't in church, Blades, I'd tell you something." He laughed and embraced me. "You just jealous. You Americans don't know nothing 'bout clothes. I keep telling you though, man. If you ask me nice, I'd give you some wisdom."

"Wisdom? I was in the Marines, remember. I know what it's like to wear a uniform."

"Man, you have no taste, that's your problem."

My father, standing a few feet away in a gray pinstripe, laughed. "You tell him, Trini."

In our corner of the courtyard an army of squirrels that had cordoned off a small area for their conference scattered in separate directions. The wind was picking up. Dust danced in a whorl around us.

"Oh, Milo, this is my father, Madison."

Milo's eyes lit up. "Your father? Well, I never thought I'd get this chance."

The two of them shook hands.

"Nice to meet you, Milo," my father said. "And I think you got style."

"Thank you. And the pleasure is mine, Madison." Milo turned to me. "Where's Anais?"

"She couldn't make it," I said.

"It's a shame, isn't it?"

"Why is that a shame?"

"No, I mean about Peltier. I only met him like twice. Once when he was campaigning. And that time he came to the store to talk to you.

But he could inspire people. And he was smart, too. I hear the police got the killer."

"That's what they say," I muttered

"You didn't mention this to me," my father said.

"I'm sorry, we never got a chance to talk about it last night. The police found the gun. The only problem is the owner is dead."

"You sound like you ain't buying it," my father said with a nod of his head.

There was a wave of activity at the entrance of the courtyard and I looked to see what was going on. The mayor and his entourage had arrived. Noah, in a dark blue double-breasted suit and black turtleneck, walked next to the mayor. When they reached us Noah stopped; the mayor and his bodyguards continued up the steps into the church. Noah and my father embraced like brothers. It was some time before they untangled from each other.

"Good to see you, Madison," Noah said.

My father nodded, seemingly too choked up to speak. Noah shook my hand.

"How're you keeping?" I said.

He made a face and tried to look brave. "I'm doing all right, man. How 'bout yourself?"

"I'm good," I replied. "How's Donna?"

He shrugged, his face flat and reserved. "You know how it is, man. Still trying to keep her back straight."

With words having little power to express what was in our hearts the three of us cross-stared awkwardly like little boys trying to make up after a fight.

"I gotta go be with Donna," Noah said. "Madison, we'll talk later."

Most of the people, who apparently had been waiting around in the courtyard for the mayor to arrive, began to filter inside. The pews were about three-quarters full when Noah, my father, Milo, and I entered the expansive church together.

The next hour was one that I would not soon forget. Noah had arranged the most elaborate tribute to his son imaginable. Using his sophisticated skills as a dramatist to produce a funny but intimate look at their relationship, Noah had written and gotten the help of some of the actors from the writing workshop to dramatize a series of vignettes showing the passage of their relationship from Ronan's early years to adulthood, including the punch that broke Ronan's jaw. My father was in tears by the end of it.

But Noah was just getting started.

The tumult of African drums began offstage and then the dancers swept into view followed by singers and musicians. Noah had somehow persuaded or paid the National Song and Dance Company of Mozambique to perform *In Mozambique the Sun Has Risen*. For what seemed like forever after the performance the crowded church was silent. Everyone was crying.

NEGUS HAD been moved from the hospital in New Jersey to New York University Medical Center on the east side of Manhattan and that's where I went after the service. His private room looking out onto 34th Street was at the end of a long bright hallway insipidly decorated with pictures of bright flowers and snow-capped mountains. I imagine some slick executive from an HMO must've done a study to prove that patients recovered faster when surrounded by genteel art and sold the idea to his chairman as a cost-cutting maneuver, earning himself a promotion and a hefty bonus for his discovery.

Negus was awake, sitting up with the aid of his adjustable bed, reading a magazine. He was hooked up to several machines by tubes attached to his arms and under his nose. It looked as if he was having a hard time keeping his eyes open or keeping his focus on the page. Boredom comes quickly in a hospital bed.

"Now, I would like to know who snuck that *Black Booty* magazine in here for you," I greeted.

He lowered his magazine. A smile swelled like a pancake on the griddle to cover his face. "Blades, my dawg!"

He tried to lift his right hand to pound and grimaced, the arm drooping slackly back at his side.

"Take it easy, big man," I said.

"You come to take me outta this fleabag?"

"What's the matter, the nurses ain't doing the midnight run these days?"

"What the fuck's the midnight run?"

"If you gotta ask then you ain't ever been to the party."

His lips were dry and cracked and there was a drabness to his eyes swollen the size of manholes, as if he'd been rubbing them all day, except they weren't bloodshot, just blank and scattered. Sun smashed a hot fist through the window chiseling vertical shadows on the walls. Despite the sun loitering in the far corner I knew that this room could feel like an old dark place and the occupant could quickly become invisible to himself when needles of pain jabbed him into denying the existence of his soul. I'd been where Negus was now, except that he seemed to be in much better spirits than I ever was when I got shot.

"You're a lucky man, cuz," I said.

He flexed an idle stare. "Tell me about it. The shit was point blank, cuz. Lucky for me, he got me on the right side. I barely twisted my body when I saw the gun. The bullet passed right through me just grazing my lung. That's why I'm still in here. My lung had collapsed."

"Did you get a good look at his face?"

"That's all I see when I close my eyes. That forehead. He looks like Frankenstein's bitch. You know him?"

"I've had that nightmare too."

His eyes flickered, then he yawned as if he was tired. "I haven't heard from River. You know what happened to her?"

"She's safe. But it's probably better that you don't hear from her."

He grimaced. "Leave her alone, man. This wasn't her fault."

I opened my mouth to speak, then ate my thought. In the affairs of the heart Negus was one of those men who followed a blind alley to its end, wherever it took him. Trying to change his course was like trying to wedge a crane from its moorings with a toothpick. No point to it. Nothing transformed a man like love, I've always heard. I looked out the window. My eyes followed the mountain of concrete that rose sharply up and then I saw how the terra-cotta carvings were etched against the bright blue sky. To me it was an allegory of this city. It's not always easy to see the beauty of New York until you're forced to stop moving.

Negus picked up the magazine with his left hand and bracing it against his lifted knee, flipped the page. "It's you she's really interested in, you know."

I leaned against the window. "Me? What're you talking about?"

"We used to spend half our time talking about you."

"The day I came to the apartment you weren't doing too much talking."

A grin slipped from the chapped corners of his mouth. "We didn't do much of that. She wanted to know everything about you. Why you left the NYPD. When did you get married. Where your mother lives. What happened to your father. Man, I was getting sick of answering questions about you. She's obsessed with you, cuz."

"You've had too many hits of that Vicodin, big man."

"I was beginning to think she had some hidden agenda with you. Like maybe you'd been tapping that ass and promised her you was gonna leave Anais and then changed your mind."

"Does she talk much about herself?"

He tilted his head to look out the window. "Naw. She's kinda secretive about her own life." He flipped the magazine across the room and turned his head. It looked lopsided somehow. "You know what I saw her do one time? I saw her put a loaded gun in her mouth and pull the trigger."

"You shitting me?"

A crooked smile slowly bled into his eyes. "She's not your average woman."

"No, she's your average madwoman."

"She's got issues."

"Are you in love with her?"

He pulled his face in behind a mask. "I really don't want to talk about this anymore, Blades. You can understand why."

"No doubt, big man. I'm gonna bounce for now."

His stare was a knife cutting through me. "Can I ask you something?"

"Shoot."

"You promise to tell me the truth?"

"I'm always straight with you, cuz."

"You fucking her?"

"No, man. Nothing like that."

"I hear you."

"It's the truth, babe."

He turned his face and closed his eyes. I looked around the room, at the shower of flowers, the small basket of fruit by the window, the get-well cards piled on the table, the little radio on a chair. I realized that the room was quiet. And that was the way Negus wanted it.

THIRTY-TWO

I didn't go there to spy on Anais. Honest. I would admit to having a jealous streak, but I do trust my wife.

After I dropped my father off to do his Ground Zero walkabout the idea came to me that I should surprise Anais and take her to dinner at Sushi Samba. Her meeting on Seventh Avenue was supposed to finish at 6:00 P.M. Around 5:30 I curbed the SUV twenty feet from a hydrant one block away.

With half an hour to kill I decided to go have a cup of coffee. Whistling one of Marley's tunes as I limped slowly back to Seventh Avenue I ran everything I knew about Ronan's murder through my mind again. Detective Riley, with a caseload heavy enough for four detectives, must've been relieved when he discovered the murder weapon and a dead suspect. It couldn't get any more convenient than that. Case solved.

I entered a small coffee shop across from the two-story building where Anais was meeting with the director of the play. It was dimly lit and empty. I plunked my tired ass down at a table near a window where I had an unobstructed view of the main entrance of the building. The pain in my knee had circled to the back of my thigh. I stretched the leg out and rubbed the area as a heavy-set elderly man came to take my order.

"Coffee. Dark," I said.

He looked at me through uninterested mud-colored eyes anchored in deep sockets, his cheeks red as strawberries. Then he turned and plodded away.

I finished three cups of coffee and a slice of carrot cake before Anais came out of the building around 6:15.

The coffee shop had attracted a few more customers by then. A young woman in a corner clucking like a bored hen into her cell phone; a mixed-race couple with a little girl, whose delight at having gotten her parents to buy her pecan pie made me think of Chez and left me smiling.

Anais exited the building buttoning her brown full-length leather coat. My knee had stiffened up and as I hurried to get up I knocked over the half cup of coffee, spilling it all over the table and floor. I left ten dollars and broke for the door before the proprietor could say anything.

Before I could call out to Anais I saw a black-caped Merkins spin through the revolving door of the building and stand beside my wife. He put his arm around her shoulder and drew her to him. From what I could tell she went willingly. He leaned his face down as if to kiss her.

It might've been just a peck on the cheek, but just the sight of him holding my wife so close infuriated me. I didn't know what to do. If I called out to her she might think I'd come spying, yet I knew I couldn't just walk away.

A taxi pulled up and Anais got inside.

Then Merkins turned and started walking away from me down Seventh Avenue. I was feeling rather stupid now and could think of nothing else to do but follow him.

He walked leisurely with an upright arrogance that only a man who believed himself to be blessed with brass balls could effect without looking stupid. After walking several blocks south he crossed the street and turned east down a tiny dim street, walking two blocks before pausing in front of an Italian restaurant at the end of the block. Then he went inside.

I reached the restaurant and stood outside trying to peer through the glass window. But it was one of those joints that took the privacy of its guests to the limit. Heavy red curtains spoiled my view. I thought of waiting until he came out but it was too cold and my knee was killing me.

The restaurant's door opened and a couple draped in the matching leisure suits of love came out. I held the door open while they smooched their way onto the sidewalk, too smitten with each other to say thank you. I stepped inside where it was warm; a violent mixture of roasted garlic and fennel smacked me in the face. Hunger leapt to my consciousness. With it, the image of Anais kissing Merkins.

I searched for him in the tiny crowded room. No sign. A waiter brushed through a thick red curtain hiding a shiny door off to my right; it wasn't the kitchen. That was directly ahead. I walked to the curtain, swept it aside, and opened the door onto another dining area, fancier, probably used for private parties or for meetings between crooked politicians and their marks, such as might've been taking place between Merkins and the dough-faced man sitting to his right.

There were only a few guests in this room. Merkins saw me approaching and sat straight up, his face turning coppery. He dipped a piece of bread in olive oil and when I was within range, like the cagey capitalist he was, went on the immediate offensive.

He turned to the pulpy man sitting next to him. "See this man; this is Anna Machel's house-husband. You remember Anna. She's that hot black chick who's playing Grace in Dennis Hector's revival. He's the last of a dying breed, this man. An honorable man. A virtuous man. Don't you know he came to my house the other day to ask me not to fuck his wife again? How does that register on your manly radar? I give it a fucking ten. He even threatened me. What do you think about that? This greasy ex-cop threatened me. But I'm not mad. He was trying to defend his wife's honor. You have to admire a man like that."

Fire erupted in my gut. I could feel acid bubbling and the walls of my stomach crumbling under my attempt to keep calm. I just wanted to put a finger in his eye and watch the blood run.

It was a bad decision to follow Merkins. Now I was here I didn't know what to do and I couldn't turn away.

Pinched-faced, he brushed a speck of lint from his black ribbed sweater. "Did your wife tell you about the time we rented a private jet and flew to Hawaii for a week?"

"No, she never mentioned that. She did tell me you had problems getting it up, though."

He looked stricken, his eyes bulged then he laughed, pointing his fork at my chest. "That's a good one. You're tough, I gotta give you that. Must be those years on the streets stealing from dope addicts. She still likes it in the ass?"

The pot of acid in my stomach boiled over, spewing up through my chest, fricasseeing my brain. I leaped across the table, grabbed him by his throat, and began to squeeze. He opened his mouth to scream but the only thing that came out was masticated bread and saliva. All over my shirt the shit flew. My fingers locked into the soft pulp of his scrawny neck, lifting him out of his chair. His hands clawed upward, his face becoming redder than a ripe berry.

I dragged Merkins across the table, sending plates crashing to the floor. His face contorted as if he was trying to squeeze something through constricted bowels.

The wimpy walrus who'd been sitting next to him jumped up screaming; the commotion had brought patrons to their feet and waiters running. Someone bashed a heavy fist against the side of my head and two men grabbed hold of my arms. I dropped Merkins on the floor to shake them off. But having achieved their objective of getting me to loosen my stranglehold on my victim, they backed away.

Merkins struggled to his knees. It was not the most graceful recovery you'll see. He was frothing at the mouth like a poisoned dog; the front of his shirt looked as if a downtown painter had used it for a canvas. He straightened up with the help of his porky friend.

He wiped a wedge of creamy drool from his mouth and tried to smile. "So, you think you're a bully?"

I stood breathing deeply, pissed at myself for losing my composure.

"But I'll forgive you this time," he said. "My present to Anais. But the truth is, Blades, I've already fucked your wife, there's nothing you can do about that. Even donning a King Kong suit won't change that."

I could feel my skin burning as if someone had whacked me with a hot stake. I had to get out of there. I turned and walked past the line of busboys and waiters who, like fighter jets from an aircraft carrier, had been scrambled by the manager to protect his establishment. At the door I passed two uniformed NYPD cops entering the restaurant. They didn't try to stop me.

I DID NOT sleep well that night. Every time I closed my eyes I felt myself swimming in a pool of dark memories: working the night shift as a narco, searching flophouses for snitches; sitting in oily foul-smelling rooms waiting for an unwashed addict to shoot up so he can remember what it was he was supposed to tell you. And then when he got high and puked all over himself, his eyes grainy as salt, his breath putrid as a rotten tomb, you feel obligated to clean him up, so that the rats didn't feast on his sodden body. And everywhere I went I felt as if there was someone watching me from the shadows, someone with an inescapably familiar smile, someone tall whose presence I yearned for and at the same time wanted to spurn; but I was powerless to resolve the stalemate.

I woke from the dream with my stomach in a knot. *And you thought when you left narcotics you left that world behind.*

It was close to midday before I crawled out of bed. Anais was preparing an omelet when I came downstairs.

She heard my shuffling footsteps and looked around. "I was wondering if I'd have to call Emergency Services to revive you."

I kissed her just as my stomach funneled gas up my throat. I turned my head to burp. "Excuse me."

"Are you okay?" She rubbed my cheek gently, the way my mother used to do when I was a boy.

"Why'd you let me sleep so late?"

"I checked in on you a few times this morning. You were out cold."

"Bad dreams."

"I was just making breakfast to bring upstairs to you. Once I'd resuscitated you I was going to fuck you back into a coma."

"I love when you talk dirty in the morning."

"You love when I talk dirty anytime."

I laughed. "Where's Dad?"

"Noah picked him up an hour ago."

"Where'd they go?"

"I don't ask two grown men where they're going, especially when none of them ain't my husband."

Anais circled juice, toast, half a block of Guido cheese around a plate with omelet and slices of tomato. I sat down and she took up a position leaning against the fridge.

"Chez left her lunch again today," Anais said.

I sliced the block of cheese with a long knife. "I used to do that all the time."

Anais hitched the sleeves of her black V-neck sweater and said nothing.

"Is there something bothering you?" I said.

"No. Why?"

"Sit down."

She walked to the coffee pot and poured a cup of coffee in a black mug.

I had not told Anais about my run-in with Pryce Merkins at the restaurant. And though she had said nothing I suspected that she knew and had somehow decided to take a wait-and-see approach, which was unlike her.

She sipped again from her black cup and looked at me, her eyes big and bright as seashells on a Caribbean beach. "I've decided to do that play."

I got up and walked to the coffee pot. Anais always let me pour my own coffee. It was a ritual in the morning that defined how I was going to approach the day. I poured a large cup and tasted it. It was sour in my mouth and I wanted to spit it out. I returned to the table where Anais was now sitting. I felt like kissing her. "I'm sure you'll be great."

She looked up; her mouth was shaped like a heart. "You're not angry?"

"I may be thin-skinned when it comes to certain things, but I'll never stand in the way of your work."

"I'm glad we didn't have to fight over this."

I smiled and looked into her eyes. "You got the power, babe."

"Okay, Blades, I know when you get that patronizing tone. What's the real deal?"

"I just wanna ask you one question. Tell me about L.A."

"What about L.A.?"

"Did you sleep with him in L.A.?"

Her voice turned salty. "So I slept with him in L.A. We were separated."

I got up from the table. "Look, if you want to do this play, go ahead. But if I end up strangling this muthafucker, it's on you."

"You are sick, Blades. You are a sick bastard."

I cut another slice of cheese, stuck the knife in the center of the block, and walked away.

I GOT a call from Toni later that afternoon while I waited to pick up Chez from school.

"Blades, are you going to come and see me when I go into the hospital?"

"When're you going into the hospital and why?"

"A week from today. For my operation."

"Which operation is this?"

"Bilateral orchietomy."

"Come again."

"That's when they remove my balls."

"Ouch!"

"No, Blades, good riddance."

"You sure you want to do this, big man?"

"Big woman, if you please. And yes, this is my dream. You know that."

"It's a hard concept for me to grasp, you understand."

"No, I don't understand."

"Aren't you scared?"

"Of what?"

"I imagine once you go flat you can't turn back."

"Hehehe. Not funny. And why would I want to turn back?"

"I'm just saying."

"You're always saying the wrong thing, dickhead."

"Hey, I'm trying to understand."

"You're a moron. You'll never understand. It's a shame you're so fucking cute, though. That's the only reason I talk to you, you know that. I have some information on that girl you're looking for."

"J'Noel Bitelow?"

"I have an associate who did some business with her departed boyfriend. He knows the girl and her mother, who lives on Foster. Seven forty-nine. The Belvedere. Apartment Nine E. You might find her there."

"Man or woman, you're still the best, Toni."

"Just make sure you come see me."

"Will I recognize you?"

He laughed. "Man or woman, I'll still be bigger than you."

"And badder, I'm sure. Even without balls."

"Hey Blades?"

"Yeah?"

"Malcolm used to roll with a character named Big-Six. He's nasty. Real heavy hitter. Would fuck his mother with a baseball bat. Watch out for him. Word is he was creeping on Malcolm's girl."

"Thanks, babe."

"Did you just call me babe?"

"Don't start, Toni."

"You can't call me babe, Blades. You can call your friends that but not me. Because I'll start thinking all kinds of shit."

"Good-bye, Toni."

After I hung up I tried to imagine the agony of Toni's life as a man all these years. I realized it was impossible for me to understand what that feeling was like. But I did know something about trying to live outside your skin. Trying to maintain the presence of blackness under your light complexion without offending your white mother or your white siblings at a time when the easiest thing in the world to do would be to feign neutrality based on the otherness of being mixed-race. But just as Toni couldn't run from his belief that he was a woman, I couldn't run from the fact that I'd always felt more comfortable in blackness. Whether or not it was society's fault for making me feel so ostracized from that other part of me, blackness remained my blanket of comfort. But contemplating Toni's plight also made me think of my father, and the one question I'd never been able to ask him: Did he ever feel guilty about abandoning his family?

THE DOOR TO the St. Paul's Academy opened and children poured out. I got out of the car and crossed the street. A flat-faced dog at the school gate nipped its tail in its mouth. The owner, doing nothing to dispel the myth that dog owners grow to look like their dogs, smoked a long cigarette not far off.

Chesney came bounding down the steps of the redbrick school. She slowed down to a casual stroll to cross the yard, but on seeing me she broke into a canter, waving her arms in the air.

Outside the gate she tumbled into my arms.

"Sweetness." I hugged her.

"I thought Mom was coming to pick me up."

"Well, I know how much you like surprises so I thought I'd surprise you."

She giggled. "What's the surprise?"

"Me," I said. "Am I not a good enough surprise?"

"Yes, but what else?" she insisted.

"This is it. Me. I'm the big surprise."

"You can't trick me, Daddy."

"Okay, Einstein junior. You're too smart for me. Guess what, we're going to Disneyland."

She held my hand as we crossed the street to the car. "Really? Let me see the tickets."

"Well, I don't have the tickets yet. They're being sent to me."

"When're we going?"

"When you get out of school in two weeks."

We got into the car and I started the engine. The Volvo hummed like a well-tuned violin. I adjusted Chesney's seat belt before hooking myself up, then eased the Volvo into traffic on Court Street.

THIRTY-THREE

The red-faced Belvedere on Foster was sandwiched between a funeral home and a church almost completely bearded with green ivy. As I parked opposite the building across from a bus stop two flirtatious young women sashayed toward me. The one in red skintight hip-hugging leather pants, slender and flat as a cactus, baited an older man who dared not get out of his truck. The other girl, her earlobes tangled with every variation of gold rings you could imagine, her thin coat unbuttoned in the front to reveal a pink shirt overlaid on breasts standing so straight out they looked as if they'd been hooked on a line, teased a half-peeled banana in and out of her mouth, her face crooked with giggles at the bantering between her friend and the man in the truck.

They crossed the street as if to enter the Belvedere and I got quickly out of the car and followed. The slender girl grilled me with deep wintry eyes as I stood waiting for her to open the door.

"Going to see a friend," I said.

She stuffed the rest of the banana into her mouth. "Who?"

"Do you know everyone in this building?"

She swallowed, ignoring my confrontational tone. "Yes I do."

I softened my voice. "She just moved in."

She held the key in the lock, not twisting. "What apartment?"

"Nine E."

"Nobody ain't moved in there. That woman been there since I been here." Then she paused. "Oh, her daughter just moved back. She's a little young for you, eh? Her mother's more your age, I believe. Or are you tapping both them asses?"

The two of them broke into laughter.

The slender one spoke again, as if speaking for both of them. It was the first time I detected a Trinidadian accent. "You look like a man with money. I bet you'd have much more fun with us," she said.

I felt as if someone had just stuffed a plum into my mouth. "I bet I would."

She twisted the key; the heavy door opened with a dirty groan. I followed the girls into a high-ceilinged foyer with puke-colored walls and peeling paint that looked like scales on the back of an alligator.

The tiny elevator was straight ahead and the three of us got in. The girl in red leather pressed 10; I pressed 9. The door clanged shut and the elevator whined like an animal about to collapse.

It smelled of musk inside the cramped space; I realized it was the girl in red leather; she was wearing some kind of men's cologne. From somewhere under her coat she produced a bag of plantain chips and broke it open with a loud pop. Exposing bright silver braces on her teeth she smiled at me with big sad bloodhound eyes and made a grunting sound.

The elevator rumbled to a stop on the ninth floor and the door croaked open.

"Apartment Ten-F. You know what the *F* stands for. Anything you want," the slender girl sang out as I got off, her voice trebled with wicked laughter. It was only then I realized her friend had not spoken one word.

AS I STOOD outside apartment 9E I wondered if I shouldn't have brought flowers considering the way my last meeting with

J'Noel went. But it was too late for symbols right now. And I was no longer in the mood for trifling bullshit.

I pressed the brass bell on the right side of the door. The syncopated brush of slippers sliding over linoleum started and reached a pitch close to the door. Someone rattled the cover on the peephole. Then after a minute of silence the bolt of the lock clacked and the door opened the width of the safety chain. J'Noel's still-swollen face shaded through the opening. Pine scent wafted through the slit.

Her eyes slashed at me. "What do you want?"

"Last time I saw you I left feeling there was something you didn't tell me."

"How'd you find me?"

"It's a long story. Let me in."

"Go away or I'll call the cops."

"Go right ahead. I'm sure they have some questions for you about your dead boyfriend. I'm not leaving until I talk to you."

Her face grew grim and her eyes wandered to the floor, as if she was trying to read something on my shoes. She closed the door. The door opened again seconds later, this time all the way. She was swallowed up in a baggy crimson Rocawear sweatsuit; the slippers on her feet were a size large.

The door closed behind me and she locked it. Staggering as if she'd just woken up, she lead me around a tight corner through a dark kitchen into a living room cluttered with boxes, too many chairs, and a glass cabinet full of china that looked like it'd never been touched. The bald green linoleum had been recycled a few times too often. She toppled onto a square couch with a quiet sigh and spread her arms wide across its back like a diva in her dressing room. Behind her was a long mirror with metal pegs in its gilded frame, from which hung several women's hats.

The rest of the furniture was that nondescript neutral variety you find in many Caribbean immigrant homes, bought from Italian furniture stores like Roma: beige and lilac chairs with pastel flowers covered with clear plastic. I sank into a beige love seat that was much too soft, leaning forward to escape the loose wire in the upholstery that was stabbing me in the back.

She stared at me as if she was looking down a drainpipe. There was a flash of loneliness in her eyes. "Do you get pleasure from bothering people?"

"This isn't fun for me."

"I feel sorry for you."

"How's your son?"

"You ain't interested in Malcolm's health so step back with that shit."

"I got a little girl, you know. She's eight."

"That's nice, but we won't be swapping any photos. I don't like you. People like you don't care who you have to hurt to get your own way."

"You don't even know me."

"I know your type. Black daddy. White mama. Probably Jewish. 'Cause if your Daddy was white and your mama was black you'd never been a cop. No black woman with a son like you woulda let him become a cop. You probably grow up trying to be just like any other nigger, but in your heart you think you better. I see the way you look around this room. You saying to yourself: *I'm glad I don't live like this.*"

"I don't know what your problem is, J'Noel, but you don't know me. My mother isn't Jewish. And even if she was what's that got to do with the price of beer?"

Her eyes darted angrily at my face. "It's all the same shit."

"The police think Malcolm killed the politician."

"Then why you here bothering me?"

"You and I know that ain't true. We both know Malcolm was somewhere bleeding to death from your carnivorous attack. So how did that gun get into his apartment?"

"I'm gonna start screaming if you don't leave."

"Go ahead. Practice the scales while you're at it. Then you can sing to the police when they get here. You weren't as careful as you think, babe."

"What're you talking about?"

"The call you made to police."

"What call?"

"The one telling them about the gun."

"You're talking shit."

"Really. It's all on tape. I listened to it. It's your voice. Easy enough to prove. The police can do a voice match in half an hour."

I was bluffing but the look on her face told me I'd caught her.

"You're a piece of shit." She stood up and walked to the window.

I breathed deeply; the air tasted of garlic. I looked at her reflection in the mirror. It was not a majestic image, but there was dignity, rough-hewn though it was with an air of sublime indifference to whatever ailed the rest of the world. Here she was living in the incestuous lap of church and funeral home, in a city swarming with charlatans, grim with the presence of cheaters and crooked freaks, a city at once baffling and absurd, for amid all of the life and art there was pain and senseless killings, and all she had to cling to was her anonymity, the passport of self-preservation in this city. It was this jungle instinct fueling her determination not to open up to me, not to get caught up in the history or drama that came with passing information because she knew that once she talked she could no longer hide.

"Did you plant the gun?"

She turned and looked at me as if weighing something heavy on her mind. "I just made the call."

"Who planted the gun?"

"I don't know."

"Who told you to make the call?"

Her mouth opened and I got the impression she was about to speak but it seemed she couldn't get her tongue off the roof of her mouth. "Malcolm has a friend," she said, her voice strained.

"Big-Six?"

"He said if I didn't make the call he'd hurt Malcolm Jr."

"You're lying again."

"Fuck off."

"Biting off your boyfriend's dick is one thing, being an accomplice to murder is something else altogether."

Her face turned dark and she looked at me as if she wanted to scratch out my eyes. "I wasn't even there."

"You made that call to the police."

"I told you he forced me."

"He was your lover. The police will never buy that. Big-Six killed the politician, didn't he?"

"I don't know."

"It's your only way out, J'Noel. You give me Big-Six for the politician's murder and you may stay out of jail."

"You're trying to scare me, but it won't work."

"Tell that to Malcolm Jr. when the cops fit you with steel bracelets."

"I had nothing to do with that politician's death."

"You made the call. You've got shit all over your shoes."

"He and Big-Six were planning to do the politician."

"Who? Malcolm?"

"Yeah."

"Who hired them?"

"I don't know that."

I stared at her, prying deep into her eyes.

"Really. I don't know. I heard them talking about it," she confessed.

"When?"

"That same night Malcolm tried to rape me."

"The night before Ronan was killed?"

"They came to the house that night. Both of them idiots was jacked on some shit. All excited and looking crazed. I heard them talking in the bedroom. Big-Six was saying he wasn't parking no politician for less than fifty loot."

"Fifty thousand?"

"Yeah."

"What did Malcolm say?"

"I didn't hear."

"Did they mention Ronan by name?"

"No."

"So how'd you know it was Ronan?"

"I'm guessing. After I saw the news."

"Did Malcolm call anybody? Did you hear him talking on the phone after?"

"I don't remember. Big-Six left shortly after. That's when Malcolm attacked me."

"He has a cell phone, I suppose."

"Yes."

"What's the number?"

She hesitated, then spoke the numbers slowly. "Nine-one-seven. Eight-three-five. Five-three-eight-eight."

I took my organizer from my inside breast pocket and jotted the number down. "Where can I find Big-Six? Where does he live?"

"I don't know."

"You were fucking the dude."

"So what? It was nothing to me. I was just using him to get Malcolm off my case. I didn't want Big-Six. I wanted Malcolm out of my life."

"Why not just leave the guy?"

"Don't you think I tried?"

"What's this Big-Six look like?"

She gave a pithy laugh. "Big dude. Light complexion. Albino-looking with freckles. You couldn't miss him if you were blind. Always wearing a black Kangol."

"Are you hiding from Big-Six?"

She sniggered. "Don't worry about me. Just don't come around me no more."

I got up and said thank you. She ignored my offered handshake and maneuvered past me through the clutter. I followed her. She had the door already open when I reached her. I stepped out into the hallway and heard the door slam behind me. It wasn't that cold in the hallway but I felt a quiet chill, like a shroud overpowering my spirit. One of those feelings of guilt that was difficult to shake off. I had lied to her but it'd been necessary. I walked toward the elevator thinking I should've listened to my mother when she told me I had the brains to be a doctor.

I CALLED Semin Gupta and asked her to find out if Malcolm Nails-Diggs had ever been on lockdown at Rikers and if so was he ever one of Dr. Heat's patients while incarcerated. It was a long shot but I still wasn't ready to give up on Dr. Heat as a suspect. I got word to Toni that I was looking for this character Big-Six. Toni maintained his accustomed distance, saying he would get back to me.

It didn't take long. The next morning I had a road map to Big-Six's life of crime.

HE EARNED the name on the streets of Baltimore where he ran with a raw crowd of gangbangers who hustled cocaine along the corridor between Philadelphia and Virginia. Urban myth had it that Big-Six took out six roughnecks from an opposing gang with an automatic on a street in Baltimore. After the Feds took down the heads of the crew through an elaborate sting leaving a leadership void, a turf war flared up pitting Big-Six, whose real name was Tracy DeRoguet, against a crew from the East Side. The east-siders won the war and Big-Six fled to New York. It wasn't easy for an albino to hide in a place like Baltimore.

In New York he packed heat for Terrence Backhouse's crew in Freeport before slicing meat for a Jamaican gang out of the Red Houses. He was linked by police to the killing of two witnesses in the Red Houses, but all the authorities could make stick was a gun charge for which he served one year. Toni's informant put Big-Six in a house on East 103rd Street in Flatlands, a neighborhood in the southeastern corner of Brooklyn.

It was a quiet-looking neighborhood, as quiet as you could find in any working-class section of Brooklyn. Once these brooding frame and stucco houses were home to many Italians and Jews; this area, like much of Brooklyn, had been invaded by the Third World and boasted a mixture of immigrants from the English-speaking Caribbean, Latin America, and the Middle East.

Parking the Volvo opposite an elementary school, I got out and leaned against the school perimeter fence to watch the kids in uniform play in the yard. Two adults, puffing on cancer-rods in one corner of the tiny schoolyard, supervised the boisterous activities. I walked back one block to a bodega at the corner, where I got a pack of plantain chips, a pack of gum, and a newspaper.

Outside the bodega I dropped a dollar in the dirt-packed palm of a homeless man even as the greasy-looking owner of the establishment tried to shoo him away. The coatless man, his shirt tattered, ranted on in a wild Jamaican accent about the many wrongs foisted on him by the world.

Stoking a wedge of gum into my mouth, I continued along the block of clean-looking frame houses. I passed the eaten skeleton of one of only two trees on the entire block. The other one stood at the other end of the block. I suspected that when the Italians and Jews lived in this neighborhood there were many more trees.

I reached the house I was looking for. An American flag flapped from the awning over the front door. In bright gold lettering the house number, 667, was plastered on the door. Music blared from the house next door.

I passed through a black metal gate and walked up the yellow-painted cement steps to the front door, where I pressed the buzzer. The semi-attached frame house had a tiny garden that was empty except for stalks. A woman wearing a bloodred tracksuit, whose face had that slack I-had-a-hard-night appearance, came to the door and looked out. I waved a phony badge in the air.

"Can I help you?" The right side of her mouth drooped heavily.

"I'm looking for Tracy DeRoguet."

"Wrong house."

"Big-Six?"

She frowned and pulled her head back to further assess my entire stature. "What's a big six?"

"I got this address from his probation officer, who said he dropped him off here just a few days ago. Tall dude. Albino-looking. Freckles."

"What's your name again?"

"Blades Overstreet."

"Detective?"

I nodded vaguely.

"You're kinda cute for a detective." She glossed a smile. "You look like an actor."

"I'm not an actor."

"I'm just saying. You coulda been an actor if you wanted to. I mean you got the looks. Though dark-skinned black men is the thing in Hollywood these days. You know, Wesley and Taye. I'm studying acting in Manhattan, you know."

"Is that right?"

"Yeah. That's right."

"I have a friend who's a playwright and a director."

"That's awesome. Is he looking for actors?"

"Actually he is. He runs a playwriting workshop and he's always looking for actors."

"My name is Julia Wells. That's not my real name. I changed it. How can you become a star with a name like Mabel Grimsley? I can give you a headshot and a bio. I've done off-off Broadway. I did a few Caribbean plays in Brooklyn, but that don't count, I don't think. Caribbean people don't understand good theater. You wanna come in while I get my headshot?"

I stepped through the door and into a foyer packed tight with potted plants. Stepping over a fat gray cat lying on the pink carpet I followed her into the living room with several movie posters on the walls, a bright Indian rug in the middle of the floor, and a sofa with an intricate Japanese design in a corner. Julia disappeared into a back room and returned quickly with a nine-by-eleven manila envelope.

She handed it to me batting her eyelids and curling her mouth in a seductive smile. "You want something to drink?"

"This is six sixty-seven east one-oh-three, right?"

Her voice broke with frustration. "What?"

"This is the address I was given."

"Maybe you didn't hear it right."

"How long you been living here?"

She hesitated. "Two years."

"You own this house."

She paused again. "Yes."

"And you live alone?"

"Yes."

"I guess you're right. I must've heard it wrong."

She sat down on the couch and crossed her thick legs. "That's what I said."

"It's a big house for one person."

Her face grew tight. "Are all detectives this pushy?"

"Actually, I'm not a detective."

"You have a badge."

"It's not real."

"You see, you could be an actor. You had me thinking you were a detective. You played the part real good. So who are you?"

"Wasn't that hard a part to play. I used to be a detective."

"What kind of plays does your friend write?"

"Plays. I don't know. He sold a movie once too. And I think he's writing another one."

"Awesome. Tell him I can play anything. Prostitute. Businesswoman. Drug addict. Anything."

"Listen, I'm sorry I bothered you."

"No bother at all. Maybe we'll meet again."

She led me out and shook my hand at the door. I walked back to my car and sat for a while thinking about my next move. I tore open the bag of chips, grabbed a handful, and stuffed my mouth full. The children had gone back into school and the street was as quiet as night.

THIRTY-FOUR

Later that morning I went running in Prospect Park, which was already alive with the cold-beaded faces of men and women jogging and walking their dogs. My knee loosened up halfway around and I was able to finish my run without pain. Patches of blooming mist covered the park; the asphalt was rain-speckled from an early shower as I breathed thick air pungent of horse manure into my heavy lungs. A cross-eyed fellow passed me going in the opposite direction. And the wild wind puffing the mist across the treetops also seemed to be blowing dark thoughts because I looked back to see if he had turned around to follow me.

Blown particles of dirt had mixed with my sweat to form a thick paste on my face by the time I'd circled twice around the park. I refueled on bottled water from a nearby bodega before limping across Flatbush Avenue, tired but spiritually reenergized. The muscles in my legs tingled and there was tightness in my back but the sweat pouring down my face and body was elixir to my soul.

AT FIVE in the evening I came out of my office at the club to find Special Agent Kraw sitting on the hood of a black Malibu. She was dressed in blue jeans, black boots, and an ill-fitting aviation jacket, her blond hair stiff bristles sticking out in the wind. I could see the bulge of her shoulder holster. She wore no makeup, and there was a rigidity to her eyes and jaw indicating to me that she might not have been in a good mood. But she smiled and jumped to the ground and thrust out her hand.

"How're you, Blades?" she greeted.

"I wish I could find the time to cruise around making social calls like you do."

She laughed. "You're irresistible, you know that?"

"Wanna go grab a coffee? I need to ask you a favor."

"I don't have time. There's something I need to tell you."

"You're refusing to have coffee with me? I'm hurt."

"How long is your father planning on staying?"

"He is an American, you know."

She leaned closer. "His life might be in danger."

I shifted my stance, scrutinizing her austere face. "Care to elaborate?"

She rested her elbow on top of the car. "You keep this pretense up, it's gonna get your father killed."

I shrugged. "You're obviously playing in another field."

"Okay, since you wanna play ignorant, let's recount the history. Twenty years ago your father testified in the trial of two Panthers who were convicted and got life. About nine years into his sentence, one of them escaped. In case you don't remember or this is news to you, his name was Carlos Peterson. Two weeks later when the police tried to recapture him there was a shootout. He got away again, but his wife was killed in the gun battle. He skipped the country with his two children. Ended up in Cuba. He managed to slip back into the U.S. at some point without us knowing. We're not sure what happened to his son but his daughter worked for the Dade County Sheriff's Department before being fired for violations involving excessive use of force against suspects. It was her troubles with the Sheriff's Department that allowed us to pick up Carlos Peterson's trail. Before we could close in he was killed by an unknown gunman on South Beach. After her father died Regina Peterson, a.k.a. River Paris, worked as a bail bondsman, bodyguard, and club manager in Louisiana and Miami before moving to New York. Do you see where I'm going with this?"

I must've had a stupid look on my face because I felt like a jerk. Boy, had I been played. A soft rain began, raindrops kissing my face, but they felt like rubber bullets. I wiped my face with my sleeve. River was Carlos Peterson's daughter. *Well, fuck me.*

Kraw circled around me. "Do you still want to protect this woman?"

"Did you know who she was all along?"

"Yes, I did."

"How long were you going to let me blow in the wind?"

"You're such a self-righteous bastard."

"I still don't know where she is."

Her stare threatened to slice me in two. Without another word she opened her car door and slid behind the wheel.

I leaned in through the open window. "I'll make you a deal."

"You think I'm worthy?" Her smile was framed in sarcasm.

"I need a printout of all outgoing calls for these two numbers the night Ronan was killed." I handed her a piece of paper with J'Noel's home telephone number and Malcolm's cell phone number.

"What do I get?"

"Regina. The queen herself."

"I need her alive." She put the paper in the top pocket of her flight jacket and started the engine. "You better not try to fuck me, Blades."

"Bite your tongue, Kraw."

I stepped back and watched as she drove off toward Flatbush Avenue.

THAT NIGHT my father was playing chess with Noah in the den. Anais was upstairs studying lines for the new play. I wanted to talk to her about what Special Agent Kraw had told me before I broke the news to my father but didn't want to interrupt her.

I bathed, washed and dried my hair, got dressed, and went downstairs.

The effort of my morning run was now beginning to exact its charge on my body. I felt drained. But I knew it was more than the run which was responsible for my lethargy. An anger brewing inside me was also sapping my energy, as was the prospect of raising the specter of the past and the imminent threat of revenge and death.

I peered over my father's shoulder the way I did when I was a boy watching him paint in our backyard in Park Slope. It always amazed me that he could sit for so long doing nothing, just staring at the canvas, deep in concentration. He was the same over the chess table, his broad back tense in concentration. Noah was about to checkmate him. No amount of concentration could save his game and he soon gave in.

"You still talk a better game than you play," Noah bragged.

My father leaned back in his chair. "You're still a lucky dog."

Noah took off his horn-rim glasses and rubbed his chin. "Another game to rub in my luck?"

"I'll take you into the park tomorrow for a game of hoops."

Twirling his glasses around by the temple, Noah said, "Now you really want me to kick your ass."

My father reached back and tapped my leg. "Listen to this fool. What do you think, Blades? University life may've sharpened up your mind, Noah, but it's left your body on the doorstep."

"I hope I'm not like you two when I get old, man," I said.

My father swiveled around to face me; Noah lifted his eyes, a sneer twisted on his face.

"After all this time, you two still trying to figure out who's got the biggest dick," I said.

"Well, we already know who that is," my father laughed.

"Carlos Peterson's daughter is in town," I blurted out.

Silence echoed like a cowbell in a chapel.

Noah was the first to respond. He fixed horn-rims back on his face and stood up. "The Carlos Peterson?"

"The Carlos Peterson."

"The one you killed?" Noah said.

I said nothing.

Noah continued. "Listen, we're all big men here. Let's stop fucking around. We all know that Carlos vowed to kill your father for ratting him out. And Blades, I know you were in Miami around the same time Carlos was killed. You two want me to think that was a coincidence?"

"What's it to you how he died, Noah?" my father said.

"I just feel like I should know the truth."

After the loud throttle of a helicopter overhead passed, I turned and spotted my eyes at Noah. "If I tell you it wasn't me, why isn't that good enough for you?"

"I'm a part of the shit, too, you know. I'm the one who convinced your father to testify."

"But my father was the one who left the country. You got to live your life."

"That was his choice, Blades. You understand what I'm saying. His fucking choice." Noah raised his eyebrows and shrugged. "You know this bitch, don't you? I can see it in your eyes. That's why you're scared."

I didn't answer. The question had caught me unprepared. There was no way to answer without sounding like a chump.

"What's the story, Blades?" My father said.

I said, "This girl's a trained killer, Pop."

"You think I'm gonna let a woman take me out?" my father scoffed.

"Did you hear what I said?"

"What?" My father squared his shoulders. "I heard you. She's still a woman."

"This ain't your average bimbo."

"Where's she now?" said my father quietly.

"I'll handle it, Pop. But you should lay low for a while. If you gotta go out let me know. I'll take you wherever you need to go."

"I don't need no bodyguard," my father said.

"Call it what you like, but you've got me," I replied.

"You think I came back here to hide?"

"Why did you come back, Pop?"

He stuffed his hand into his pockets and walked across the room. Erect as a post, he turned his back, staring out the window. Hard light bounced off the side of his face, and a limp shadow fell at his feet. He turned around, his lips pursed.

"I came back because I was tired of living a lie."

At that moment he became the father I remembered. I was looking at the man who'd left twenty years ago. The calmness of his eyes was back. The toughness in his voice was there. And though his face had been reshaped over the years by the burden of shame and now looked as though the flesh would soon fall off, that barren, grotesque remoteness had disappeared.

He folded his arms. "I used this threat against me as an excuse to run from my own self. I've failed at everything I've ever done in my life. I wasn't even good at being a rebel. And I certainly wasn't any good at being a husband or a father. So after Peterson escaped it was easier to run. I could've stayed and fought for the things that should've mattered. You. Your mother's love. Even your sister and brother. I didn't fight for their love." My father came back to the center of the room. "I had a long talk with your mother the other day. She's an amazing woman. She told me that though everyone told her to do it she refused to declare me dead. Not because she was expecting me to come back to her. She did it for you. Said she couldn't declare your father dead unless she saw a body. I'm not running anymore. After running so much there comes a point when you realize that you can't run away from death. Eventually death will catch up with you. And as you get older you realize that the only way to face death is with courage. And because it's inevitable the best you can do is prepare to leave by making the burden less for the people who love you. The people who will grieve. Have all your papers in order. Have enough money to bury you. Those things you can do while you're alive."

"Are you trying to tell me something, Pop?"

"I'm not afraid. I let Noah here talk me into ratting out my friends. My brothers. Well, you know what? It looks like I've come full circle. But I promise you, if I gotta die, I ain't dying running. Like a rat."

"Let me tell you something, Madison," Noah exclaimed. "I'm not ashamed nor will I apologize for what I did back then. We're talking about two men who ambushed a cop and killed him. Any way you smoke that it's cold-blooded murder. Brother or no brother, they got what they deserved."

"I'm not blaming you, Noah. It's on me," my father said.

Noah jumped up, knocking the chess pieces off the board. "That sounds very noble and shit, but it's a bunch of crap. If you didn't blame me how come all these years you never once sent me a fucking postcard. Tell me that."

The chess pieces had rolled across the polished floor, the queen coming to a stop near my father's feet.

"Gentlemen, it's too late for all this soul-searching," I said. "Tomorrow I will go climb a tall mountain and shake a tree. Hopefully nothing will drop."

"What if something does?" Noah said.

"I'll have to sweep it up."

I left them to their memories and regrets and went upstairs to kiss my daughter goodnight. I wanted to get a good night's sleep. Tomorrow was shaping up to be a trying day.

THIRTY-FIVE

Day dawned with a slimy coal-gray scowl on its face, its breath frosty as glass with portents of snow. After downing a piece of toast and coffee I drove Chez to school, kissed her before she got out in her bright Red Riding Hood coat, and told her Anais would pick her up. I waited for her to enter the school door before driving off.

Waiting for the lights to change at Franklin and Union I noticed something that made me smile. On this Friday morning, cold and ugly as it was, a crowd clogged the sidewalk to watch students reenact the crucifixion story on the steps of the Middle School of Brooklyn. Noah would've been proud, because here was theater as pageant, theater for the people; the kind of theater he'd always advocated.

At the change of the light I took one last glimpse catching a partial view of the procession led by Jesus bearing his cross. That's when it hit me. Toni Monday's ears were so attuned to the ripple in the cesspool where sewer rats bred that he knew with accuracy when one miscarried. If Toni put Big-Six at a job there was a ninety-nine percent probability that he was at that location when Toni got a fix on him. Which meant Julia Wells was a better actor than I gave her credit for.

I made a U-turn and throttled my trusty old machine through the crackling cold streets of central Brooklyn. Approaching Grand Army Plaza I called Toni Monday but got his voice mail.

I MADE IT to East 103rd in twenty minutes. It was 8:45 when I parked outside Julia Wells's house.

For about five minutes I had my finger jammed to the tiny black button on the front door before I got a response. Traveling voices looped behind me in boisterous conversation. Out of the corner of my eye I glimpsed a group of young boys stumbling to school, jeans wobbling below their hips.

Movement inside the house incited me to press the buzzer harder. I heard a sound, like someone cursing; it had that distinct throaty flavor of a man who'd just woken up.

Julia opened the door wrapped in a dusty purple terrycloth robe tied at the waist with a long sash. On seeing me she glanced furtively up the stairs behind her.

"Do you know what time it is?" she said.

"Time for slugs to eat salt." I knocked her flat as I bulldozed my way into the house, reaching the stairs in a bound. Two at a time, I darted up the steps. By the time she recovered her voice and screamed Big-Six's name I had already gained the top. I drew the Glock from its sheath under my coat. In front of me was a dark tight passageway made even more constricted by the presence of large boxes packed on top of each other on my right.

Big-Six must not have heard Julia's siren because he came out of the bathroom naked as a manatee, his face lit up with a smile. I could only think he must've been expecting a morning present from his girlfriend. When he saw me his eyes froze and his body went awkwardly limp. He may've lost all motor senses for that instant.

I'd seen it happen to many hardened criminals, men you'd think would be immune to such a reaction just by the nature of their way of life. One guy even lost control of his bowels in the shock of having a bunch of weary-eyed narcos, smelling of last night's funk, bust in on him while he was fucking his girlfriend at five o'clock in the morning. I can't imagine any woman finding anything romantic about a man nutting and shitting at the same time, especially if that's the last memory you'll have of that man for a while.

I slithered up to Big-Six, my gun pointed directly at his eyes. Julia was still screaming and I could hear her scrambling up the stairs.

My mouth inches from Big-Six's ear, I said, "Where's the bedroom?"

He blinked and nodded his head away from me.

I pushed him forward. "Move."

He stumbled and fell against the boxes, bouncing off and twirling down the corridor on jellied legs. I followed at his heel into the room at the end of the hall. I pushed him inside and closed the door, leaning against it to keep Julia at bay.

"Who paid you to park the politician?"

He sat at the edge of the rumpled bed. The light in the room came from a low-intensity bulb in a walk-in closet whose door was open; thick purple blinds were drawn covering the two windows. I could feel his thought tumbling out through his almost colorless eyes.

He sniffled as if he had a cold. "You the man?"

"I got the gun, asshole. That makes me the man. Who paid you?"

He got up and stepped toward the closet.

"Don't move."

"Man, can I get some clothes to cover my shit?"

Julia had reached the bedroom; she began banging at the door screaming, her voice shrill. "Open this muthafucking door or I'll call the police!"

It seemed that her voice was all Big-Six needed to morph into his bravura street persona. A rigid smile scuffed his pale face and his sculpted body slumped into a leaden defiant posture. "So, you ain't the man. You must be the freak who came looking for me yesterday."

"Sit your stupid ass down."

"Man, I shit punks like you in my dreams."

"I don't care if you blow smoke rings out your ass on Good Friday. This ain't no dream. And if you don't sit your ass down I'll turn that little thing you got there into a freaking memory." I pointed the gun at his dick.

That thought sucked the defiance out of his eyes, which clouded with doubt.

"Sit down," I ordered.

He scotched again at the end of the bed. Something smacked against the door outside, the impact echoing inside the room like a bell in a belfry.

"You open this door right now!" Julia screamed.

"If you got proof I baked this dude why didn't you bring the weight?" Big-Six said.

"I wanna know who paid you."

"Your shit's punk, man, and you know it. Unless you plan to do something other than wave that toy in my face you better get outta my sight. I'll forget that you're trespassing. I may be the one undressed but you're naked, cuz."

I could tell Big-Six was about to try something by the edgy lean that fell from his shoulders. He rushed across the room, head down. I sidestepped and clubbed him behind the neck, sending him asprawl on the floor. But the attack forced me to shift my weight from against the door, giving Julia time to barrel her way inside.

Her unwieldy swipe at my head with what looked like a clothes iron missed as I ducked out of the way. I grasped a clump of her hair and twisted. She spun twice around screaming, swinging her weapon in a wide arc. The clump of hair came off in my hand. Extensions. I made another grab at her and latched on to the sash of her robe and tugged. She lurched toward me. The sash released and her robe fell open. Her huge breasts lay flat on her chest like deflated footballs, her stomach protruding as if she were pregnant.

Big-Six had gotten to his feet and before I could stop him, he rushed past me through the open door. I turned to go after him, but having recovered from the minor embarrassment of her abrupt striptease

Julia took another swing at me. I ducked, caught her by the waist, and threw her to the floor.

I rushed down the stairs. By the time I got to the street he'd disappeared. The street was empty. I went back inside the house as Julia came down the stairs.

She smiled, keeping the robe wrapped close to her body with crossed arms. "Listen, that was all an act. I had to do it. Otherwise he'd be on my ass for not doing anything to help him."

"It wasn't very convincing," I said.

"Really?"

"You should try method acting."

"I thought that's what I was doing."

"Here's some advice. Write that loser out of your life."

"I got bills, you know. Acting don't pay the bills."

"You may pay with your life if you don't get away from that guy."

Before she could react I opened the door and went out into the softening mist.

I WAS crossing the Brooklyn Bridge when my phone rang. It was Agent Kraw.

"I've got your phone records."

"That was quick," I said.

"You complaining?"

"Not on your life. I'm passing that way."

"You don't know where I am."

"I stand corrected. Where are you?"

"A diner off the BQE, near La Guardia. I can drop this off at your house this evening."

"No, I'll pick them up if you're gonna be there for the next fifteen minutes."

"I'll be here."

"What's the name of the place?"

"Lucky Stars. Exit Five A. Can't miss it."

. . .

TWENTY-FIVE minutes later I pulled into the Lucky Stars parking lot, which was next to one of those hot-sheets motels that always seemed to point the way to airports. I stepped through the aroma of fried bacon inside the chromed pit stop, crowded with tattooed truck drivers and beer-bellied Port Authority cops. Agent Kraw sat alone at the back of the mobile-home-styled eatery, which was roomier inside than I'd expected.

When she saw me she closed the green folder she was reading and pushed it to the side. Approaching her, I unbuttoned my leather jacket and smiled. She peered over her glasses as I sat down in the red vinyl booth. In front of her was a plate with remnants of what looked like hamburger.

"So, you are a meat eater," I joked.

She winced. "Not wild meat though."

I laughed. "What brings you out here?"

Her voice was flat and sour. "None of your business."

"Sorry. You've got something for me?"

"After you give me what I want."

"I can't give you what I don't have."

She took off her glasses and dangled them in front of her face. "Then I have nothing for you."

"I think I can get what you want, though."

She licked her lips. "That's not good enough."

"It's the best I can do."

"You're a goddamn liar, Blades."

"I thought you Midwesterners were supposed to be polite people. Give me until morning."

She reached for the green folder, pulled out two pages stapled together, and slid them across the table. I sensed a shadow over my shoulder and looked up. A lanky waitress with a bird face was standing behind me, a pained expression on her face as is she'd been working a double shift and needed to sit down.

"Nothing for me," I said. "Just visiting."

She glared down at me for a second then lofted her gaze over to Agent Kraw.

"Can I have some more coffee, please?" Kraw said.

After the waitress had hustled away on swollen ankles, I stood up, folded the pages in half, and stuffed them in the inside pocket of my jacket.

"I'm through playing games with you, Blades. If I don't hear from you by tomorrow morning, I'm coming to arrest you," Agent Kraw said.

"On what charge?"

"Obstruction for starters. I'll think of something else by then. Let's see how cute your smile is when I fit bracelets on you."

I turned to leave.

"By the way," she started. "Just to show you what a good sport I am, I got you bonus coverage."

"On what?"

"The numbers. I got you a month of calls instead of the one night."

I buttoned my jacket and smiled.

I GOT BACK onto the BQE southbound making sure I wasn't followed. Crossing into Manhattan I drove north along the FDR, streaking by the dark apartment buildings of the Upper East Side, my mind slowly adjusting to the prospect of facing off against River. The ponderous East River showed no signs of life. No presence of barges or ships, just flat cold water. I checked once more to see if I had a tail before crossing Washington Heights and getting onto 9-A. I slipped Mingus into the cassette player and turned up the volume. It was going to be a long drive and I wished I'd brought something to eat.

A GRAY FOG drifted across the Hudson. Birds lifted off a jetty near Ossining, and like a dazzling squadron of fighters disappeared into the darkness. The black water shimmered, the gray mountains reflecting off its face. Wind shook the water and the flat silent waves broke out into ripples like tiny holes being pierced in black skin.

My cell phone jingled and I answered. It was Semin.

"Blades, I was about to hang up."

I turned the music down. "Sorry Semin, I didn't hear the phone."

"Where the hell are you? On a train?"

"In my car."

"Listen, I did find out that Malcolm Nails-Diggs spent some time on the island about the same time Dr. Heat was doing her charity stint. He was waiting to go on trial for a murder charge which was later dropped because a key prosecution witness developed water on the brain. But he was never her patient."

"Thanks, Semin."

"Sure."

And she was gone.

As much as I hated to do it, I had to rule out Dr. Heat as a suspect in Ronan's murder. That left the Russians. Ronan had been killed because of his business association with Rupert Chernin. What other explanation was there?

Still there was something nagging at me. I couldn't get past the idea that there was a connection between Marjorie Madden's death and Ronan's. I felt like I'd overlooked something. Like somewhere a clue was staring me in the face and I was staring blindly back at it. Right now, I was staring at something even more ominous. What was I going to do about River?

A BARGE crept painfully upriver greeting a tug boat at Croton-on-Hudson. At once the sun slashed through the mist, slicing the river in two. One half light. One half dark. Near the next town mountains rushed to life, dark and majestic; twin peaks like two red gods facing each other, changing the air around them. Another town appeared before me. Bleak buildings with FOR SALE signs all around.

. . .

TWO HOURS LATER when I reached the cabin in Albany black mist stretched tight across the sky covering the sleeping trees. It was six in the evening and everything seemed to be in suspense. Negus's Bronco was parked below the cabin. I pulled up behind it and killed the Volvo's engine, which whined and chugged as if it couldn't believe the long journey had come to an end. I slipped the safety off my Glock before tucking it into my waistband under my thigh-length jacket. Then I got out and walked around the back of the cabin.

The lake there was silent, green, and deadened by black mist. Beyond the lake ghostlike trees huddled together in sleep. Far in the distance I saw the tip of a light streak across the lake; it was the only dazzle to the evening.

I walked back to the front door. River was already standing there. I could see her shadow but not her entire body. Even from where I was I sensed a rigidity to her body that told me her guard was up. I assumed it was the paranoia the came with being hunted, a condition I was certainly familiar with. She opened the door as I got to it and stepped back. Her right hand, hanging at her side, held something dark.

I glanced down. "That's a big gun for a woman. Going hunting?"

"Just making sure you didn't have company," she said.

I laughed as the door closed behind me. She walked ahead of me through the dark house into the living room.

"What kind of gun is that?"

"FN forty-nine."

"Nice. Tested one of those once. Didn't like it. Heavy trigger pull."

"It does take some strength, yeah."

"What's the payload?"

"Forties. Nine ems."

"You ever killed anybody with it?"

"Not this particular one. I used one like this when I was a cop in Miami."

We stood eye to eye in the center of the room warmed by a fire in the hearth a few feet away. That savageness I'd seen in her eyes when she told me about the ambush was there now. Pulled back and tied into a ponytail, her long locks had been glossed with some kind of gel and smelled fresh.

"Don't the lights work?" I said.

"You afraid of the dark?"

"I try to stay away from dark places with beautiful women who're not my wife."

She pursed her lips and smiled. "You want some coffee?"

"You gonna put that forty-nine shit down?" I said.

"You gonna put the safety back on yours?"

I lifted up my coat, pulled the Glock from my waist, safetied and restored it. She stuffed her pistol into the waist of her black jeans.

"Do you take milk?" she said. "The coffee's fresh."

Feeling cornered I nodded. She left me in the living room and went into the kitchen. This woman was sharp; she'd observed every one of my actions in the car.

She returned with two New York Yankees mugs. I took one and sipped, tasting more milk than I liked in my coffee, but I wasn't in the mood to complain.

She sat down in a worn yellow sofa. "What brings you up here?"

I leaned against the curved archway, contemplating for a moment how to respond. There was no bullshitting this woman, and there was no way to be subtle or diplomatic about my concerns.

"Did you try to kill Noah?"

Her expression didn't change; it was clear that the question didn't surprise her. And that told me everything I needed to know. This was a moment she'd foreseen. It was becoming clear that this River was deeper than any ocean. She knew that I knew.

"I don't have a beef with him."

"Do you have one with me?"

"Did you kill my father?"

I hesitated. "It was self-defense. I had no choice."

Her voice was tight, guttural. "I can respect that."

"What does that mean?"

Her face became a mask in the shadows. "It means I have no beef with you."

I didn't quite believe her. "What about my father?"

"He's a rat and must suffer the fate of a rat."

I shifted the mug from my right hand to my left, readying myself to reach for my Glock with my right. "You'll have to kill me first."

"I don't want to have to kill you, Blades," she said.

"Your father was a murderer."

"My father was a revolutionary."

"He ambushed a cop."

"There was a war going on. It was justified."

"Look, I'm not interested in that debate. It's old. What went on between your father and my father has nothing to do with you and me. A lotta shit went down between those folks back then. A lotta milk turned sour. My father may've been a rat, but he's still my father. And I'm not gonna let you or anybody else kill him if only on that principle. I'm sure you can appreciate that. The question is, Where does that leave you and me?"

Her gaze dissolved inwards, so that even though she was facing me it was as though she wasn't there, as if she'd gone asleep, and then all at once, as if she awakened from a fitful sleep, her eyes were open, the red eyes of some ancient reptile, shiny as stones.

"Then I'm sorry," she whispered.

I did not see how it got there but the gun was in her hand.

It was not the first time I've had a gun pointed at me. More often than not, however, I was the one who got the drop on my adversary. For a second I considered going for my Glock. In a dark room sudden movement might make it difficult to get off a good shot. But I was a big target. And the steadiness with which River held that gun, and the calm directness of her eyes, told me I'd be taking a big chance.

"I don't think you want to kill me," I said. "You and I have a different history from our fathers. We don't have to repeat their mistakes."

"My father lived his life for revenge. And more than anything else that's what he taught me. Revenge is good. Revenge is cleansing."

"Your father abandoned his country. My father abandoned his family. I think you got the better of the deal. At least your father took you with him."

"I would rather have stayed behind. Playing with my dolls. Double-Dutching in the rain. Making ice cream and cake with my mom. But I had no mom. They took her too. All because of the lies your father told."

"Let's end this, River. Right now. Without any more killing."

She flinched slightly and opened her mouth to speak then closed it moistening her lips noisily. But a sliver of doubt seeped through the cloud of her hard stance. Her eyes wavered. "I don't see how that's possible."

"The thirst for revenge is self-destructive," I said. "Look at what happened to your father. If you kill me and my father how long will the satisfaction last? Where will it end? Will my daughter grow up to hunt you?"

"Your father cost me my family. My mother. My friends. Took away my life and sent me to hell. I hated Cuba. Hated the language. When we hopped over to Jamaica that was no better. I wanted to be in America. I wanted to be home. I hated everybody. So, you see, my father didn't have to work too hard to convince me that your father didn't deserve to live."

"Walk away from it, River."

"I've never walked away from anything in my life."

"Have you ever killed a friend?"

"I don't want to kill you."

"I've stuck my fucking neck out for you. The FBI or the Russians would have your ass right now were it not for me. My father has lived a miserable existence since then. Killing him will bring you no peace because you must kill me too. Can you really do that?"

My phone rang. The musical chime made her flinch. I put my hand up to say take it easy.

"Can I answer my phone?" I said.

She nodded. "Unbutton your jacket and open it so I can see where your hands are going."

I stooped to put the mug on the floor then I opened my jacket. My phone hung from my belt. I unclipped it slowly, flipped the mouthpiece down. "Yeah?"

From the other end came a sneering voice that raised the hair on my arm. "I warned you about fucking with me, Blades."

"How did you get this number?"

"How else? Your darling wife. She's here shitting her panties."

"You better be kidding."

"Tell me where the bitch is and you just might see your wife and daughter alive."

"I will shit on your coffin, you lizard."

"Fuck you!"

"Let me talk to my wife."

"Right now the only chips you have are the ones I loan you. Get me the girl or my money. Then we can play swap. You've got four hours."

"How do I know you have my wife?"

"Are you a gambler?"

The line went dead. I stared helplessly at River. The gun was still pointed at me, but it didn't matter anymore. I was walking out of there. If she wanted to shoot me, then that was her choice.

"He's got your family?"

I nodded. "He wants you or my family is dead. You wanna shoot me you're going to have to shoot me in the back because I'm going to get my family."

She lowered the gun. "I'm coming with you."

"I don't need you."

"You do. I have information that might help you."

"Like?"

"How to find Parkoff."

"You know where he is?"

"Remember I told you I wasn't running because I was afraid for myself? I knew he was capable of doing something like this if he found out that Papa Smooth was my brother."

By now I should've been immune to her surprises, but the shock must've registered on my face.

"I'll explain on the way," she said.

THIRTY-SIX

I hated leaving my car 300 miles away in the middle of nowhere, but taking the more powerful Bronco made sense. River drove like the devil had his horns stuck up her ass.

The Bronco was equipped with radar jammers and could easily notch 120 on six of its eight cylinders. River busted 90 before we hit the highway, tripping the speedometer as high as 110 as we flew down I-87. Her face was as intense as I'd ever seen it.

I called my house. Nobody answered. Next I called Kraw. Gave her a description of my wife's car. Parkoff claimed he had both my wife and my daughter, which meant he must've grabbed them sometime after three, the time Chez got out of school. My last call was to Lieutenant Terry Doyle in Queens. I explained what was going on. By the time I hung up an APB was out on my wife's car.

When I finished my calls River began to speak.

"Smooth and I are very different."

"Meaning he's not as bitter as you?"

"He's found an outlet for his pain. He sulked just about every day of the three years we spent in Cuba. But he liked Jamaica. Took to the culture right away. The music. The food. Didn't wanna leave. To him that's home. He thinks of himself as a Jamaican. I never forgot America. I never forgot what it did to my father."

"Who does Parkoff work for?"

"Some people in Miami. Maxwell was a consular officer stationed in Miami before he became deputy ambassador. Maxwell loved the good life. His wife had even more expensive tastes in clothes, jewelry, and all things luxurious. They had a house in Boca Raton and one in Long Island. Plus a bank account in Switzerland. But he was lazy. And had a pimp's mentality. The life of a diplomat for a tiny Caribbean island isn't very stressful, but it also doesn't pay all that well. He was always looking for another hustle."

"You said he was a transporter."

"For a few special clients."

"And his cargo?"

"Mainly dirty laundry. But he'd take anything as long as the money was right. Even drugs. The night he got popped he was bringing three quarters of a million dollars he'd picked up in Arizona to be deposited in a bank in the Bahamas."

"Belonging to Parkoff's people?"

She nodded.

"Did Parkoff kill Ronan?"

She took her eyes off the road momentarily to look at me. "I don't know."

"Did he kill Chernin?"

"I don't know that either. He could've. That's what he does."

"So where's the money?"

"Maxwell didn't have the money when he got to New York. The bag he was carrying was stuffed with paper."

"Wouldn't he have checked to see what was in the bag before he left Arizona?"

"He never checks the bag. Principle."

"Why would they give your boyfriend a bag of tissue and then pop him?"

"Maybe they knew something was wrong."

"Something like what?"

"I don't know."

"Why would Parkoff be after you for money they've already crooked?"

Then I recalled the story she told the night her boyfriend was killed. The bag had been switched in flight. I would bet anything the young man who'd sat next to Maxwell on the flight was her brother Smooth.

"Did Smooth and your boyfriend know each other?" I said.

She took a while before answering. "No."

"You had Smooth switch the bags, didn't you?"

She stared straight ahead, but her body had momentarily stiffened, that telltale sign of being caught unawares.

"That money is tainted with FBI blood. It's probably marked. It's no use to you."

She glanced sharply in my direction but said nothing.

"What's your involvement with these people?" I said.

"None. Not anymore. They own the club I used to manage in Miami. That's where I met Maxwell. And that's where I met Ronan."

I tried to keep the shock from infiltrating my voice. "You knew Ronan?"

"How do you think I found you? Ronan came into the club one night with Maxwell. Maxwell invited me over to their table. But he had to leave early. Ronan stayed. He was pretty drunk. Started talking about his father. It was just another story to me. I've heard them all. Until he mentioned that his father used to be a cop and had helped catch the infamous Carlos Petersen. After I got what I wanted I drove him back to his hotel."

"Did you fuck him?"

"Didn't have to. He'd already told me what I needed to know. How to find you."

WE MADE IT back to New York City in two and a half hours, having to cut across town because of an accident on West Street. The city seemed less alive. The lights had lost their dazzle, the people on the street were lethargic, without rhythm. New York had no vigor and I was deaf to its music.

There are times when your life is like a crippled animal dragging a steel trap through the woods. It needs help but can't ask for it. And it can't escape without help. And without help it will die. I was lucky to have people to go to for help. I called Kraw and Lieutenant Doyle. Nothing had changed. Neither the FBI nor the police had located my wife or her car.

"So how do I find Parkoff?" I said to River.

"He's got a joint in Red Hook. I'll take you there."

THIRTY-SEVEN

River piloted the Bronco toward Brooklyn. The heavy truck scrubbed the frozen crust off the New York night, the vivid scrawl of lights on the Manhattan skyline receding in the background as we boomed across the Brooklyn Bridge. At any moment I expected to hear police sirens chasing us. But River didn't seem to care. Neither did I. I was determined to find my family. Nothing was going to stand in my way. And knowing I had a kindred spirit in River, someone as stubborn as I was, comforted me.

My throat got dry and bubbles of sweat broke out all over my body as we blasted through Boerum Hill's hive of streets closing in on Red Hook. I was beginning to feel lightheaded, part tension, part hunger, as I hadn't eaten in a while.

We crossed beneath the elevated highway separating Red Hook from Carroll Gardens and drove for six or seven blocks along a quiet stretch of dark warehouses. At the next light we made a right turn onto Dikeman Street and crawled along.

"Right there on the right," River sang out. "Two twenty-four."

She drove past to the next block and stopped.

"You stay here," I said, unlatching my seat belt.

"You shitting me, right?"

I turned around to look at her. "My family might be in there. I don't want them dead."

"You think I'll screw things up?" She stared at me as if measuring my resolve. "I'm coming in with you. What if the cops roll up and see me sitting here like a shithead?"

"The cops don't venture into this neighborhood unless they've been called."

"I got you into this, Blades. And fuck me if you think I'm gonna sit here while you go in there alone."

"How'd you know about this house?"

"Maxwell brought me here once. He had to pick something up from Parkoff."

I readied my Glock, racking the slide to send a jacket into the chamber, and stepped out of the truck.

THE COBBLESTONE STREET was uncommonly dark; it appeared that several streetlights were dead. Red Hook was a rough neighborhood, long the domain of street gangs and wannabe wiseguys. Recently I'd read that similar to what was happening in Williamsburg, gentrification was beginning to sink its teeth in the tattooed ass of this neighborhood, as young artists shut out from SoHo, drawn by Red Hook's empty warehouses they could rent for a song, were settling in large numbers. You couldn't tell from surveying this street.

The air smelled of burning gasoline. A Pabst Blue Ribbon sign dangled from a building. Country and western music spilled out into the night but I couldn't tell where it came from. A pack of stray dogs steamed along in single file in front of us. The amplified *whoosh-whoosh* of fast-moving cars tearing along the highway overhead made the darkness more disquieting.

Walking quickly, upright, River was two lengths ahead of me, her right hand holding her pistol straight down at her side. She glanced left to right intermittently as she raced toward the detached brick ranch house.

I caught up to her on the frozen front lawn. We slid up to the front door in single file, our eyes tuned to the darkness by now.

No lights in the house.

I leaned ear to door listening for movement, but not a mouse squeaked.

I tested the door. Locked.

"Step aside," River whispered.

I turned. She was stuffing the gun into her waist. A tiny penknife appeared in her hand. She moved forward to the door, thrusting the tiny point into the keyhole. In a few seconds, *plick,* the lock released.

A helicopter appeared, its engine barking overhead. I stepped inside. River eased in behind me. We stood in the darkness; our ears testing the air for sound anywhere.

It smelled of paint or turpentine inside the house, but it could've been my senses still locked on the burning gasoline smell from outside. We were standing in a large room containing a sofa and little else. When my eyes had grown accustomed to the dark I stepped tentatively to the right up one step into the kitchen. I could feel River's warm breath on my neck as she followed close behind.

My phone rang.

"Shit!" I yanked it from my belt and turned it off. We hunched down expecting lights to be turned on. But nothing happened.

"I don't think there's anybody here," she whispered.

My gut told me she was right, but I had to be sure. "I'll check the back. Stay here."

She tapped my shoulder.

Wind blew in through an open window somewhere; I could almost taste the cool slap on my face. I crept along, my back stapled to the wall, my eyes focused down the corridor ahead. I reached the first bedroom. The door was open. I stuck my head inside. No sign of life. I crouched to one knee and peered inside to make sure there was no one hiding. The bed was made up with shiny white sheets. Through an open window I could see a woman moving in the house next door.

I backed out of that room. Two steps down the corridor was another bedroom, smaller than the first, but just as empty. Across the hall was the bathroom. I could hear the heavy drip of a leaking faucet.

It took only a few minutes to determine there was no one inside the bathroom either. From the unlived-in look it was clear that nobody had been in this house for a while.

I stepped into the hallway and felt a gray clamping pressure in my head. It wasn't a headache. It was as if someone was inserting bubbles into my skull. On the edge of panic I was having trouble breathing, keeping my focus. Where was my family?

I walked back along the corridor. River was not where I'd left her. I heard scuffling feet to my left and dipped to a knee, the Glock ready in firing position. River came out of the kitchen, her gun hanging at her side.

"Anything?" she said.

"I thought I told you to stay here."

"I was checking around. There's a little storeroom behind the kitchen. It's empty."

"I told you to stay here!"

"Jesus! What's your problem?"

"Let's get out of here."

She stuffed her gun into her waist and cleared her throat but said nothing. We stepped outside into the clear cool night. The wind blew up hard from the east, releasing the smell of gasoline trapped over the highway. I reached for my phone to call Kraw. Before I could dial it rang.

"Hello?"

"Blades! Oh thank God!"

"Anais! Where're you?"

"Home. We got away. Oh, Blades. I've never been so happy to hear your voice."

"Who's there with you?"

"The police. There're here."

"I'll be there in a minute."

"I love you, Blades."

I rang off from Anais and fell into River's arms.

BUSTING JUST ABOUT every traffic light or sign on my way, I made it home in fifteen minutes. Several police cruisers were parked on the block. One cop in uniform stood on the sidewalk, his fingers hooked inside his gun belt.

"I'm not coming in if that's okay with you," River said.

"That's fine. And thanks."

She smiled and patted my hand. She was really a beautiful woman when that savageness was gone from her eyes. I got out.

The uniformed cop on the sidewalk started to yell at me as I raced across the lawn. Several more policemen in uniform guarded the door; one of them went into a crouch, reaching for his weapon when he saw me barreling toward them. Then as if he recognized me he straightened up and stepped aside, opening the door. I ran straight into the living room, past my father leaning on the doorjamb.

Flanked by two detectives and a sergeant with notepads, Anais scotched on the edge of the couch as if she was an intruder, a criminal waiting to be hauled away by police. She stood up when she heard me come in. I ran to her, clasping her in my arms. Feeling her heart throb against the force of my body took my breath away.

After a while I said, "Where's Chez?"

"Upstairs."

"How is she?"

"Asleep." She began to cry.

She had just picked Chez up from school after purchasing dark unsweetened chocolate and a few other items at the gourmet market on Court Street.

After making sure Chez was buckled into her seat she turned

around to start the car. But she had made a mistake not locking the doors right after getting in.

The man who yanked the back door open must've approached from the rear because she did not see him. She felt the large shadow present in the car about the same time he levered the gun at Chez's head. She spun around. A large yellow hand was clamped around Chez's mouth. His eyes were a speckled gray, as if they'd been doused with ashes.

"Scream and her brain is dog food," he said.

There was no snarl on his face, no bark in his voice. In fact, his demeanor was so calm you'd think he had come to invite them to a meditation workshop at the Healing Center around the corner.

She couldn't have screamed even if he hadn't ordered her not to. Her voice was caught up in her throat, entangled with briars of fear. Chez's eyes were frozen stiff in shock.

He massaged Chez's temple with the shiny gun. "Drive."

Anais remained paralyzed in that position. She couldn't turn around. She couldn't take her eyes off Chez's face.

"Drive," he said again.

Still hadn't raised his voice. Soft and almost polite as before. How could a man so ugly not have hidden fangs? How could a man so vile as to put a gun to a child's head and threaten to kill her not have a snarl?

But as much as she wanted to obey him she couldn't move.

"Drive, bitch!"

There was the evil snarl she expected. Just like in the movies it activated her motor neurons. And her voice came back.

"Who're you?" Her voice was unrecognizable to her. She was wheezing.

A smile broke out at the chapped corners of his fat red lips. "Call your husband. I'm sure he remembers me."

"What do you want?" Anais begged.

"I want you to drive the fucking car. Now!"

She turned around, away from the scream of his face, away from the shock in Chez's eyes. Away from the reality of danger but smack up against the prospects conjured in her mind by fear. Were they going to die?

She jerked the ignition key but the SUV's engine refused to kick, as if it somehow knew it would be transporting illegitimate cargo. But the BMW's dalliance would only be temporary. It was too sophisticated a machine to suffer engine failure, especially one inspired by its owner's fear. The engine spurted; she slid the car into drive.

He directed her to the BQE; they drove south then east for an hour. He remained quiet throughout, giving her time to collect her scattered emotions. Perhaps he wasn't going to kill them after all. But what did he want?

Somewhere heading east on the Long Island Expressway he asked for her cell phone and asked for my number. She unhooked it from her belt and handed it to him.

After he rang off he leaned back and laughed. "If your husband loves you as much as he hates me you're a lucky woman."

She didn't answer, glancing into the rearview mirror to see if Chez was okay. That stricken look had not left Chez's eyes.

He opened the bag she'd placed on the backseat and after rummaging around got hold of the bar of chocolate. "Ah, chocolate." He read the label. "European, eh? I must say you have good taste for a nigger."

He stripped the wrapper away and bit off two nuggets of the dark bar. His tiny eyes lit up. "Have you ever tried Korkunov? You'd like that one."

He offered chocolate to Chez, who just stared at him. He shrugged and bit off another chunk, bopping his head as he hummed a tune, his eyes boring into Chez.

"You have a family?" She spoke to distract him, to get his focus away from Chez.

"No. I'm too ugly to find a wife," he said, laughing in a self-deprecating way. "But this is America. Money can buy anything you want. Even a wife."

"You have an accent. Where're you from?"

"Just drive the fucking car. Where I'm from is of no importance to you." He turned to Chez. "What's your name?"

"Where're we going?" Anais said quickly.

"We're just out for a drive like a happy American family."

In the rearview mirror she could see him staring at Chez.

"You're a very pretty girl," he said to Chez.

"Do you like America?" Anais interrupted.

He chuckled. "I hate America. You people don't know how to enjoy life. You think you own the world. You have too much of everything. You can't appreciate life that way. It's all too easy. You know how to spend money, but you don't know how to enjoy life. You don't even know the meaning of life."

"People enjoy life better in your country, I suppose."

"Of course. They have less money, but they know how to enjoy life. Russian girls are happier back home than they are in America. You know why? Because they can be women in Russia. They come over here and they want to be like men. Women weren't made to be like men."

"Is that where you're from? Russia?"

He opened the window and stuck his head out and screamed at the wind rushing by. When he pulled his head back inside his eyes were ragged-looking, no nuance whatsoever about the stupid look on his face, his mouth slack as a wilted flower.

"I used to have a family," he said with a sibilant slur.

"What happened to them?"

"What do you think?" He laughed. "You are so stupid. You Americans with your optimism. You want the whole world to think like you. And when they don't you bomb them. And you think you're so rational. You can't figure me out, so stop trying."

"Is it irrational for me to think that only a man with a lonely heart could do what you're doing, or what you plan to do?"

"I did it for years. Somebody did it to my family."

"Somebody killed your family?"

He stared at Chez. "She doesn't look like you. My daughter looked like me."

"How were they killed? Was it in a war?"

"It doesn't matter. My wife is dead. My daughter is dead. And I will kill you and your daughter if your husband doesn't hand over my stuff. It's not personal."

EVENING HAD slithered away into the Long Island Sound by the time he instructed her off the Expressway and through a small fishing town. There weren't any noticeable landmarks, and having spent little time on Long Island, Anais had no idea where she was.

They drove along a narrow gravel road up to a small cottage. He made her park next to a wooden shed behind the house and ordered her to wait in the car while he got out, lifting Chez out with him, his thick arm around her waist. The minute he touched Chez she started crying. The distraction gave Anais time to open her bag and position the .25 within easy grasp. When he opened the driver's door for her after putting Chez on the ground, she hooked the handbag over her arm and got out, staring into his eggshell-colored eyes. She was still scared but now she had a plan.

In single file he marched them up to the cottage. There he handed her a key to unlock the door. His fingers were short and thick and he was missing his pinkie finger on the left hand. The chug of a motorboat beat the silence into submission, the wind icy on her face. She could see a fire growing in the distance beyond the black flat body of water reflecting lights from houses around.

There was hardly any furniture inside. A few broken down chairs and little else. The air was musty; the odor of old unwashed socks that had been locked away for months filling the house. He herded them into a bedroom and flicked on the light on the wall.

He said, "You can relax in here. Don't close the door and don't try to open the window. We'll call your husband again in fifteen minutes to see if he's ready to make a deal."

He closed the door. She listened to his footsteps retreating until there was silence. Chez was still crying and Anais drew her close. Beside the unmade bed, the tiny bedroom only held a small mirror on a bureau.

"Shhh! It's gonna be okay." She smoothed Chez's hair, leveling it around her face. "Sit on the bed."

She waited until Chez was sitting on the bed, then she drew a deep breath. Her heart was pounding. Her mouth was dry and hot. Opening her bag she took out the .25-caliber pistol and hid it behind her back. She went to the window and banged on it with her handbag until it shattered.

He came storming into the room.

She fired.

He fell to the floor.

Grasping Chez by the hand she stepped over him and flew from the house. In the BMW she wasted no time with seat belts, locking the door as soon as they were inside. She powered the SUV through the gravel, spitting up a white cloud of dust and noise, refusing to look behind her until she was already speeding along the tiny street leading to a ramp onto the highway.

Half a mile down the highway she saw a Nassau County police cruiser heading her way.

Flashing her emergency lights and honking her horn she managed to draw their attention. She didn't want to go back but the police needed her to show them the location of the cottage since she hadn't been alert enough to log street names in her memory.

When they got there Parkoff was gone.

THIRTY-EIGHT

What do you mean he was gone?" I exclaimed. "Didn't you shoot him?"

"I think so. He fell down."

"How close were you when you fired?"

"About ten feet."

"Are you sure you hit him?"

"Jesus, Blades, I don't know. I didn't have time to check for exit wounds."

"I'm sorry, honey." I took her in my arms.

"I'm just happy to be alive."

I closed my eyes and held her, trying to blot out the wolves howling in the dark behind my eyes, trying to stir visions of her smile, but all I saw were Parkoff's lizard eyes. I kissed her neck and tasted the salt of her fear. I imagined it was his blood.

"I'm going upstairs to look in on Chez," I said. "Then I'm going out again. I won't be back until I know that fucker is dead."

The police sergeant creased his weathered face and folded his lips inward. "We can't let you do that, Mr. Overstreet."

"Can't let me do what, Sergeant?"

A tortured smile got trapped at the corner of his bloodless lips as he frowned. "You've just threatened to kill a man. That could get you arrested."

I stood erect, a head taller than he was, and smiled. "I didn't threaten to kill anybody. I said I wouldn't be back until I know he's dead."

I FOUND Chez fast asleep. Tempted to wake her though I was, the sight of her so calm and relaxed after her ordeal tempered my desire to hold her in my arms. As I was about to leave the room, Anais entered. She came directly to me, enclosed me in her arms, and began to sob.

"It's going to be all right, baby," I reassured.

She clung to me as if she was drowning and I was a lifeboat. "I've never felt anything like that in my life," she wailed.

"It's over now."

"I can still see his eyes. I can still smell him."

I held her, doing my best to absorb the fury of her shock, unable to find any words to take away her pain.

She stepped away from me, wiping her eyes with long slender fingers. "Please don't go out tonight."

"The police will be guarding the house. You'll be safe."

"Blades, I need you tonight."

"I'm here." I bowed my head.

ANAIS TOOK two sleeping pills and was knocked off her feet by 12:30. I called Lieutenant Doyle. Parkoff hadn't shown up at any hospital. I suspected the bullet might've grazed his head, stunning him briefly, but nothing more. I looked out the bedroom window. A police cruiser sat outside. I got dressed, checked the clip in my gun, stuffed it in my waist, and went downstairs to get my jacket. I found my father playing chess with himself in the kitchen.

He looked up when I entered the room. "How's Anais?"

"Laid out like a corpse. Where were you today? I called here and nobody answered the phone."

He leaned back against the chair. "I don't like that tone."

"I'm sorry."

"I spent the day with your mother."

"Really?"

"Really. We had a nice long talk."

"About?"

"Things. Life. Death."

"Death?"

"It's all around us these days. Can't you see? And you? Where're you going?"

I buttoned my jacket but said nothing.

"You're going out to hunt that man, aren't you?" he said.

"What would you have me do, Pop? Run and hide?"

"One day I hope you forgive me for running away," he said quietly.

"There's nothing to forgive."

"Stop trying to be so goddamn tough, Carmen."

"You don't know me."

"I know this person you're trying to be. That's not you. That's you trying to not be me."

"You gave up the right to talk like you know me."

His eyes fell back to the chessboard. When he lifted them again they held ingots of pain. I could see the effort in his face to mask the anger. He stood up. "Yes, I ran away. But I never stopped loving you. You wanna be a tough guy? Stay home with your wife."

I walked toward the door, lifting my keys out of my pocket and twirling them on my finger. Sour bile surged up to my throat and I felt a burning in my stomach. I knew what it was but tonight I would ignore it. Let my stomach burn. The only thing that could settle my stomach was removing Parkoff's stench and the nightmare of his soulless eyes from my wife's consciousness.

. . .

MY FIRST STOP was an all-night deli on Flatbush where I got two packs of Big Red. It'd been awhile since I'd felt like this: armed, a little crazed, a hunter with a cause. It'd been a long time since I chewed Big Red, the gum that kept me company on long stakeouts when I was a narco. Somewhere in the pith of my consciousness I knew I should've felt ashamed for getting so amped about this hunt. Any rational thinking person would. But I'd lost patience with rationalism; sometimes being an animal was less taxing on the brain.

I'd always thought that my brother's drug addiction and the sight of him buying drugs in the park on Fourth Avenue was what spurred me into the NYPD. My thinking was that if I could get rid of all the drug dealers then my brother would be safe. Of course, experience quickly snuffed out those romantic notions. It became clear that keeping drugs off the street was a Sisyphean task and my job became more about the chase, outwitting and outthinking the dealers. It became more about inflicting pain and punishment on barbaric men and women who didn't care who they hurt in their thirst for money than about bringing them before the courts, because we knew that there, justice didn't always prevail. We were sometimes brutal, often looking the other way if a member of the team decided that thumping on a suspect was more efficient than arresting him. I thought I'd put that savage life behind me. But this adrenaline rush I was getting told me I was a long way from being cured. I'd been living a big lie. Out here, in the bleakness of this cavernous New York night, armed to kill under a sky that sprouted ghosts, I somehow felt freer than I'd ever felt.

My jaws pumping relentlessly, I funneled my wife's SUV through the hollow darkness of Red Hook's silent streets, refusing to let my dark mood be subdued by the constant swooshing of traffic sailing along at high speeds on the elevated Gawanus Expressway.

Popping another fresh stick of gum into my mouth, I parked under a broken streetlamp on Dikeman half a block away from the house

River and I had searched earlier. I hadn't told the FBI nor the police about this house.

A hooded bowlegged youth came toward me walking a white pit bull on a long leash. I let them pass, then turned my head to watch until they were out of sight before stepping out of the truck. Sliced in half by a batch of wandering black clouds the silvery moon sailed high above as I crept up to the house. I was calm, in control of my emotions now. Big Red had worked its magic on me.

The house was still bathed in darkness. I tested the door. It was still unlocked, the way we'd left it. I suspected that Parkoff wasn't there but I rang the bell anyway. No response from inside.

I stepped back onto the linen of dirt on the lawn.

AN HOUR LATER I was running out of gum. My mind began to fill up with scenarios that I had no way of certifying. Parkoff could be dead. Or there might be another safe house somewhere that River didn't know about. Maybe he'd decided to leave the city. I popped my last piece of gum and resolved to wait until daybreak. My Glock lay on the seat. The cold was beginning to get to me.

ABOUT THREE-THIRTY my phone rang.

"Blades, where're you?" It was Kraw.

"In my bed."

"Don't lie to me. Are you stalking Parkoff?"

"That's your job, isn't it?" I said sarcastically.

"Yes, it is. And you can stuff that sarcasm up your ass. Where's she?"

"Gotta go."

I hung up the phone because headlights from a vehicle that had just turned the corner illuminated my car. Lowering my head out of sight I waited for the vehicle to pass. After it went by I inched up until I could see without showing my full head. The black Jeep slowed down then turned, chugging to a stop in the driveway of Parkoff's house. I hefted the Glock off the seat. It was warm and comforting in my hand.

As soon as the driver killed the Jeep's lights I got out of my car. Glock in hand, in a deep crouch beneath the visual plane of the occupants, I darted up to the rear of the vehicle.

With my back pressed to the Jeep's skin I checked to see if anything or anyone else was coming down the block. Slowly, I rose up enough to peer into the truck. I made out one head: the driver. It appeared that he was alone, but I couldn't tell if it was Parkoff. Adrenaline surged through my veins.

Heart racing.

Chest tightening.

A dog after a bitch in heat.

For a second I felt lightheaded. Taking deep puffs of cold air to water down the thick adrenaline rush I waited for the driver to get out.

I heard the door open. This I knew would activate the roof-light of the car, so I quickly bobbed my head up hoping it'd be enough to get a look at the driver. It was Parkoff. I glanced quickly around the edge of the taillights to see his dark clad leg land on the running board. Gripping the gun firmly with two hands I slid around the black skin of the Jeep just as Parkoff finished donning his cap. His legs were out of the Jeep but his body leaned inside.

I jammed the gun into his back. "Don't move!"

He froze. I grabbed his coat and pulled his head and body into view. He had a large bag of potato chips in one hand and a quart of gin in the other.

"Drop them," I ordered.

The bottle and bag fell to the ground, the bottle exploding with a thick *splat*.

"Keep your hands up where I can see them."

He slurred. "You better shoot me now if you're going to kill me."

I frisked him and found an automatic jammed into his waist. I removed it, stuffed it into my belt, and pushed him forward. "You can't wait to die, I'm sure."

A swirling gust of wind swept the street as we crossed the tiny front lawn, picking up strands of loose paper and tossing them over the fence of the house next door. Zooted into next week, Parkoff wobbled up to the front door, his legs seemingly going in a different direction than his body.

"I have to take my hands down to get my keys," he said, his voice thick and almost unintelligible.

"Kick it. It's open."

He kicked the door and fell facedown inside. The door slashed open, banging hard against the wall, the sound vibrating around the howling wind. I stepped in and closed the door. Knowing the location of the light switch proved advantageous. I was able to flick the switch without taking my eyes off him. Perhaps expecting me to be lost in the dark he rolled over and tried to leg whip me. I hopped over his thrashing legs.

Grasping the hood of his down coat I dragged him to the middle of the room. He rolled onto his stomach and groaned.

It was cold in the house. I sat at the edge of the dusty sofa, my mind softening at the sight of Parkoff curled up on the floor. He sat up slowly and turned to face me. His face was white as a mime's mask, his tiny eyes bulging wider than a frog's. There was a tiny spawn of blood caked on the side of his head below a flesh wound. I suspected that was where Anais's bullet had grazed him.

"Did you kill Ronan?" I said.

"Somebody else got to him first."

"Who?"

"Whip me if I know or care. Politicians make all kinds of enemies." He groaned again and smiled, his upper lip cocked sinisterly. "You could've prevented all of this. All I wanted was the money."

"What you gonna get is a bullet."

His expression didn't change, but his eyes sunk deep into his skull. He blew his nose in his hands, then scrawled his scum-filled hands across the front of his jacket. "Your wife couldn't kill me. And you can't either."

"You stink so much she probably thought you were already dead."

"So pull the trigger if you've got the balls. Because if you don't I'm going to kill you unless you give me the girl or my money."

He saw the hesitation in my eyes and laughed, unbuttoning his coat as he struggled up off the ground. "Your wife's got more balls than you."

I stared at his leering face and realized I couldn't pull the trigger.

"See you around." He dropped his coat to the floor and turned to walk away.

"Stop." I unhooked my phone to call Agent Kraw.

He stumbled a few more steps.

I got up and followed him, pressing the gun into his neck. "I said stop."

With a quick shift of his head he ducked and spun bulldozing into me. The blow sent me lurching backward. I stumbled, attempting to regain my balance. He was on me with the viciousness of a rabid dog, following up his shoulder tackle with a kick to my groin. The pain flew straight to my head setting off bells ringing in my ears and the gun slipped from my fingers as I slammed into the floor. He leapt on me, scooping up the gun, which had fallen near his foot. He put the gun to my head, his eyes wild, his shirt open exposing a nest of tiny snakes.

"They say when you die you don't feel a thing," he sneered.

"Then enjoy your trip to hell." The woman's voice came from behind us.

Parkoff spun around. River shot him twice in the head.

I grabbed the gun from Parkoff's hand as he fell to the floor. I rolled away from his twitching body and when River refocused on me my gun was already pointed at her heart.

"What're you doing?" she said, still crouched.

"What're you doing here?" My eardrums pulsed from the reverb of the big gun exploding.

She straightened up and brought her gun down. "I spoke to your father. He said you went hunting. Figured this was the game."

"I'm going to ask you one more time and don't lie to me. Did you try to kill Noah?"

"That wasn't me."

"Who was it?"

"Look, Blades, my head's been fucked up for a long time; I'd be the first to admit that. Yeah, I got close to you because I wanted to find your father. But I've learned something from you. People can change what's in their heart if they want to. You've been a friend to me. And I want to change what's in my heart because I care about you. And I love Chez. I didn't try to kill your friend and I have no intention of trying to kill your father. I stepped off that battleship when I saw how lost you looked after you got that call from Parkoff. I knew I'd have to kill you if I took out your father. I couldn't imagine what that would do to Chez."

"What about your brother?"

"You don't have to worry about Smooth."

THIRTY-NINE

We lodged Parkoff's gun into his hand and squeezed off two rounds into the wall. Then we called the police. The story we gave them was credible enough: I'd come to see Parkoff to ask him to stay away from my family. He pulled a gun and threatened to kill me. We struggled and I was fortunate that River arrived in time to save my life.

As we left the scene together, foaming wind fanned the oatmeal-thick fog which had settled over Brooklyn like a giant gleaming spaceship, whipping at Brooklyn's dusty corners, threatening to uproot trees, sucking up every loose scrap of dirt and paper off the ground and turning them into tiny missiles.

"You okay?" River said to me, standing next to my car.

"As a horse."

She smiled, her loosened dreadlocks swept by the wind. "You better clean that shit off before you go home."

"Where're you going?"

"Somewhere to get drunk."

"That helps you forget?"

"Nothing helps you forget, you must know that. It just makes the time go by faster. Or at least it seems that way. Death is lamentable.

Once you kill another person you're wounded for life. But people like Parkoff are lesions, cancers. Sometimes you have to kill it to save a life."

I saw the ache in her eyes before she walked away, struggling against the wind.

"Hey," I called.

She paused, turning slowly.

"You better give the FBI their money back. Call their field office in Manhattan and ask for Agent Kraw. She might even give you a finder's fee."

Without a reply she turned and walked away. I lost her in the fog. A few minutes later I heard the heavy purr of the Bronco waking up. I was already in my car when she rolled by, steaming the vapor with powerful lamps.

I SAT IN the X5 for some time reliving the nightmare trying to think of how I was going to bind Anais's anger. The raw smell of death finally made it past the stubborn centurions guarding my senses.

My jacket had been scorched with blood and tissue from the close-range blast of River's big FN 49; my eardrums still shivered. I took the jacket off and flung it across the passenger seat. Something spilled from the pocket onto the floor. I reached over and picked it up.

My mind was so far away from reality, for a moment I looked at it not recalling what it was and where I'd gotten it. It was a list of telephone numbers. Then I remembered meeting Kraw earlier. I perused the list making a mental note to call on J'Noel Bitelow later so we could go over the list.

My eyes caught a number that seemed vaguely familiar. I stared at it for a while thinking. I'd called the number recently. But when?

Like a rod between the eyes it hit me. I took out my wallet hoping to find the piece of paper on which I'd copied the number Noah had given me. I still had it. I compared the two numbers. Perfect match. What were my eyes telling me?

I continued to stare at the number. The call was made on the same night and roughly half an hour after Ronan was gunned down. And then I noticed something else. The number appeared more than once. In fact there was a pattern of repeated calls late at night over a month. I checked the calling number. J'Noel's home number. And then it occurred to me that based on the frequency these calls were probably not made by Malcolm Nails-Diggs, but by J'Noel Bitelow herself. Besides, Malcolm was in no condition to call anyone the night Ronan was killed.

What could J'Noel and Dr. Palmer have in common to be calling each other so often? What strange bed had J'Noel and Dr. Chris Palmer made together? I now saw that J'Noel had been the link all along. She'd done a good job lying to me.

I closed my eyes and leaned my head back against the headrest. I didn't want to think about this shit anymore. The adrenaline burnout left me exhausted and my head felt too heavy to lift up off the headrest.

HIGH WINDS scattered rain down the mountainside. I was drenched, yet my throat was parched and I felt as if I'd been running all day and night. There were voices above me, loud singing in a language I could not understand. And there was a strange sound like the wings of large birds beating the air. I looked up but whatever it was that hung above me was made invisible by the thick rain clouds. I kept running up the mountainside until I reached a clearing at the top. The singing had stopped. And the beating sound had disappeared. There standing under the wide wings of a massive oak, his eyes whiter than daybreak, was Billy Franklin, an unarmed drug dealer I'd shot to death when I was a cop.

I WAS JERKED out of the dream by bells ringing. The faint light of dawn had slipped past me leaving a soft glow. I blinked several times before I realized my phone was ringing. When I answered it was Anais crying.

"Where're you, Blades? Come home."

"He's dead, Anais."

"I don't care. Come home."

"Did you hear what I said?"

But she'd already hung up.

SLY DAWN toting a slate gray sky shadowed the low-slung buildings to the east. A pickup truck, its engine sputtering like a mad cow, wheezed toward me. I started the SUV and drove off feeling a welt thickening in my throat that ordinarily might signal the beginning of a cold. But I knew what had brought on this feeling.

I had just participated in the death of another human being. This was my mind telling my body that all was not well with my conscience, that I could not easily absolve myself of guilt though I knew Parkoff was an evil man.

I had crossed the Gowanus Bridge and was about to weave my way into the burgeoning traffic on the Prospect Parkway when I remembered the telephone list. There was one thing left for me to do before I went home to Anais.

I ARRIVED AT J'Noel's apartment building around 6:25, as Brooklyn stuttered from sleep. Nearby, Flatbush Avenue clamored with buses rumbling over rutted roads setting the morning humming. I knew I smelled like shit. Looking like shit was no big deal, but I hated to smell bad. Right now it couldn't be helped.

I had to buzz the door downstairs several times before anyone answered. The intercom squawked and a woman's voice still trapped in sleep spat irritation.

"Police," I barked. "Open up."

"What you want?"

"Just open the door, lady."

The intercom went dead.

Bzzzzz went the door.

I pushed and entered, releasing the heavy metal door to bang shut behind me.

The elevator was waiting. I rode up alone, wondering what it took for these two women from such different backgrounds to form their murderous tryst. How much money did it take to secure J'Noel's streetwise expertise?

Parkoff didn't kill Ronan, for I believed him to be the kind of killer who proudly claimed his scalps. I was convinced that the telephone calls between J'Noel and Ronan's ex-wife were for one purpose, and if what I suspected was true then J'Noel Bitelow would be long gone.

Standing in front of apartment 9E I banged firmly on the door.

A woman's raspy voice. "Who there?"

"Open the door. Police matter."

"What wrong?" she spat back.

"Ma'am, you don't want us to break down your door, do you?"

She must've been standing behind the door because it cracked open seconds later.

A plump face, swamped in confusion, sleep-red eyes fixed in a startled stare, peeked out at me. "You the police?"

"Are you J'Noel's mom?"

"She ain't here."

"Where's she?"

"Is this about that crazy man she was seeing?"

"Can I come in?"

"She ain't here, I tell yuh."

"I still need to come in." I said.

She opened the door wide enough for me to slip into the passageway. It smelled of puke.

"Look, I telling you the truth. J'Noel not here. She pack she suitcase and take off yesterday morning. If you want to search the house you could search it but you ain't go find she in here."

The woman's morning alcohol-laced breath fanned out above my nose.

I stepped to the side. "Where did she go?"

She stepped back. Probably got a whiff of my funk.."Trinidad. She and Malcolm gone to stay with my mother."

"Is that where she was born?"

"She come here when she was three. Ain't never been back since."

Her voice was passionate and sincere. I concluded she was telling the truth.

"Thank you, ma'am."

"I know why she run back. She afraid of his family. They threaten her. He deserved it, that fella. He was always beating her. I woulda done the same thing if it was me."

I turned away, walking toward the elevator. I didn't have the heart to tell her that her daughter was a murderer.

TEN MINUTES LATER I saw Dr. Palmer come out of her house as I pulled the truck curbside. I got out and silently approached as she was locking her front door. She was dressed smartly in a tan pants suit; a light-brown raincoat flopped in the crook of her left arm, a brown leather briefcase slung over her right shoulder. When she turned around I was there, two feet away on the porch.

"Good morning, Chris."

Startled, she stiffened like a soldier at inspection, her keys clanging to the floor. "My God! You gave me such a fright."

I bent down to pick up her keys. "Sorry. I have to talk to you."

She stepped back, eyeing me with a lean of her head. "I'm late for the clinic. It'll have to wait."

"I'm afraid not." I handed her the keys.

She took the keys and began to walk past.

I latched on to her wrist, stopping her dead.

"Are you out of your mind? Release me."

But I didn't. "I just spoke to J'Noel."

My lie hinged on the hope that J'Noel hadn't given her a heads-up about her plan to skip.

Her face tightened. "I said release me."

"Let's go inside, Chris. You can hear what J'Noel told me alone, or you can hear it in handcuffs from the police."

Her left eye twitched, her eyes turned frosty, as she tried to hold my gaze in a show of defiance. Her body trembled vigorously.

I took the keys from her hand and she made no attempt to resist me.

I released her to unlock the door. She stood quietly behind me until I was done. I pushed the door open and waited for her to enter. I followed her inside.

She shed her briefcase and coat on the sofa and walked into a room off to our right which might've been used as a study. Heavy wine-colored drapes hung from the wide windows. A folded treadmill braced a far wall. There was a laptop computer on an L-shaped desk and folders stuffed with papers piled on the floor. She turned to face me, leaning on the edge of the desk.

"Why did you kill him?" I said, not giving her a chance to speak.

Her chest rose high as she breathed deeply. Holding her breath like an underwater diver, her eyes welled with frustration and anger. Then she exhaled, but said nothing.

"J'Noel confessed everything," I lied. "She told me how you paid her to hire somebody to kill your ex-husband and his girlfriend."

"If you don't get out of my house this minute I will forget that you are a friend of Noah's and call the police."

I took the phone list from my pocket. "You spoke to J'Noel twelve times last month. Twice the day before Ronan was gunned down. And then half an hour after he was killed. I would bet the record of withdrawals from your bank account would back up J'Noel's story about the sum you paid her."

There was a knot of defiance in her laughter. "If you know so much, why didn't you bring the police?"

"They're on their way. So's Noah. You should be glad I got here before Noah did. Based on the conversation I had with him, I would be more afraid of him than the police, if I were you. He's not coming to give you a medal. He's drunk and he's armed. I'm here because I don't want to see him get in trouble. Donna has already suffered enough."

She walked to the window and drew the drapes back, looked out.

A whimpering sound as if she was crying. She turned around, her eyes as harsh as ever, her voice unyielding. "How well did you know Ronan?"

"Can't say I knew him that well. I gather he was a clever businessman. And a good politician."

"The things that made him a good politician made him a terrible husband. He wasn't trustworthy. He was manipulative. He trusted no one. He said he didn't want children. That's what broke us apart. Claimed he wouldn't be a good father. I begged for a child. He said he'd rather divorce. And we did. Yet, I still loved him. Do you understand how painful that is? I loved him so much I was willing to confuse our friendship by continuing to sleep with him. Even after we divorced. Then he tells me his girlfriend is pregnant. I couldn't live with it. Just couldn't live with it."

FORTY

My father returned to Barbados a week later. I cancelled my reservations to Disneyland and Chesney and I accompanied him. Anais was busy rehearsing and couldn't make it. My mother, who'd never been to Barbados, came too. So did Noah and Donna. He thought the surroundings might put some spirit back into her smile.

Before we left I got a call from Kraw. She sounded as if she was sitting in a rainstorm.

"Hey Blades, I know you don't hear this often, but thanks."

"You're welcome. But what are you thanking me for?"

"I got a call yesterday. Got a tip that the money was in a locker in the George Washington bus terminal. Proved to be a good tip."

"I had nothing to do with it," I said.

"Take care of yourself, hot shot."

IN THE WEEK we stayed on the island my mother did all the tourist things: the museum, the island tour, Harrison's Cave, and the Andromeda Gardens. I spent most of my time with old friends. Chesney was happy to see her uncles and aunts and grandmother and I let her stay with them until it was time to leave.

Two days into my stay in Barbados my father and I strolled along a quiet road near his house on the eastern part of the island. It was early evening, not yet dark; the sky paved a dusty vermilion. We'd just had dinner together on his verandah, from which one could see the sea slowly change from pale blue-green to orange as the sun swept over it.

"Do you like that house?" he said.

"Your house?"

"Yeah."

"Great view."

He nodded. "I'm thinking of selling it."

"Why?"

"I'm moving back to the States."

I stopped short. "Why?"

My father kept walking. When he realized I wasn't following and had no intention of continuing our walk until he answered me he turned around. He walked back and stood a few feet away, his arms folded across his chest. "Remember what you said to me when you picked me up at the airport?"

I looked into his dark eyes.

"You said, 'Welcome home.' It felt good hearing that from you. I used Ronan's death as an excuse to do something I've been thinking of doing for a long time. Come home. I do love Barbados. I love the people. But New York is my real home. I need to go home."

"Why now? After all this time?"

"This is the right time."

"Bullshit!"

"More than anyone I want you to understand, Blades. I need to do this."

"There's something you're not telling me."

"It's really not that complicated."

"Has this got anything to do with Mom?"

His brow knotted. "No. It's about me needing to close some issues. It's about me needing to stop running. As long as I stay here I'll feel like I'm still running. I need to come home. And I need you to understand that."

"There's nothing for me to understand. It has nothing to do with me."

"Yes, it does."

Pause.

"Blades, I can feel your anger."

"I'm not angry at you."

"We'll see. So you want to buy a house with a great view or not?"

I tried to laugh.

THE DAY BEFORE we returned to New York, Noah and I stood on the beach just beyond the hotel where we were staying. Dressed touristy, in floppy hat and sunglasses, his three-quarter-length swim trunks were as colorful as a clown's costume. I wore shorts, white tee and sandals, waiting for my friend, Salty, a young businessman on the island, to pick me up for lunch.

"You know, Blades, it's kinda ironic," Noah began.

"What is?"

"That it took the loss of my son to bring your father back to you."

"It was his time," I said.

"Yeah, I suppose. I went to see Chris in jail. You know what really hurts? She still claims she loved him. What kind of bullshit is that? Twenty grand she paid to kill my son. And she claims she loved him."

"Jealousy is like a force of nature."

"Remember the shooting at the funeral home? Was a setup. They weren't really shooting at us. It was part of her plan to throw any suspicion off herself. Clever, huh?"

"Not clever enough. Any news on this fella, Big-Six?"

"The police picked him up at a bus station in Buffalo but had to let him go. The only person who can tie Big-Six to the killing is that girl who skipped the country."

"I'm really sorry it turned out this way, Noah."

I looked at him and then let my gaze wander off to where the sea melted into the horizon.